Rise of the Queen

By V.J.O. Gardner

V&E Enterprises

www.ve-enterprises.com

ISBN: 9781313686349

V&E Enterprises
Springville, UT 84663

Table of Contents

Their faces unseen and voices unheard,
starving and beaten they labor unloved.
Their only hope of freedom is through death.
Without them an entire nation might fall.

Chapter 1 – She Lies Beneath the Dirt

Li was exhausted as she lay down on her sleeping mat. It had been a very long day. She who bore Li had not been able to do much lately. Li had noticed that she had not eaten at all during the day. She had insisted that Li eat the scraps of food and soured milk that Father and Rowan had left for them to eat. Li slept soundly until about midnight. She woke suddenly and sat up. It was very quiet in the small kitchen. She placed her hand on she who bore her's shoulder and found it to be cold.

"An," Li whispered, fearing to wake Father and Rowan. "Are you alright?"

There was no response. She could feel no breath and no life in she who bore her. She felt the tears begin to run down her cheeks. Silent sobs wracked her body as she buried her face in her hands. It took a few minutes before she could get up to open the kitchen door. She drug An on her mat out the door. She quietly shut the door before going next door to wake Ti. She was the wife of Dreggen.

Li quietly entered through the kitchen door to kneel beside the sleeping woman and whisper, "Ti, wake up."

The woman opened her eyes and sat up.

"An is no more," Li whispered as tears ran down her face.

"Oh, Li," Ti whispered and put her arms around Li. "We must go wrap and lay her beneath the dirt."

Li led Ti to where she had left An. They lifted her off the mat and began to unravel it. The mat was made of scraps of cloth sewn together in a long strip, and then loops were formed by pulling the fabric through previous loops using a wooden hook until the mat was formed. The women of Mannton would use the scraps that were too worn to be left in their dresses to create the mats. Their patchwork dresses were made from scraps of fabric left over from the men's clothes.

"Start at her feet," Ti said as she handed the end to Li.

They wrapped the long strip of cloth around An until she was completely covered and there was no more left. They then carried her to where the women were laid beneath the dirt. Although there were no markers, every woman in Mannton knew every grave by heart. They each took a flat stone and began to dig the shallow grave. Li cried as she dug. It was hard for Li to cover An's body with dirt knowing she would never see her again. It was nearly dawn by the time they finished.

Li brushed the dirt from the front of her dress before getting the bucket to draw water from the well. There were already women and girls at the well drawing water.

"Wait your turn!" a woman said as she pushed Li back toward the young girls waiting a short distance from the well.

Most of the women pushed the young girls aside until they had gotten their own water. It would be a few more years before she was considered old enough for a man to take her as a wife. Li listened to the chatter of the women and ocean waves in the nearby harbor as she waited until the older women had left. She filled her bucket and helped several of the youngest girls fill theirs before returning home to start breakfast.

She had breakfast ready and on the table for Father and Rowan before they awoke. She stood quietly in the corner looking down at the floor as was customary, listening to them eat. She heard the scraping of the chairs, then saw Father's boots approach her.

"Where is An?" Father asked. "She has gotten so lazy."

"An is no more," Li said, knowing he would be angry.

He slapped her face, knocking her down.

"She's run away, hasn't she?" Father's angry voice asked.

Li struggled to her feet and replied, "She is no more."

Father hit her again before he turned and left. Li curled into a ball and cried for a few minutes before carefully looking around the floor. She found that both Father and Rowan had left. She quickly gathered the empty bowls and cups from the table. They had not even left her a single scrap of food. She quickly washed the dishes and went outside. She had watched which plants the animals ate and soon learned which tasted better than the others. She turned over a few rocks and found a couple of large white worms. They tasted bitter, but it was better than nothing. As she made Rowan's bed, Father returned.

"I'll ask you again, where is An?" Father's voice was angry.

"She is no more," Li replied. "She lies beneath the dirt."

"Don't lie to me," Father growled and hit her with the staff he was holding.

"She is no more," Li repeated as she lay on the floor at his feet.

He kicked her and stomped out of the room. Li lay on the floor for a while sobbing as she tried to catch her breath and waited for the pain subside. Eventually she got up and went into the kitchen to prepare lunch. This time Father hit her before sitting down to eat. Again there were no scraps left for her to eat. She had just finished washing the dishes when Father entered the kitchen.

"Where is An's mat?" Father asked. "Did she take it with her when she ran away?"

"An is no more," Li said. "She lies beneath the dirt in her mat."

Father began to beat her. She offered no resistance. She knew that he would eventually either quit or would beat her until she was no more. She didn't much care which. When he did finally stop, she stayed where he left her until she was certain he was gone. She saw Rowan's boots stop at the kitchen door, then turn and walk back into the main room. She washed her face and arms before carefully stitching up the gash he had left in her arm. It burned like fire every time the needle pierced the skin, but she was used to pain. She got the bucket and went to the well to get water. Ti was there.

"Your father has beaten you?" Ti asked as Li passed between the houses.

"He thinks An ran away," Li said as she looked up at Ti's kind face. "He was very angry when I told him she was no more."

Ti nodded her head and said, "I heard Kenner ask Dreggen if he or Anunik had seen An leave."

She left with her bucket of water. Li drew her bucket full of water and returned to the house. She began to scrub the floor. It was hard work to clean her blood from the kitchen floor, but she knew Father would be even angrier if she didn't. By the time she had finished, it was time to prepare supper. Father had left a yard fowl on the table. Li plucked it, saving every feather in a bag that already had feathers in it. By the time it was plucked, the bag was filled. She put the yard fowl on to cook and began slicing the vegetables that were left with it. While they cooked, she sewed shut the bag of feathers and placed another over it. She took it in to Father's bed and placed it at the head of the bed as a new pillow. She returned to the kitchen and made some biscuits. Father came in as she was setting the table.

"Where is she, Li?" Father asked.

"I can show you," Li said. "You will see she is no more."

"You'll just try to run away too," Father said angrily and slapped her.

She fell to the floor, but he drug her into the kitchen and tied her to the table leg. She felt the ropes cutting into her flesh as she sat there. She tried to stay as still as possible so that the ropes wouldn't tighten any further. It seemed like a very long time before she saw Father's boots approach her. He untied her then tied the rope around her waist.

"Wash the dishes," Father said as Rowan brought the empty plates into the kitchen. "Watch her, Rowan. Tie her up before you go to bed."

She began washing the dishes knowing she probably wouldn't get any sleep tonight either. She was glad when she had finished the dishes.

"Why won't you tell Father where An has gone?" Rowan asked as he began to tie her to the table leg.

"An is no more," Li said. "She has not run away, she lies beneath the dirt."

"You know Father will beat you until you tell him the truth," Rowan said.

"I told him the truth," she replied. "An is no more. He can beat me until I am no more, but the answer will remain the same."

Rowan left and she heard voices in the other room, but could not make out the words. She was grateful that Rowan had not tied her nearly as tightly as Father had. She drifted in and out of sleep during the long night. She was relieved when she at last saw Father's boots coming towards her. He stood before her and kicked her feet.

"I am awake, Father," Li said. "I have no desire to run away. I do not know of anywhere that I could go. I know that if I tried you would beat me until I am no more."

"Go get the water and fix breakfast," Father said as he untied her.

When she tried to move, her arms and legs wouldn't cooperate. She fell over on her face. She forced her arms under her and finally her legs. Her steps were weaving and unsteady as she picked up the bucket and opened the door. At least he hadn't kicked her before she got onto her feet. On the way to the well she turned over a rock and found three large white worms to eat. She also ate a couple of flowers. By the time it was her turn at the well, she was feeling a little better. She returned home and prepared breakfast. She placed the plates on the table and stood in the corner waiting.

When he was finished eating, Father said, "Li, if you will not run away, I will not tie you up today. An was becoming useless anyway. Maybe it's for the best that she is gone."

"Yes, Father," Li said, trying to not sound relieved. "I will not run away. There would be no one to care for you and Rowan if I did."

Father and Rowan left. Li was surprised to find a few scraps of food left and even some milk. She gratefully ate them and washed the dishes. The rest of the day, she worked hard as she waited for Father to beat her again, but he did not. The next few days were about the same.

Chapter 2- Something the Healer Did Not Know

Li had thought often about An over the last couple of years. As she sat sewing a new shirt for Rowan, she thought about An. Li missed her, but knew that she had sacrificed herself so that Li could live. She had taught Li almost everything she knew including that if she was to survive she should never look up at a man's face.

She finished the shirt just before it was time to prepare supper. She hurried towards Rowan's room to place the shirt on his bed. She was carefully folding it as he entered the room.

"What are you doing in here?" Rowan asked.

"I have brought your new shirt," Li said. "It is larger, just as you asked."

Rowan tossed his old shirt on the floor before picking up the new one.

"Take away that old shirt," Rowan said.

"Thank you," Li replied and picked up the shirt before leaving.

After supper and the dishes were washed, Li used the scraps from the new shirt to patch her dress. She then took the best pieces of Rowan's old shirt for wash rags before cutting the rest into strips to be sewn together and added to her sleeping mat. She had grown and her feet were beginning to hang off the end.

The next morning brought rain. Li was completely drenched by the time she returned from the well. She wrung her dress out as completely as possible before starting breakfast. Rowan and Father both had capes to keep them dry in the rain, but she did not. None of the women in Mannton wore capes or even boots. Once she had finished washing the breakfast dishes, she began her day's work. By afternoon the rain had quit and the skies were beginning to clear. She was just starting to prepare supper when Rowan and Anunik came in the kitchen door. She saw blood dripping on Rowan's boots as they made their way to a chair.

"You are injured, Rowan," Li said.

"He cut his forehead when he tripped on a tree root," Anunik explained.

"Can you stitch it shut?" Rowan asked. "I've seen you with stitches in your arm before."

"Let me get some of the numbing herb," Li said. "The needle is very painful."

She ran out the door and soon brought back a handful of leaves from the numbing herb. She ground some up and mixed in a little water before spreading the paste on Rowan's forehead. She carefully and quickly stitched shut the wound. Just as she was washing the paste off his forehead, Father entered.

"What are you doing to him?" Father asked in an angry tone before he struck her with his fist.

She fell to the ground and waited to be beaten, but heard Rowan say, "She was stitching shut the cut on my forehead."

"He tripped and fell," Anunik said. "He asked her to stitch the wound shut."

"Let me see," she heard Father say. "It looks like it will heal without much of a scar. Where did you learn to do that, Li?"

"I once got a cut on my arm that was bleeding," Li said as she carefully stood back up. "I thought that if I could stitch it shut it would stop bleeding. It was later that I discovered which herb would numb the pain."

"How would you find that out?" Father asked.

"My mouth went numb after I ate it and my bruises quit hurting," Li replied.

"Why were you eating plants?" Father asked.

"I was hungry and had seen the animals eat it so I thought I could too," she said. "When there is not any food left for me, I eat plants and some white worms until there is food again."

The room fell silent. She wanted to look up, but it was forbidden for a female to look upon the face of a man.

She waited to be hit, but nothing happened.

"Fix supper," Father said and the three men went out the kitchen door.

She finally got to her feet and washed her hands before finishing supper. She put the plates on the table and waited in the corner as usual. Father and Rowan came in and ate in silence. When they left, she was surprised to find they had left her quite a bit of food and even some fresh milk. She ate quickly and washed the dishes before she scrubbed Rowan's blood off the floor. She found Rowan's boots next to the door and cleaned the blood off them. She hoped his new shirt didn't have blood on it.

****

Kenner led Rowan and Anunik outside. Rowan sat down and pulled off his boots. He set them next to the door for Li to clean.

"I've seen her lifting up rocks and picking up something, but I didn't realize she was eating worms," Anunik said.

Rowan turned over a rock and there was a white worm under it. He picked it up gingerly between one finger and a thumb. It squirmed in his grip. Kenner's stomach turned at the thought of actually eating such a thing.

"I noticed how thin and bony her hands are," Rowan said. "An's were thin like that just before she vanished. I always thought that she kept food out for herself when she cooks. If she's eating these she's not saving out food for herself."

"I did too," Kenner said. "She must be really desperate to eat that. I can't imagine eating random plants just because I saw an animal eating them. There's a whole garden of vegetables that she could have been eating, but obviously she hasn't."

Rowan put the worm down and stood up.

"We should start leaving her more food," Kenner said. "She shouldn't have to eat worms and plants."

The following morning Kenner and Rowan went to the healer's to have him look at Rowan's wound.

"What did you do?" the healer asked as he looked at the stitches. "Who did this to you?"

"My daughter Li stitched the wound shut," Kenner said.

"Why would she do such a thing?"

"I asked her to," Rowan said. "I've seen her with stitches on her arm or leg before."

"I want to ask her who taught her to do this."

"She's at home," Kenner said. "You can come now."

****

The next morning Li found Rowan's shirt and pants, dirty and bloodied. She went quickly to the well for water before washing the clothes. She prepared breakfast as soon as she had hung the clothes to dry. She was glad they were not torn. After Father and Rowan had eaten, she was surprised to find that they had again left her some food. She wasn't certain why there was so much left since she had prepared the same amount as usual. She had just made the beds and was sweeping the floor when she heard men's voices enter the kitchen.

"Where are you, Li?" Father's voice asked.

"Here, Father," Li replied as she hurried to the kitchen.

She saw Father's boots and another pair she didn't recognize.

She saw Rowan's boots behind them.

"She's the one?" an unfamiliar voice asked as the boots turned.

"Yes," Rowan's voice replied.

"How did you learn to stitch wounds shut, girl?" the voice asked in an insulting tone. "Who taught you?"

"I learned it by myself," Li replied. "I got a cut that went through my sleeve and into my skin. As I was stitching shut the hole in my sleeve, I realized how similar the cloth was to skin. I thought that like cloth helps keep dirt off the skin, the skin must keep the dirt outside the body. I have had wounds get infected and take a long time to heal. I thought that if I could stitch shut the skin it might not get infected. My needle had gotten bent on the tip, but I found that it worked well for stitching the skin, since the skin cannot be folded up and you cannot get under it to complete the stitch with a straight needle. Later I found the numbing herb."

"There is no herb that numbs," the man said angrily. "If there was I would know about it."

She suddenly heard the sound of someone being hit.

"Let go of my arm!" the man said, sounding even angrier.

"She is mine, Jasper," Father's voice said in a tone she recognized.

She knew that even Rowan did not dare contradict Father when he used that tone of voice.

"I will beat her and no one else," Father said. "You will not lay a hand on her. Li, go get some of the numbing herb."

"At once, Father," Li said and quickly left.

9

She was very surprised to realize that Father had stopped the man from hitting her. She ran to where she knew there were several of the plants and carefully dug up a small one, keeping the dirt around the roots. She held it in both hands as she ran back to the house. She held it out for the man to see. She noticed that Rowan had left.

"If you chew a leaf, it will take away pain," Li said. "If you grind it and add water, you can make a paste that will numb where you spread it on the skin."

"What would a mere female know of pain?" the man said in an insulted tone.

"We feel pain," Li said and again heard the sound of someone being hit. "Women and girls spend most of their lives in pain. We feel the pain from being hit and kicked. We feel pain when our skin is torn. We feel pain when we are hungry and when we bear children."

"You lie," the man said in a disgusted tone.

"I know that if I lie, I get beat," Li replied. "I do not like to be beaten, so I never lie even if I know I might get beaten for telling the truth. You can tell the men that you discovered the herb if you like. No one would believe that I was capable of discovering anything. I am just a female and therefore of little importance. When I am no more, no one will mourn for me."

She saw hands held out under hers and she dropped the plant into them. The man stomped out of the house.

"Thank you for not letting him beat me, Father," Li said.

"When you die, I will miss you, Li," Father said and left.

Li stood in surprise for a while as Father's words repeated in her head. Although she had not heard the word before, she realized that die must mean to be no more. She washed her hands as she thought about it. She worked extra hard that day and was rewarded by Father and Rowan both leaving food for her at lunch and dinner. She was still thinking about it as she fell asleep.

Chapter 3 – Death of the King and Becoming a Wife

As the years passed, Li grew into a woman. Father rarely beat her anymore and she was grateful for that. She also got more to eat and no longer had to eat plants and white worms. She worked hard to repay Father and Rowan for their kindness.

One afternoon, Li was at the well getting water. She heard shouting and confusion among the men. She hurried home to prepare supper. Father and Rowan barely ate.

"What is the matter, Father?" Li asked. "Why did you not eat?"

"King Tokar died in battle with Brinley today," Father said. "His son, Prince Yitzhak will now become king. Tomorrow there will be a procession from the palace. Prince Yitzhak will lead the horse pulling the wagon holding the body of his father. He will lead it all around the city until all the men have assembled behind it. When he returns to the palace and King Tokar has been buried, he will become king."

"Prince Yitzhak must have great pain in his heart as he mourns for his father," Li said.

"What would you know of that?" Father asked.

"I felt great pain in my heart when she who bore me was no more, when she died," Li replied.

"An really didn't run away?" Father asked in a surprised tone as Li shook her head. "I didn't realize that is what you were saying when you said she was no more."

"I did not know the word that men use," Li said.

She felt Father's large hand on her shoulder for a moment before he turned and left. She had never felt such a gentle touch from Father before. She ate some of the food before she wrapped it in some scraps of cloth and took it back to the well. She knew that the women who were too weak to fight for water came after the others left. She found several women there. They cried as they ate the food. She filled their buckets for them as they ate. She saw a man's boots standing a short distance away. She wondered why he

11

would be looking the direction of the well. The boots had designs pressed into the leather.

Another man's boots approached the man.

"Tomorrow will be a long day, Prince Yitzhak," a man's voice said.

"Yes, it will, Yuri," came the reply as the boots turned and left.

She hurried home as she thought about the sadness in the voice. She knew she was right about Prince Yitzhak mourning his father's death. She washed Father and Rowan's best clothes and polished their boots before going to sleep. She awoke early even though she had not gotten to sleep until well into the night. She made several trips to the well for water so that the large tub would be filled with water for Father and Rowan to wash themselves with before preparing breakfast. She was relieved when she saw that they had eaten almost the normal amount of food.

"We will not be home until supper, Li," Father said. "You may prepare yourself something for lunch."

"Thank you, Father," Li said. "I will have supper ready at the regular time."

"You will have to catch and kill the yard fowl yourself," Father said. "You will have to pick the vegetables as well."

"I will, Father," Li said. "I will not disappoint you."

"I know you won't," Father said before he left with Rowan.

Li cleaned the house and went out to the garden to pick a few vegetables for her lunch. She ate them without cooking them because she did not feel right cooking only for herself. She then went out to the yard fowl pen and carefully slipped in through the gate. They all gathered around her feet and began pecking the ground. As a large one pecked her foot she grabbed its neck to stop it. It began to squawk and kick its feet so she shook it. She heard the neck snap and the fowl went limp. She waved it at the others and they scattered allowing her to leave the pen.

Li wiped her feet on some grass before going to the house. She left it on the table before she picked up the basket Father left the vegetables in. She went out to the garden and found the vegetables that Father usually picked to go with yard fowl. As she returned to the house, she heard sad music playing. She peeked around the corner of the house to see a procession of men. It was the first time she had actually looked at much more than their boots except when she had stitched Rowan's forehead. She saw a young man leading the horse pulling the only wagon in the procession. His head was bowed and she saw him wipe at his eyes. She felt her cheeks flush as she realized she found his appearance pleasing. She was glad that none of the men looked at anything besides the road that passed the front of the house. She quickly went into the house knowing she would be beaten if any man knew she had dared look at any of their faces, especially Prince Yitzhak. She would not recognize her own father by his face. Rowan she would know only because of the faint scar on his forehead.

Li worked hard to have supper ready for Father and Rowan when they returned. There was silence as they ate and went straight to bed. She ate the food they had left her and washed the dishes. She went out the kitchen door and sat down on the back porch. She hugged her knees as she thought about her day. It had been very different than any other she could remember. She remembered the sadness of the music and Prince Yitzhak crying. She wished that someday men would realize that women felt the same things that they did and could learn more than cooking and cleaning. She remembered when Father had taught Rowan to read and write. She had stolen a look at the strange markings on the paper. She knew that somehow these markings said words. She wished she knew how to read them, but knew that knowledge was forbidden to women. She sighed as she stood up and returned to the kitchen. She lay down and went to sleep.

****

It was almost a year since King Tokar had died. Li was too busy taking care of Father and Rowan to think much about that day and the man who was now King Yitzhak. Most women did not even know the name of the king. It was a hot afternoon as she stood filling buckets for the young girls. As she filled her bucket, she saw a man's boots approach. She placed the bucket on the step around the well before kneeling. She recognized the boots from the patterns pressed into the leather. It was King Yitzhak who stood before her.

"I want some water," she heard his voice say as he put one boot on the well step.

She dared not speak as she took the ladle from its hook on the side of the well and filled it with water. She felt hands take it from her. She could see the dirt on his boots and ripped a piece of cloth from her dress. She wet it with water from the bucket and began to wash his boots. She carefully dried them with another piece of cloth from her dress. As she finished, she saw the ladle being lowered to her. It was empty as she held her hands out for it. She felt a gentle touch on the top of her head before King Yitzhak turned and left. She found her hands trembling as she carefully hung the ladle on the hook. She picked up the bucket of water and headed home. As she walked, she thought she heard a horse follow her, but she did not dare look.

She hurried into the kitchen and began to prepare supper. It took her a very long time to get to sleep that night. She could remember King Yitzhak's touch on her head. She had been very surprised when he had put his hand on her head for a moment. She was still tired when she woke up the next morning. After breakfast, she heard a knock at the front door and Father's voice. The door shut and she did not hear any more voices. She cleaned the house and tried to forget what had happened yesterday at the well.

****

Kenner was surprised to find a palace guard at the door when he answered.

"King Yitzhak requests you meet with him," the guard said.

"Now?" Kenner asked and the man nodded. "Why?"

"He didn't say," the guard replied.

Kenner followed the guard to the palace. He wondered why the king would want to talk to him. He was led to an office where King Yitzhak sat at a desk writing something.

"Come in and sit down," King Yitzhak said as he looked up. "Your name is?"

"Kenner," he replied.

"You have a son and a daughter."

"Yes."

"What is your daughter's name?" King Yitzhak asked to Kenner's surprise.

"Li," Kenner replied.

"Tell me about her," King Yitzhak said as he set down his pen. "How old is she?"

"Seventeen I think," Kenner replied. "She's a good cook and keeps the house very clean. She's very smart for a female. She's very brave as well."

"Smart? Brave?"

"She learned to stitch shut her own wounds," Kenner said. "She realized that by stitching shut torn skin dirt will be kept out of the wound so it will heal without becoming infected. She wasn't afraid to tell Rowan and me that we needed to leave her more food."

"Interesting," King Yitzhak said. "I've seen her at the well. I noticed that when my father died, she brought food and shared it with the women there. She helps the young girls fill their buckets sometimes."

"When I heard that King Tokar had died, I just couldn't eat. I gave her the food. I had no idea that she would share it with others."

He couldn't tell why King Yitzhak would be so interested in Li.

"It's time for me to take a wife," King Yitzhak said and Kenner's heart sunk. "I've been watching Li at the well for a while now. Yesterday I wondered what she would do if I asked her for a drink. She knelt and gave me a ladle of water. She cleaned my boots while I drank. I was not expecting that reaction from her at all."

"You want Li for your wife?" he asked.

"What do you want for her?" King Yitzhak asked.

"I'll need to think about it," Kenner said. "I'd certainly miss her if she were gone."

"I'll give you a week to think about it," King Yitzhak said. "Come back then and we'll talk some more."

Kenner nodded and stood up. He felt a bit numb as he walked out of the palace gate. He didn't want to go home just yet. He walked down to the harbor and watched the water swirl around the pier pilings. He had thought about An often since she vanished and would walk into the kitchen expecting to see her there. Before she died he used to go into the kitchen while she slept to look at her face since she never looked up at him. Now Li would be taken from him too. He knew King Yitzhak would not give up until Li was his.

He didn't even know what to ask for her. He shook his head and turned towards home. He thought about maybe asking for a couple of horses and a cow as he reached home.

"Where have you been, Father?" Rowan asked as he opened the door.

"At the palace," he said as Li came in to put the food on the table. "Go outside sit on the back porch while we eat."

****

Father's voice sounded strangely to Li. She wondered what was wrong as she sat down on the porch to wait. It seemed like a very long time before the back door opened.

"We're finished," Rowan's voice said.

"Am I in trouble?" Li asked.

"I don't know," Rowan replied. "Father spent the whole morning at the palace, but wouldn't say why."

Li was worried as she quickly ate the scraps of food and washed the dishes. Father didn't speak to her for the rest of the day. She knew she must be in trouble for something as she lay down to sleep that night.

For the rest of the week, Li sat on the back porch while the men ate. After each meal, Rowan would bring Li a bowl of food to eat. When she was allowed back in the house, the dishes had been washed. Rowan would sit in the kitchen while she prepared supper. He would not say why he was watching her, nor did she dare ask. Something was wrong. That much was certain, but Li couldn't figure out what. Father wouldn't even speak to her. He didn't beat or hit her either. She was growing more worried every day.

One morning, as she was putting breakfast on the table for Father and Rowan, Father said, "Li, get your things together and get in the carriage out front."

"You are sending me away?" Li asked. "Who will take care of you and Rowan? Please at least tell me what I have done wrong."

"I have no choice, Li," Father said in a voice that sounded almost sad. "Just do whatever you are asked."

"I will, Father," Li said. "I will miss you and Rowan."

Li gathered up her few belongings. There was the small bag holding two needles and some thread along with her wooden hook. It also held the tip of a broken knife that she used to cut cloth and the small flat stone she used to keep it sharp. The only other things she owned was her dress and her sleeping mat. She rolled up the mat and went out the front door for the first time in her life. There were two men by the carriage and one on the driver's seat. She got into the carriage and the two men mounted horses. She dared not look up as the carriage took her away from home. It went through a gate in a thick stone wall before stopping. The two men dismounted and led her into a building made of stone. They led her into a room and shut the door behind her.

As she heard the door being locked, she at last dared to look up. The room was as large as the kitchen and main room of Father's house had been. There was a fireplace with wood stacked beside it and a medium sized pot that could be hung over the fire on a hook that swung from a joint on the front corner of the fireplace opening. In front of the fireplace sat a table and two chairs. On the other side of the room was a bed flanked by two tables with lamps. Opposite the door she had come in was another door with a bucket sitting next to it.

She stood there not knowing what to think. Certainly this was not the dungeon she had heard about. She put the bag on the table before putting the sleeping mat under the foot of the bed. As she slid the mat under the bed, she noticed what Father called a chamber pot. He sometimes used it in the winter and she had to go out to the outhouse to empty it. She always had dreaded doing it, but knew better than to complain.

She sat down on the floor next to the fireplace to wait. The room was very clean and smelled freshly scrubbed. Next to the door she had come in, she noticed a picture of King Yitzhak on the wall. As she sat there, she studied his smiling face and it gave her comfort. It was several hours before she heard the door unlock. She stood up and watched boots walk over to the table, then turn around and leave. As she heard the lock, she looked up and discovered a tray of food had been left on the table.

It wasn't much, but it was fresh. She gratefully ate it. When she had finished, she checked the bucket near the other door and found it had water in it. She washed the dishes and returned to sit near the fireplace. She could not tell how much time had passed before she heard the lock turn again. She stood and waited for the man to come and go. Again she found that food had been brought to her. A little more this time than last time, but she was grateful to get any food at all. She still wasn't certain what trouble she was in as she washed the dishes. She was just placing them on the tray when the door opened again. She recognized the boots and quickly knelt at King Yitzhak's feet.

"You are my wife," she heard him say. "Stand up so I can have a good look at you."

She felt herself trembling as she stood up. She stood still as he walked around her. She felt his hand beneath her chin, lifting her face.

"Are you afraid?" King Yitzhak asked as she kept her eyes averted.

"It is not allowed for a woman to look at a man's face," she said. "Those that did got beaten."

"I want to see your eyes," King Yitzhak said. "Look at me."

She looked up to see him staring at her. He gently brushed the hair from her face. She dared not move as he continued to look her over, touching her gently as he did. She wasn't certain what to expect next. He was not acting as most men did. She knew from An and Ti what to expect when a man took her for his wife, but they had said nothing of this.

"Are you afraid of me?" he asked. "You are shaking."

"I belong to you and you have the right to do whatever you please with me," Li said. "If I displease you, you will beat me. I will not purposely displease you for I do not like to be beaten. I will never lie to you either, for you will beat me if I do."

"I have learned from your father that you are very clever for a woman," King Yitzhak said. "I see no need to beat you. You will learn what you need to without being beaten."

"Thank you," Li said feeling relieved.

"This is your home now," King Yitzhak said. "There is a small garden courtyard out that door. There is a well for you to draw water from. There is a chamber pot for you to use since there is no outhouse. This will be emptied for you and firewood will be brought in for you."

"I was not certain where that door led, but did not dare try it," she said. "I did not want anyone angry with me. You do not need

18

to lock the door. I will never try to leave. I knew someday a man might take me for his wife, but I did not expect that man to be you. I do not deserve the honor of being the wife of King Yitzhak."

"You know who I am?" he asked in a surprised tone and she nodded.

"I remember you standing near the well after your father died," she said. "I remember your boots and that a man called you Prince Yitzhak. I remember the sadness in your voice and thinking about how your heart must hurt mourning him dying. I also remember when you asked for water at the well and I cleaned your boots."

"You are very clever for a woman and only such a clever woman deserves to be my wife," King Yitzhak said with a smile.

His hand was gentle as he took her arm and led her over to the bed. It was then that he did what she had expected him to do as he took her as his wife. She was surprised by his gentleness. When he left, she opened the door to the courtyard and drew more water from the well. There was a washtub on a table and a rope stretched tight between two posts. She washed the sheets before hanging them over the rope to dry. She unrolled her mat at the foot of the bed and was soon asleep.

****

"You're in a good mood, My King," Yuri said as Yitzhak walked toward his chambers.

"My wife arrived today," Yitzhak said. "Her name is Li and she is very clever for a woman. She was very cooperative and was not afraid."

"All women are afraid," Yuri said. "They fight and sometimes bite until you beat them."

"Not Li," Yitzhak said with a smile. "She even knew who I was. I think she is worth what I paid for her. Her father was reluctant to give her up and I can see why."

Chapter 4- A Dress of New Cloth

When Li first opened her eyes, she didn't recognize where she was, but then remembered. She stood and went over to the picture of King Yitzhak. She smiled as she remembered how kind and gentle he was with her. She was not afraid of him beating her. She drew fresh water from the well before making the bed.

When lunch was delivered to her, there was some cloth delivered as well. She ate and washed the dishes before she looked at the cloth. It was a reddish brown color and softer than any fabric she had felt before. She had noticed that King Yitzhak was about the same size as Rowan, so she laid out the fabric and began to cut out a pair of pants and a jacket. She carefully drew some thread from the longest of the scraps left and began to sew. She sewed very carefully knowing that the King of Mannton would not want to wear poorly sewn clothes. It took several days to complete the sewing. When she finished, she took the knifepoint and carefully carved buttons from a piece of firewood.

When supper was delivered on the day she completed the buttons, there was some of a vegetable that was red. She knew that the juice would stain things red. She carefully mashed the vegetable before putting the buttons into it. She ate the rest of the food before washing the buttons in water and setting them out to dry. The next morning, she was pleased to find the buttons matched the fabric well. She carefully sewed them securely in place. She folded the pants and jacket before placing them on the bed.

****

It was almost a month before King Yitzhak came to visit her again.

"What happened to the cloth I sent to you?" he asked.

"I finished the pants and jacket for you," she said. "I will adjust them if they do not fit right."

"You what?" he asked in a surprised tone.

She picked up the clothes and held them out to him. He took the jacket and held it up.

"You sewed this?" he asked.

"Yes, King Yitzhak," she replied. "That is why you sent the cloth isn't it?"

He was silent. She glanced up at him and found him frowning.

"Oh, I have displeased you," she said as she felt the first tears begin to run down her cheeks.

"I sent the cloth so you could make yourself a dress," King Yitzhak said.

"Such a waste of cloth is not allowed," Li said. "New cloth is for men's clothes."

She dropped the pants on the floor as she saw him draw his knife. She trembled as she waited for the pain to come. King Yitzhak grabbed the neckline of her dress and sliced through the fabric until he could pull it from her. She stood naked as she watched him roll the dress into a ball and throw it in the fire.

"Now you must make yourself a dress out of the cloth I will send to you," he said before picking up the pants and jacket.

He left the room and shut the door behind him. She collapsed to the floor, crying. Although he had not laid a hand on her, his anger had hurt her even more than his knife could have. She did not move or look up when the door opened again.

"Are you hurt?" a woman's concerned voice asked as Li felt a hand on her back.

"I have angered him," Li said as she shook her head.

"He told me to give this to you," the woman said as she placed some brown cloth on the floor. "And these."

The woman held out her open hand. On it were six brass buttons.

"He did not want to send these with a man," the woman said. "He did not want another man to desire you as his own."

Li slowly sat up until she could see the woman's soft, kind face.

"My name is Ta," she said as she brushed Li's hair back. "I was wife of King Tokar."

"You are she who bore King Yitzhak?" Li asked in surprise.

"Yes," she said. "I had not seen him since his father became no more, but today he came to me. He was upset. I was worried that he might have hurt you."

"He sent cloth to me," Li said. "I thought that it was to make him pants and a jacket. I worked very hard to make them. I even made the buttons and dyed them to match the cloth. I did not know the cloth was to make me a dress. The man who brought it has never spoken to me."

"No one told you?" Ta asked.

"King Yitzhak is the only man to speak to me since I left my father's home," Li said. "When he cut the dress from me and threw it in the fire, I felt as though he had stabbed me in the heart with the knife."

"Oh, my dear," Ta said. "You love King Yitzhak."

"Yes," Li admitted. "I saw him crying as he led the horse when he led the procession to place King Tokar beneath the dirt. Once he asked me for water at the well. He handed me back the ladle and touched my head before he left. When he took me for his wife, he was very gentle."

"He will not stay angry with you," Ta said. "My room is next to this one. If you clear away some of the vines in your courtyard, you will be able to see into mine. We can talk anytime you want to."

"Thank you," Li said.

"You have a lot of sewing to be done," Ta said. "I must return to my room now."

Li put the buttons on the table before laying out the cloth to be cut. It was at first difficult to know where to start since the only dress she had ever worn had been pieced together from scraps. At last she began to cut the cloth. Ta delivered her meals to her until the dress was at last complete.

"It is a beautiful dress, Li," Ta said as she put the tray of food on the table. "He will be pleased."

"I hope so, Ta," Li replied. "I do not wish to anger him."

****

It was the cold season before King Yitzhak came again. She was surprised to see him wearing the jacket and pants she had sewn for him.

"Thank you for the cloth, My King," Li said. "It is so much softer than the old dress."

"You are very good with a needle," King Yitzhak said. "Rowan told me of you stitching his forehead. He had to point out the scar. Although I was angry at first, I like the clothes you made for me. They fit very well. I might have you make some more."

"I will do whatever you ask of me," Li said. "When the man brought the cloth, he did not say anything to me. That is why I did not know it was to make a dress from."

"He was supposed to tell you," King Yitzhak said.

"You are the only man to speak to me since I arrived here," she said. "Ta is the only other person to speak to me at all."

"I will talk to him about that," King Yitzhak said. "If he cannot do the job properly, then I will find someone else. I've been curious as to where you got the buttons."

"I made them and dyed them myself," she replied.

"How could you make buttons?" he asked.

She got her box and drew out the knife point and held it out on the palm of her hand.

"I used this to cut the cloth and make the buttons," she said as he picked it up.

"No scissors or knife?" he asked as he put it back on her hand.

"What are scissors?" she asked.

He went to the door and opened it for a moment before shutting the door and returning.

"The guard will bring a pair of scissors," King Yitzhak said. "They will help you cut cloth."

"I would like that," she said. "It is hard to use the knife point. I would very much like to sew more clothes for you. There is not much for me to do since I do not prepare your food. During the warm months I liked to sit in the courtyard and tend the plants, but it is too cold to go out for very long now. I go out to draw water and that is about all."

"What do you do during the day?" he asked.

"After I have cleaned the room, I like to sit and look at your picture," she said.

Just then there was a knock at the door.

"Come," King Yitzhak said.

She saw a man's boots enter before he knelt at King Yitzhak's feet with something held out in his hands. He left once King Yitzhak had taken the shiny thing from him. It was long and pointed on one end, but there were two loops on the other end. King Yitzhak put his fingers through the larger loop and his thumb through the smaller one. He then opened and closed his hand causing the pointed end to split in two, and then return together. He handed it to her.

"These will cut cloth much faster than that bit of metal," he said as she tried to do what he had done.

As she placed the knife point back in the box and set down the scissors on the table, he took off his jacket.

"Now, My Wife," he said. "I have had enough talking. Take off your dress."

She smiled as she understood what he wanted. It was something she had been wanting too.

Chapter 5 – Poisoned

It was a week later that the man delivered her food to her and some cloth along with some buttons. The man cleared his throat before speaking.

"King Yitzhak sent cloth and buttons to be sewn into clothes for him," the man said with a growl.

It was the same tone the healer had used when he had learned she could stitch skin and knew something he did not.

"You are angry," she replied. "Why do you hate me?"

"Because of you, I spent all last week in the dungeon," the man said in an angry tone.

"Because you did not tell me I was to sew a dress, not clothes for King Yitzhak," she said. "If you would have told me, King Yitzhak would not have had any reason to be angry with either of us."

"I shouldn't have to speak to a mere woman," the man said. "I shouldn't have to wait on you either. You're hardly more than a stupid beast. He only needs you to bear his heir."

With that the man turned and stomped out, slamming the door behind him. She went to the table. The food was not fresh, but even so it did not smell like it should. She tasted a couple of bites and it did not taste right either. She decided that she should not eat any of it. She began to lay the cloth out on the floor, but she felt dizzy. She went to the courtyard door hoping some fresh air would clear her head. Instead she felt her stomach tighten and suddenly what she had eaten came back up. She rinsed her mouth out with water and laid down on her sleeping mat. She had never felt like this before. She did not know what was wrong.

****

"My King!" the guard shouted as he came running into the room. "There is something wrong with your wife!"

Yitzhak felt his heart skip a beat. He followed the guard with Joris and Yuri following behind.

"I went in to get the tray at the usual time and the food was still there," the guard said. "The courtyard door was open and she was lying on the floor on a mat next to the cloth you sent. She looked pale. I shook her shoulder, but all she did was moan."

He burst into the room and was alarmed at what he saw. Li was lying very still on a mat at the foot of the bed. The cloth was half spread out on the floor. He crossed to the courtyard door. As he looked out, he saw something on the ground that was similar in color to the uneaten food on the tray. He shut the door and went back to where Li lay on the floor.

"Send for the healer," Yitzhak said as he carefully lifted her off the mat.

Li groaned softly as she turned to lay her head against his shoulder. The guard left as Joris pulled down the covers. He placed her gently on the bed and covered her up. She was so cold. Her eyes fluttered open and her hands felt the blankets and sheets.

"Bad taste," she murmured as she tried to get up.

"Lay down," Yitzhak said. "The healer is coming."

"Not allowed to sleep on bed," she muttered as she again tried to get up.

"Lay down, My Wife," Yitzhak said. "You will stay in this bed."

Her hand reached up towards his face. He took her hand in his and placed it on his face. She smiled faintly and finally relaxed into the bed.

"My wife would have scratched my face," Yuri commented as the healer entered.

"A woman?" the healer asked in an annoyed tone.

"You will treat her," Yitzhak said as he stood up.

The man's eyes widened and he quickly knelt.

"It appears that she ate a few bites of food, then threw up," Yitzhak said, not waiting for Kon to stand. "She said something about bad taste. She is very cold and pale. She is not completely conscious."

"Bad taste?" Kon asked and looked at the food. "Yes, I suppose this would taste bad."

He put his finger in some fluid on the plate and sniffed it.

"Now, that smell I recognize," Kon said. "It is a poison. It can be lethal if enough is eaten. Milk helps dilute it, but a man would be ill for several days. I don't know about a woman."

"Get me a pail of fresh milk and a cup," Yitzhak ordered as he pointed to a guard. "Now!"

The man hurried off.

"Bring Nokar here," he said, pointing to the other guard, who quickly left.

The second guard soon returned with Nokar, who looked nervous.

"Sit down and eat, Nokar," Yitzhak said as he grabbed the man by the arm and pushed him into the chair.

"I . . . I . . . I'm not hungry," Nokar stuttered as he began to tremble.

"You poisoned my wife," Yitzhak said and the man seemed to shrink into the chair.

"She's hardly more than a stupid beast," Nokar said. "I should not have to wait on a stupid beast."

Yitzhak's blood was boiling with anger as he hit the man with the back of his hand so hard that Nokar and the chair were knocked over. The guard bringing the milk barely avoided being knocked down as Nokar fell at his feet. Yitzhak took the cup and pail from the guard and went over to the bed. He set the pail on the floor before scooping out some milk in the cup. He gently put his hand under Li and lifted her until she was almost sitting.

"Drink this, My Wife," Yitzhak said softly as he pressed the cup to her lips. "It will make you feel better."

Obediently, Li drank the milk and two more cups. He let her lay back down and arranged her comfortably. He walked over to where Nokar still lay on the floor.

"It's obvious that you are incapable of a simple yet important task," Yitzhak said. "Take him to the dungeon. If she dies, he dies. If she lives, he will be released, but he will never work in this palace again."

The two guards drug Nokar from the room. He knew he must now find someone he could trust to bring food to Li. He threw the plate and food into the fireplace. As he leaned on the mantelpiece, he said a silent prayer that Li would live. There was something special about her that had made her different than other women. There was an intelligence and kindness that most women did not display. If Nokar had been talking about Yuri's wife, he would have been right, but not Li.

"My King," he heard Joris say.

He turned to find Li trying to sit up again. He quickly crossed to the bed and sat on the edge.

"Lay down, Li," he said softly to her.

"King Yitzhak?" she asked.

"I am here," he replied.

"Where is my sleeping mat?" she asked. "That is where I should be, not here in your bed."

"My bed?" he asked in surprise. "You don't sleep on the bed? Where do you sleep?"

"On my mat at the foot of the bed," she responded. "Before I came here I slept on my mat in the kitchen near the fireplace. That is where women sleep."

"No blanket or pillow?" Yitzhak asked in shock.

"Those are for men," she replied.

"Nokar tried to poison you," Yitzhak said. "Until you are well, you will sleep in this bed, not on the floor."

"I will obey," she said. "I feel awful. I've never felt like this before."

"I will find someone I can trust to bring you your food," Yitzhak said.

"He said I was hardly more than a stupid animal and that he shouldn't have to talk to me," she said and began to cry.

"Oh, My Wife," Yitzhak said gently. "It is he that is an animal and you should not have to talk to him. He will never be able to hurt you again."

"Could Ta bring my food and even eat with me?" Li asked.

"Yes," Yitzhak said. "I like that idea. Perhaps Yuri's wife should come stay with you for a while. I think it would be good for her to come and learn from you."

"I would like that," Li said. "I get so lonely sometimes."

"I will come visit you more often," Yitzhak said and she smiled. "Sleep now. I will bring Ta to care for you. You will drink as much of the fresh milk as you can."

"I will," Li said as she closed her eyes.

He gently stroked her face before standing up. He gestured for the other men to leave the room with him.

"Bring Ta," Yitzhak said as the guards returned.

"Why do you need my wife to come if she who bore you is here?" Yuri asked. "I have never seen a man treat their wife like you treat Li. You act more like she is your son."

"Maybe if women were not beaten so much, they might not try to scratch and bite every time you went to them," Yitzhak said. "When she was first brought here Li told me that I would beat her if I was displeased with her. I was shocked. She told me she did not like to be beaten and would try not to anger me. I've begun to look around and noticed women and girls being beaten even out in the streets. I also noticed that there appears to be many more men than women."

"So?" Yuri asked.

"It's always been that way," Joris said.

Just then the guard returned leading Ta.

"Li has been poisoned," Yitzhak said. "She will be sick for several days. Can you please tend to her? She does not trust a man to bring her food that is safe to eat. Make certain she drinks lots of fresh milk."

"I will care for her," Ta said and went into Li's room.

Yitzhak led Joris and Yuri back to the meeting room.

"There are fewer men in Mannton than there used to be," Yitzhak said. "Brinley is crowded and may be looking for more land. We need to make certain they do not take over Mannton."

"I heard that King Burkhart has never taken a wife," Joris said.

"He's probably the smart one," Yuri commented as he rubbed a scratch on his face that was healing. "I heard that his father's wife still lives in the palace and would rule if he died. I can't imagine a woman being a king."

"They call a woman ruler a queen," Joris said in a condescending tone. "Still, I doubt a woman could be capable of ruling a kingdom."

"Certainly a woman would not know how to defend a kingdom," Yitzhak said. "If Burkhart were out of the way, we could have Brinley."

Chapter 6 – Calling a Truce

Li woke up to hear women talking. She had been sleeping for almost three days. She sat up. King Yitzhak had insisted that she sleep on the bed while she was getting better. She still didn't feel right about it. Ta was at the table talking to a younger woman.

"Are you feeling better?" Ta asked and Li nodded. "This is Yuri's wife."

"What is your name?" Li asked as she got slowly out of the bed.

"I was never given a name," the woman said.

"We should give you a name then," Li said.

"Yuri would be angry," the woman said. "He is always angry."

"What difference would he know?" Li asked as she sat down and began eating the food that was on the table. "We should name you Ki."

"I like that name," the woman said. "I am now Ki."

"What are you doing here?" Li asked.

"I'm not sure," Ki said.

"King Yitzhak said she was coming to learn," Ta said.

"Learn what?" Li asked and Ta shrugged her shoulders.

"I don't know, but you could ask him," Ta replied. "He usually comes by around this time of day to check on you."

They ate in silence for a moment before the door opened up.

"It is so good to see you out of bed and eating, My Wife," King Yitzhak said in a pleased tone of voice.

"I am feeling much better, My King," Li replied as she stood up.

The other two women remained seated with their heads bowed.

"Ta has taken very good care of me."

"I knew she would," King Yitzhak said with a smile.

"I wanted to ask you something, My King," Li said. "Ki said she was sent here to learn but didn't know what she would learn."

"You probably were too sick to remember," King Yitzhak said. "Yuri didn't understand why you do not try to bite or scratch me and why I don't beat you. I am trying to make Yuri understand that women do not need to be beaten and that they are much better than stupid animals. I thought that perhaps his wife might learn some things from you that would help her stop trying to bite and scratch him."

"I would never bite or scratch you, My King," Li said. "You treat me kindly and touch me gently. I am not afraid of you. Although I had been told what I should expect when you took me as your wife, you did not act as I was told you would act."

"What do you mean?" he asked in a surprised tone.

"You were not rough or mean," she replied as she tried to think of the right words to make him understand. "You did not hit me or tie me up. You spoke to me and touched me gently. You did not make me feel forced to do what you wanted me to do. After the first time, I look forward to your visits. I enjoy making you happy."

"I can see that Yuri needs to learn as much as his wife," King Yitzhak said. "Perhaps even more."

"Tell him her name is Ki," Li said. "Do not let him be angry with her. They should learn to not be angry and want to hurt each other before they see each other again."

"You are most clever, My Wife," King Yitzhak said as he smiled. "I do not have time now, but I will come to visit you again in a few days. I am finding a man that I can trust to bring your food to you who will be kind to you and not try to harm you."

"I will be waiting for you, My King," Li said. "Tell Yuri that he should have Ki look at his face. Most women never get to see a man's face, only their hands and boots. I would not recognize my own father by his face, but I would recognize your face. It is good to see the face that goes with the voice."

King Yitzhak smiled as he softly stroked her face before leaving. As he shut the door, she turned to find the two women staring at her with their mouths hanging open.

"I can't believe you look at his face," Ta said.

"I can't believe that you dare speak like that to him," Ki said. "You speak like a man speaking to another man."

"When I first arrived here, I was very frightened and thought I was in trouble," Li said as she sat back down. "But King Yitzhak came to me and told me I was his wife. He was kind as he spoke to me. He told me he wanted to see my eyes, so I finally looked up at him. He even smiled at me. He touched me gently and said that he did not see any reason to beat me."

"He does not beat you?" Ki asked in a tone of disbelief.

"Not even when he got angry when I made pants and a jacket for him with the cloth he sent for me to make a dress for myself," Li said as she shook her head. "His anger hurt me as though he had stabbed me in the heart instead of cutting my old dress off of me. I realized then that I love him."

"Men are evil," Ki said. "They don't care that they hurt us. They think we are stupid. I hate them all."

"Men are not evil," Li said. "They are the ones who are stupid about some things. They do not understand women's words. I wish for a day when every woman dares to look men in the eye and say what is truth without fear of being beaten. When she who bore me became no more, my father thought she had run away. Even after I told him that she was no more he did not believe me. Later I realized that Father did not understand my words. To a man, to be no more is to die and to lie beneath the dirt is to be buried. It was only much later that I learned the right words to make him understand."

They sat in silence for a while. She hoped that Ki would understand what she was telling her. Even more she hoped that Yuri would understand what King Yitzhak wanted him to know. Ki stayed even after Ta returned to her room. King Yitzhak brought one of the guards named Lucjen to replace Nokar. Lucjen was not angry when she looked up as other men would be, instead, he smiled at her. He spoke kindly to her and even asked her what foods she preferred. King Yitzhak came twice to visit before bringing Yuri with him. Li answered Ki's questions as best she could after King Yitzhak's visits. Ki was beginning to see that men were not evil.

"You dare look at me?" Yuri asked as Li stood and did not look at the ground.

"I dare look at King Yitzhak," Li said. "I do not care whether I see your face or not, but King Yitzhak's face pleases me."

"And your face pleases me, My Wife," King Yitzhak said with a smile. "Yuri, have you ever even seen your wife's face?"

"No," Yuri admitted. "But I have seen her fingernails."

"I have seen your fists as you beat me and your boots as you kicked me," Ki said as she spoke for the first time. "You hit me before you even spoke to me."

"Yuri," King Yitzhak said. "If you bought a new horse and treated it that way, it would try to bite you. How can you expect your wife to act any differently? If you treat her like an animal, she will behave like an animal. If you treat her like a person, she will behave like a person. Now, Ki, look up at Yuri."

"He will hit me," Ki said, still looking down.

"Yuri, you will not touch her," King Yitzhak said in almost a growl.

"N . . . No, My King," Yuri replied and Ki suddenly looked up.

"I see you are both scarred like warriors," King Yitzhak said. "You can battle each other until your deaths or call a truce."

It was very hard for Li to not laugh as they both looked at King Yitzhak.

"Now, Yuri," King Yitzhak said. "This is how you should touch your wife."

King Yitzhak reached out and placed his hand on Li's cheek softly. She smiled as she leaned her cheek on his hand.

"Ki, you should not try to scratch or bite Yuri," Li said. "You should do this."

Li reached up and softly stroked King Yitzhak's face before letting her hand slide down onto his chest. He smiled at her and she understood the look in his eyes. She wished that Ki and Yuri would leave. She was certain that he did too.

"You will not scratch me if I do not hit you?" Yuri asked.

"You will not hit me if I do not scratch you?" Ki replied.

Slowly Yuri reached out towards Ki's face. Li could see her tremble as she waited. Once Yuri's hand was on her cheek, she seemed to relax. Ki carefully reached out towards Yuri. Li could see his eyes follow her hand until it rested on his cheek. Yuri looked back at Ki's eyes as Ki's hand slowly slipped from his cheek to his chest. King Yitzhak led Li out into the courtyard. It was a bit chilly, but not too cold. He led her to the bench and sat down. She saw that he had left the door ajar and they could hear quiet talking.

"When I first spoke to Ki, she thought men were evil," Li said quietly. "Even though my father was sometimes cruel, I could not hate him. I learned that men use different words for some things than women use. Sometimes this is why men think women are stupid. They don't understand what the women are trying to tell them."

"You have taught me things I did not know, Li," King Yitzhak said. "I know that there is a problem, but I still don't completely understand why."

"There are so many things I wish I could tell you," Li said. "Some I cannot, because I am still learning the words men use. Others I cannot because I see that you are not ready to understand them. I hope in my heart that someday you are, for I know that you are the one person who can make things change. Although you are kind and gentle most of the time, I see that sometimes you get very angry. I know that even men do not dare disobey you then. I could see it in Yuri's eyes and hear it in your voice."

They were interrupted by the creaking of the door. Yuri stood in the doorway with Ki behind him.

"If it pleases you, I will take Ki home now," Yuri said.

"Ki, do you want to return to Yuri's home?" King Yitzhak asked.

"Yes," Ki said. "We have done what you said, called a truce."

"I'll see you tomorrow, Yuri," King Yitzhak said and the two left. "Would you like me to stay longer, Li?"

"Yes, My King," Li replied with a smile as they went back inside. "I think that you want to stay for a while."

"Yes, I do," he replied as he placed her hand on his chest.

Chapter 7 – Proving Her Life is His

Yitzhak looked over the reports from Brinley again. King Burkhart was slowly withdrawing from all but the most essential duties and appearances. She who bore him hadn't been seen outside the palace for almost a year, but was apparently still alive. General Caddaric was reported to have travelled north to bury his father. Maybe it was time to take advantage of this vulnerability.

"Guard," Yitzhak said and the door opened. "Time to assemble the army."

"At once!"

He went to the armory and soon Lenar was there to help him put his armor on. He was just about ready when Joris arrived.

"A word with you, My King," Joris said in a tone he recognized.

"It's got to be now, Joris. General Caddaric is two days travel or more away. I need to strike fast and hard."

Joris gave him a look that revealed his disagreement.

"I know," Yitzhak said. "We'll strike early tomorrow morning near Weston. It's a farming community. We'll take it quickly and move into the city from there."

It was nearing nightfall when they arrived across the river from Weston. The river would be easy to ford just east of Weston where it widened out. They made camp and had a good supper. He sat watching the fire as the moon rose through the trees.

He hated this part, the waiting. He knew Joris didn't approve of him leading the battle when he had no heir. He had to try. He knew if he didn't it would not be long before Brinley would try to attack and take Mannton from him. He went to his tent and lay down hoping to sleep. He lay awake thinking about Li.

Yitzhak woke before dawn. They had a quick breakfast before mounting up to cross the river. They were greeted by King Burkhart and a small army. This was unexpected, but as the sun rose, he ordered the attack. It was midmorning when he faced King Burkhart on foot.

"Why continue this futile tradition?" King Burkhart asked as they dueled. "Go back to Mannton where you belong."

"And wait for you to take Mannton for yourself? You don't have an heir," he replied.

"Neither do you," King Burkhart countered as the reflection off his sword blinded Yitzhak.

"At least I have a wife," he said just before King Burkhart struck a solid blow that caught him off balance.

The sun was glinting off what appeared to be two swords before King Burkhart slashed his side through his armor. He stumbled backwards into someone.

"Take your wounded and dead back to Mannton and stay there," King Burkhart said as he held his sword up and twisted it back and forth several times.

"Get me a horse," Yitzhak said. "Sound the retreat."

King Burkhart was still standing nearby. The horse was panicked. King Burkhart sheathed his sword and took the reins from the soldier. He stroked the horse's face and whispered something into its ear. Soon the horse settled down and he pulled down and back on the reins until the horse knelt, then lay down. Two of his men helped Yitzhak to mount before King Burkhart pulled gently up on the reins. The horse stood.

"Don't leave this life with regrets," King Burkhart said before he turned and left.

"Don't leave anyone behind," Yitzhak said before turning his horse towards Mannton.

A couple of men followed him on horseback as he rode straight to the palace at a gallop. He was getting light headed and knew he was losing a lot of blood. Li would be able to take care of him while he healed. He thought of her beautiful face and urged the horse on faster.

When he reached the palace he practically fell off the horse before the men could dismount. He staggered through the door and down the hall to Li's room.

****

As he promised, King Yitzhak visited with Li more often, but still not often enough. She wanted to bear his child but was beginning to become worried that she never would. The last time he had visited he had been quiet and distracted. That had been a month ago. The warm season was drawing to a close and soon it would be cold again. She had just finished washing her lunch dishes as the door burst open. King Yitzhak staggered in wearing strange metal and leather clothes. He was spattered in blood.

"My King!" she exclaimed as she ran to him. "Are you injured?"

He did not answer as she took him over to the bed. He sat down on the edge and pulled off the metal that covered his head. She began looking for a way to take the rest of the metal off as the thing that had covered his head dropped to the floor and rolled under the bed. He unbuckled his belt and his sword clattered to the floor. Bit by bit she got the metal and his boots off. She began removing the leather that was under the metal. She could see the damage to the metal and leather and knew he was wounded. She removed his shirt and found a gash in his side that was oozing blood. She helped him to lie down before she ripped his shirt into pieces and got a fresh bucket of water. She cleaned his wound and stitched it shut before washing the rest of his body. She found bruises beginning to form. There were other minor wounds that she washed and bandaged. He was unconscious as several guards entered the room. She gently covered him up.

"King Yitzhak," one of the men said, then stopped.

"His wounds have been cleaned and bandaged," she responded as she looked at King Yitzhak's face. "He must rest to heal. I will care for him. You may send in the healer if you feel it is necessary."

The guards left and soon another man came in. This man checked the bandaged wounds and found the stitches.

"Who did this?" he asked as he pointed to the stitches.

"I did," Li replied. "It was bleeding."

"King Yitzhak will be angry," the healer said. "I am the only one to treat his wounds. It will not heal like this."

"He came to me, not you," Li said. "He knows that I have stitched skin before. If the cut in Rowan's forehead healed after I stitched it, then this wound will heal as well. I cleaned it before I stitched it shut. Stitching the skin shut will keep the dirt out. If clothing is stitched when it is cut or ripped, then why not skin?"

There was a long silence before the man spoke.

"If he dies, you die," the man said with a growl.

"I would gladly die to preserve his life," Li said.

"Li," King Yitzhak whispered and his eyes opened a little.

"I am here, My King," Li replied as she placed her hand on his face.

"My side," he said a little louder.

"I stitched the wound shut, My King," Li said and he smiled. "Sleep now. I will watch over you."

King Yitzhak closed his eyes again.

"I will allow no harm to come to him," Li said. "My life is his and that is as much by my will as it was his and my father's. I will ask the guards for you if he needs you, but if you wish to stay or check up on him, that is your choice."

"I've never seen a man trust his wife when he was so badly injured before," the healer said. "I've got other wounded to attend to. The war went badly. I will be back tomorrow."

"I will expect you then," Li said.

The man left, shutting the door softly behind him. Li was worried. She had heard of war before. She knew that often war meant that some men died and other men would take their wives as their own. She sat on the edge of the bed watching King Yitzhak sleep, but he did not stir before her supper was delivered.

"How is he?"

She recognized Yuri's voice as he spoke.

"His wounds are cleaned and bandaged," she replied. "He sleeps now. I will not leave his side for more than a moment until he wakes."

"I know you will take care of him," Yuri said.

"The healer was not so certain," Li said. "But King Yitzhak came to me, not him."

"I will return tomorrow," Yuri said and left.

Li sat on a chair next to the bed as she ate. She knew it would be a long night. She lit the lanterns on the tables next to the bed. She held his hand in hers in case she fell asleep. The hours crept by slowly, but King Yitzhak did not stir. By dawn, she was very tired. As breakfast was brought in, he at last began to stir.

"Li?" King Yitzhak said as his eyes opened.

"I am here, My King," Li said as his hand closed around hers.

"I have not left your side. I will not leave you while you heal."

He smiled.

"The healer and Yuri will be here sometime today," Li said. "They both came last night. Are you hungry?"

"Just a little," King Yitzhak said.

"Do you think you could sit up to eat?" she asked. "If not, I can bring it here to your bed."

"I don't quite feel up to sitting at the table," he said after trying to sit up.

"I have an idea," Li said.

She got her rolled up mat out from under the bed and unrolled it. She then folded it up until it was almost the same size as the pillow on the bed. She helped King Yitzhak to sit up while she rearranged the pillow with her mat under it. She then helped him to lean back against the pillow.

"Better?" she asked.

"Yes," he replied. "I think I can eat now."

She went over to the table and found two plates instead of one.

There was a plate similar to what she used to prepare for Father and Rowan in addition to her usual breakfast. The milk was fresher than she usually got as well. She placed her plate on the table before taking the tray over to the bed. She set it gently across his lap. He tried to raise his right hand to eat, but winced before he could get it to the tray.

"I will feed you, My King," she said as she picked up the fork.

She fed him and even held the cup while he drank until he was full. She took the tray back over to the table and set it down. She returned to the bed.

"How are you feeling?" she asked. "Are you in pain?"

"Yes," he said.

"I'll be right back," she said. "I know what will help."

He nodded and she went out into the tiny courtyard. She had noticed that there was a numbing herb growing in a back corner and had been carefully tending it. She plucked several leaves from it and washed them in fresh water before returning to King Yitzhak.

"Chew on these and swallow them," she said. "They are bitter and make your mouth numb for a while, but it will ease your pain."

"How do you know this?" he asked. "The healer has never given me this before."

"Women spend most of their lives in hunger and pain. I watched animals to learn what they ate. I saw them eating this plant once. I tried it and found out what it does. It is not much good for food, but it is good to ease pain," Li said but could see the uncertainty in his eyes. "I would never do anything to hurt you. I would gladly give my life to preserve yours. You have shown me a kindness far beyond any I had thought possible. You have given me a better life than I had ever hoped for. You have even saved my life when no other man would. My life is yours."

"I trust you Li," King Yitzhak said. "When I was wounded, all I could think of was getting to you."

"The healer said the war went badly," Li said as he chewed on the leaves.

"Brinley is larger than Mannton," King Yitzhak said after swallowing. "They have many people and I have worried that they would want Mannton. King Burkhart has no wife and no heir. It is said that when he became king, he drove away his only brother. No one knows where Prince Langward went. Most people think he is dead, perhaps even killed by his own brother. It was King Burkhart that cut my side."

"Such a man does not deserve to have a wife or an heir," Li said as she helped King Yitzhak lay back down. "He deserves to die alone, ill in his bed, not in battle. Your father died an honorable death in battle protecting Mannton. King Burkhart is not worthy of such an honor."

"You are very wise for a woman," King Yitzhak said. "I know that one day you will bear me an heir and he will be a very wise king."

"Sleep now," Li said with a smile as she made certain he would be comfortable. "I will always be nearby."

He reached up with his left hand and stroked her face softly before closing his eyes. She ate while he slept. She washed the dishes and began to clean the leather and metal outfit he had been wearing when he arrived. She was just finishing as lunch was delivered. Again there were two plates. She went to the bed and placed her hand on King Yitzhak's hand. He opened his eyes and smiled at her. Again she fed him. She was just finishing when the door opened up.

"My King," she heard two men's voices say.

"Your color is better today, My King," she heard a man say and recognized the healer's voice.

"I am feeling better, but still in pain," King Yitzhak replied. "Could you please bring me more of those leaves, Li?"

"At once, My King," she said and went out to the courtyard.

"What leaves?" she heard Yuri's voice ask.

"They ease the pain when you eat them," Li heard King Yitzhak reply. "Li gave them to me."

"You're certain she's not poisoning you?" she heard the healer ask. "Women can't be trusted, My King. My wife has tried to poison me several times."

"Li can be trusted," King Yitzhak said as she entered with the leaves.

"I told you before that I would take care of King Yitzhak," Li said. "I do not want him to die."

She heard the healer make a noise as she approached the bed.

"Don't you dare," King Yitzhak said with a growl. "She is my wife. You will not touch her."

Li smiled at him as she handed him the leaves.

"My wife does not dare speak like that," the healer said in a disgusted tone.

"Li," King Yitzhak said. "I think it best that I speak to these men in private."

"I will go out to the courtyard and shut the door," Li replied as he stroked her face. "I might lay down to sleep. I stayed awake all last night to watch over you."

"I will have Yuri open the door when we are finished," King Yitzhak said. "You can come back in when you wake. I will be alright while you sleep."

"Yes, My King," she replied and left the room.

****

After the door shut, Yitzhak said, "I know you hate women, Kon, but you must understand something about Li. She is not like most women."

"They're all evil," Kon replied. "They're only good for three things; cooking, cleaning and bearing children. We keep them around only because we have to. I can't eat what my wife cooks because she tries to poison me."

"It's because of men like you that most women think men are evil," Yitzhak said, watching Kon's expression betray his surprise. "They are so much more intelligent than you think. Although they are not allowed to speak, doesn't mean they don't think."

"He is right," Yuri said. "I used to think that women were evil. My wife was always scratching and biting me. I had to beat her daily just to get her to prepare my meals. King Yitzhak and Li helped me and my wife call a truce. Since then she has not scratched or bit me even once. I have not felt the need to beat her either. I can relax in my own home knowing I'm safe. I have discovered that my meals are better and my house cleaner."

"When I first noticed Li at the well, I could see that she was different," Yitzhak said. "She acted differently and even helped the other females. When my father died I felt lost. I wandered until I reached the well and Yuri found me there. Later she told me she remembered the sadness in my voice and knew my heart must have hurt from mourning my father's death."

"She understood?" Kon asked, then stopped.

"Yes," Yitzhak said. "A year after the funeral I realized I needed to have a wife soon. I had thought of her often since first seeing her, so I decided to see what she would do if I asked for a drink. She handed me a ladle of water and then cleaned my boots as I drank. I knew then that I wanted her for my wife."

"When I came yesterday, she had already cleaned and dressed your wounds," Kon said. "I noticed your side was stitched up and asked her about it. She said you knew she would stitch the wound closed."

"Yes," Yitzhak said. "I expected her to."

"She had also washed you so thoroughly that if not for your wounds, no one would realize you had been in battle," Kon said. "I see that your armor has been cleaned as well. Did she do that too?"

"She must have," Yitzhak said. "As you can see, she wants to please me. I know that Li will never purposely do anything that would harm me because she loves me. She would never purposely do anything to make me angry, even though she knows I will not beat her."

"I did not know that women would have such feelings," Kon said quietly. "Yesterday she said that her life was yours and that was as much by her will as it was by yours and her father's."

"They feel pain and sorrow just like men do," Yitzhak said. "Go and think about it. Perhaps if you spoke to your wife instead of beating her, you might find out why she tries to poison you."

Kon bowed and left.

"I know you don't want to hear this again, My King," Yuri said. "But, Li has not born you any heir. Perhaps you should consider taking another wife. If you had been killed, the kingdom would not have a prince to eventually take your place."

"I know, Yuri," Yitzhak said with a sigh. "Joris has told me the same thing."

"You need to think about it," Yuri said. "If Li cannot bear you an heir, then you need to get rid of her and take a new wife."

"I need to rest, Yuri," Yitzhak said. "Help me to lie down and then open the courtyard door."

****

Yitzhak was quiet as Li fed him dinner. He could see the same worry in her eyes that he had seen in Yuri's. He slept fitfully, dreaming strange dreams. He suddenly awoke in the middle of the night. He heard a soft voice. He could not understand the mumbled words at first, but then heard his name. He slowly and carefully sat up. His head was not as dizzy as he had expected it to be. He slowly stood and made his way to the foot of the bed. He could see Li in the light of the lamps and fireplace. She was lying on her side on the mat. He sat down on the edge of the bed and watched her as she slept. Her legs and arms twitched as she said his name again. He saw the smile on her face as she began to relax. Soon he could tell that she was sleeping deeply again.

He thought about what Yuri and Joris had been telling him about taking a new wife. He could not do that to Li. If Kon had repeated her words correctly he knew that she would rather die than leave. He slowly got back into bed. He wondered what he should do. The cold season was swiftly coming and from all the signs it would be a harsh one.

Chapter 8 – Haunting Memories

It was a cold morning several months after Mannton's last battle with Brinley when a soldier came bearing news of King Burkhart's death. He said that she who bore King Burkhart had sent messengers to find Prince Langward. Yitzhak wished he could attack now that Brinley was without a king, but the army was still recovering from the last battle. His wounds had healed, but he knew it was too soon to go back into battle. He needed an heir. He wished he had more time to spend with Li, but so many other things got in the way. The warm season was approaching, but it didn't feel like it outside.

Yitzhak was also worried about Ta. She had fallen ill and was not doing well. He walked down the stairs to go to her room. The guards let him in. Li was at Ta's side as she lay on the mat at the foot of the bed. He shook his head wondering why she would not sleep in the bed or even accept a blanket to cover her. He knelt next to Li and placed his hand on Ta's cheek. Her face was pale and cold, but she still lived.

"King Yitzhak is here, Ta," Li said softly and Ta's eyes fluttered open for a moment.

Ta smiled faintly, and then was still.

"She is no more," Li said quietly as a tear ran down her face. "She is dead. She waited to see you one last time before she died."

Yitzhak put his arm around Li and was surprised as she buried her face against his shoulder. He could feel her body shudder as she cried. He remembered his sadness at his father's death. That night, he had not slept. He had cried all through the night. At last Li sat up and wiped her eyes.

"She must be wrapped before she is laid beneath the ground, buried," Li said. "When she who bore me died, Ti helped me wrap her and bury her."

"I will help you," Yitzhak said. "We will bury her next to my father. Although it has never been done before, I feel that is what we should do."

Li nodded and said, "Help me to lift her from her mat."

He helped, not knowing why Li wanted her off the mat. He watched as Li began to loosen a piece of cloth from the mat and pulled it. The narrow strip of cloth got longer as the mat got smaller. When Li reached the end, she began to wrap the cloth around Ta's feet. No words were spoken as Yitzhak helped Li wrap she who bore him. He was beginning to realize what a dismal existence most women must have to know they were sleeping on the very cloth that would be used to wrap them for burial.

They carried her through the palace halls and out to the small cemetery within the outer wall. Li picked up a flat stone from the low stone wall separating the cemetery from the garden. She knelt next to the wrapped body and began using the stone to dig the grave. He thought about getting a shovel, but then picked up a stone and silently joined her. It took a long time to dig the grave. Several guards had followed them, but he waved them away. He felt this was to be done in private, not that he was ashamed to be doing it. He was very tired by the time they were finished.

"Usually a woman is buried at night," Li said as she looked at the mound of dirt covering the body. "Those who have buried her return home to wash up and start breakfast. When she who bore me died, my father beat me all day, not understanding that I was telling him she was dead."

"I am seeing that life is not easy for women," he said as they walked back towards her room.

"My life here and Ta's life are better than most women have," Li said quietly as the guard opened the door. "For that I am grateful. It is more than I could have hoped for. Most women only hope for more food, fewer beatings and death."

With that, Li turned and went into the room shutting the door softly behind her. Yitzhak thought about what she had said as he stood staring at the door. Joris and Yuri thought he was insane to listen to a woman, yet Yuri was glad his wife no longer bit or scratched him. Yitzhak had not thought it was possible for any woman besides Li to have much intelligence, but perhaps they could. He wandered back into Ta's room. The room was clean and felt as though it had been empty for years in spite of the fire in the fireplace.

He noticed a bag sitting on the mantle. He stroked the worn fabric softly before picking it up and taking it over to the table. Inside the bag he found a bit of sharpened metal, two needles, a stick with a hook carved in the end of it, two stacks of fabric sewn together on one edge and several sticks with various colors of thread wound around them.

Yitzhak picked up one stack of fabric and folded back the first layer to find an image of his father stitched in thread. On the next piece he found a picture of an infant. As he turned the pieces of fabric he saw himself grow from a child to a man. The last stitched piece was an image of Li. He picked up the second stack of fabric and found an image of a woman who looked a bit like Ta but different followed by one of his grandfather and several of his uncle. Ta had certainly loved the family she left to be his father's wife. She had also loved him and his father.

Yitzhak left the items laying on the table and left the room. He wandered the halls of the palace thinking about Ta. After going up several staircases in his wanderings he was walking along a hall and where it turned there was a cold breeze that startled him. He looked around and realized he didn't recognize this area of the palace at all. The section of wall seemed poorly made of rough stones and didn't match the rest of the walls. As he felt along the edge that butted up against the corner one of the stones came out in his hand. There was light on the other side of the wall that was bright enough to be sunshine. He put the stone down and tugged at the one above it. That stone came loose and the ones above it began to shift. Yitzhak jumped back as the top portion of the wall collapsed to the floor revealing a staircase with small windows along the right side. Several servants came on the run.

"I'm fine," he said as he pushed down more of the wall. "Haul these stones out."

He went up the stairs to arrive at a small landing. There was a dusty table with a lamp and two small rods on it. To the left was a large door. He tried the door, but it was locked.

"There you are, My King," Lenar's voice echoed in the staircase. "I didn't expect to find you in the servants' area of the palace knocking down walls."

He soon joined Yitzhak on the landing.

"What is this room?" he asked as he pointed to the door.

"Possibly storage since this should be the attic level," Lenar said. "My father mentioned his father said something about the attic containing the ghosts of the past. Perhaps. . ."

Lenar pulled a ring of keys out of a pouch that hung from his belt. After trying a couple of keys the lock turned. As Yitzhak opened the door Lenar scraped the rods together creating a spark to light the lamp. Yitzhak pushed the door open further not knowing quite what to expect. He was greeted by a confusing jumble of furniture and trunks. Lenar held the lamp higher and he realized it was quite a large room with a peaked ceiling. Yitzhak placed his hand on something tall covered by a large cloth. He felt carvings under the cloth.

"The guards mentioned you and your wife burying something large next to your father's grave. Then you sort of vanished. I've been looking for you for hours. It is well past suppertime."

"She who bore me died," Yitzhak replied as he rubbed the carvings through the cloth. "We buried her next to Father."

He heard Lenar shuffle his feet like he was uncomfortable.

"I. . . I," Lenar began.

"Yeah, I don't know quite how I feel about her death," Yitzhak said softly.

He turned and walked toward the door. Lenar followed him. He shut the door as Lenar blew out the lamp.

"I'll take supper in my chambers," he said when they reached the main hall of the palace.

Lenar hurried off as Yitzhak walked towards the royal chambers. When he arrived he looked around the elegant but comfortable rooms that contrasted the bare room that had served as Ta's home. Lenar soon arrived with the tray of food. He sat down at the table to eat.

****

Kenner sat at the table in the kitchen staring at the floor in front of the fireplace. He missed An and Li. While both he and Rowan shared the cooking and cleaning, it wasn't the same as before. He was still learning to sew, but wound up paying Dreggen to have Ti repair their clothing or make new clothes.

Anunik had built a home a half day's ride away on the shore of the ocean and had built a boat. Rowan sometimes spent a week at a time out on the boat with Anunik. It was then that Kenner really missed An and Li. He sighed as he went out to pick some vegetables. He cleaned them and started some soup. He'd be able to eat it for several days. As he stirred in some herbs to flavor the soup he heard something outside. He went out the kitchen door and found Rowan tying up his horse.

"You're home sooner than I expected," he said.

"It was a good trip," Rowan said as he pointed to the other horse loaded down with bags. "I brought dried fish to sell. I'll split the earnings with Anunik."

"I'm making some soup. Come in and eat."

When they sat eating supper Rowan looked at him and said, "What's wrong Father?"

"Just thinking about An," Kenner said with a sigh. "I look around and see so many women with thin hands just like she had. I wonder why I never really noticed until it was too late."

"I never noticed either," Rowan said.

Kenner gathered up the dishes and began washing them while Rowan took some fish over to Dreggen. Rowan spent the rest of the week selling the dried fish. Kenner spent a lot of time out in the garden because the house reminded him of An.

"Anunik and I are going fishing again," Rowan said as he put some money on the table one morning. "Are you going to be alright?"

"I'll be alright," he replied. "It's just so empty now."

Rowan put his hand on his shoulder. He looked up into Rowan's worried eyes.

"Maybe you should write down what you are feeling," Rowan said. "I've noticed you haven't been sleeping well."

"Just be careful. I worry when you're out there fishing."

"Maybe you should come with."

"No, I'd just be in the way," he said. "Besides, who would feed the animals and tend the garden?"

Rowan patted his shoulder and went to his room to pack. Kenner knew he would be gone for a week or more leaving the house empty of everything except memories. Even during the cold season, Rowan would be gone fishing with Anunik a couple weeks each month.

Early in the warm season Dreggen invited Kenner over to eat supper. Their sons were out on another fishing trip. Kenner made certain he left some food for Ti.

When Ti came to clear the table, he said, "Thank you Ti that was really good.'

"You barely ate," Ti said.

"I'm just not very hungry," he replied. "I miss An."

"I do too," Ti said before she took the plates from the table.

"We should spend a couple of days out hunting," Dreggen said.

"There's no one to feed the animals and milk the cow," Kenner said.

"Ti, if Kenner and I went hunting could you milk his cow and feed the yard fowl?"

"Yes," Ti replied.

"We'll leave tomorrow morning."

Kenner woke early and packed a few things for the hunting trip. Dreggen was waiting for him near the back door. It felt good to be getting away from the house and its memories. They passed a square of ground surrounded by stones on the outskirts of town. It was bare other than scattered stones. There were a couple of women scraping dirt into a hole.

"Ti says that's where the women lie beneath the dirt. I didn't realize before now that she meant it's the women's cemetery," Dreggen said.

Kenner realized that was where An now was. They rode all day and made camp about an hour before sunset. They ate in silence and sat watching the fire. Kenner got out his journal and began to write about how he felt about An. Before long he could no longer hold back the tears.

"We've known each other too long for you to not feel that you can tell me anything. I've known for a while that something has been troubling you. You've changed. You spend more time outside than inside."

"It's just so full of memories of An. I know she died because I didn't leave her any food," Kenner said as he stared at the fire. "It's like a part of me is missing."

"I think I know what you mean," Dreggen said softly. "I would be completely lost without Ti."

"I loved her, Dreggen." Kenner sobbed. "I still love her. I dream about her. Everything I see reminds me of her and that it is my fault that she's dead. I never gave her enough to eat. I never asked her if she kept food out for herself. I never told her how much I love her. I killed her just as surely as if I took a knife and plunged it into her heart."

He sobbed into his hands as he felt Dreggen's hand on his shoulder.

"Since I've been going to the well, I've noticed how thin all the women and girls are," Kenner finally said. "I always thought An and Li kept food for themselves before serving Rowan and me. I found out that everything they prepared got put on the table in front of us."

"Ti eats before I do," Dreggen said then paused. "At least that's what I think Ti is doing."

"Make certain that she gets more food."

"I've been thinking about another infant, maybe even a girl."

"You should," Kenner said. "Don't wind up like me, alone and heartbroken."

"Get some sleep, my friend," Dreggen said as he gently closed the journal. "The past can't be changed."

It took him a long time to fall asleep. The following days were filled with setting traps and collecting their catch. They skinned all the rabbits and other small animals before cutting the meat into strips and smoking it for hours over a fire to cure it. They started curing the hides while waiting for the meat to cure. After a week they had the horses so laden that they would have to walk home leading the horses.

"Anunik and Rowan are probably back by now," Dreggen said as they walked towards home.

It took a long three days to get home. When they got there they were greeted by Ti.

"I haven't seen Rowan yet," she said. "I thought he would be back by now."

Kenner checked all through his house, but it was just as he left it. As he and Dreggen sold the cured meat and hides, Kenner got more worried as each day passed. By the end of the week he wondered if he'd ever see Rowan again.

Chapter 9 – At Last Ready to Hear the Truth

As the cold season gave way to the warm season, Li thought often of Ta. Li asked one of the guards if she could go to Ta's room to clean it and he let her. He said she could go between the rooms until her supper was brought to her. Li found Ta's bag with its contents strewn on the table. She smiled as she looked through the pictures Ta had shown her of King Yitzhak growing up. She gathered the things back into the bag and put it back in its place on the mantle. She noticed the seat under the window was lifted up so she went over to shut it. She looked inside and saw some bedding that looked like it was in better condition than what was on King Yitzhak's bed in her room. She took it out and put it on the table to take back to her room.

When Li looked inside the empty compartment she noticed a front corner of the bottom was missing. Curious, she carefully put her finger in the hole and lifted. The whole bottom came out revealing another compartment full of something she had seen at her father's home. Sometimes she saw Father making marks in one of them. She leaned the wood against the wall and carefully picked up one of the items. The inside was completely full of markings. She heard footsteps in the hall so she quickly put the item back and replaced the piece of wood before shutting the lid. She picked up the broom and began sweeping the floor.

When all was quiet she was tempted to look again inside the compartment, but didn't want to be caught so she scrubbed the floor before taking the bedding back to her own room. She spread out the bedding and confirmed it was in good condition before using it to replace the bedding on King Yitzhak's bed. King Yitzhak was very busy and seldom visited her. She had heard Joris tell him to take a new wife the last time he came in to visit her. She did not say anything, but he seemed distracted and worried.

She wished with all her heart that she could bear King Yitzhak an heir. She had not slept well since that night. King Yitzhak had mentioned attacking Brinley again. It worried her because the last war with Brinley had almost killed King Yitzhak. Lucjen mentioned going with King Yitzhak but promised the remaining guards would treat her kindly and bring her food. It was almost time for her lunch to be brought when a guard came into the room.

"King Yitzhak sent word that you are to be taken to Brinley," the guard said and her heart caught in her throat.

He was at least still alive. She took her rolled mat from under the bed and the bag from the table. She followed the guard out to a waiting wagon. She placed her mat and bag beside the trunks in the wagon. She heard Joris and Yuri talking as she climbed up to the seat of the wagon. One of the guards led the horses pulling the wagon and they left the palace wall. She tried to be brave, knowing that King Yitzhak must have decided to take a new wife. She did not look up as they traveled. She heard the guards talking about Lucjen having wings and a woman with a sword. It didn't make any sense to her.

At night Li unrolled her mat next to the wagon away from the men. They gave her some food after they had eaten. After eating she lay down, but woke to every noise fearing the men would leave her behind. By morning she was very tired. The second night was not much better. It was a very long ride, but at last they reached Brinley's city on the third day.

Li knew that by the buildings that she saw out of the corner of her eyes. She could see many men, women and children as they passed by. It was strange to see men and women walking together. It was also strange to see girls playing, not working. Just after they entered through a gate in a stone wall, the wagon suddenly stopped.

"Welcome to Brinley," a woman's voice said.

Li looked up suddenly to see King Yitzhak and a man standing beside a woman who was wearing a very beautiful dress. Between them and the palace was a large, winged beast.

"Haskell will not eat you, nor harm you in any way," the woman said.

"This is Queen Marriah of Brinley and Burton," King Yitzhak said as he indicated the woman.

Li was amazed. The man said something.

"And this is King Archelaus of Burton and Brinley," King Yitzhak said as another man rode up leading three horses.

The man dismounted and knelt at the woman's feet. The woman spoke and the man stood. She spoke again and the man mounted and rode away very quickly. King Yitzhak mounted his horse as the man he had called King Archelaus clasped his hands together and stood beside one of the other horses. The woman placed one foot in his hands and mounted the horse with both legs on the same side. Li gasped in surprise. She had never known a woman could ride a horse.

"I see that women in Mannton do not ride horses," the woman said.

"No, they don't," King Yitzhak replied to Li's surprise.

They followed as the woman led them to the palace. When they reached the courtyard, a man surrounded by four men walked in through another door. As they stopped a short distance away, Li could see the wagon the man was pulling. The man quickly laid out flat on the ground at the woman's feet. Li had never seen a man behave this way. He acted more like some of the women she knew in Mannton.

"Rise," the woman said.

He rose to his knees with his head bowed, and said, "Wise and Compassionate Queen, I know that I am unworthy of your presence. My life is yours to command. Only by your kindness I still live. I humbly present you with this gift to demonstrate my faithful compliance with the terms of my sentence."

"Present your gift," the woman said.

He got to his feet and went to the wagon. He removed a blanket revealing a stone statue of a creature. As she approached the wagon, he dropped again to his knees. She circled the wagon, looking closely at the statue.

"Your gift pleases me," she said as she stopped before him. "When you are skilled enough, I will have a project for you. One which you will be paid for upon completion." The man looked up at last.

"I will work hard to gain the required skills, Great Queen," he said. "I will not disappoint you."

He then laid down again.

"I will find a place suitable to display this," the woman said. "You are dismissed."

The man got to his feet and returned to the four waiting men. "How?" King Yitzhak asked in an amazed tone. "What?"

"I had learned much about Tarl and his cruel methods of teaching by the time Archelaus and I were married. I challenged him to a dual. He soon discovered himself disarmed with both swords pointed at his throat," the woman said as they entered the palace. "He learned that he and his father had played a part in encouraging my uncle to abuse my father and to not respect him. That is what made my father decide to leave Brinley."

"Most thought Prince Langward was jealous or cowardly," King Yitzhak said.

"He was neither. He was never trained to fight as King Burkhart had been. It also explains why he never fought Larkin before the day of his death," the woman said. "Garman will show you to your rooms. I will see you at supper."

The man who had brought the horses led them up some stairs and down a hall to a large room with chairs and tables in it. She followed King Yitzhak into the room. She saw a woman come out of a single door near the ones they had entered through. Inside was a small bedroom. Li took her box and mat with her through the door to the first room with a bed. It was barely large enough for her to spread her mat next to the bed.

"What are you doing in here?" the woman asked her.

"This is where I will stay," she replied.

"This is the servant's quarters," the woman said. "You are King Yitzhak's wife aren't you?"

"Until he says I am not," Li replied, trying not to choke on the words.

"Shouldn't you be staying in the same room as King Yitzhak?" the woman asked.

"No," she replied in confusion. "It is not done. This is the only other sleeping room I saw. This is where I will stay."

The woman looked frustrated and shook her head as she left. Li began to cry. She just knew that King Yitzhak would leave her here and take a new wife. She did not know what would happen to her then. She knew she must be strong. She wiped away her tears and looked around the tiny, plain room. Suddenly she heard a knock on the door. As she turned, she saw the woman who was Queen Marriah standing in the doorway. Li fell to her knees at Queen Marriah's feet. She suddenly felt a hand on her chin and her face being lifted up until she looked up. She could see Queen Marriah looking at her.

"You need not kneel before me, Li," she said in a gentle tone. "You are in Brinley and things are different here. In Brinley, because you are King Yitzhak's wife, you are Queen Li. As Queen Li, you are a sister to me."

"You are very powerful to have King Yitzhak address you directly," Li said. "I am nothing. I am not worthy of your attention."

"We are not so different, you and me," Queen Marriah said.

"Less than a year ago, I thought as you that I was nothing."

Li sat up in surprise.

"My father and I had been slaves to a cruel man for eight years. He beat us and tortured us. My father died at this man's hand that I might escape. The man had decided I would be his wife."

"You . . . you were beaten?"

"Every day," Queen Marriah said. "Sometimes even whipped. When I escaped, I was rescued by Haskell, the dragon, and Regis Bryant of Glynis, Lord Dracona."

"Did Haskell eat . . . ?" Li said, then trailed off.

"No," Queen Marriah said. "But since dragons speak through thought, he helped me tell what I had been through and Regis Bryant executed the man. While I was in Dracona, I was taught to read and write. I also learned that I was not a slave, that I was equal to others and worthy of being loved."

"You can read and write?" Li asked in amazement.

"In three languages," Queen Marriah replied. "We are setting up schools in Brinley and Burton so that everyone can learn to read and write."

"I have wanted to learn to read and write," Li said. "But I dare not ask."

"I have spoken to King Yitzhak and he has agreed to try Brinley's way of doing things while staying in Brinley," Queen Marriah said. "You have the opportunity to show him that you are much more than he ever imagined. Change won't come easy, but it must start somewhere."

"I won't have to stay in this room the whole time I'm here?" Li asked finding it hard to believe what Queen Marriah was saying.

"My husband, King Archelaus, told him that in Burton and Brinley if a man is not sharing a bed with his wife that it is because he has angered her," Queen Marriah said.

"You sleep in a bed?" Li asked. "In the same bed with King Archelaus?"

"Yes," Queen Marriah replied. "And tonight you will not be sleeping in this room on the floor nor in this bed. Come with me."

Li followed Queen Marriah out of the servants' quarters and into the bedroom.

"You will sleep in this bed. If King Yitzhak doesn't like it, he can sleep on the floor," Queen Marriah said. "You will come and go as you please. You will have two women who will attend to your needs. You will eat in the dining hall seated beside your husband."

"That is allowed? I couldn't," Li said. "King Yitzhak wouldn't."

"See this sword?" Queen Marriah said as she lifted the sword at her side and Li nodded. "With this sword, I disarmed King Yitzhak and held both swords to his throat. He will not dare to argue right now. He knows that in Brinley my word is law and obeyed without question. He is my guest and must abide by my rules."

"You didn't hurt him, did you?" Li asked with a tremor in her voice, frightened that he had been injured.

"No, I just wanted to get his attention," Queen Marriah said. "I slid the flat of the blade across his chest so he could see that I was capable of hurting him if I desired to. He found that he could not ignore me."

"I'm glad you did not hurt him," Li said with great relief.

Another woman entered followed by two men carrying large piles of cloth. They put them on the bed before kneeling at Queen Marriah's feet.

"Rise," Marriah said. "Inform the Ministers and District Governors that they are to bring their wives to dine at the palace tonight. Aurella, some may need their children fed and watched during supper."

"It shall be done," the woman replied and they left.

"What are these?" Li asked.

"You will not be wearing that plain brown dress to supper," Queen Marriah said. "First you need a bath, and then you can choose a dress from these to wear. The rest will be put in the closet for you to wear during your stay."

Li couldn't believe her eyes as Queen Marriah led her into another room with a large pool of water in the center of it that was fed by a stream of water falling from a shelf on the wall.

"This is what I will bathe in?"

"Yes. Get undressed and get in. I brought something to show you."

Wild ideas were racing through her mind as she removed her dress with trembling hands. When Queen Marriah returned with her drawing board, Li was in the water. As Li bathed, Queen Marriah showed her several drawings and they talked about men. Li told her about how women in Mannton lived and were treated. She revealed that women often starved or were beaten to death. She began to cry when Queen Marriah showed her the picture of a man carrying a woman in his arms. Queen Marriah told her about how much this man loved his wife.

"I have wanted King Yitzhak to care for me in that way," Li said as she felt her heart ache.

"You love him," Queen Marriah said.

"He has been very kind to me," Li said as she nodded. "He has never beaten me and he gave me the cloth large enough to make an entire dress. That brown dress I was wearing is the first one I have ever worn that was not patched together out of scraps."

"He says he cares for you, but that he doesn't really know what love is. Perhaps you can help him learn."

"But how?" Li asked as she stepped out of the water.

"When you follow your heart, you will know," Queen Marriah said. "You will have to make him understand what you want from him. I will have Aurella put out a bowl of sweet oil for you. But first you need to make him see you differently than he ever has before."

"What is sweet oil for?"

"I think you'll figure it out. It tastes good and feels good."

"Oh," Li said with a smile as she blushed slightly realizing what Queen Marriah meant.

The piles of cloth turned out to be dresses more beautiful than Li had ever imagined. They looked through the dresses and Li tried several on. She finally settled on a blue-green dress with silver trim. Queen Marriah brushed Li's hair until it glistened. She then braided it around Li's head.

"Now look," Queen Marriah said as she led Li to the polished shield. "This will get his attention."

Li's hand went to her cheek as she saw her reflection. She could not believe the beautiful woman looking back was really her. She looked more like Queen Marriah than herself.

"Stand tall and proud," Queen Marriah told her. "Let's go join our husbands. I can't wait to see King Yitzhak's face when he sees how beautiful you are."

Li realized that when she said husbands she meant King Archelaus and King Yitzhak.

"Do you think he'll notice?" Li asked.

"He would have to be blind not to," Queen Marriah said as they walked down the hall. "The guards at the door noticed."

Li smiled, hoping that she was right. King Archelaus opened the door at Queen Marriah's knock. Li heard men's voices that suddenly stopped as she stepped into the room. King Yitzhak had his back to her, but turned as the man facing him stared at her with his mouth hanging open.

"Li?" King Yitzhak asked in a surprised tone as he stood.

"Yes, My King," Li replied and he quickly crossed to stop before her.

He stood looking at her with a shocked expression on his face.

At last he reached out and gently stroked her face.

Li stepped closer and asked, "Are you pleased?"

"Yes," he replied in a whisper as he leaned down and his lips met hers.

Li felt herself tremble as he put both his arms around her and drew her body against his. As his lips met hers again, she felt like she had melted inside and her arms closed around his neck for support. He at last released her from his arms with a smile. He took

60

her hand and led her to where Queen Marriah and King Archelaus stood with the man who had stared at her.

"Regis Bryant," King Yitzhak said as she recognized the man from Queen Marriah's drawing. "Queen Li."

Li felt like her heart had leapt into her throat as Regis Bryant bowed to her and she returned Queen Marriah's smile. They walked over to where Lucjen was sitting on a bench. He said something in a strange language and Queen Marriah replied in the same language.

"I heard the guards talking about you having wings," Li said.

"Yes, I have wings, Queen Li," Lucjen responded. "I am feeling too weak to show you mine, but perhaps Regis Bryant will show you his."

"I would like that," Li said. "Could you ask him if he would?"

Regis Bryant smiled and nodded at the translation. He removed his shirt and turned his back. She felt King Yitzhak put his arm around her waist as Regis Bryant's back began to change and soon he had large wings very much like Haskell's.

"Amazing," Li said as Regis Bryant turned around. "May I touch them?"

He nodded at the translation. During the next hour, they discussed the similarities and differences between their peoples. Li listened quietly and answered when they asked her a question. She was very happy that if King Yitzhak did not have his arm around her, he was holding her hand. At supper, King Yitzhak seemed very interested to see how the other men treated their wives. Li was glad to see the other men treated their wives kindly and with respect. Not long after supper Regis Bryant left with the dragon. King Yitzhak took Li to his room soon afterward. As she turned to face him, she saw a look in his eyes she had not seen before. It was an almost hungry look.

"You are so very beautiful, Li," King Yitzhak said softly and put his lips on hers again.

This time the sensation was even more intense than before. She felt dizzy as their lips parted. She laid her head on his shoulder while she caught her breath. She could hear his heart beating rapidly. She remembered Queen Marriah calling it a kiss when lips met like that. She could feel his hands on the buttons on the back of the dress. She began to unbutton his shirt. It was very exciting to her as they undressed each other. She saw the bowl of sweet oil on the table next to the bed. As she began to spread the oil on his skin, she felt a tremor go through him. She realized that now was the time to actually do the things she had only dared dream of. King Yitzhak yielded to her touch and seemed to understand what she wanted.

By the time they were finished, it took some time for Li's breathing to return to normal and her heart to slow down. It felt so good to lay with King Yitzhak's arms around her. She looked up at his face and found him looking at her with a contented look in his eyes.

"My Dear Wife," he said. "I like this change in you."

"The only change in me is that I dared try what my heart had desired, My King," Li replied.

"I've noticed that Queen Marriah does not use King Archelaus' title when she speaks to him," King Yitzhak said. "She only uses his name. I think I would like it if you called me by name, not title."

"I would like that," she replied. "I like the change in you. I did not expect you to call me, Queen Li."

"I want you to tell me the things that you have wanted to, but have not dared," he said. "I think I am ready now that I have seen Brinley for myself. I have seen that Queen Marriah is treated with so much more respect than I have ever seen a king receive. I have seen that she has earned that respect. I know that Mannton will slowly die if changes are not made. I need you to help me understand what must be done and I need you to help me do it."

"Right now it is as though there are two kingdoms in Mannton," Li said. "The kingdom of men and the kingdom of women. The men build the houses and grow the food, but the women clean the houses and prepare the food. The men eat the food and maybe give what is left to the women. Sometimes the only food women have to eat is moldy or soured. Usually there is very little food given to the women. Most women starve to death because they do not have enough food. That is how she who bore me died. She insisted that I eat what little food was given to us. She grew weaker every day and Father beat her more every day. Most of the women who do not starve to death die by being beaten to death."

Yitzhak had an angry look on his face, but she knew she must continue.

"Sometimes when I was given nothing to eat, I would find white worms under rocks and eat them. There were plants and flowers that could be eaten as well," she said.

"You ate worms?" Yitzhak said in a surprised and almost disgusted tone.

"When your stomach is empty and your head dizzy you will eat almost anything to survive," she replied. "Those that lost their will to live simply quit eating. For a woman life is hard work, painful beatings and little food. Most women have no hope of anything better. There are fewer infants born every year. Only the women who get enough food have infants that survive. The boys are raised by their fathers and taught to beat and starve the women. The girls are raised by the women and taught to clean, cook and sew. The girls are taught that they are nothing. They have no voice and no face. Women are not allowed to see the face of a man. Many women only recognize their husband's boots and fists. Those that fight back are killed."

Yitzhak rose up to a sitting position and stared at her.

"Although born of the same woman and man, Rowan and I were always treated very differently," Li said. "Rowan has never known hunger. He has never been beaten or tied up. Any time he fell he was helped up. When he was injured the healer took care of him. He learned to read and write. He learned to ride a horse and grow food. I was always hungry. I was frequently beaten and kicked. I have even spent entire nights tied so tightly to a table leg that I could not even sleep. If I fell down I was almost certain to be hit or kicked. I learned to heal my own wounds and there were many. I learned to clean the house and the men's clothes. I learned to cook meals. I learned to make the mat that someday I will be wrapped in before being buried. I had no hope of anything better until I became your wife, but I knew that there were others that were treated worse than I was."

"When you first told me that I would beat you if I wanted to, I was shocked," Yitzhak said softly. "I went out into the city and saw it differently than I had ever seen it. I saw the men beating the women and girls in the streets and in the houses. I saw the women's bowed heads and thin hands. I began to notice that there were hardly any children, but the boys were happily playing while the girls carried buckets of water that were almost bigger than they were. I began to realize that something was wrong. I just don't know what to do."

"Because you are king, the men will listen to you," Li said as she sat up. "Queen Marriah said that change can be difficult, but it must start somewhere. You once told Yuri that if he treated his wife like an animal, she would behave like an animal, but if he treated her like a person, she would behave like a person. All the men need to be told that. Queen Marriah said that the first thing that must change was for you to see me differently than you ever had before."

"I have always thought of you as a person," Yitzhak said as he reached out and softly stroked her face. "I have always thought your appearance was pleasing and did not want other men to want you as their own, but today I saw you entirely differently. I saw your beauty and I saw you not just as a person, but as someone equal to myself. When Queen Marriah confronted me I was angry that a mere woman would dare tell me what to do. When she disarmed me, she told me that I was to treat her with all the respect that I was due. It was at that moment that I began to understand I was wrong. She knew how to set and splint broken bones. Every man from Brinley listened to her as she spoke and instantly obeyed her every request without protest or question. I began to see something of you in her."

"What do you mean?" Li asked in surprise.

"She was confident and not afraid to speak," Yitzhak said. "She has a commanding presence like my father had. It was something I never expected to see in a woman. I saw Brinley's sword instructor lay face down in front of her and tell her that he was not worthy of her presence. I don't know what she did to him, but I do know that she knows how to use that sword of hers better than any man I've seen. She can draw better than anyone I've seen including the royal painter. She is a very amazing woman and I wonder what Mannton's women could do if only they were allowed to."

"First the men must begin to see women and girls as people," Li said. "In time they will see them as equal, but a change that big cannot happen all at once. For now it is you who can make the law and change the law. It is you who can change how women are treated."

"When we wrapped and buried she who bore me, I thought about what kind of a life a woman must have knowing that she was sleeping on a mat that would be used to wrap her for burial," Yitzhak said as a tear began to glitter in the corner of his eye. "I began to realize that I had never really known her as I had known my father."

"What is important is that you now understand these things," Li said.

"When you die, I do not want you wrapped in the cloth from the mat you slept on," Yitzhak said. "You will be wrapped in the finest cloth there is. It will be new cloth that has never been used before. I want that mat burned and I want you to share my bed every night. You will be able to go everywhere I go. Never again will you be made to stay in one room. I can't imagine how you could stand to be locked up in that room day after day."

"I knew that was my place as your wife," Li said before he leaned over and kissed her.

She felt him gently lay her down before his lips wandered from hers to her neck.

Chapter 10 – A Different Man Than He Had Been

Yitzhak woke up feeling incredibly good. Li was still asleep in his arms and he realized that he loved her enough to do what she was asking him to do. He would begin making changes in Mannton so that eventually women would be equal to men. He lay there for a long time just feeling her body pressed against his and her movement as she breathed. He thought about the conversation they had last night, but his mind kept returning to what they had done before they started talking. He had never known anything that had felt so intense and so good all at the same time. When she did wake, she turned over and smiled at him.

"What time of day is it?" she asked.

"I don't know and I don't care," he said with a smile. "All I care is that I woke up with you in my arms."

"I am hungry," she said.

"So am I, now that you mention it," he said.

"I have been afraid to ask before now, but I would like to learn how to read and write," Li said as she sat up.

"I can teach you when we get back to Mannton," he replied as he sat up.

He kissed her before getting out of bed. He put on one of the robes that were hanging on the back of the door. She got out of bed and smiled as he put the other robe on her. He opened the doors to find Garman and a woman waiting for them. There was a tray of food on one of the tables. After they ate, Garman helped him bathe in a pool of water in the next room before getting dressed. Li and the woman went into the room with the pool and he went out to the balcony. He smiled as he looked out over the city. He remembered seeing how busy it was compared to Mannton. Men and women worked together while children played. He knew that today he was a different man than he had been when he woke up yesterday morning. He heard men's voices in the sitting room.

"Did you have a good night?" he heard King Archelaus ask.

He turned around and said with a smile, "Very."

His advisors dropped to their knees.

"Joris, Yuri," he said. "Last night I realized that we have been making a big mistake for many years."

The men looked puzzled as they stood up.

"Mistake?" they asked in unison.

"When we return to Mannton, I will start to correct our mistake by decreeing that the wife of the King will hold the title of Queen of Mannton and will be treated with the same respect the King is due."

The two men stood with their mouths hanging open.

"Also, women will be allowed to attend public meetings," he added. "From now on, my Queen will share my bed every night."

"The palace staff will talk, My King," Joris said. "What will the men think?"

"I'm expecting them to talk," he said as he opened the door to go inside. "You are beautiful this morning, My Queen."

As he crossed the room to take her hands, he heard Joris ask in an alarmed tone, "What have you done to him?"

"Why is he acting so strangely?" Yuri added as Yitzhak kissed Li on the lips.

"He's acting like a man who has discovered he is in love," King Archelaus replied. "He is learning that a woman can do more than bear children."

"She has been his wife for two years and there are no children."

"Give them six months," was the reply. "She will be with child by then."

Yitzhak smiled at the thought. He led Li over to where they were standing.

"We want to thank Queen Marriah," he said.

"And I would like to learn to ride a horse," Li said. "If it is not too much trouble."

"Garman?" King Archelaus said.

"I will see to it personally, My King," Garman replied.

"When we return to Mannton, Queen Li wants to learn to read and write," King Yitzhak said.

"But, My King," Joris protested. "Women are not capable of such things."

"If Queen Marriah can speak, read, and write in three languages, I can certainly learn to read and write in one language," Li replied.

"Three?" Yuri asked.

Both King Archelaus and Garman nodded.

"It is nearly lunchtime," Garman said.

"Take us to Queen Marriah," King Archelaus responded.

When they reached the room, there were men beginning to leave and Garman left with them.

"We wanted to thank you personally," Yitzhak said as he bowed to Queen Marriah. "In the two years she has been my wife, we had barely spoken to each other before last night. I learned many new things about the women of Mannton and their importance."

"I will be learning to ride horses and when we return to Mannton, I will learn to read and write," Li said. "Thank you for giving me the encouragement I needed and for letting me borrow the dresses."

"Aurella said they have been in storage," Queen Marriah said. "You are welcome to keep any that you want. I'll have a trunk found for you to put them in while returning to Mannton."

"Thank you," she replied. "I would like that."

"So would I," Yitzhak added before kissing her hand.

He listened to Queen Marriah and King Archelaus speak in the language of the northern kingdoms as they followed a woman to the dining hall. Although he had heard it spoken before, he had never learned it. He had been told it was a difficult language to learn, yet Queen Marriah spoke it just as easily as she did their language or the one that she had spoken to Lucjen in. He was still getting used to the idea that a woman could know more than a man, yet he had no doubt that Queen Marriah could do many things that he could not.

After lunch he took Joris and Yuri with him as he met with Queen Marriah, General Caddaric and another man. Queen Marriah quickly made it very clear what she expected to be included in the peace treaty. Yitzhak was very impressed by her intelligence and fairness. Joris and Yuri tried to protest some of the points, but soon ran out of arguments. She even got them to concede on some of the things they had adamantly argued. She never wavered and never raised her voice. He knew that the treaty was fair and that if King Archelaus proposed the points of the treaty, Joris and Yuri would have had no arguments. Early on she had smiled slightly and given an almost imperceptible nod letting him know that she realized why he remained mostly silent. Joris and Yuri were learning what he had already discovered, that women were capable of ruling a kingdom. By the time they were finished meeting, Joris and Yuri had at last fallen silent.

"You are one of the toughest negotiators I have ever seen," Joris said to Queen Marriah as they walked toward the dining hall. "I never realized a woman could be capable of much of what you do."

"Thank you," Queen Marriah said. "When I arrived in Dracona, I was nearly dead. Before escaping Larkin, I believed that I was nothing, much like Queen Li believed before yesterday. In Dracona I learned the truth about the importance of every individual person, including me. They healed my body and my mind, but it was Archelaus who healed my heart and made me whole again."

"King Archelaus mentioned that he had served as a scullery boy and was beaten before gaining Burton's throne," Yuri said.

"Yes," she replied. "He still bears the scars."

"Why keep them if Dracona's healers could remove them?" Yuri asked. "And why have you kept the one on your arm?"

"Archelaus chose to keep his scars as a reminder of what our people could suffer," she replied as they entered the dining hall. "And this scar I got while saving the life of one of Brinley's new sword instructors."

"It's about time," King Archelaus said before taking her hands and kissing them both.

"Although we were enemies, I had great respect for your father, King Yitzhak," General Caddaric said. "He was a worthy adversary. Adamok knew him as well."

"He was a good father to me," Yitzhak replied as the other man joined them. "I still miss him."

"I met with him a couple of times," Adamok said. "We never quite saw things the same way, but I respected him. I think the only thing about him that really bothered me was the way women were treated in Mannton."

"It has been that way for longer than anyone can remember," Yitzhak said. "I never really noticed it until after I took Li as my wife. Her fear of being beaten opened my eyes to what was happening."

"I think that has always been the one thing that men from Brinley did not understand," General Caddaric said.

"I now know that it is very wrong and I must change the way women are treated in Mannton," Yitzhak said. "It will be a difficult task, but it must be done if Mannton is to survive."

Queen Marriah and King Archelaus joined them.

"Your wife is a tough negotiator," Yitzhak said.

"She had to be tough to survive Larkin's cruelty," King Archelaus said as he put his arm around her waist. "It's one of the things I love the most about her."

As they took their places at the table, Li said, "The wives of Brinley's sword instructors make and sell wood carvings. They have been able to make a lot of money selling their carvings.

This surprised Yitzhak. It was another thing that he had not imagined a woman would be able to do. But he remembered how the buttons Li had made were very skillfully carved. As they ate, he watched the two women Li had pointed out sitting with the two men who had helped Queen Marriah set Lucjen's bones. He could see that these men loved their wives very much. The four of them seemed very happy together.

As they were finishing their meal he said, "My queen tells me that the wives of your sword instructors sell wood carvings."

"Yes," Queen Marriah replied. "They are very skilled. General Caddaric has one of their carvings in his office and has ordered several for his home."

"The one in my office is of Davon and Dallon wrestling," General Caddaric explained. "I consider it a trophy of sorts. After all, it was posing for that carving that helped them decide to get married and then they promised not to rig any more buckets of water over my office door."

Everyone began laughing over that admission. The thought of General Caddaric drenched in water was actually quite funny. When the meal was finished, they went to their suite. Yitzhak was relieved when the servants finally left.

"How did you do with learning to ride a horse?" Yitzhak asked Li as they sat down on a settee.

"It was very hard at first," Li said as he put his arm around her shoulders. "But I soon realized what I was doing wrong. Garman said that I did very well for my first time riding. How did the negotiations go?"

"Quite well," Yitzhak said with a smile. "The treaty will be almost exactly as Queen Marriah first proposed it. She is very intelligent and very fair. Joris and Yuri had to argue every point though. I was surprised that she didn't get angry with them."

"I suppose it will take some time for them to get used to a woman being capable of more than cooking, cleaning and bearing children," Li said with a laugh.

"I think they are finally realizing that," Yitzhak said. "When she first went over what she wanted in the treaty, I was ready to sign it once it was written out. I let Joris and Yuri do all the arguing and they eventually ran out of arguments. I think Queen Marriah understood that I was letting them discover for themselves that she is very capable of being queen and ruling a kingdom."

"Maybe someday every man in Mannton will understand that," Li said.

"Even though it was Queen Marriah and I that were negotiating the treaty, I think that it would be a good idea for you and King Archelaus to sign the treaty as well," Yitzhak said. "I know it takes time to learn to read and write, but I think I could teach you to write your name tonight."

"You really want to do that?" she asked in surprise.

"Yes, I do," he replied. "In fact I think it is important that you and King Archelaus sign the treaty."

He got up and went to the table where he had seen a pen and some ink. He opened several drawers in the table and soon found some paper.

"Come here," he said. "I'll teach you right now."

Li looked a little unsure as she sat down in the chair at the table. He pulled another chair over to sit beside her.

"First, you take the pen and dip just the very end of it in the ink, like this," he said as he dipped the pen. "Now you have to hold it this side up. This is how you write 'Queen Li.' Always start at the top and left. Now you try."

Li took the pen and carefully dipped it in the ink. She copied the letters very carefully. It was a little shaky, but not bad for a first attempt.

"Try it again," he said. "I remember it took me a while to get used to the pen. I sometimes got ink all over myself."

"You did?" Li asked.

"Yes," he replied, laughing at the memory. "You're actually doing quite well."

Li smiled as she tried again. This time the letters were clearer. He sat patiently as she copied the letters over and over again until they were smooth. He took out a new piece of paper and folded the old one in half.

"Now try it again," he said.

Li dipped the pen and began to write. She hesitated only once as she wrote 'Queen Li' on the new paper.

"Perfect," Yitzhak said. "I knew you would be able to do it. Joris and Yuri will be so surprised. We should be going to bed before much longer."

"I've had an exciting day," Li said as she laid the pen on the paper. "I'm too excited to sleep just yet."

Yitzhak smiled as he led her to the bedroom.

Chapter 11 – Seeing Her Father's Face

The next morning they wrote the peace treaty out and signed it. Yitzhak insisted that Li and King Archelaus sign it. Queen Marriah seemed pleased at his suggestion. Li signed her name perfectly. She was very happy to see the look of surprise on Joris' and Yuri's faces.

After lunch, Queen Marriah showed her paintings to Yitzhak, Li, Joris and Yuri. Li was very amazed that she could paint so well, especially from memory. Yitzhak asked if she could paint one of him and Li. This made Li very happy.

"I would be happy to," Queen Marriah replied as Joris and Yuri looked surprised.

"Queen Marriah told us that you have scars on your back," Yuri said. "Would you mind showing us your scars?"

"Of course not," King Archelaus said as he began to remove the tunic he was wearing.

Li gasped as he turned his back towards them. She could see the scars that were left by a whip.

"Were your scars this bad, Queen Marriah?" she asked.

"I had scars, bruises and fresh wounds all over when I arrived in Dracona." Queen Marriah replied and Li saw the men's faces go pale. "That is why in our kingdoms, abuse is not tolerated."

"We are setting up schools to educate our people in the hope that there will be less abuse and other crime," King Archelaus said. "Every man, woman and child will have the opportunity to learn to read, write and speak both Brinley's and Burton's languages."

"And once the people of Glynis have left for their true home, all of Dracona and Merton will be given to us," Queen Marriah said. "Since Brinley has a serious problem with overcrowding, the people of Brinley will have the first opportunity to move there."

"To tell the truth, I have known about Brinley's problem of overcrowding and have been worried that Brinley would invade Mannton," Yitzhak said. "That is why I thought I would seize control of Brinley before Brinley took over Mannton."

"That makes sense," Queen Marriah said. "But I'm glad I was able to change your mind."

"So am I," he replied with a smile before kissing Li's hand.

The next morning, as they were preparing to leave, Queen Marriah presented them with a side saddle for Li, a trunk for the dresses she had decided to keep, and samples of sweet oil. Joris and Yuri asked what it was for and Yitzhak promised to explain it to them later. They were in the courtyard packing the wagon and saying goodbye when their attention was drawn by a flapping sound.

"Tasia!" Queen Marriah exclaimed in a surprised tone as she looked out to where the sounds had stopped.

When Li reached Queen Marriah's side she saw the dragon that had taken Regis Bryant home and another smaller one that was gold colored with black stripes. A man climbed down from the large one's back.

"There is more than one dragon?" Joris asked.

"Fifty two more," Queen Marriah confirmed as they crossed the draw bridge. "This is Tasia, queen of the dragons."

As they approached the dragons, Queen Marriah said something to the man in the strange language that she had spoken to Lucjen in.

He replied in the same language as he dropped to one knee before her.

Lucjen spoke as he stepped forward.

The man looked up in surprise.

"Lucjen!" the man exclaimed as he leapt to his feet before speaking in the strange language.

Lucjen replied as the man hugged him and pounded his back. They spoke rapidly to each other.

"He is the man who taught you to use a sword?" Yitzhak asked.

"And that maneuver that I used to put you on the ground," Queen Marriah confirmed.

"I've seen her win a duel with him several times," King Archelaus said.

"You can beat him?" Yitzhak asked in amazement. "I'm glad you only wanted my attention."

"Queen Li, Tasia wants to meet you," Queen Marriah said. "She has a prediction for you."

They walked over to where the dragons were waiting. She was surprised to see King Archelaus kneel on one knee before the small golden dragon while the woman named Aurora who had been with Lucjen curtsied.

Queen Marriah led Li forward and said, "Tasia doesn't know the language of Brinley and Mannton, but you will be able to hear her voice in your mind and see some images. I will translate for you."

"I am glad to meet you in person, My Sister," Queen Marriah said after Li heard a strange woman's voice in her mind. "You and Marriah will lead your people into a great era." Li looked from Tasia to Queen Marriah.

"You will end the suffering of your women, Li. Your works will serve as an inspiration to generations to come," Queen Marriah said as Yitzhak walked up to them. "This one will provide you five beautiful children."

Li could see glimpses of happy healthy children and an older Yitzhak. She looked at Yitzhak and smiled.

"How do you know that?" he asked, looking at Queen Marriah.

"Not me," she replied. "Tasia can foresee the future."

Queen Marriah looked at Tasia's large eye as she stroked the dragon's cheek.

"Edgard," Queen Marriah said then spoke in the strange language.

The man who had come with the dragons said something in reply. He drew a rectangular piece of gold from the pouch he had been carrying and handed it to Queen Marriah.

"What did he say that was for?" Yitzhak asked.

"He was told only that I would know what it was for," she replied. "I believe it is meant for you to present to Queen Li when you return to Mannton, but not in this form."

"A crown?" he asked. "That would take several days at least."

"Lucjen, come here a moment," Queen Marriah said. "I'm guessing that you are able to shape stone and metal."

75

"How did you know?" he asked.

"Otherwise, Regina Sonje would have made the crown herself," she replied as she handed him the gold. "You might want Edgard to give you some of his energy."

Lucjen sat down on the ground. Edgard knelt behind him and placed his hands on Lucjen's shoulders. They gathered around to watch. Soon he held in his hands a delicate crown of gold shells matching the one Yitzhak wore. A row of pink gems were set just above the bottom of the crown.

"Perfect," Yitzhak said.

"The first time it is placed on her head, it will adjust to a perfect fit," Lucjen said as he handed the crown to him.

"When we arrive in Mannton, I will proclaim you Queen Li of Mannton," Yitzhak said as he faced her. "Then I will place this crown on your head."

Li began to cry.

"What's the matter?" he asked as he handed the crown to Yuri.

"I'm so happy," she said as he put his arms around her. "I was so frightened when I was summoned to Brinley. I was afraid that you would leave me here and take a different wife. I never expected to become Queen of Mannton."

"I would never do that," he said. "I negotiated with your father for a week before he agreed to give you to me."

"Father said nothing to me about it," she said. "One day he just told me to get my things and get in the carriage outside the front door. There were two guards who didn't even look at me."

"You didn't know?"

"They led me to my room and locked me in. I thought I must have done something wrong. I was surprised when lunch and supper were brought to me. I recognized your boots as you stood in front of me and I knew you were king. Then I heard you say that I was your wife."

"I had seen you at the well several times," he said. "I noticed how kind you were. I was curious to see what you would do if I asked for a drink, but I never expected you to clean my boots."

"I'm glad I did," she said before he kissed her.

As they walked back to the palace, Yitzhak drew a ring from his finger and held it out to Lucjen.

"I want you to have this," Yitzhak said.

"Your father's ring?" Lucjen asked. "That should go to your son."

"I shall never forget you and I don't want you to forget us," Yitzhak said. "You volunteered to take Nokar's place and kept your promise that you would treat Li well. It is important to me that you have this to pass to your son. I know I have learned a lot from you in these last few days. I'm sorry that I did not get to know you better sooner."

"I promise that I will pass this to my son," Lucjen said as he took the ring. "I understand your reaction to my having wings. When I saw my wings in the reflection of my shield I wondered if I was turning into a monster. I will always remember you. I know that you will change Mannton so that men and women will be equal."

Soon they were on their way. This time Li rode on a horse beside Yitzhak while one of the guards drove the wagon. She did not bow her head but looked around at the busy city. The women looked happy and healthy, not thin and sad. All the children, both boys and girls, were playing together and looked happy. This is how she hoped Mannton would one day become.

"Joris, Yuri," Yitzhak said, and they drew their horses beside his. "This city is busy and full of life. Everyone is happy. The women and girls are not being beaten. They are not thin and fearful, but happy and healthy. They look at the men's faces and not at their feet. They speak to the men and the men listen. This is the way that Mannton should be, not sad and dying."

"For a while I thought you were going insane," Yuri said. "Even though I am grateful my wife doesn't bite or scratch me anymore, I still couldn't see anything was wrong with how we had treated women. Now I am beginning to see what you have been trying to tell me."

"I can see it too," Joris admitted. "I will support any law you pass that will make Mannton more like this, including giving the king's wife the title of queen."

Li smiled. The things she had always hoped for would someday come true. She enjoyed the trip back to Mannton. There was so much to see when one wasn't looking at the ground all of the time. A tent was set up for Yitzhak and her to sleep in, but everyone else slept outside around the fire. As they approached Mannton's city, she could see the empty houses and the empty streets. She could see how very different Mannton was from Brinley. She glanced at Joris and Yuri to see them looking around with stunned expressions.

"Would it be possible for me to see if Ti is still alive?" Li asked.

"Of course," Yitzhak said. "The others can go on ahead of us."

She and Yitzhak rode to her old house. It looked different than she remembered, but then she had never seen any of it above the doorknobs. She dismounted as the front door opened and a man came out. He stopped with his hand still on the doorknob. She glanced at Yitzhak.

"Th . . . that's not," the man said in a shocked voice.

"Yes," Yitzhak responded. "This beautiful woman is your daughter and my wife, Li."

Li was silent as she studied the face she had never seen before. She was surprised to see much of her own face in his.

"You allow her to look into men's faces?" Father asked.

"She is allowed to look at anything and anyone she wants to. She will speak to anyone she pleases and they will reply with all the respect that I am due. Since she has left your house, she has not been beaten and she has eaten better," Yitzhak said as he put his arm around her waist. "That is by my command."

"Father," Li said, and he looked at her. "Although you were sometimes cruel to me, I cannot hate you for that. I know that you did not understand that women are people just like men are. I know that sometimes you thought I was stupid, but it was because I had not yet learned the words men use to say certain things."

"I," he said then paused as he looked down.

"I am stronger willed than most women, but I think that I got that from you, Father," Li said.

"And for that I am grateful," Yitzhak said, and Father looked up at him with a surprised expression on his face. "I have learned a lot of things from Li. Things that will make Mannton a better and happier place. I am grateful that she had the courage and determination to tell me what I needed to hear."

"Do you know if she who bore Anunik still lives?" Li asked.

"She should be coming back from the well soon," Father said. "There she is now."

Li turned around to see Ti approaching with a bucket full of water.

"Ti," Li said as she walked towards her.

"Yes?" Ti replied as she glanced up then looked back down. "I am Ti."

"Set down your bucket and look at me," Li said.

"He will be angry if I am late," Ti said.

"He will not," Yitzhak said. "As King of Mannton, I will not allow it."

"Look at me Ti," Li said as Ti finally put her bucket down.

Ti looked up and gasped.

"Li?" she whispered. "You still live?"

"Yes," Li replied as she hugged Ti. "I am so happy to see you again. I had wondered if you still lived."

"You are so beautiful," Ti said as Li released her. "And you look happy."

"I am happier than I thought possible," Li said. "I must leave now for there is much work to be done. I will see you again, Ti. I promise. Things will be better."

Ti looked at her with questioning eyes.

"Things will be better," Yitzhak said. "I promise they will."

Li could see the tears in Ti's eyes as a man approached with an angry look on his face.

"Why aren't you preparing supper yet?" the man said and Li recognized Anunik's father's voice.

"You will not be angry with her," Yitzhak said. "We have delayed her."

"Yes, My King," he said and dropped to his knees.

"Tonight you will allow her to eat the same amount that you do. She will eat fresh food, not spoiled or moldy food," Yitzhak said. "And you will not beat her."

"I will obey," the man said as he stood up and looked at Li for the first time. "Who?"

"This is my wife, Queen Li." Yitzhak said as Anunik's father looked stunned. "You knew her as Rowan's sister."

With that he led Li back to the horses. He clasped his hands as Li had seen King Archelaus do for Queen Marriah to mount. She stepped into his hands and mounted her horse. She glanced back to see Father staring at her with an open mouth. She smiled, pleased with what had just taken place.

When they returned to the palace, Yitzhak led her up some stairs to a dining hall similar to the one in Brinley. There was much muttering and talk among the guards and servants as she ate sitting next to Yitzhak. After the delicious meal, Yitzhak took her hand and led her down the hall to an enormous room that had chairs and tables along with a large fireplace. She was surprised to see her mat in the corner next to the fireplace.

"Now, this entire palace is your home," Yitzhak said. "Before I show you the bedroom, I think we should burn that mat."

"I will be glad to sleep in a bed now," Li said. "But only if you are sleeping beside me."

"I wouldn't want it otherwise," Yitzhak said as she picked up the mat.

She placed the mat carefully on the fire in the grate. As they stood and watched, it began to burn. She suddenly felt very happy knowing that she would never have to sleep on that mat again. They watched it burn until there was nothing but ashes left of the mat.

"Now, My Dear Wife," Yitzhak said. "It is time we go to bed. Tomorrow will be the day that I officially declare you Queen of Mannton."

He led her into a room that was almost as large as the last one. The bed was a very large one and she found it to be very comfortable as she fell asleep in Yitzhak's arms.

Chapter 12 – Mannton's First Queen

"Good morning," a man's voice said soon after Li had begun to awaken.

"Good morning, Lenar," Yitzhak replied.

"My King!" the man exclaimed with a gasp. "What is she doing here in your father's bed?"

Li opened her eyes to find a man standing next to the bed, staring at them. She felt Yitzhak's arms tighten around her briefly before he replied.

"This bed is no longer my father's bed," Yitzhak said. "This bed is no longer my bed either. It is our bed, mine and my wife's."

"But," the man began in protest.

"The time has come for us to change how we treat women," Yitzhak said.

"What have they done to you in Brinley?" Lenar asked. "Were you tortured?"

"No," Yitzhak said and began to laugh.

"What has happened to you?" Lenar asked.

"My eyes were opened and I now see things clearly for the first time in my life," Yitzhak explained. "Li had been trying to tell me that we were wrong in how we treated women, but Queen Marriah of Brinley proved it to me. She is so completely amazing, Lenar. Every man in Brinley obeys Queen Marriah without question or hesitation. They respect her and she deserves that respect. I saw the sword instructor, Tarl, lay himself on the ground at her feet."

"Tarl?" Lenar asked in a surprised tone. "The one Joris calls an arrogant braggart?"

"The very same," Yitzhak said. "I'm certain that if she had handed him a knife and told him to plunge it into his own heart, he would have done it without hesitation. I'm not certain what she did to make him behave that way, but I can tell you he is a changed man. I can also tell you that Queen Marriah knows how to use a sword better than any man I know, myself included."

"A woman with a sword?" Lenar asked.

"I discovered no one can ignore Queen Marriah," Yitzhak replied. "Yet she is one of the kindest people I have ever met. When she slid the flat of her blade across my chest before disarming me, I realized that I would have been dead if she had wanted to kill me."

"Where did she come from?" Lenar asked. "I heard King Burkhart died before producing any heirs."

"He did. She is the daughter of Prince Langward."

Lenar shook his head.

"We'll both need robes and a bath this morning, Lenar," Yitzhak said as he released Li and sat up.

"My King," Lenar said in a surprised tone. "You're."

"We both are, Lenar," Yitzhak said. "Go get the robes."

The man hurried off and soon returned with two robes. He laid them on the bed before helping Yitzhak put on one of the robes.

"Now go get the bath drawn."

Li was glad when the door shut behind Lenar. Yitzhak held the robe for her as she got out of bed. She put on the robe and he tied the sash around her waist.

"He acted very shocked to find me in bed with you," Li said at last. "And that we were not wearing clothing."

"He'll get over it," Yitzhak said. "They all will."

Yitzhak led her to another room off of the bedroom. There was one large tub with water in it. Several men waited but glanced at each other as they saw her.

"I think we can bathe ourselves this morning," Yitzhak said, and the men looked relieved.

They quickly left. Yitzhak helped her get into the tub before helping her to wash. The water felt good as she bathed. When she had finished and was dry, she put the robe back on and Yitzhak got into the tub. Once he was in his robe he went to the door.

"Now, let's go choose a dress for you," Yitzhak said with a smile as he opened the door.

She heard men's voices in the bedroom that suddenly went silent.

"Where are the trunks from the trip?" Yitzhak asked and Lenar pointed to a door.

Yitzhak opened the door to reveal a room with clothes hung around the walls. There were trunks under the clothing, but there was one trunk left in the center of the room. Yitzhak opened the trunk to reveal the dresses carefully folded. He looked through the dresses and finally selected one that was a deep maroon color with gold trim.

"This one, I think," he said as he held it up. "And I shall wear this."

He held up a jacket that was the same color. It was hanging on a strange wooden thing with a curved piece of metal coming out of the top. She could see pants underneath it. She smiled.

"Lenar, we shall need hangers for Li's dresses," Yitzhak said. "Get rid of anything of mine that is wearing out or too small."

"It shall be done, My King," Lenar replied. "Do you wish our assistance in dressing this morning?"

"After I have helped Li get dressed," Yitzhak said. "We will have to find a woman to assist her in the future. What does your wife do during the day?"

"I . . . I don't know," Lenar replied with a confused expression on his face.

"Ask her," Yitzhak said. "I think you'll be surprised."

Lenar knelt before leaving. Soon Li was dressed and she watched as the men dressed Yitzhak. While she watched, she braided her hair as one of the women in Brinley had taught her to do. She knew that how she looked today was very important. She was suddenly nervous at the thought of all the men staring at her, but she knew she needed to do it for the women of Mannton. She thought about the beautiful crown that matched the one that Yitzhak settled onto his head.

"Lenar," Yitzhak said. "I want an announcement made to all of Mannton. Today all people, including women and girls, will meet in the plaza just after lunch."

"Yes, My King," Lenar said although he looked confused.

"It is very important that the women and girls are there, Lenar," Yitzhak said sternly. "The men may protest, so have them told it is by my direct command that the women and girls are to attend this meeting."

Li noticed the other men glancing at each other with puzzled looks as Lenar knelt before leaving. Yitzhak led her down to the dining hall where there was a large breakfast waiting for them. For the rest of the morning she sat with Yitzhak while he read through various reports. She was surprised that he read them aloud to her as he ran his finger along below the markings and asked her opinion. She answered as honestly as possible considering she was not always certain what he was talking about. When she asked questions, he patiently explained things to her. At last it was time for lunch.

"Thank you for not being angry with me for asking so many questions," Li said as they walked towards the dining hall.

"I know it will take time for you to learn things," Yitzhak said with a smile. "You were actually a big help today. You look at things differently than I do and your questions made me think about things differently. I can see that what I had first decided to do wasn't always the best thing to do."

She smiled as they entered the dining hall. Joris and Yuri were already there. Ki was standing in a corner with another woman. Both looked frightened.

"Why do you want the women and girls to attend the meeting?" Joris asked in an almost angry tone.

"It is important for them to see Li crowned Queen of Mannton," Yitzhak said. "It is important for women to know what is going on in the kingdom. The men need to begin to see women as people, not stupid animals. The women need to begin seeing themselves as people and not possessions."

"Since we usually have lunch here, I thought we should bring our wives so we don't have to go back home to get them," Yuri said.

"There should be enough food for everyone," Yitzhak said. "Li, I think it best if you explain to their wives what is going on and that they are allowed to sit beside the men to eat."

Li nodded and went over to the corner where the women huddled.

"It is good to see you again, Ki," Li said, and Ki looked up at her.

"Li?" Ki asked. "Is that really you?"

"Yes," Li answered with a smile. "It was hard for me to believe, too. Today is a very important day for women in Mannton. Things are going to change and eventually women will be equal to men."

"Why are we here?" the other woman asked.

"You must be Joris' wife," Li said, and the woman nodded. "What is your name?"

"My name is Fa," the woman replied.

"You are here to watch King Yitzhak declare that I am now Queen Li of Mannton," Li said, and the two women looked confused.

"What is a queen?" Fa asked.

"A queen is the wife of the king," Li said. "A queen is a ruler just like a king is."

Their expressions went from confused to shocked.

"Today you will sit beside Joris and Yuri to eat the same food that they do," Li said. "You will not eat what they leave behind, but your own food from your own plate."

"Joris will be angry," Fa said.

"King Yitzhak will not allow him to be angry," Li said. "Joris has seen in Brinley that women eat sitting beside the men. Queen Marriah of Brinley showed both of them women are smart and can be leaders that even men obey."

"Men obey a woman?" Fa asked in a shocked tone.

Even Ki looked shocked as Li nodded. She saw the servers bring in the food.

"You will see," Li said. "Things will change. Come and eat."

Ki and Fa followed her to the table. Yitzhak gave her a questioning look and she nodded as Ki sat down next to Yuri. Fa carefully sat on the chair next to Joris. As the men and Li put food on their plates, the two women watched. Li could see that they did not dare reach for any food for themselves. She was pleased as first Yuri, then Joris began to put food on their wife's plates. The meal was eaten in strained silence. Once it was finished, Yitzhak stood up. Joris and Yuri scrambled to their feet as Li stood up. The two women stood as well.

"It will soon be time," Yitzhak said with a smile. "Let's go to the balcony to see if the people are assembling."

Yitzhak led them to a wide balcony overlooking the city. There were people starting to gather. There were groups of men and boys talking while the women and girls stood quietly behind them. All of the women and girls were looking at the ground.

"The women need to know that they are allowed to look up to see what is going on," Li said.

"Yes," Yitzhak said as he looked out over the plaza. "I will take care of that. I want the women and girls to see how beautiful you are. I want them to begin to realize that they can be beautiful too. I want the men to realize that you are beautiful and perhaps their own wives can be beautiful as well."

"I learned from Queen Marriah that because I am your wife, you are my husband," Li said.

"Husband," Yitzhak said with a smile. "I like the sound of that. It seems that both men and women need to learn new words."

Li glanced at Ki and Fa. They both looked stunned. She smiled and nodded to them. Yitzhak led them down to the palace courtyard and to a stand built against the palace wall. Lenar was waiting for them next to the stairs. He was holding something covered by a cloth.

"Where did you get the crown?" Lenar asked.

"Remember Lucjen?" Yitzhak said and Lenar nodded. "I learned that he has some extraordinary talents. I also learned where he came from. He was a good man and I will miss him now that he has returned to his own people and the dragons they live with."

Lenar looked confused but nodded as Yitzhak led her up the stairs. Lenar followed behind them.

"People of Mannton," Yitzhak announced loudly, and silence fell. "As you have probably heard, I have just returned from Brinley. While there I signed a peace agreement with their ruler. I learned some very important things from this ruler and my stay in Brinley."

There were murmurings amongst the men.

"One of the things that I have learned is that women are capable of much more than we thought," Yitzhak said, then paused until it was quiet again. "Queen Marriah of Brinley is a very capable ruler who is respected and loved by all of her people. She is also very skilled with a sword."

There was more talk among the men. It was quite a while before they settled down.

"Since I took Li as my wife, I had noticed that she was intelligent. She knew of things that most men do not," Yitzhak said.

"Some of what she was able to tell me is that women use different words for some things than men do. While a man would say someone had died and was buried, a woman would say that the person was no more and lay beneath the dirt."

Again he was forced to pause. This time even the women were murmuring.

"Women are not stupid, nor are they mere animals," Yitzhak said. "Part of what has divided Mannton into a kingdom of men and a kingdom of women is we speak differently. We all need to learn to communicate with our wives with words instead of just beating them."

The men were getting louder.

"I know that change is not easy, but I now can see it is necessary for our survival," Yitzhak said. "Part of the peace agreement is that Brinley will never invade Mannton nor take over any of our land, but if we do not change, Mannton will die."

This time there was stunned silence as Yitzhak paused.

"One of the first changes is that from this time on, women and girls will be allowed to attend public meetings," Yitzhak said. "They need to know what is happening just as much as the men and boys do. I have learned that most women never see the face of the man who took them as his wife. The girls never see the face of their father. Women and girls have not had a face, nor a voice before today. That must change. From now on women and girls will not be punished for looking at a man's face."

There was some murmuring amongst the men.

"Now today I want to officially give all women and girls a face and a voice to represent them in ruling this kingdom. I have asked that they are here so that they can see this with their own eyes. I want all of the children including the girls to come forward so they can see clearly," Yitzhak said and paused as the boys followed by the girls moved to the front of the group. "Men, you will not hit any female for looking at me. Now I ask every woman and girl to look up so they can see my face and what I am going to do."

Li saw the women and girls begin to look up at last. Yitzhak held out his hand to her and she stepped forward to take it. The men stopped murmuring as she came into view.

"This is my wife, Li," Yitzhak said. "From this day forward she shall be known as Queen Li and be treated with all the respect that I am due."

He motioned Lenar forward and removed the cloth covering the crown. Li heard gasps among the crowd as Yitzhak raised the crown in his hands and placed it gently on her head. As it settled in place it fit perfectly.

"Queen Li will be the face and voice for the women of Mannton," Yitzhak said. "If you will look around, you will see that there are many more men than women. If you look closely you will notice that there are not many children either. I know that change will take time, but it is urgent that we make changes before it is too late. The kingdom of Brinley has as many women as men and the streets are filled with the laughter of children. In time Mannton can be that way as well."

"May I speak?" Li asked quietly.

"Yes," Yitzhak replied with a smile.

"Women of Mannton," Li said loudly, and she heard a collective gasp from the men. "Change is not easy and takes time, but do not give up hope. I will work very hard to help King Yitzhak make the changes to the laws so that life will be better for all of us. Although it has been more than two years since I lived among you, I have not forgotten what your life is like. It is because I had a strong will and courage that I stand before you today. I will make certain that your voice is heard."

"And I will listen closely," Yitzhak said. "As you return home, remember that women are just as important as men are to any kingdom."

As they reached the bottom of the stairs, they found Li's father waiting for them. He knelt and stood back up before speaking.

"I wanted to tell you that the men were all very surprised to see your beauty," Father said. "They aren't too certain about the idea of a queen, but like you said, change is not easy."

"We know it will take time and that we must proceed carefully," Yitzhak said.

"I wish that Rowan had been here to see you," Father said. "I know he cared a lot about you. Sometimes he would even defend you when I was angry with you."

"I never knew that," Li said. "Where is he?"

"He and Anunik went out on Anunik's boat to catch fish, but they have been gone far too long," Father said in a worried tone. "I hope that he still lives."

"I do too, Father," Li said as she put her hand on Father's arm.

She was surprised as he smiled and patted her hand. She was glad to know that at least Father would accept the changes they wanted to make. The days that followed were busy ones. Li was learning to read and write, but more importantly she was learning about ruling a kingdom. Yitzhak sometimes seemed frustrated, but never spoke harshly to her. She tried very hard to understand what he was trying to teach her. Lenar's wife, Ka, began helping Li bathe and dress. Li was grateful for her assistance and her friendship.

Chapter 13 – Past and Present

Yitzhak was quite pleased with Li's progress learning to read and write, but today she wanted to spend some time alone in the garden. Yitzhak wandered into the throne room and looked at his throne sitting on the dais. He noticed the throne seemed to not be centered. It was something he had never noticed before. He walked up the three steps and put his hand on the back of the throne. The carvings were familiar under his hand. His mind flashed back to the storage room in the attic of the servants' area.

Yitzhak found his way back to the attic storage room. He lit the lamp and opened the door. He soon found the piece of furniture he had come to examine. He found a safe place to put the lamp and started moving the items and trunks that were around and sitting on it until he could remove the cloth that covered it. He noticed that many of the things appeared to belong to a woman. When he moved the last small flat box from it something inside the box slid and clattered softly. He opened it and found a tangle of gold and smashed bits of seashell. He shook his head and set it aside.

"I saw you come this direction," Lenar's voice said behind him as he pulled the cloth off the piece of furniture.

"What is this?" Yitzhak said as he moved aside so Lenar could see it.

Lenar came closer.

"Why would there be a throne here?" Lenar asked. "It is a twin to yours. It makes no sense at all."

"No, it doesn't," Yitzhak agreed. "I am glad it is here though. I think it is time Li has a throne of her own so she can participate in audiences."

"It's too wide to get through the door we came in," Lenar commented as he glanced back at the door. "It had to get in here somehow."

Yitzhak picked up the lamp and made his way around piles of things to the other end of the room. There were large double doors at the other end of the room. Lenar tried them but they were locked. He used the key, but when he pulled open the doors they were greeted by a stone wall.

"Obviously this room was meant to be forgotten," Yitzhak commented.

"I recognize this stone," Lenar said pointing to one with distinctive dark stripes on it. "There is a landing and another attic storage room on the other side of this door. There is also a wide staircase."

"I wonder if this wall is as poorly made as the other one was." Yitzhak commented as he pushed at the stones near the top.

"Maybe this will help," Lenar said as he held up a hammer. "It might be a stone mason's hammer that was sealed in when the wall was built."

Yitzhak traded the lamp for the hammer and used it to tap the stones at the top. One dropped out of sight followed by another. Soon several stones at a time were coming loose and they began to see the doors in the opposite wall along with the worried faces of several servants.

"Haul away these stones and finish tearing out this wall," Yitzhak said. "Lenar will show you what I want brought down and where it goes."

The servants picked up some of the stones and quickly left.

"I agree with your grandfather," Yitzhak said. "This whole room has a story to tell about our past. It might take quite a while to uncover the truth of why this was hidden. Curiously much of what is in here appears to belong to a woman. I've not seen much up here that would belong to a man."

"I'll let you know when we have the throne in place. It might need cleaning."

"I want it ready for her to use before showing it to her. I'll be in my office."

Lenar bowed as Yitzhak headed back toward the small door. When he reached his office he searched the shelves for the oldest books.

"What are you looking for?" Li's voice startled him.

"Some very old books," Yitzhak said as he turned to face her. "Maybe something hidden even."

Li looked puzzled.

"Something only the king would have access to, but from a very long time ago," he said.

Her eyes widened and she whispered, "I wonder."

"Wonder what?" he asked as she turned and left.

He followed her down to Ta's room. She went to the window and lifted the front of the wooden bench. She reached inside and pulled out a piece of wood.

"Is this what you are looking for?" she asked.

He looked inside the compartment and found the bottom filled with books.

"This might be it," he said as he met her eyes. "How did you know to look here?"

"I found it after Ta died but didn't dare say anything. What is this about?"

"Ghosts of the past," Yitzhak said, and she tilted her head. "Something happened long ago, and I need to find out what and why."

She helped him gather the books and carry them upstairs to their quarters. They spread them out on the table in the sitting room. Yitzhak opened each book and found what appeared to be the oldest and written by a young boy. He began to read it out loud.

"I hate it when Father calls me Amby. My name is Ambrose. I've been dreaming about she who bore me again. I remember so little about her. The last time I asked Father what happened to her he beat me. There are many boys my age and younger, but no girls. There are no women allowed in the palace. I asked Father why three days ago, but he beat me until I had to be carried back to my room by the servants. I can finally sit long enough to eat and write this."

Yitzhak looked up to see Li shaking her head.

"This seems to be a few days later," Yitzhak said and continued reading.

"Father insisted I accompany him out into the city. As we passed a woman, she looked at us and Father grabbed her by the hair. He declared that any woman who looked at his face would die. He then drew his dagger and slit her throat. The women fled into the homes and the men knelt. He called women worthless and then drug me back to the palace. I don't know what to think, but he is king and he makes the laws."

"What would make a king act that way?" Li whispered.

"I don't know, but I think something awful happened," Yitzhak replied as he put down the journal and picked up another one. "It will take some time to figure this out. It might explain why women were treated so badly for so long."

"There has to be some of Ambrose's father's journals somewhere or some record of what happened," Li commented as she picked up a journal. "I wonder if they are hidden too."

She set down the journal and went into the bedroom. Yitzhak followed her. She tossed the cushions from the window seat and lifted the bench. She emptied the bench onto the floor but found no hidden compartment. She shook her head and put the things back in place.

"I don't think this has always been the royal quarters," Yitzhak said. "There's a locked door behind a tapestry in the throne room. It is opposite the dining hall. I found it when I was young but didn't think much about it before now."

Lenar entered and met Yitzhak's eyes before glancing at Li.

"A matter needs your immediate attention, My King," Lenar said.

"Go on," Li said as she picked up one of the journals. "I will see if I can read one of these."

Yitzhak kissed her forehead before leaving with Lenar.

"Li found some journals in Ta's room. I think they hold clues to what we found in the attic," Yitzhak said.

"We were so concentrated on the wall that we didn't notice what was on the doors," Lenar said as they entered the servants' area of the palace.

When they reached the top of the stairs there were men and women moving things around in the attic. Lenar closed the double doors.

"In memory of Queen Lodena," Yitzhak read aloud. "It looks like it was hastily painted. I found a box with some twisted gold and fragments of seashells. I wonder if it is what remains of her crown. I wonder if her death has something to do with how women have been treated in Mannton."

"Perhaps it does," Lenar said as the doors opened. "I've had a couple of servants cleaning the throne while the rest cleared a path to the doors."

Two large men carried the throne out of the doors. Yitzhak and Lenar went down the stairs ahead of them. Once they reached the bottom of the stairs the men had to rest.

"I need to show you something, Lenar," Yitzhak said and led him towards the throne room.

When they reached the throne room Yitzhak went over to the large tapestry opposite the dining hall and went behind it.

"Why are you. . . a door?" Lenar asked.

"I wonder if one of your keys fits it."

Lenar drew out his keys and tried each one, but none fit.

"No luck. This lock is different. The keyhole is shaped differently," Lenar said. "The lock plate feels carved. It's too dark to tell for certain."

Yitzhak held the tapestry out further allowing more light to fall on the door. The lock plate was topped with what looked like his crown. The keyhole was curved with the ends curling opposite of each other and a rounded part in the center. Something about it was familiar, but Yitzhak didn't know why.

"Obviously we're not getting this opened until I find the key," he said. "I wonder if there is another door in the main hall."

"Perhaps there is," Lenar said. "I never really noticed that there is a room missing."

As they came out from behind the tapestry the men entered with the throne. Yitzhak climbed the dais and pointed to where the throne should go. As they set the throne down it seemed to slide a bit before settling into place next to his throne.

"Like it was always meant to be there," Yitzhak commented and Lenar nodded.

On the way back to the royal quarters he checked behind the tapestries in the hall and found a set of double doors matching the ones for the throne room and dining hall, but the lock plates matched the one on the other hidden door. When he arrived, he found Li reading one of the journals.

"I have a surprise for you," he said when she looked up.

"What is it?"

"It's in the throne room. Did you learn anything more?"

"The original royal quarters were next to the throne room, but Ambrose's father locked them up and covered the doors with tapestries. He was forbidden to mention them and she who bore him," she said as she stood and placed the journal on the table.

"I found one of the doors when I was a boy, but had forgotten about it until now," Yitzhak said as they left the room. "I need to find the key before it can be opened. Lenar has some keys that seem to fit every other door in the palace, but this one is shaped differently than any key I've ever seen."

"Show me the door so I can be watching for the key as well," she replied.

When they arrived at the throne room she suddenly stopped.

"A throne?" she asked, and he nodded. "Where did you get it?"

"I found it in an attic storage that had been sealed off," Yitzhak said as they crossed the room. "I believe it was removed when she who bore Ambrose died. Her name was Queen Lodena."

She climbed the steps, stopping in front of the thrones. He joined her and sat in his throne. She sat down beside him.

"Now you can be here for audiences," he said as she stroked the carvings on the armrest on her throne. "It's important that the men see you as my equal."

****

Kenner was glad that Li was happy and King Yitzhak treated her well. He was still not certain about some of the changes that King Yitzhak had been making, but since Kenner no longer had a wife or daughter it really didn't matter much. He thought about how different Li had looked when he last saw her. Most women's hands were thin and bony, but Li's had looked more like a young man's hands. Her hair was no longer matted and shinier than he remembered as well.

He picked up the empty bucket and headed towards the well. He stopped as he saw the crowd of women at the well. Some of them looked so very thin and frail like An had before she had died. Some had open wounds and their hair was dull and matted. He realized that they must not get much to eat. He thought about the white worms that Li had admitted to eating when there was no food left.

A man came as a woman began moving her bucket of water away from the well. She had to set it down every few steps. The man looked very angry.

"This is ridiculous," he said in an angry tone. "Pick it up and carry it!"

Kenner went over as the man raised his arm to strike the woman. He caught the man's arm before he could bring it down.

"What do you think you're doing?" the man asked in the same angry tone.

"Look at your hand and then at hers," Kenner said as he took the woman's wrist and brought her hand next to the man's. "Tell me what you see."

"Hands," the man muttered.

"Look how thin and bony her hand is next to yours," Kenner said. "What her dress covers is probably the same. What food do you give her?"

"She cooks the food and eats first," the man said angrily as Kenner released her arm.

"That's what I thought for years, but I found out that my wife and daughter were not eating first at all. Everything she cooks gets set in front of you. When is the last time you left her any food at all?"

"A couple of days ago," the man replied in a softer tone.

"If you want her to be able to carry this bucket of water, I suggest you start making certain she eats something at least once a day. If you don't, she'll soon die just like my wife did. Then you'll be cooking your own food and cleaning your own house just like I am."

"Ka," the man said, and the woman glanced up at him. "What have you been eating?"

"Only what you leave for me," Ka replied.

"I had no idea," the man shook his head. "I'll carry the bucket today. Keep out some food for yourself so you don't have to eat what I leave."

The woman collapsed to the ground sobbing into her hands.

Kenner knelt next to her and said, "Don't give up. I know that Queen Li will keep her promises and so will King Yitzhak. I know that Queen Li never lies because she is my daughter."

She began to look up at him but stopped.

"You can look at my face, Ka. I don't mind," Kenner said, and she finally met his eyes. "Don't give up hope."

"Thank you," she whispered.

Kenner and the man helped her up to her feet. The man met his eyes with a surprised look on his face. Kenner nodded realizing that the man could feel just how thin and bony she was. Kenner noticed that the women at the well were watching as he picked up his bucket. They backed away from the well as he approached. The two women who were drawing up the bucket dropped the rope. He took the rope and drew up the bucket before filling one of the women's buckets.

"Ka's man didn't know she put all the food on the table for him," Kenner said as he dropped the bucket down the well to draw more water. "Men think that the women eat before setting the food on the table or keep some out to eat later."

"We would be beaten if we did that," one of the oldest women said softly.

"Would he even notice?" Kenner asked. "If he asks tell him you are tasting it to make certain it is good enough for him to eat. You'll get something to eat every day and he'll think you're doing it to take better care of him. Even if it's only a little, it's much better than nothing."

"Why are you at the well?" one woman asked as he filled her bucket.

"Because my wife is no more and lies beneath the dirt. Queen Li is my daughter," Kenner said. "I miss An very much. I know that I should have made certain she got enough to eat before she became no more."

"You know women's words."

"Queen Li taught them to me."

He filled the rest of the women's buckets before returning home. The house was so empty with Rowan gone. The worst part was not knowing if he was still alive.

Chapter 14 – Rescued

One day while they were looking for more journals in Yitzhak's office, a man came bearing a message from Queen Marriah. As Yitzhak opened the scroll, Li gasped to see a drawing of two men that looked like they were in pain. One's features reminded her of Father. Yitzhak frowned as he read the scroll, then seemed relieved.

"Rowan and Anunik were rescued from the ocean by the people of Merton," Yitzhak said. "They are badly sunburned and weak but should recover in time. Queen Marriah and King Archelaus will bring them back to Mannton. They have healers that will be able to heal their burns."

"They look like they are in pain," Li said as she looked at the drawing. "This one must be Rowan."

She pointed to the one who looked similar to Father.

"Yes," Yitzhak said as he drew paper out of the drawer.

"When they return, it will show the people that the treaty with Brinley is working," Li said. "I know that Mannton has been at war with Brinley many times in the past. It would be something to celebrate that Brinley is demonstrating they are no longer an enemy."

"You are right," Yitzhak said. "Perhaps we could organize a feast. It will take them about ten days to reach Mannton."

"Would it be possible to have the women eat at the feast sitting beside the men?" Li asked. "Both Ki and Fa have said that their husbands now let them sit with them at meals and eat what they want to. Yuri and Joris have begun listening to their wives too."

"Yes," Yitzhak said. "That is a very good idea."

Yitzhak wrote out a reply to Queen Marriah's message and sent the messenger on his way. They then sent guards to bring Father and Anunik's father, Dreggen, and his wife to the palace. They were just going to the dining hall when they arrived.

"We have some good news to give you," Yitzhak said. "Come join us for lunch."

The two men stared as Li sat next to Yitzhak to eat. Ti stood in the corner looking at the floor.

"Come sit down to eat with us Ti," Yitzhak said, and Ti glanced up. "You must be hungry too."

"Yes, My King," she said quietly as she cautiously approached the table.

She took her place next to Dreggen after the men had sat down.

"Rowan and Anunik have been rescued," Yitzhak said. "They are badly sunburned, but the people who rescued them are treating the burns. They will be brought safely to Mannton by Queen Marriah and King Archelaus. We will have a feast when they arrive."

"That is very good news," Father said with a tone of relief in his voice.

"Why have a feast?" Dreggen asked. "Certainly they are not that well known."

"Li pointed out that when Queen Marriah and King Archelaus return Rowan and Anunik to Mannton it will demonstrate to the people of Mannton that Brinley is no longer an enemy," Yitzhak replied as he began to eat.

The two men looked at her in surprise.

"I have been aware of Mannton being at war with Brinley many times," Li said. "I thought that this demonstration of peace would be something worth celebrating."

They glanced at each other before looking back at her.

"I was beginning to wonder if," Dreggen said then stopped.

"If I was going insane?" Yitzhak asked with a grin. "I'm certain that is what every man is wondering right now. Li suggested that the women should sit with the men at the feast. They need to see how King Archelaus treats his wife. I may even invite Queen Marriah to demonstrate her skill with the sword. If that doesn't convince the men that things need to change, I don't know what will."

During the rest of the meal, Father asked Li a lot of questions. Some were about when she lived in his house and some were about since then. He was very amazed when she told him about Brinley. She could tell Ti was listening closely as was Dreggen. When they left, Li realized that she had never been able to speak to her father like that before. It made her feel good that Father was finally realizing that she was worthy of being Queen Li.

They made plans for the feast as they waited anxiously for Queen Marriah and King Archelaus to arrive. Li hoped that Rowan and Anunik would learn from the time they spent with them. She frequently looked out over the city from the balcony. She watched the women as they went to the well for water. Although it was not easy to see at first, she could see that the women had changed. They looked up more than before. They were still shy about looking at men for more than a moment, but at least they were beginning to look up. The men did not beat them for looking up at their faces. It was encouraging, but there were still men beating women and girls even in the streets.

****

Yitzhak could tell that Li was excited. Yesterday they had received a message that King Archelaus and Queen Marriah were in Brinley and would arrive in Mannton today. He took four guards with him to greet them. As he approached, he saw Queen Marriah kneeling next to a young woman. Captain Davon and Captain Dallon both stood with swords drawn facing a man holding a hoe on a half of a handle. Beside him stood a boy.

Queen Marriah stood and faced the man. The man dropped the hoe and stood with a shocked expression. She did not turn away from the man as Yitzhak pulled his horse to a stop and dismounted.

"You would do well to listen to Queen Marriah," Yitzhak said. "She is very wise. I have asked her and King Archelaus to help me make changes in the way women are treated here in Mannton before it is too late."

The man and his son knelt. Captain Davon and Captain Dallon sheathed their swords before bowing to Yitzhak. Queen Marriah turned to face him.

"Thank you for coming," he said as he bowed to her.

Yitzhak heard many gasps from the men who had assembled to watch.

"We are happy to help," she said as she curtsied. "Leda and Lyla have brought something."

Captain Davon and Captain Dallon hurried to help their wives from the wagon and remove the tarp.

100

"We bring a gift from the women of Brinley to the women of Mannton," Leda said.

"Dresses to replace the patchwork ones they must make from rags and scraps," Lyla said.

"We also brought carvings for you and Queen Li," Leda added.

Lyla took two dresses from the pile and took them to where the young woman still knelt on the ground.

"These are for you," she said as she handed the dresses to the woman.

"Thank you," she said as tears began to run down her cheeks.

Yitzhak knelt next to the woman and saw how thin her hands were.

"Can you stand?" he asked as he noticed the drag marks in the ground leading up to the bucket of water next to her.

It was only half full. She nodded. He gently took her elbow and helped her to stand.

"Women are vital to the survival of a kingdom," Yitzhak said loudly. "A woman needs to eat or she will starve to death. All women and girls will be allowed to eat the same quantity and quality of food that the men and boys eat. Women will sit with the men to eat each meal. Also, from now on any man found beating a woman or girl will face time in the dungeon."

Yitzhak saw the man's face go white.

"You two help distribute these dresses," Yitzhak said pointing at two guards. "You two escort him home. He is to remain under guard until I decide what to do with him."

The young woman was trembling as she clutched the dresses to her chest.

"I will carry you since I don't think you could walk right now," Yitzhak said to the young woman before turning to Queen Marriah. "Please come to the palace. Rowan and Anunik's fathers are waiting for them there."

Queen Marriah and King Archelaus walked with him, followed by the others. He was surprised by how light the young woman was. He could see how thin her hands were.

"It was very thoughtful to bring dresses," Yitzhak said.

"It was Leda and Lyla's idea," Queen Marriah explained.

When they reached the palace courtyard, Li was waiting with the two men.

"Bring her inside," she said as she saw the young woman. They all went inside and down the hall. They entered the room that had been Li's. Li pulled the covers down and Yitzhak placed the woman on the bed.

"I'll send for the healer and some soup," he said as he went to the door.

"Get me some rags with a bucket of cold water," he heard Queen Marriah say. "I can keep these bruises from swelling further."

Yitzhak returned with two men following him. One was carrying a pot and the other a tray of food. He saw Rowan and Anunik talking with their fathers. Queen Marriah moved away from the bed while Li and Yitzhak helped the young woman to eat. When the healer arrived, he looked a bit annoyed.

"You will see to her injuries," Yitzhak said in a stern tone and Kon nodded.

He and Li went over to where Queen Marriah and King Archelaus stood with Rowan, Anunik, their fathers and Ti.

"What she needs now is rest," Yitzhak said.

Rowan and Anunik both dropped to their knees at Li's feet.

"Rise," she said as she smiled at Queen Marriah. "I see that you have benefitted from your time spent with our friends King Archelaus and Queen Marriah."

"Yes, My Queen," Rowan said. "We have learned the error of Mannton's men. I hope you can forgive me for how I treated you. You always took such good care of us."

"I do forgive you," Li said as she put her hand on his shoulder. "All of you. But I do expect you to share what you have learned with the other men."

"It won't be easy," Yitzhak said. "But things must change if we are to survive."

"I have something to present to you," Rowan said. "It's out in the wagon."

"We're not leaving her alone are we?" Anunik asked.

"Kora and Ethan could stay with her," Queen Marriah said.

"We would be happy to," the servant woman said.

When they got out to the wagon, it was mostly empty. Rowan opened the tailgate of the wagon to reveal a marker stone.

"When King Archelaus told me that our mother, she who bore us, starved to death, I felt terrible," Rowan said. "I know there is no way to make up for that, but this will help to remind others to not make the same mistake."

"An, beloved mother of Queen Li," Li read aloud. "May she always be remembered that no others go hungry."

"Oh, Rowan," Li said as she hugged him. "Thank you."

"We could take it to the cemetery now," Yitzhak said. "Supper will be ready when we return."

Yitzhak was very interested to see the women's cemetery. It was covered by rocks and there was a border of rocks around it. Li walked straight to a particular spot. It was the only place where there was a small flower laid on the ground. Li looked up at Ti.

"I had been thinking about how proud she would be of you," Ti said. "I woke up early this morning and put the flower on her spot."

"Thank you, Ti," Li said as she hugged her.

Rowan and his father placed the stone just above the flower. Father and son stood silently looking at the stone and flower before looking at each other. Yitzhak could see conflict and guilt in both of their eyes. He knew that they would be of great help making the changes needed. By the time they returned to the palace Captain Davon, Leda, Captain Dallon and Lyla were waiting for them. They were waiting beside their wagon.

"Leda, Lyla, I'm so glad you could come," Li said as she approached the wagon.

"We brought gifts for you," Leda said as she reached into the bed of the wagon.

"We hope you like them," Lyla said as she took the carving Leda handed her.

"They are beautiful," Li said.

"I have never seen birds like these before," Yitzhak said. "What are they doing?"

"These are birds that live in the marsh where we grew up," Leda said. "They mate for life, but each spring they dance before mating."

"Then when the chicks hatch, both parents feed and care for them," Lyla added.

"I think that we should display these in the main hall so everyone visiting the palace will see them," Yitzhak said as he put his arm around his wife.

"Yes," she said as she smiled at him. "I like that idea."

Just then Joris came out of the palace and bowed.

"We were wondering where you were, My King," he said. "Everything is ready and waiting."

"Let's go eat," Yitzhak said.

Soon they were seated in the dining hall. Servants brought food out and kept their plates full until they could eat no more. Yitzhak noticed that Ti seemed to enjoy the meal, but Anunik seemed distracted.

"What's the matter, son?" his father asked.

"I wonder if the young woman would like some of this food," Anunik said. "She is so thin."

"She would probably enjoy some bread and a few vegetables," Queen Marriah said. "But I doubt her stomach could handle much else yet."

"May I be excused to take her some?" Anunik asked.

"Of course," Yitzhak said.

Soon Anunik had left with a plate of food.

"He is certainly acting strangely," his father said. "I wonder what's wrong."

"I think I understand what is going on," Archelaus said with a laugh. "I doubt that he realizes it yet, but I think he is falling in love."

"With the young woman?" Ti asked.

Archelaus nodded.

"Tomorrow afternoon, we had planned to take you to visit the ocean," Yitzhak said. "My Queen has only seen the harbor up close. She has seen the ocean from a distance. We could bring the young woman with us if she feels up to it."

"I could work on your portrait in the morning," Queen Marriah said. "But, tonight I am feeling tired."

"Let me show you to your rooms," Yitzhak replied.

Chapter 15 – A Visit to the Ocean

The next morning Queen Marriah began painting the portrait of Yitzhak and Li. Eventually King Archelaus entered leading Anunik who was carrying the young woman. Captain Davon and Captain Dallon followed behind.

"Are you feeling better?" Yitzhak asked.

"A little, My King," the young woman replied. "I wish to ask something of you."

"What would you like to ask?" he answered.

"May I see my father?" she asked. "I don't trust him, but I have some questions for him."

"I can have him brought to your room," Yitzhak said, and she nodded. "Anunik, Captain Davon and Captain Dallon will keep you safe."

"Thank you, My King," she said.

"Guard, go fetch her father to the palace and bring him her room," Yitzhak said.

"Yes, My King," the guard replied and left.

King Archelaus kissed Queen Marriah's cheek before following the others.

****

Anunik followed the guard as he carried the young woman in his arms. They returned to her room and he set her on a chair. She looked different than the frightened woman sitting in the dirt yesterday. Her dress was clean and not patched together. She was beautiful with her hair brushed and braided into a crown around her head.

The door opened and he turned to see a man who didn't look up led in by a guard with two more trailing behind. He knelt at the young woman's feet when they stopped in front of her. Anunik moved to stand behind her and put his hands on the chair. Captain Davon and Captain Dallon stood to either side of her and King Archelaus stood off to the side near the fireplace.

"Father," she said, and the man finally looked up. "I wanted to see that you are alright."

"I have been treated better than I deserve after how I treated you and she who bore you," he replied quietly.

"I have some questions for you," she said.

"I will answer if I can," he responded.

"What is my name?" she asked and Anunik was surprised by the question.

"I don't know," he answered after a moment. "What did she who bore you call you?"

"Only daughter or girl. I guess I have no name."

Anunik's heart ached to think she had no name at all. Prince Langward's wife's name came to his mind as a beautiful name for a beautiful woman. He moved beside her chair and knelt.

"Queen Marriah's mother was named Carita," he said as he took her hand in his.

"Carita," she repeated softly.

"I think she would be honored if you chose to make Carita your name," King Archelaus said.

"I will ask her permission. Father, I need to know that when you are released, that you will teach Amasas that you were wrong in how you treated me and she who bore me."

"I swear I will. I sent him to live with Queen Li's father for now," he responded fervently. "Since yesterday I have eaten nothing but bread crusts and drank only water so I can better understand what you went through. I won't eat anything else until you have healed."

"When I am well, I will not be returning home," she said.

Anunik worried about where she would live or who would take care of her.

"I understand," her father said. "And I don't blame you. I have spent all night thinking about what happened yesterday. I do not deserve a wife, nor a daughter, but I want to make certain you have a better life than I gave you."

Anunik's heart began to pound as he gathered up his courage knowing she might refuse his request, but he had to try. The thought of her alone and defenseless broke his heart.

"If you think I am worthy, I want to take care of you," Anunik said as he looked into her eyes.

"Would you expect me to be your wife?" she asked.

"I expect only to take care of you," Anunik said as his heart ached to have her for his wife. He felt a tear roll down his cheek. "It would be for you to choose my place as either your servant or your man. I promise I will never force you to do what you don't want to."

She looked from Anunik to her father.

"It is up to you," her father said. "Although you are my daughter, I deserve no control over your future."

"I will need time to think about it," she said. "I am not accustomed to thinking about my future, let alone making decisions about it."

"I will provide you anything you want," Anunik said as hope began to grow in his heart. "All you need to do is ask."

She nodded and said, "I am tired. Take him home."

Her father stood and followed the guards out of the room.

"Can you sit me on the bed? It is much softer."

Anunik gently lifted her from the chair hoping she didn't notice how fast his heart was beating. She was so very thin. He prayed she would survive and eventually want to be his wife.

"I'll see if there is a nice soft chair you could use," Anunik said as he put her on the bed. "I'll be right back."

His head was swirling with the possibilities as he went to find a palace servant for help finding a softer chair.

****

To Yitzhak it seemed like a very long time before King Archelaus returned.

"I'm nearly finished," Queen Marriah said as he kissed her cheek. "How is the young woman?"

"She is doing better," he replied. "She wants to ask you something."

"You can finish tomorrow morning," Yitzhak said. "Do you mind if we have a look at it?"

"Not at all," Queen Marriah replied as she cleaned her brush. "Tell me what you think."

He was very pleased with the portrait.

"It's beautiful!" Li exclaimed. "Do I really look like that?"

"You are very beautiful, My Dear Wife," Yitzhak said and kissed her hand. "This portrait shows your beauty perfectly."

"I'm glad you like it," Queen Marriah said as she stood up. "I'm going down to see what the young woman wanted to ask me. What is her name? We can't just keep calling her 'the young woman.' It just isn't right."

"That's what she wanted to see you about," King Archelaus replied. "She has no name."

"No name?" Yitzhak asked as a shock ran through him.

"Some women are never given a name of their own," Li acknowledged. "They are known as wife of this man or daughter of that man."

"That will have to change," Yitzhak said as they arrived at the door.

"How are you feeling today?" Li asked as they entered the room.

"Better," she said as she stood up and then knelt. "I have something to ask of Queen Marriah."

"What would you like to ask?" Queen Marriah said as the woman sat back on the bed.

"Anunik said that your mother's name was Carita," she said. "He suggested that you might consent to let me use that as my name."

"That would make me very happy," Queen Marriah said. "Anunik was thoughtful to suggest it."

"He has offered to take care of me," Carita said. "He even said that he would be my servant if I didn't want to be his wife."

"How do you feel about him?" Li asked. "He seems to care a lot about you."

"I think I can trust him," she replied slowly.

"I know what you mean," Queen Marriah said as she sat on the bed near Carita. "When Regis Bryant rescued me from Larkin, I didn't trust anyone, not even Regis Bryant. For a while, they didn't know if I would live, but then I saw how much Regis Bryant loves his wife. Knowing that there was such love in this world gave me the courage I needed to survive. Soon after that I met a man whom I could trust enough to become his wife."

"King Archelaus?" Carita asked.

"Yes. I soon discovered that although we had just met, he was more concerned about me than his title or kingdom."

"Kora told me about your wedding," Carita said. "Does everyone in Brinley and Burton have a wedding when they take a wife?"

"Not nearly as large or elaborate as our wedding," Queen Marriah said. "But, yes, everyone has a wedding."

"If I decide I want to be Anunik's wife, could we have a wedding also?" Carita asked.

"I don't see why not," Yitzhak said, liking the idea. "It would be the first wedding Mannton has seen, so we would have to decide what would be involved."

"We would be happy to help," Queen Marriah said as Anunik walked in.

He dropped to his knees.

"Rise," Yitzhak said. "Carita was just telling us that you have offered to care for her. Do you realize you would be making a lifetime commitment?"

"Yes, My King," Anunik replied. "I have thought of little else. It is what I want to do. I am prepared to sleep on the floor at the foot of her bed until she is ready to make my house her home and I have built a second bed. I will even build a new house if mine doesn't suit her."

"You are welcome to stay in the palace until she is ready to leave," Yitzhak said. "I will have a room assigned to you if she is willing to let you stay here."

Anunik went over and knelt at Carita's feet.

"May I stay here to care for you?" Anunik asked as he looked up at her. "You can say no if you are not comfortable with me staying."

"You may stay," she replied. "I know that I will need to learn to trust you."

"I have spoken to the cobbler, and he might have some sandals that would fit you," Anunik said. "I checked on Amasas and he asked if you are alright."

"There are a few things I would like to get from my house, but I don't want my father in the house with me," she said. "I would like to see your house."

"We can pick them up after seeing the cobbler," Anunik replied as he stood up. "I brought a horse. My home is outside of town by the ocean"

"We are going to visit the ocean and you can come with us. Don't be gone more than an hour," Yitzhak said. "We will be leaving soon."

"Yes, My King," Anunik said as he picked up Carita.

Yitzhak led them back upstairs where they talked about different weddings. He was surprised to hear that Brinley, Burton and the village of Langward all had very different weddings. There were several things that he liked about each ceremony.

Li said, "I like the idea of the man and woman's hands being bound together. It would help remind the men that they are bound to the agreements made in the ceremony."

"Yes," Yitzhak said. "And I like the agreements made in Langward's ceremony and Brinley's wish of joy and happiness."

"I do hope that Carita decides to let Anunik be her husband," Li said.

"I still find it hard to believe that she had no name before today," Yitzhak said. "I can't imagine what it would be like to not have a name."

"My grandfather did not have a name until my grandmother gave him his name," Queen Marriah said. "I have learned that he was called by his title or by military rank until then. He apparently felt very frustrated to not have a name. The sons of the palace staff teased him about it all the time. He was always fighting or alone in his room. The girls wouldn't even talk to him."

"All women and girls should be given names," Yitzhak said.

"Yuri's wife did not have a name until I gave her the name Ki," Li said.

Yitzhak was shocked.

"So that's why you told me to tell him her name was Ki," he said as they walked towards the courtyard.

"She was afraid that he would be angry," Li said.

They were in the courtyard when Anunik returned with Carita and his parents. Anunik gently lifted Carita down from the horse. He helped her into the waiting carriage before taking a pair of saddlebags and a rolled up mat into the palace. Anunik's father helped Ti into the carriage. Leda and Lyla took their places in the carriage as they mounted their horses. Soon Anunik returned and they left the courtyard.

They passed the harbor near the well on the way out of town. After an hour traveling south they reached a wooded hill overlooking a stretch of sand leading to the ocean.

"My house is just east of here," Anunik said. "It's a little closer to the water than this."

"Lead the way," Yitzhak said.

Anunik led them through a gate and to a modest house with a porch on the west and south sides. There was a small barn to the east and a pasture. A couple of horses paused in their grazing to see who had come.

"This is your house?" Carita asked as he helped her from the carriage. "May I see inside?"

"Of course," he replied with a smile. "There is a path from the south porch to the beach. We'll be down in a few minutes."

"She seems to be taking his offer into serious consideration," Captain Davon said as they walked down the path.

"What offer?" Ti asked.

"He offered to care for Carita," King Archelaus said. "Either as her husband or her servant."

"He mentioned he was staying in the palace for a while," Dreggen said. "He has been very concerned about her."

"She asked about having a wedding if she decides to let him be her husband," Queen Marriah said. "I think she is beginning to trust him."

When they got to the beach Captain Davon, Leda, Captain Dallon and Lyla began running along the edge of the water and laughing. Leda pushed Captain Davon into the water, and he pulled her in with him. Captain Dallon began to laugh, and Lyla pushed him in. She ran up the beach with Captain Dallon close behind her. Anunik and Carita arrived just as Captain Dallon caught Lyla.

"Will he hurt her?" Carita asked in an alarmed tone.

"Watch," Queen Marriah said as Captain Dallon pulled Lyla to the sand on top of him.

She tried to get up as she laughed, but he caught her again. He laid her on her back on the sand and kissed her.

"Dallon would never do anything to hurt his wife," Queen Marriah said. "Neither would Davon. But they all enjoy playing jokes."

"They do look happy," Carita commented as Lyla pushed Captain Dallon off onto his back before kissing him. "I didn't realize that any woman could be so happy being a wife."

"There was a time when I felt the same way," Queen Marriah admitted. "But Archelaus has made me happier than I knew was possible."

King Archelaus leaned down and kissed her lips. As he did, she put her arms around his neck.

When they broke off the kiss, Carita asked, "Do all husbands and wives do that?"

"Kiss?" King Archelaus responded. "Yes."

"What does it feel like?" Ti asked.

"It's hard to describe," Queen Marriah said.

"It is something I really enjoy," Li said. "You should try it."

Anunik's parents turned to face each other. Hesitantly they kissed.

"Oh," Ti said before her husband kissed her again.

Yitzhak smiled as he saw Anunik watching his parents. Carita was looking up at Anunik. With her hand, she turned his face towards her. He met her gaze for a while before leaning down to kiss her lips.

"You may be my husband," Carita said. "But only if we can have a wedding."

"Husband? Wedding?" Anunik asked with a confused expression on his face.

"We'll do it tomorrow just before the feast," Yitzhak said. "All you have to do is show up."

"Davon, Dallon and I will make sure of that," King Archelaus said.

"I'll do anything you want," Anunik said as he looked into Carita's eyes.

"Set me down on my feet," Carita said.

Once she was standing, she turned to Anunik and put her arms around his neck. He put his arms around her and held her close.

"Now kiss me again," she said.

Yitzhak noticed that his parents looked pleased as they watched. The rest of the afternoon they explored the shoreline. Captain Davon and Captain Dallon caught fish which Anunik cooked for supper. By the time they returned to the palace, it was dark. Carita was already asleep when Anunik carried her into the palace.

Chapter 16 – Mannton's First Wedding

The next morning, Yitzhak went to his office and studied the wedding ceremony after having breakfast while the women were getting Carita ready for the wedding. When he returned to the sitting room, Carita was ready for the ceremony.

After kissing Li, he turned to Carita and said, "You look beautiful. There is an hour before time for the wedding. Is there anything you want before then?"

"I want my father and brother to see my wedding," Carita said. "But I want to speak to my father first."

"I'll have him brought here at once," Yitzhak said. "Then I will send two guards home with him while he cleans up. They will get him here in time for your wedding."

Yitzhak stepped out and told the guards to bring Carita's father to the palace before returning to the sitting room. Queen Marriah was working on the portrait when Carita's father was brought in. He did not look up as he was led in. He knelt in front of Carita when they stopped before her.

"Father," Carita said. "Look at me."

He looked up and gasped.

"I have taken the name Carita and will become Anunik's wife today," she said. "I want you and Amasas to attend our wedding."

"I know Anunik will care for you as you deserve," he replied. "I will do anything you ask of me."

"I do have several conditions," she said. "First, you will not attempt to make any contact with me. I may someday be ready to forgive you, but right now I do not trust you."

"I will do as you say," he replied. "I will see to it that Amasas follows the same rule."

"Second, you will get a marker stone for the grave of she who bore me."

"I do not know where it should be placed," he said. "But I will get the marker."

"She who bore Anunik knows where she is laid beneath the dirt."

"I will do as you have asked," he said. "Is there anything else I can do?"

"Just go and get cleaned up for the wedding," she replied.

"These two men will see that you return for the wedding," Yitzhak said and the two guards nodded. "Another will be sent for your son."

By the time Carita's father and brother returned, it was time for the feast and Queen Marriah had completed the portrait. Yitzhak went to get King Archelaus, Anunik and the others. Li would lead the women down a few minutes later. He led the men out to the plaza where the feast was set up. He was glad to see that the men had brought the women and girls with them.

Yitzhak said, "Today is an important day. Not only are we feasting to celebrate our new friendship with Brinley, but we are also celebrating a new beginning for Mannton. Our new friends have shown us that there are better ways to treat our women before we lose them entirely."

He waited for the crowd to settle down before continuing.

"Today we will put into practice some new traditions. The first is that the women of Mannton are here to sit beside the men as we feast. The second is Mannton's first wedding. Since most of us are unfamiliar with what a wedding is, I have asked King Archelaus to explain it to us before we begin."

"In other kingdoms, when a man decides to take a wife, not only does he ask her father, but he asks the woman that he intends to marry," King Archelaus said and was forced to pause. "Since this is a decision that will affect the rest of her life, she is given a choice in the matter. The wedding is a public ceremony recognizing the promises made between husband and wife. A marriage is a partnership with husband and wife sharing equally in responsibility and decision making."

King Archelaus paused to let the murmuring stop.

"In my experience, women are equally intelligent and capable as men. They deserve our respect and admiration," King Archelaus continued. "Women are vital to the future of any kingdom, for they alone are capable of bearing children. We must remember to cherish the birth of a daughter as much as the birth of a son."

Yitzhak was pleased with what King Archelaus was telling them as he saw some of the men nodding.

"We are ready to begin," King Archelaus said. "King Yitzhak and Queen Li have chosen aspects of weddings from several kingdoms to make a ceremony unique to Mannton."

"Stand before me, Anunik," Yitzhak said.

Anunik stepped forward and turned to face him. Queen Marriah led Carita forward to stand beside Anunik.

"Please join hands," Yitzhak said.

Anunik took Carita's left hand in his right hand. Li brought a cord made of shining threads and held it up.

"Today is the beginning of a new life for Anunik and Carita," Yitzhak said. "Their hands will be bound together with this cord to symbolize that instead of two individuals, they will become one, having equal rights, privileges and responsibilities."

Li wrapped the cord around their hands.

"Do you, Anunik, take Carita as your wife, promising to love, honor and cherish her until the end of your days?" Yitzhak said.

"I do," Anunik said. "I promise to care for her, putting her needs before my own."

Yitzhak smiled, pleased with the addition, and said, "Do you, Carita, take Anunik as your husband, promising to love, honor and cherish him until the end of your days?"

"I do," Carita said as she turned to look at Anunik. "I promise to care for him, putting his needs before my own."

He could see tears in both of their eyes as he said, "As king of Mannton, I officially declare Anunik and Carita to be husband and wife. May their happiness grow each day and joy be with them always. Anunik, you may kiss your wife."

He saw the startled reaction of the crowd as Anunik and Carita kissed.

"At their first meal as husband and wife they will feed each other while their hands remain bound. Now let us feast!" Yitzhak announced.

Soon they were seated at the tables laden with food. Yitzhak could see that the women were not reaching for food to put on their plates. He motioned to one of the servers. The man nodded after he told him to have the servers put food on the women's plates. He spoke to several other servers and soon the servers began to put food on the plates of all the women. As they ate, a group of men began juggling different objects. There was a lot of talk among the men. Yitzhak could see that it would take a while before all the men would be convinced of his plans.

"I hope you are enjoying your visit," Yitzhak said.

"Very much," Queen Marriah replied, "But, we must be getting back to Brinley soon. We have a lot to do before we must return to Burton."

"I'm glad I only have one kingdom to run," Yitzhak said. "I don't know how you manage."

"We hope to get to the point we are not traveling so much," King Archelaus said. "Hopefully within six months."

"So soon?" Yitzhak asked.

"I don't want Marriah to have to travel the last two months before our first child is born," King Archelaus replied. "And I don't want to travel without her."

"You are with child?" Yitzhak asked in surprise. "And yet you risked your life to save Carita's. You could have ordered Captain Davon and Captain Dallon to do it."

"Yes," Queen Marriah said. "But I wanted the people of Mannton to see that a woman was capable of defending herself. Sometimes something is hard to believe when you hear about it for the first time."

"Actually, I had considered asking you if you would mind demonstrating your skill with the sword," Yitzhak admitted.

"Captain Davon?" Queen Marriah said.

"With pleasure, My Queen," Captain Davon replied.

Captain Dallon quickly left the table and was soon back with two practice blades. Yitzhak stood as the jugglers finished.

"In order to help you understand that women are capable of more than what we have allowed our women, I have asked Queen Marriah to demonstrate her skill with a sword," Yitzhak said. "In addition to this, she also reads, writes and speaks three languages. She is a gifted artist. Most importantly, she is loved and respected by the people that she rules, men and women alike."

Queen Marriah led Captain Davon and Captain Dallon to the area where the jugglers had been. Captain Dallon gave a blade to Captain Davon before kneeling with Queen Marriah's across his palms until she took the blade from him. As soon as Captain Dallon left, Queen Marriah and Captain Davon began to duel. Yitzhak was mesmerized by the speed of the swords as they dueled. He could tell from Captain Davon's expression that he was determined to win. They fought for a while before Captain Davon knocked her blade from her hand. Yitzhak saw many of the men and women rise to their feet as she dropped to her hands while hooking behind his knee with her foot. As he fell, he lost his sword. Queen Marriah caught it before it hit the ground and soon had it at Captain Davon's throat.

"Excellent strategy, My Queen," Captain Davon gasped as she moved the sword from his throat.

Queen Marriah offered her hand to Captain Davon to help him up. He smiled and took her hand.

"As you can plainly see," King Archelaus said as Yitzhak and Li followed him to where Queen Marriah was standing. "There is little chance of forcing Queen Marriah to do anything she doesn't want to do."

Yitzhak saw some of the men nod as King Archelaus put his arm around her waist and he stepped beside her.

"I would like to suggest that by treating your wife with love and respect, you will be rewarded with her love and cooperation," he said. "I highly recommend that you do this at least once a day."

King Archelaus turned Queen Marriah to face him as Captain Davon took the sword from her. She put her arms around his neck as he drew her closer and kissed her. When their lips parted, she sighed and let her head fall against his shoulder. Yitzhak could tell she was trying to catch her breath.

"If you will try these things, you will not regret it," Yitzhak said as he and Li stepped beside them. "I would not go back to the way things were."

"You are welcome to visit Brinley to see for yourselves how women are treated and how the men feel about it," Queen Marriah said. "You will notice that there are many children in Brinley and the women work beside their husbands."

"And they work just as hard," King Archelaus said. "Captain Davon and Captain Dallon are Brinley's sword instructors. Their wives, Leda and Lyla, make and sell wood carvings."

"We were very grateful to be offered the position so our wives could continue to carve," Captain Dallon said.

"We are very proud of them and the fact that they make as much from their carvings as we make teaching at the Military Training Camp," Captain Davon added.

"I know that this is a big change," King Yitzhak said as he saw the looks of surprise on the people's faces. "But please at least try it."

Yitzhak could see many of the men nodding.

"I know that you must leave for Brinley now, but you are welcome to visit at any time," Yitzhak said.

"Thank you," Queen Marriah said as their horses were brought.

There were some gasps as Queen Marriah mounted her horse.

Yitzhak was grateful that they had come. He knew that seeing Queen Marriah for themselves would help change the men's opinion of women better than anything else he could do.

"It has come to my attention that there are some women and girls that have never been given names," Yitzhak said. "From now on every infant born will be given a name. Every woman or girl who does not have a name should either be given one or choose one for themselves."

Some of the men looked shocked. The women looked pleased.

"I have also learned that the women and girls of Mannton have been sleeping on mats made of strips of cloth," Yitzhak said. "This is not acceptable. Some of you may have heard that my wife, Queen Li, sleeps with me in my bed. This is not a rumor. The only thing about it that is not correct is that it is not my bed. It is our bed."

There was much talking among the men. It took some time for them to quiet down.

"For those of you with wives, I would recommend that you share your bed with your wife," Yitzhak said. "I want all women and girls to sleep in beds with blankets and pillows instead of on the floor. If a woman dies, she is not to be wrapped in the strips of cloth from her mat; I want her wrapped in new cloth to be buried."

He could see the look of shock on the men's faces. He could see some of the women begin to cry.

"If Mannton is to survive, we men must treat our women with kindness and respect," Yitzhak said. "As King Archelaus said, women alone can bear children. If women do not get enough to eat, they cannot bear children. If they cannot bear children, then we all eventually die leaving Mannton empty. While in Brinley, I learned what must be done to insure Mannton's survival. Some of you may think that I may have been tortured or forced to sign the peace treaty, I can assure you that neither is true. The only thing I was forced to do is to pay attention to Queen Marriah when she first spoke to me. Once I saw her as an equal to myself, I began to realize what I needed to do for Mannton's survival. The peace treaty is very fair and quite generous. It was signed with very few changes from Queen Marriah's original proposal."

"The changes King Yitzhak is proposing have nothing to do with the peace treaty," Joris said as he and Yuri stepped beside them.

"I have learned that there has been a battle between the men and women of Mannton for many years now," Yuri added as he rubbed his scarred cheek. "Recently my wife and I called a truce and have been working out our own peace treaty. I can tell you that life is a lot better for both of us now. I now ask her if she will share my bed. I ask her if she would agree to the same things that Anunik and Carita just did."

Ki came out of the crowd and around the tables. She stopped in front of Yuri.

"Yes, Yuri," Ki said. "I will."

Yuri stepped cautiously forward and leaned forward to kiss Ki. He drew her into his arms as Ki put hers around his neck.

"If these two can declare peace, then the rest of you certainly can," Yitzhak said.

Slowly the crowd began to dissipate.

"I'm glad she agreed," Li commented as they watched Yuri walk off with his arm around Ki.

"So am I," Yitzhak said. "Thank you, Joris, for your comments."

"I know it won't be easy," Joris said. "I've begun trying to treat Fa better. She seems afraid of me though."

"Most women are afraid of men, especially their husbands," Li said. "If you promise her you will no longer beat her, it might help. Even when Yitzhak was very angry with me, he did not beat me. That is why I now trust him. Let Fa look into your eyes as you tell her that you will not beat her. Earning trust takes time."

"I will try," Joris said as Fa came towards them. "Fa, I have something to tell you."

Fa stopped in front of Joris but looked down at his feet.

"Fa, look at my face," Joris said and she at last looked up. "I promise you I will never beat you again. You can even sleep in my bed with me if you want to."

"You will not beat me?" Fa asked.

"I will not," Joris replied. "I know you don't trust me, that you are afraid of me."

"I do not wish you to be angry with me," Fa said and a tear began to run down her cheek.

"I will not be angry with you," Joris said as he reached out towards her face.

Yitzhak could see her tremble as he gently wiped the tear away.

"I will get you cloth to make yourself a new dress," Joris said. "I want you to be beautiful like Queen Li and Carita."

"I could never be that beautiful," Fa said with a tremor in her voice.

"I never dared tell anyone before now, but I chose you as my wife because I thought you were beautiful," Joris said. "I wanted beautiful sons and now I want beautiful daughters too."

"You do?" Fa asked as Joris stepped closer.

"Yes," he replied before he kissed her.

Fa suddenly burst into tears as she put her face against Joris' shoulder. Joris looked panicked. Yitzhak glanced at Li who smiled and nodded.

"Perhaps you should take Fa home, Joris," Li said. "Let her burn her sleeping mat."

"Her sleeping mat?" Joris asked as Fa looked up.

"Think about how you would feel knowing that the very mat that you had slept on every night of your life would someday become your burial wrapping," Yitzhak said. "Every night as you laid down to sleep you were reminded that someday you would either starve to death or beaten to death and be wrapped with the cloth from what you slept on."

"That's horrible," Joris said.

"That is what the women of Mannton have been doing all their lives," Li said. "Every one of them. Until now they had no hope for anything better. They went from being beaten and starved by their fathers to being beaten and starved by their husbands. Like Yitzhak, you and Yuri must be an example to the other men. You must help them learn to make life better for the women and they will find that life will be better for them."

"I will try," Joris said. "Let's go burn that mat, Fa."

Fa smiled as she and Joris left.

Chapter 17 – Uncovering the Past

As time passed, Li could see that life was better for most women in Mannton. Every day she would spend some time on the balcony watching. If she saw a woman or girl being beaten, she would point and soon the guards would be bringing the man to put him in the dungeon. She was glad that the guards had decided to obey this silent command. She did not know if they would obey any other command she made, but she was satisfied with that much.

They continued to search for the strangely shaped key and for more information about what happened to Queen Lodena. As they read more of Ambrose's journals it became obvious that he never learned what happened to her.

"Listen to this," she said to Yitzhak before reading aloud from one of the journals.

"Today I buried Father and became King Ambrose of Mannton. Before he died I asked Father about where his journals were hidden and what happened to she who bore me, but all he would say is that the past is buried. I know I must have an heir, but there are no women my age or younger."

"That is strange," Yitzhak commented. "Certainly there were girls being born."

"There's more," she said and continued to read.

"I walked around the town and wound up at the harbor. One of the old fishermen commented that I seemed troubled. When I pointed out that I needed a wife, but there were no women he nodded. 'I can bring you a woman to make your wife,' he said. 'I know where there are women that we can get so all the young men can have wives.' I thanked him and promised to pay him when he delivered a woman to me."

"The next entry is a week later," Li said.

"The old fisherman was true to his word. Today he delivered a woman to me. She was tied up with a gag in her mouth. He said that she bites but would bear me an heir. She glared at me through matted hair. It will take time to tame her, but I need an heir. I locked her in my old room."

"That's how it began," Yitzhak said softly. "I wonder where the old fisherman got the women from."

"Perhaps we should ask some of the fishermen. One of them has to be descended from him," Li suggested. "It's curious that Ambrose's father said that the past is buried."

"That just means he won't talk about it," Yitzhak said.

"I know, but we've even gone through everything in the attic storage room and haven't found any of his journals. We haven't found any other hidden compartments in any of the rooms either. What if he meant buried in the dirt?"

Yitzhak stared at her for a long time before speaking.

"I suppose it's possible, but where do we even begin to look? We don't even know where she is buried."

"It must be somewhere within the palace walls, because he wouldn't want her or any of his journals dug up by accident."

"It wouldn't be in the garden because there's always digging going on caring for the plants."

"It wouldn't be in the king's cemetery because you have to dig to bury someone. It's not going to be marked with a gravestone as angry as he obviously was."

Yitzhak nodded and said, "If you buried a body under the courtyard cobblestones they would eventually collapse."

"Maybe we should ask Lenar or one of the other palace servants," Li suggested. "It might be within the palace itself.

"I've been down to the dungeon," Yitzhak said. "I don't know if there are any other rooms under the palace."

Yitzhak spoke to one of the guards at the door and soon Lenar arrived.

"What can I assist you with, My King?" Lenar asked as he bowed.

"Besides the dungeon are there any other rooms or chambers under the palace?" Yitzhak asked and Lenar nodded. "Do any of them have dirt floors?"

"No," Lenar replied. "Why do you ask?"

"We are still searching for answers about Queen Lodena," Yitzhak said. "We think if we can find where she was buried we will find the journals and maybe even the key we are looking for."

"We're certain she was buried in a hidden spot that wouldn't be disturbed accidentally," Li said.

Lenar looked at Li and then at Yitzhak before staring at the window.

"Maybe," he whispered. "That would explain . . ."

"Explain what?" Yitzhak asked.

"There are storage rooms under the palace that are accessed through the kitchen," Lenar replied. "There is one that most of the servants avoid going in unless absolutely necessary. Something about the room makes my skin crawl."

"Sounds like we should take a look," Yitzhak said.

Lenar led them to the kitchen. He stopped where several lanterns sat on a shelf in the corner. He lit three before handing one to Yitzhak and another to Li. He led them through a door and down some stairs.

"It's a maze down here," Lenar said as he led them down a short hall and through a room.

Li noticed all the floors were stone as Lenar led them through several more rooms. He stopped short at a door.

"Here it is," he said. "We don't keep much in here because no one wants to have to go in very often. Sometimes it smells like something is rotting even though there isn't any food kept in here. Some of the things haven't been touched for as long as I can remember."

Yitzhak stepped into the room and stopped short. Li followed him. The air in the room seemed heavy and unwelcoming. She held up her lantern and looked around. There were boxes and trunks of various dimensions along the walls along with some furniture which seemed purposely placed near the back corner.

Li walked over to the chair and table. There was a lamp on the table next to a pen and a small jar with a stopper. The end of the pen looked oddly worn and the tip was black with dried ink. When she touched the pen she felt overwhelming sadness. Yitzhak joined her and looked at the trunk that sat beside the table.

"This is odd," he said. "Most trunks have a latch on them or a keyhole but this one just has a small hole."

She picked up the pen and handed it to him.

"Try inserting this into the hole."

"It is the right size," he commented as he put the end into the hole.

As he reached the end of the wear marks there was a click and the lid lifted a little. He opened the lid to reveal piles of books and an odd looking piece of metal.

"I think this is the key we've been looking for," Yitzhak said as he picked it up.

Behind the trunk were two sealed boxes, one large and one small.

"The bottom box is large enough," Li said and stopped.

"I think we found Queen Lodena," Yitzhak nodded. "We'll take the trunk up to the office so we can read the journals, but let's not disturb the boxes just yet. Take this pen. We'll need it to open the trunk. Lenar, get a couple of men to come carry this trunk up to my office."

Lenar hurried off but was soon back with two men. They seemed eager to get out of the room once they had picked up the trunk. Once in the office Li felt very tired.

The following morning Li's stomach was very unsettled.

"You look a bit pale," Yitzhak said as he helped her put her robe on.

"I don't feel well," Li said. "I was up a lot last night."

There was a tap on the door.

"Come," Yitzhak responded.

Lenar and Ka entered.

"You look pale, My Queen," Ka said. "Do you have a fever?"

Li shook her head but the motion made her stomach churn. She ran for the bathing chamber and threw up into an empty bucket. Ka followed her and patted her back softly.

"Were you up at all last night?" Ka asked her.

Li pointed to the chamber pot. Ka lifted the lid and put it back on.

"You might be with child," Ka said. "If so, you'll just have to get used to this. If you're lucky it won't last the whole time you are carrying your infant."

"How will I know for certain?" Li asked.

"There are certain signs," Ka said. "You are showing two of them so far. I'll let you know if you are showing the rest."

"Signs of what?" Yitzhak asked from the doorway.

Ka gave Li a questioning look.

"Ka suspects I might be with child."

"Are you sure?" Yitzhak sounded excited.

"It's too early to tell for certain," Ka said.

"Let's keep this to ourselves for now until you are certain Li is with child," Yitzhak said.

Ka and Lenar nodded. By the time they sat down for breakfast, Li felt better and very hungry.

"I've never seen you eat that much," Yitzhak commented as Li finally put down her spoon. "Let's see if we can talk to some of the fishermen and see if they know anything about where Ambrose's wife and the other women came from. I asked Lenar to have a carriage ready for us."

"Yes," Li said as she stood up. "I am most curious about that."

"This afternoon we'll hold audiences," Yitzhak said as they left the dining hall. "I want to read some of the journals we found before using the key we found with them."

"I agree," Li replied, feeling apprehensive about what they might find behind the doors that had remained locked for so long.

There was a carriage waiting when they left the palace. Soon they were on their way to the harbor. There were only a couple of boats at the docks, but there were several old men talking as they worked with large nets. Some young boys were playing nearby. The men fell silent as they noticed Yitzhak and Li getting out of the carriage. They glanced at each other as Yitzhak and Li stepped onto the dock.

"Good morning," Yitzhak said in greeting to the men.

"Good morning," the oldest man replied. "What brings our king and queen to the docks today?"

"We seek information about the past," Yitzhak said. "Information that might have been passed down through generations of fishermen about Ulric and Lodena."

The men glanced at each other.

"We recently discovered that long ago there was a tragedy that happened and all the women who were not a man's wife along with all of the girls vanished from Mannton," Li said. "When the king of that time died and his son took the throne there were no women for him to take as a wife."

"A fisherman brought some women back to Mannton and presented the king with one to take as his wife," Yitzhak said.

"There is a legend about an island of women that is spoken of," one of the men said.

"My father swore it was no legend, but the truth," another said.

"Aye, it is the truth," the oldest man said. "I have seen the island for myself."

The old man whistled a series of notes loudly and the tallest boy came on the run.

"Marvin, run get the black bag out of my chest," the old man said.

"The one with no opening and the fancy stitching?" Marvin asked.

The old man nodded and the boy touched his forehead before running back to the shore.

"This bag has been passed down through my family," the old man said. "It was sewn shut long ago to safeguard what's in it."

"What are you doing with the nets?" Li asked.

"We are mending them, My Queen," one of the men replied. "Sometimes they get torn by the fish."

"We long for the ocean but are too old to go out for more than a day or two," another said. "Here we can enjoy the salt in the air and the sound of the waves against the wood."

"It is good to feel useful," Li said. "Busy hands can make a heart happy."

"Aye, you speak the truth," the oldest man said as the boy returned.

He held out the bag to the old man who pointed to Li. Marvin turned and offered the bag to her. As she took the bag the light caught the shiny threads creating the design on the bag.

"Lodena!" she read aloud.

"That's why I thought of it," the old man said.

"She who bore the king who needed a wife was named Lodena," Li said.

"Queen Lodena to be exact," Yitzhak said. "Women went from being equals to being slaves as a result of her death. We are searching for any records from that time to explain exactly what happened."

"I hope you find what you are looking for," the old man said. "The bag has been kept hidden in a chest for as long as I can remember. I think it is time for their secrets to come to light."

Li nodded and followed Yitzhak back to the carriage. Once they returned to the palace Li and Yitzhak went to his office. Li sat down at the small table that was in the back corner.

The bag held something hard within it.

"I need a knife or pair of scissors," she said after examining the tight stitching along the top of the bag.

"Which would you prefer?" he asked.

"A small knife would work best."

He opened a desk drawer and drew out a small knife. He passed it to her hilt first. Li carefully found and cut the stitches one by one until she could open the bag. Inside she found a brown spotted shell about the same shape as the egg of a yard fowl, but just a bit larger. It was split by metal and joined with a hinge and clasp. She took the shell out of the bag and set the bag aside.

"It's beautiful, but a strange thing to turn into a box," Yitzhak commented as he pulled another chair up to the table.

Li gently opened the box and found it held tightly folded paper. She carefully pulled the paper free and set the box on the bag. The paper remained tightly folded. She tugged at a corner, but the paper cracked.

"That's not good," she muttered as there was a tap on the door.

"Come," Yitzhak said, and Yuri entered.

"I saw you down on the docks at the harbor," Yuri said. "I was curious as to why."

"We are researching the past," Yitzhak said. "We discovered that women were once equal to men until the queen died suddenly. We are trying to piece together what happened."

"This might hold some important information," Li said as she pointed to the folded paper on the table. "It's too brittle to safely unfold."

"Paper is made from wood pulp," Yuri said. "My neighbor has a box to soften wood so it will bend. I could ask him how it works."

"That would be very helpful," Li said.

****

Ka confirmed Li was with child the same day that Yuri announced that his wife was with child. Yitzhak and Li invited her father and Rowan to the palace for dinner to announce it to them. Father was very happy. Rowan mentioned Anunik and Carita were wanting to visit Brinley and had invited him to go with them. He offered to take a message to Queen Marriah and King Archelaus with them. Yitzhak asked him to pick up the message in the morning.

They were gone for two weeks. When they returned, Rowan came to the palace bearing a message of congratulations from King Archelaus and Queen Marriah.

"I wanted to ask about the peace treaty," Rowan said as he sat down in the sitting room with Li and Yitzhak.

"What about it?" Yitzhak asked.

"While we were in Brinley, I met a woman," Rowan said. "Her brother, Garman, serves Queen Marriah."

"He taught me to ride a horse," Li said.

"Garsha is very beautiful and I think I am falling in love with her," Rowan said as he blushed. "I even kissed her before we left. I couldn't stop myself. She told me that she had hoped I would kiss her. She didn't want me to leave, and I didn't want to leave."

"What does this have to do with the peace treaty?" Yitzhak asked.

"Did it say anything about someone from Mannton marrying someone from Brinley?" Rowan asked.

"No," Yitzhak answered and began to laugh.

Rowan blushed even more. Li began to laugh too.

"You would have to ask her father for her hand in marriage before you asked her," Li said. "Queen Marriah said that is how it is done there."

"Garsha wants me to write to her," Rowan said.

"I doubt there would be a problem if you decide to marry her," Yitzhak said. "What matters is how you would treat her. You must understand that her father will want to make certain that you will treat her the way a man in Brinley treats his wife."

"I have met her father and mother," Rowan said. "One night, her father and I talked about that most of the night. He knows that I would treat her like a man in Brinley treats his wife. I just did not want to break any agreement of the peace treaty."

"If it would make you feel better, I'll let you read our copy of it," Yitzhak said. "But, I can assure you that it does not say anything about marriage."

"We could even send a message to Queen Marriah to ask her if you would like," Li said.

"There were some other things I wanted to ask about," Rowan said. "I would like to ask you, King Yitzhak."

"Please, Rowan," Yitzhak said. "You do not need to use my title, we are brothers now."

From the look on Rowan's face, Li thought she understood what he wanted to ask about.

"I am feeling tired," Li said. "I think I'll let you two talk and I will go to bed now."

"Go ahead, My Wife," Yitzhak said before kissing her. "You need your rest."

"Good night," Rowan said with a relieved look on his face. As she shut the bedroom door behind her, she was certain Rowan wanted to talk to Yitzhak about what a man should do when he took a woman as his wife. She was glad that Rowan was talking to Yitzhak and not their father.

****

After a month, a message came from Brinley. Rowan and Garsha were to be married in two weeks. Li smiled as she read the message. The evening before they left Yuri delivered a strange device to Yitzhak. There was a wooden box on legs. Attached to the legs on one side was a kettle, but the spout went into the side of the box. Below the kettle was a metal bowl on legs.

"He said to put water into the kettle and build a small fire in the bowl below it," Yuri said. "Put the paper inside the box and close the lid. The steam from the kettle will soften the paper and allow it to be unfolded."

"We don't want to have the ink run," Yitzhak commented.

"He sent this with it," Yuri said as he opened the box.

Inside was a piece of paper with sharp creases but it was flattened out and had writing on it.

"He tested it with this paper," Yuri said as Yitzhak examined the paper. "I mentioned the information on the paper you had is probably very valuable. He said you can keep it as long as you need it but wants it back when you are finished with it. He wants to use it for small pieces."

"Thank you," Yitzhak said as Joris showed up. "This will be most helpful."

"Yuri mentioned you've been working on something but wouldn't say what," Joris said. "I've been wondering where you found a second throne."

"Come inside and I'll explain," Yitzhak said. "Guards, set this out of the way just inside the door and notify everyone it is not to be touched without my order."

The guards saluted as Yitzhak led Yuri and Joris into the palace. He took them up to the attic storage room and showed them the doors.

"Queen Lodena?" Joris asked. "Queen Li is not the first queen Mannton has had?"

"It is a long story that we are still uncovering, but it was Queen Lodena's death that started all of this," Yitzhak explained as he opened the doors.

He told them everything they had discovered so far. The men silently stared at him for a long time when he finished.

"So you believe that this king's grief and anger over the death of his wife is the cause of our women being treated like. . .," Joris said.

"Animals," Yuri finished quietly.

"Yes," Yitzhak said. "We've begun reading through King Ulric's journals. We'll know more when we finish them. We want to know everything about what happened before announcing this to the kingdom. People, especially the women, will want to know why."

"Yes," Joris said. "I've heard people talking about that very question – why did it happen?"

Chapter 18 – Admission of Guilt

The next morning Li and Yitzhak took her father along with Carita, Anunik and his parents to Brinley for the wedding. Garsha was beautiful in her white dress and Rowan very handsome in the white suit he was wearing. They both looked very happy. After the ceremony, people were congratulating the couple. Li noticed Father slip out a door. Li followed and found him sitting in a chair with his head in his hands. He did not look up as she placed her hand on his shoulder. She could feel him shaking.

"What's the matter, Father?" Li asked.

He just kept crying. She was puzzled and worried. She sat down on a chair next to him. She patted his back and sat waiting for him to say something.

"I miss her, Li," he at last whispered hoarsely. "She probably hated me for how I treated her."

"An did not hate you, Father," Li said. "I think she loved you even when you beat her."

Father began crying harder.

"It is my fault she is dead," Father said in a strained voice. "I have been trying to not think about it, but it remains true."

"While that is true, it is also true that she would not try to eat the white worms and plants as I did to remain alive," Li said. "She once told me that she wished you could love her. Sometimes I would awaken in the night as she came to lie down. I asked her where she had been and she finally told me that she had gone into your room to look upon your face as you slept. What is now important is that you understand that what you did was wrong and you are trying to help other men understand it as well."

"I don't know if I can live with it much longer, Li," Father said. "Sometimes I can't force myself to eat."

"I had noticed you seem thinner," Li said. "Starving yourself will not bring her back. She would not want you to do this to yourself. Queen Marriah said that she honored her father by helping others. Her father allowed himself to be beaten so that she could escape. He knew he would die even as he told her to run away. You can best honor An by teaching the men of Mannton that they need to allow their wives and daughters to eat as much food as they want and to never beat them. Starving to death would not honor her."

Father looked up at her as tears streamed down his face.

"I do not know how you came to be so wise, Li," Father said. "You are right, it would not honor An to starve myself to death."

"Queen Marriah read in her grandfather's journal that when he had a heavy burden on his heart, he would go to the grave of his wife's father to talk to him about what was troubling him," Li said. "When we return home, you could go to An's grave and talk to her. I know that she would want that."

"I will," Father said as he began to wipe his tears with a cloth from his pocket.

"This is where you are," Yitzhak's voice said behind Li. "What's wrong?"

"Li has made things clear for me," Father said. "Always listen to her. I do not know how she came to be so wise. Certainly it was not from me."

"Father misses An," Li said. "It burdens his heart to know he caused her death. I told him he must now honor her by teaching others to treat their wives and daughters as equals. He must not starve himself, because that would not honor An."

"A month ago, I had a long talk with Rowan," Yitzhak said. "I know that you have told him that how you treated An and Li was wrong and he should not treat his wife that way. He said that you would not talk about when you took An for your wife. He asked me if I would tell him about when I took Li as my wife."

"I knew that what I could tell him would be wrong," Father said quietly.

"I told him that a man must always touch a woman gently," Yitzhak said. "I told him that he should make certain she was not afraid of him. I also told him that he should do what she wanted him to do and that he would be very happy if he did that."

"Thank you for talking to him," Father said. "And thank you for telling me. I now know what I should say if I am asked. I have worried that someone would ask me. I also wanted to thank you for how you have treated Li. I am glad that she is your wife."

"Thank you for giving her to me as my wife," Yitzhak said with a smile. "She has taught me more than I thought possible. It is because of her that Mannton will survive. If not for her I might not have listened to Queen Marriah."

"Father, I had wondered where you had gone," Rowan's voice said from the door. "What's the matter?"

"I am a foolish old man, Rowan," Father said with a sigh. "My heart aches knowing I caused An's death. Always listen to Li and Yitzhak. Do exactly as they tell you for they are far wiser than I could ever be."

"I have worried about you, Father," Rowan said. "I knew something was troubling you. I had noticed that you haven't been eating much lately."

"Li has made things clear for me and I know what I must now do," Father said as he stood up. "I do not want to make you unhappy on such an important day for you."

"We are invited to go to Garsha's parents' house for lunch before returning to Mannton," Rowan said. "I hope that Garsha likes the house I built near Anunik and Carita's house."

"She will love it because you are there," Li said as she and Yitzhak stood.

Li was glad to see Father was cheering up. When they sat down to eat, he ate slowly, but finished what was on his plate. Although she was worried about him, she was glad that he at last realized what had really happened to An and was willing to admit it was his fault.

"Rowan told me how things have changed in Mannton," Garsha's father said.

"Women are treated much better now," Yitzhak said. "Kenner has been a great help. I've gotten several reports about him helping the women at the well and even confronting men to prevent them from beating their wives."

"Most men didn't know that their wives put all the food prepared in front of the men and only ate what was left," Father said as everyone looked at him. "I told the women they should eat first and if asked should tell their men that they are tasting the food to make certain it is good enough for the men to eat. Now most of the women say their men let them sit at the table to eat with them."

"I have wondered why the women were treated so badly in Mannton," Garsha's mother said.

"We recently discovered that once women were treated as equals," Li said. "When Queen Lodena died suddenly her husband made the laws against women."

"Lodena?" Garsha's father asked. "Queen Lodena?"

"Yes," Yitzhak replied.

He suddenly got up and left the room. Li was puzzled. Everyone looked confused except Garman. He returned with an old leather pouch which he handed to Li.

"Open it," he said, and she found a book inside.

On the cover was etched 'The Lodena' followed by 'Ship's Log'.

"That has been passed down through my family," he said. "It seemed really odd to me since we are nowhere near the ocean. I've even read it, but the last couple of pages are ripped out. It just stops mid-sentence after mentioning live cargo."

"If this ship was from Mannton around the time of Queen Lodena's death the captain and crew might have been a target for King Ulric's anger," Yitzhak said. "Perhaps they destroyed the ship and moved to Brinley."

"Why not rename the ship?" Li asked.

"It's bad luck to rename a ship," Anunik said. "When I started building my own ship I started thinking about what to name her. It was as I was putting the sail on her that I knew what the name should be. My new ship will be named 'The Carita'."

"I thought he was joking at first," Carita said. "Now I am happy he gave her my name."

"It's time to get going," Yitzhak said. "Thank you for the ship's log. I'm certain it will help our research. We can return it to you when we are done."

"Let me know what you learn," Garsha's father said. "I'm very curious to know its story."

****

When they returned home Yitzhak was anxious to try to get the paper from the shell box unfolded. Li seemed fascinated by the steam box Yuri had delivered. They had the guards take it out into the courtyard.

"Perhaps we should make certain we know how to use it before risking putting the paper in," Li suggested.

"I've got an old map that got folded up that we could try it on first," Yitzhak said. "I have more updated maps so I wouldn't feel bad if it got ruined."

Lenar brought a bucket of water and some sticks of wood. With Lenar's help they got water heating in the pot. Yitzhak went to get the map. By the time he returned with the map and shell box there was steam when they opened the lid of the wooden box. Yitzhak placed the folded map into the box and shut the lid.

"I wonder how long we should wait," Li said.

"That's a good question," Yitzhak said. "Probably not very long since paper is thin."

They waited a few minutes before opening the box again. Already the map was starting to unfold on its own. Yitzhak tugged gently on the corners and the map unfolded more, but the folds that had been in the center were still stiff.

"Put it back in for a few more minutes," Li said. "How is the ink?"

Yitzhak rubbed one of the lines and it didn't smear under his thumb.

"Good so far," he said as he put the map back in. "Do you want to try the paper in the box? I think it will be alright if we do it only a few minutes at a time."

Li took the paper out of the shell and placed it in the box. Yitzhak shut the lid. It was hard waiting since he was anxious to read what was on the paper. At last he opened the lid and found the paper was starting to relax and unfold. As he picked up the map it unfolded the rest of the way. Li carefully picked up the paper and tugged at a corner. The paper unfolded a bit more.

"It isn't breaking like it did before," Li said as she set it back in the box.

"Good," Yitzhak said as he shut the lid. "I feel it has to contain something really important to have been saved. Obviously it was something that needed to be kept a secret."

"I noticed that one edge of the paper seems torn rather than cut," Li said. "Like it was torn from a book."

"What are the chances that it is the missing pages from the ship's log?"

She shrugged her shoulders and said, "Both the shell and the ships log are tied to the ocean. Most men would probably make a box from wood, but a fisherman might make one from shells he found."

Yitzhak opened the lid again and the paper had unfolded a little more. Li gently tugged on the paper to coax it to unfold more. It yielded a bit more before she shook her head and put it back in the box.

"It's far older than the map," Yitzhak commented. "We need to be patient."

After several more tries the paper finally unfolded revealing there were two pieces of paper.

"Just a little longer and it should flatten out." Li commented. "It says something about an island and women. I wonder what that means."

"We'll know soon enough."

Finally the pages flattened out. Yitzhak carefully poured water from the bucket to douse the fire.

"Make certain no one touches that," Yitzhak told the guards as they took the papers and map back into the palace.

When they got to the office they discovered that the torn edges matched where pages were torn out of the ship's log.

"I think we need to read this next," Li said. "Maybe not the whole thing, but maybe we can find mention of Queen Lodena's death and start reading from there."

Yitzhak nodded and sat down at his desk.

"We really need to get you a desk," Yitzhak commented. "You need a place you can sit down and work. That table is way too small and has no drawers."

"That would be really nice," Li said. "You said you found the throne up in the attic. What else is up there?"

"I really haven't had a chance to look," Yitzhak replied. "Let's go take a look."

Yitzhak stood and led her to the attic. Li softly stroked the letters painted on the doors before opening them.

"There's more in here than I expected," Li said. "It's like her entire life was packed away up here."

"I think it was, along with anything that would remind King Ulric of women."

Lenar showed up and asked, "Can I help you with anything?"

"We wanted to find a desk for Li," Yitzhak said. "I thought this would be a good place to look."

"I'll send a couple of strong men up to help move things around for you," Lenar said and left.

Soon two men showed up.

"It's such a jumble," Li commented. "This corner doesn't have much in it, so as we move things let's pile the boxes and trunks in rows against this wall. Leave room for someone to get in between the rows."

Soon there were four rows of stacked boxes and trunks. That left most of the furniture unburied. Li directed the men to move things and where to put them. They were half way through the room when they found a desk. The men tried to lift it to move it to the doors, but it was too heavy.

"Maybe if we take the drawers out," Li suggested.

The drawers were packed with books. The bottom two drawers would not budge.

"They're locked shut, My Queen," one of the men said. "This is such an odd keyhole."

Yitzhak knelt and held a lantern close. The keyhole plate was a tiny replica of the one for the hidden door in the throne room. A shock ran through him as he remembered the box of twisted gold and broken shells. That's where he had seen the shape before. He stood and soon found the box where he had left it near the door at the far side of the room. He brought it back to the desk and opened it. Li set the lantern onto the desk.

"I think this was her crown," he said as he opened the box. "But that's not the only thing in here."

He searched around among the fragments and found what he was looking for. It was a small brass key curved to fit the locks on the desk. He handed it to Li. She knelt and tried it in the keyhole of one drawer. There was a soft click and she was able to pull out the drawer. She soon had the other drawer unlocked. Both drawers were full of books and other things. Once the drawers were pulled out the men tried lifting the desk again.

"That's much lighter," one of the men commented.

"Take it down to my office. It will need to be cleaned up," Yitzhak said. "Take the drawers down without emptying them. We'll look for a chair."

The men soon were hauling the desk down the stairs. Near where the desk had been found was a chair that matched the one at Yitzhak's desk.

"I wonder what is in the drawers," Li commented. "There is still so much to go through up here."

"There's time for that later," Yitzhak said as he set the chair next to the drawers. "You are really good at organizing. The way you had them arranging what they had moved will make it easier to go through it later."

"It made no sense to just pile it without sorting it," Li said as they went down the stairs. "I'm really hungry."

They met Lenar near the kitchens.

"Lunch is ready when you are," he said as he bowed. "You've had a busy morning."

"Yet productive," Yitzhak said. "We are ready to eat immediately."

"Let's take lunch in our quarters," Li said. "I'm suddenly tired."

After eating lunch Li laid down to take a nap while Yitzhak went to his office. He began thumbing through the ship's log while a couple of women cleaned and polished the desk and chair. The drawers were stacked near the desk.

"My King," one of the women said just as he found mention of Queen Lodena giving birth to an infant girl. "The drawers need to be emptied so we can clean them."

Yitzhak tucked a blank sheet of paper into the logbook to mark the page.

"Is there a box or trunk the things can be put in?" he asked. "We need to go through them to see if there is anything important that needs to be kept."

"Some vegetables were delivered today in a wooden box," the other woman said. "We've got a couple boxes waiting empty for the farmer to pick them up."

"Bring them up," Yitzhak said. "And send some men to help me rearrange the office to make room for the second desk."

The women bowed and left. Soon some men showed up and Yitzhak had them shift his desk to the side to make room for Li's desk. The women returned with the wooden boxes and began to empty the drawers. While the women cleaned the drawers, Yitzhak had the men place Li's desk next to his and the chair behind it. Soon the drawers were cleaned and put back in the desk. He had the men move the small table to between the chairs that faced the desks before they left.

Yitzhak began to sift through the things that had been in drawers. He found some blank paper, a pen with a stand and an ink bottle, but the ink was dried up. There were a few other things that Li might find useful to have in her desk, but the rest seemed to be journals and decorative pieces.

Yitzhak settled back into his chair and picked up the logbook again. Two days after the announcement of Queen Lodena giving birth was another entry that told of both Queen Lodena and the infant suddenly dying. The entries told of King Ulric's anger and erratic behavior.

"Oh! It's perfect," Li's voice said from the doorway.

"We'll need to get some ink, but I found a pen for you and some paper," Yitzhak replied as she sat down at her desk. "I had the drawers emptied into those boxes."

"Something's wrong," she said.

"What?" he was confused.

"The tone of your voice tells me something is troubling you," she said.

"I've been reading the logbook," he said. "Apparently Queen Lodena gave birth to a daughter, but she and the infant died about two days later. King Ulric's personality changed."

"Keep reading while I go through the things in the boxes. Read anything important out loud," she replied.

The next entry he read out loud.

"I don't know if Mannton will survive. Yesterday King Ulric killed a woman for looking at his face. Today an official proclamation came out that all infant girls were to be killed. Everyone is questioning his sanity, but he is our king. I'm afraid it won't be long before he remembers this ship is named after his wife."

"That's awful," Li said.

"There's more. Part of this entry is in the logbook and the rest on the torn - out pages," he replied and kept reading.

"We had a late night town meeting. On my voyage tomorrow I will be taking live cargo to an island. I know of where there is a small group of primitive people living. I have been friends with them for several years now. I will load all the infant girls and the young women onto The Lodena and take them to the island. There they will be safe. I will take one captain with me so he will know where this island is. Once the delivery is made we will return to a point east of the town. The captain will transfer to his ship there.

We will then sail to a place east of the point where the water is deep even close to shore. Our wives will be waiting with wagons packed. We will drop the masts and chop holes in the hull to scuttle her. From there we will move to Brinley's city. It is a busy place and easy to blend in. I pray for the day that things will be made right and women will again be welcome in Mannton."

"That explains some of it and fits with Ambrose's entry about there being no girls or women," Li said. "It also explains how a ship's logbook wound up in Brinley's city."

"The rest are details of the journey and directions I don't understand," Yitzhak said after skimming through the torn-out pages. "This is the last entry."

"I don't want these outcasts to be forever lost to us. If you are reading this, keep safe the location of these lost souls until it is safe for them or their descendants to return to Mannton. Captain Burney."

"We need to read more of King Ulric's journals to find out why Queen Lodena died," Yitzhak said.

"It sounds like the people didn't agree with his new laws, but had to follow them," Li said softly. "By the time Ambrose took the throne the old ways were being forgotten."

Chapter 19 – The Healer's Wife

It was well into the cold season when they received a message from Queen Marriah and King Archelaus announcing the birth of their son, Bryant. By then Li knew it would not be much longer before she would give birth to Yitzhak's child. Although the dresses Queen Marriah had given her no longer fit, Yitzhak had new ones made that were just as beautiful. Lenar's wife had been helping her bathe and get dressed. Li was grateful for the help.

Li and Yitzhak were just getting ready for supper when an angry looking man came in dragging a woman by the arm.

"Kon, what is the meaning of this?" Yitzhak asked in a stern tone.

"She tried to poison me again!" the man said as he pushed the woman forward and released her arm.

The woman stumbled and fell. Li recognized his voice as the healer that had come to treat Yitzhak's wounds.

"Have you beaten her?" Yitzhak asked.

"I've wanted to, but I have not," Kon replied.

"Does she have a bed to sleep in with blankets and a pillow?" Yitzhak asked.

"Yes, yes," Kon said in an impatient tone. "And all the food she wants, yet still she wants to poison me."

"Go wait in the hall, Kon," Yitzhak said.

"What?" Kon sounded angry.

"Now!" Yitzhak said with a growl as he suddenly stood up.

Kon backed away with a stunned look on his face while the trembling woman curled up and covered her face. Li could see her flinch as Kon slammed the door behind him. Yitzhak looked at the woman and then at Li. She nodded and got up from her chair. She went and knelt beside the woman.

"Do not be afraid," Li said softly as she stroked the woman's hair. "What is your name?"

The woman uncovered her face and looked up at Li.

"What is your name?" Li asked again.

"Fi," the woman replied.

"I know that Kon has not treated you well," Yitzhak said as he slowly knelt beside Li. "Even though he is a healer, I know that he has much to learn about women. I want you to tell us why you try to poison him. I want to understand what is happening between you and Kon."

"You will be angry," Fi said with a tremor in her voice. "He will be angry."

"Do not be afraid, Fi," Li said gently. "We can help you if you will tell us what is happening. Has Kon been beating you?"

"Not with his hands or with his feet," Fi said as she finally began to sit up. "He has been beating me with his words."

"With his words?" Yitzhak asked.

"Kon tells me that I am stupid, ugly and worthless," Fi said. "He complains about everything I do. Nothing I do is right."

"If you were stupid, you would not know how to poison Kon," Yitzhak said. "You are not ugly and no one is worthless."

"Perhaps Kon does not deserve a wife," Li said. "At least not until he can change."

"I think you are right," Yitzhak said. "I have noticed that you need more help now, Li. Perhaps it would be best if Fi stayed here in the palace to help you until the infant is born."

"Kon would try to drag me back to his house," Fi said. "He would be very angry."

"I think it is time that Kon learns to take care of himself," Yitzhak said. "I think that it is time that he visits Brinley, but I think he needs more than even that."

"Perhaps we should send him to deliver a message to Queen Marriah," Li said. "She would know what to do with him."

"I like that idea. If she can get Tarl to lie down at her feet and obey her every word, she should be able to change Kon's mind about women," Yitzhak said with a laugh. "Kon will be furious, but it won't do him any good. I'll send a couple of guards with him and I think I know just the ones to send. They will make certain he obeys me."

"He would leave?" Fi asked. "I could be safe from him?"

"You will stay here and be safe," Li said. "You can help Lenar's wife, Ka. You will learn many new things."

Yitzhak helped Li to stand back up. He held his hand out to Fi. She looked frightened as she looked up at Li. Li smiled and nodded. Fi cautiously put her hand in Yitzhak's and stood up.

"Why don't you write a message to Queen Marriah explaining why Kon is being sent to her," Yitzhak said. "Fi, you can go through those doors into our bedroom. There is no one in there right now. You can leave the door open a little so you can hear what is going on, but Kon cannot see you."

Fi nodded and went into the bedroom. Li got out a piece of paper and sat down at the table. Yitzhak went out into the hall.

> Dear Queen Marriah,
> I send this message to ask you for your help. Although most of the men in Mannton are now treating women more like they should, the man delivering this message to you is not. Kon is a healer, but he still does not understand that women are people just like men and deserve to be treated with respect. Although he has obeyed the law and no longer beats his wife with his hands, he beats her with his words. He tells her she is stupid, ugly and worthless. He complains and tells her she cannot do anything right. Yitzhak and I hoped that perhaps you could show him how wrong he is. His wife will be staying in the palace to assist me until my infant is born. If Kon cannot change, then we will not let him take her with him.
> Your friend,
> Li.

She looked up to see Yitzhak and Kon enter.

"What is she doing with a pen?" Kon asked with a sneer. "She'll just get ink everywhere."

"Do you want to read the message before I seal it, Yitzhak?" Li asked, ignoring Kon's angry stare.

Yitzhak took the paper and read the message with a smile.

"Perfect," he said as he handed it back to her.

Li rolled the message into a scroll and sealed it with wax imprinted with the ring that Yitzhak had given her.

"Kon, I need you to deliver this message to Queen Marriah in Union," Yitzhak said as he picked up the scroll. "Fi will be staying here in the palace while you are gone."

"Does your horse have a message you want me to deliver as well?" Kon replied in an angry tone. "I have more important things to do than deliver messages for women."

"I'll give you a choice, Kon," Yitzhak said calmly. "You will take this message to Queen Marriah now, or you can stay in the dungeon until you decide to deliver the message."

"What lies has that stupid, ugly, worthless woman told you?" Kon asked as his face turned red.

"Fi has not lied to us," Li replied. "You, yourself just confirmed the truth of her words."

Kon did not speak as he glared at her, but Li could see his clenched fists. As Kon brought his fists up in front of him, Yitzhak suddenly drew his sword and placed its point at Kon's throat. Kon looked surprised.

"Now, you will deliver this message to Queen Marriah in Union," Yitzhak said in a commanding tone. "You will stay there until she sends you back to Mannton with a message. I will give you this warning, Kon; Queen Marriah will not tolerate your attitude. She is very kind and very wise, but every man in her kingdom will obey her without question. They would risk their own lives to preserve hers, not that she cannot defend herself."

"A woman men would die for?" Kon asked in a surprised tone.

"One already did," Yitzhak replied. "Her father, Prince Langward, was beaten to death, allowing her to escape. One man rode horseback for three days with a broken leg after she saved his life. He and his brother would give their lives to preserve hers without hesitation. Do you remember her sword demonstration at the feast?"

"I did not attend the feast," Kon said.

"That explains a lot," Yitzhak said. "You will notice that she carries a sword. It is not decoration. She knows how to use that sword much better than any man I know, myself included."

"Brinley's sword instructor, Tarl, could beat her," Kon said.

"I watched him lay down at her feet, Kon," Yitzhak said as Kon's eyes widened with surprise. "I have no doubt that he would take his own life at her command. She disarmed him on the fourth attack and caught his sword in mid-air before bringing both points to his throat."

"No one can catch a sword in mid-air," Kon argued.

"I watched her do that very thing before I felt both my sword and hers pointed at my throat, Kon," Yitzhak said. "She easily could have killed me if she had wanted to. It's time you met Queen Marriah and learned the truth about women. I have known you for a very long time, Kon. You may know a lot about healing, but you know nothing about women. Make your choice, deliver the message or sit in the dungeon."

"I'll take the message," Kon said at last.

"Good," Yitzhak said as he sheathed his sword. "When you get back, I will decide if you deserve a wife or not. Go get packed. I will send two men to accompany you. You will behave yourself and follow orders or they will make certain you do."

Kon nodded and left. Yitzhak went out into the hall for a while before returning.

"Do you think he will change?" Li asked as he took her hand. "What if he does not?"

"If he does not change, then he certainly does not deserve a wife," Yitzhak said. "We will make certain that Fi is safe and will be happy."

"Thank you, King Yitzhak," Fi said as she opened the bedroom door.

"Come to supper with us, Fi," Yitzhak said. "Queen Li's father is already waiting for us."

Fi followed Li quietly while Yitzhak instructed the two guards who would take Kon to Union. When they entered the dining hall, Father was waiting.

"You're looking better, Father," Li said as she hugged him.

"You look very happy, Li," Father replied. "Who is this?"

"Father, this is Fi," Li replied. "Fi, this is my father, Kenner."

"I am pleased to meet you, Fi," Father said with a smile.

Fi looked at Li with a surprised look on her face.

"Fi is nervous around men," Li explained. "She is the wife a man who is very cruel to her. We are sending him to meet Queen Marriah, but Fi will be allowed to decide if she wants to remain his wife or not."

"Let me know if there is anything I can do to help you, Fi," Father said as Yitzhak entered. "Li has taught me that I was wrong in how I treated her and she who bore her. Although I know I caused my wife, An, to be no more, I now honor her memory by teaching other men the right way to treat women."

"You know women's words," Fi said in surprise.

"Yes," Father said as he held a chair for Fi to sit in. "Li taught them to me."

Father sat down next to Fi. He put food on her plate before putting food on his own plate. Li was pleased. Fi seemed surprised.

They talked as they ate, but mostly Father and Fi talked. Fi helped Ka get Li ready for bed before going to Li's old room.

"I was surprised at how quickly Fi relaxed while talking to your father," Yitzhak said as he got into bed.

"So was I," Li said. "If she and Kon cannot call a truce, I think she could find a new husband that she would not want to poison."

"Perhaps even your father," Yitzhak said.

Li fell asleep thinking about it.

Over the next week Fi learned how to help Ka in her duties as Li's maid. She seemed happy most of the time, but occasionally she would try to hide her eyes that were red from crying. Li was a bit worried about her and did her best to reassure Fi that she was safe.

Li spent some of her spare time reading King Ulric's journals. Fi asked Li what she was doing and Li began teaching Fi to read.

Chapter 20 – Welcome News

It had been a week and a half since Yitzhak had sent Kon to Queen Marriah when a messenger came from Union. Fi was brushing Li's hair as Yitzhak read the message. He suddenly started laughing.

"What is it?" Li asked.

"It . . ." Yitzhak began but couldn't stop laughing.

He finally handed her the message to read for herself. The message was from Queen Marriah and King Archelaus.

> Dear King Yitzhak and Queen Li,
> We were out riding when Kon delivered your message to us. His horse bumped into him and knocked him to the ground, and he broke his arm on a stone. When Marriah set the break he tried to hit her, but when she cut the stone in half with her sword he quickly handed over the message. We understand why you sent him to us. We are sending for Tarl to come spend some time with him while he is healing. It might take some time for him to see a new point of view and mend his ways, but we won't give up.
> Your friends,
> Archelaus and Marriah

As she read it Li began to laugh. Perhaps now Kon would begin to change his opinion of women.

"May I ask what is so funny?" Fi said.

"Let me read this to you," Li said before reading the message out loud.

"It's too bad he fell on his arm instead of his head," Fi said. "Even if he does change, I do not think I could ever trust him. I do not want to be his wife."

"I don't think you should be his wife either," Yitzhak said. "We are going to visit Queen Li's brother and his wife today. Would you like to go with us?"

"Yes," Fi said. "Would Kenner be going too?"

"Yes, he is," Yitzhak said. "He will have breakfast with us before we leave."

Li noticed Fi's smile. She followed them to the dining hall. Father was waiting at the door.

"Fi will be coming with us today, Kenner," Yitzhak said, and Father smiled.

"I was going to ask if she wanted to come with," Father said. "I thought she might like to see the ocean. I even brought a warm cape for her to wear."

"I would like to see the ocean," Fi said as they sat down to eat.

Yitzhak seemed pleased as he watched Father and Fi talking during breakfast. Li noticed that Father seemed happier than she ever remembered him being. Fi rode with Li in the carriage and seemed very interested in everything she saw.

"Everything is so beautiful," Fi commented.

"Just wait until the leaves come out on the trees and the flowers bloom," Li said. "I noticed that you and Father seem to get along well."

Fi blushed and nodded before saying, "He is so kind to me. I have never known a man to be so kind."

"He has been very sad since he realized that he caused she who bore me to starve until she was no more," Li said. "But he is happy when he is with you. I know that he has learned what he did wrong and would never do it again. I know that she who bore me loved him even when he was cruel. He is a good man."

"If I were the wife of a man like him, I would trust him and not feel like I needed to poison him," Fi said.

Li smiled as they stopped in front of a large house. Yitzhak helped her from the carriage before Father helped Fi get out of the carriage. Rowan came around the side of the house with an armload of firewood.

"Come in," Rowan said with a smile. "Lunch is almost ready. Carita and Anunik are already here. I wanted them to hear the good news as well."

"Rowan," Father said as Rowan put the firewood down next to the fireplace. "This is Fi. Fi, this is my son, Rowan and his wife Garsha. This is Rowan's friend Anunik and his wife Carita."

"Welcome to our home, Fi," Rowan said with a smile. "We're glad you came. I think I've seen you before. You were taking water to Kon's house."

"I was Kon's wife, but I do not want to be his wife anymore," Fi said.

"I never liked Kon very much," Rowan said. "He always thought he was better than anyone else. I remember he always had a sharp temper and never would admit it when he was wrong."

"We sent Kon to meet Queen Marriah," Yitzhak said as they began to sit around the table. "He broke his arm and Queen Marriah set it. He was insulted that a woman dared touch him, but she took out her sword and told him to behave himself or lose his head. When she cut the stone he had broken his arm on in half with her sword, he finally realized he had best obey."

They all began laughing.

"I sent a message today telling Kon that Fi was no longer his wife," Yitzhak said. "He will be angry, but there is nothing he can do about it. He does not deserve a wife. He must change a lot before he deserves another wife."

Li noticed Father smile at what Yitzhak had said. Perhaps Yitzhak was right about Father and Fi.

"So, what news do you have, Rowan?" Anunik asked as they began to eat.

"Do you want to tell them, Garsha?" Rowan asked.

"I'm with child," Garsha said.

"That's wonderful," Li said.

"I am, too," Carita said.

"We just found out a couple of days ago," Anunik said.

They talked about infants while they ate, but Li noticed Fi was a bit quiet and her smile seemed forced. After they had finished eating, Fi insisted on washing the dishes. Li went in to where Fi was washing the dishes and noticed she was crying.

"What's the matter, Fi?" Li asked.

"I want to be with child, too," Fi said quietly. "But I never wanted Kon's child."

"You are still young, Fi," Li said. "You could be someone else's wife, someone whose child you want to bear."

"I know whose child I want to bear," Fi said even quieter. "But I don't dare ask."

"I have noticed how well you and Father get along," Li said and Fi looked up at her.

"I want to bear Kenner's child," Fi said.

"Yitzhak and I have thought that you might want to be Father's wife," Li said. "We could even have a wedding."

"What is a wedding?" Fi asked.

"A wedding is a special ceremony where a man and a woman make promises to each other and become husband and wife," Li said.

"Husband?" Fi asked.

"A man with a wife," Li explained. "Yitzhak is my husband and I am Yitzhak's wife."

"What promises?" Fi asked.

"Promises to love, honor and cherish each other," Li said. "Promises to care for each other."

"I would definitely want a wedding," Fi said.

****

"Li's been in there a long time," Kenner said. "What's going on?"

"Give her some time to talk to Fi alone," Yitzhak said as he tried not to laugh. "I've noticed that you seem to like Fi a lot, Kenner."

"Yes," Kenner said. "Right before I first met Fi, I had a dream. I had gone to talk to An that day. I told her how lonely I was without her. I told her how sorry I was for how I treated her and how terrible I felt about starving her to death. That night I dreamed that as I lay in bed I opened my eyes to see her standing near the bed watching me sleep. She said that she was happy that I at last understood. She said she wanted me to be happy and that she would like it if I took another woman as my wife. I woke suddenly and looked around the dark room. I thought I saw a shadow move across the moonlit wall. I could not sleep the rest of the night. The next day I met Fi."

"Kon does not deserve a wife and I don't think Fi could ever trust him, but I think she trusts you," Yitzhak said. "She seems much happier when she is with you."

154

Just then Li and Fi came out of the kitchen.

"Are you alright, Fi?" Kenner said in a concerned tone as he crossed to where she was. "You are crying."

"I," she began, but covered her face with her hands and cried harder.

Yitzhak smiled as he watched Kenner put his arms around Fi and drew her close. Fi leaned against him as she cried. Li smiled as she took Yitzhak's hand.

"She wants to bear Father's child," Li whispered to him.

"Do not cry, Fi," Kenner said. "No one will hurt you now. I will make certain they will not."

Fi looked up suddenly.

"Even when you cry, you are so beautiful, Fi," Kenner said. "If ever I took another woman as my wife, I would want that woman to be you."

"You want me as your wife, Kenner?" Fi asked.

"Yes, I do," he replied before softly kissing her on the lips.

"You would want me to bear your child?" Fi asked. "We would have a wedding and make promises to each other?"

"Yes, Fi, anything you want," Kenner replied.

"I want you to be my husband," Fi said and put her arms around his neck.

This time they kissed longer than before. Rowan and Anunik walked in as Kenner and Fi kissed. They both grinned.

"We need to plan a wedding," Yitzhak said.

****

The day before Li's father and Fi were to be married, they received a message from Union. Yitzhak was surprised to see that it was from Kon.

> King Yitzhak,
>
> I have spent the last week with Tarl. He told me about what happened when he first met Queen Marriah. You were right about her skill with the sword. I watched her as she dueled with several men, beating one after the other.
>
> King Archelaus told me about Prince Langward's death. When I was training to be a healer, my parents and brother left Mannton. I never

heard from them again. I found out that Father beat
she who bore me to death in front of my brother,
Larkin. Larkin then beat Father to death. He also
beat his wife to death before leaving Brinley. It was
my brother, Larkin, that killed Queen Marriah's
mother and father. I am beginning to understand the
changes you are making in Mannton.

I received your message telling me that Fi
was no longer my wife. I now understand why she
wanted to poison me. I learned that Larkin's wife
was the sister of one of Brinley's District
Governors. When I have healed, I will not be
returning to Mannton. I feel there is still a debt to be
paid to Kervyn. Queen Marriah suggested that I go
to Brinley to become his servant.

Please tell Fi that I finally understand and
admit that I was wrong in how I treated her. I am
learning how hard she worked to clean my house
and prepare my food. Tell her to find a new husband
who will treat her properly. Tell her that I will never
see her again.

Sincerely,
Kon.

Yitzhak was very surprised at Kon's revelations. He was
glad that he finally understood that he was wrong. He knew that the
message would make Fi very happy. Li had been spending a lot of
time in bed. He had not realized a woman with child could get so
very large. She had been having pains this morning and had not
slept much last night. He hoped that everything was alright. He
headed towards the royal quarters to check on her before his
meeting with Yuri and Joris.

"King Yitzhak!" a guard came running down the hall
towards him. "Come quickly!"

"What's wrong?" he asked with alarm.

"Nothing is wrong," the guard said. "It's just amazing!"

Yitzhak was puzzled as he followed the man to the sitting
room. Fi was at the bedroom door.

"I did not know it was possible for a woman," Fi said.

"What?" Yitzhak asked, now completely confused and concerned.

"Come see for yourself," Fi replied.

He followed her into the bedroom and to the bed. What he saw made him drop the letter he was carrying. Li smiled at him as she held not one, but two infants.

"Two?" he asked, stunned by the sight.

"A boy and a girl," Li said. "We need to give them names."

"What about An for the girl?" Yitzhak said.

"And Tokar for the boy," Li said with a smile.

"Yes," he replied. "May I hold one?"

She nodded and he carefully took one of the infants from her. It was the most beautiful sight he had ever seen.

"That is An," Li said.

"She is so beautiful," Yitzhak said.

"In Brinley, a daughter of the king and queen is called a princess," Li said.

"Princess An," Yitzhak said with a smile before kissing the tiny forehead.

The feeling of love he had for Li and his children was more than he had ever imagined possible. He felt so very happy. He heard a knock at the door and Fi speaking to someone.

"Joris and Yuri are looking for you, King Yitzhak," Fi said.

"Tell them to come in," he said as he stood up.

"We wondered why you were not in the meeting room, My King," Yuri said.

"I want you to meet Prince Tokar and Princess An," he said as he turned to face them.

"Two?!" Joris exclaimed.

"It's not possible!" Yuri added.

"Possible or not, it happened anyway," Yitzhak said, pleased with their shocked expressions.

"Never in Mannton's history have two infants been born at the same time to the same woman," Yuri said.

"I always told you that Li was not like other women," Yitzhak said with a smile. "I think that our meeting can wait until the day after tomorrow."

"Why not tomorrow?" Joris asked.

"Li's father, Kenner, will marry Fi tomorrow," he explained.

"Kon's wife?" Yuri asked.

"She is no longer Kon's wife," he said as he pointed to the message where he had dropped it on the floor.

Joris picked it up and read it. He just shook his head. Yuri read it and seemed very surprised.

"What message is that?" Li asked.

Yuri handed it to her. She smiled as she read it.

"Fi, Kon wants you to know that he understands now and admits that he was wrong to treat you the way that he did. He said that he wants you to find a new husband who will treat you right and that you will never see him again. He will be living in Brinley to serve a man whose sister was killed by his brother," Li said. "He now understands why you wanted to poison him."

"He is never coming back?" Fi asked. "I can be Kenner's wife and Kon will not try to take me away from Kenner?"

"Exactly," Li said with a smile. "Why don't you take this to show to Father. He can read all of it to you."

Fi had tears in her eyes as she left with the message. Joris and Yuri left, too.

"I can't remember ever being so happy," Li said. "Since the day you took me as your wife I wanted to bear your child. I had heard Yuri and Joris tell you that you should take another woman as your wife if I could not bear you an heir. I was afraid that you would not want me anymore."

"When I was injured, I woke up in the middle of the night and heard you say my name in your sleep," Yitzhak said as he sat on the edge of the bed. "I knew then that you loved me and that you would rather die than leave me. I also knew that I could never send you away. Although I did not understand love at that time, I think I did love you from the moment I first saw you."

"I stole a look at you as you passed my house on the way to bury your father," Li said. "I realized that I found your looks pleasing. When you asked for the drink at the well and then touched my head, I knew that if I had a choice, I would want to be your wife. I loved you when you told me that I was your wife."

"I now understand that is why my anger hurt you so," he said. "I never wanted to hurt you."

"I know," she replied as she reached up and stroked his face softly.

They spent the rest of the day in the bedroom. Yitzhak held the infants while Li slept. Joris and Yuri came after supper and brought two cradles with them. Yitzhak was surprised how many times the infants woke during the night and had to be fed. They were both tired, but happy in the morning. He was glad to see that Li felt like she could attend Kenner and Fi's wedding. They had the wedding in the plaza. Many people attended. After the wedding, Yitzhak announced the birth of Prince Tokar and Princess An. He saw Kenner cry as he held An and kissed her forehead.

"Thank you for naming your daughter, An," he told Li.

"It was Yitzhak's idea," she replied.

"Thank you," Kenner said as he turned to Yitzhak. "It means so much to me that you would honor An by naming your daughter after her."

"I could see that she deserves to be honored," Yitzhak replied. "Because of An's sacrifice, Li lived to become my wife. Without Li, I would not have known what changes were needed to keep Mannton from dying. That is why I named my daughter after An."

Chapter 21 – Searching for Hidden Memories

The wife of one of the palace guards volunteered to help Li with the infants. Ni was very surprised when Yitzhak started paying her. Li and Yitzhak worked on reading King Ulric's journals when their busy schedule of meetings and audiences left them some time. Yitzhak was confused since King Ulric often spoke of his love for Queen Lodena. Eight months had passed when they finished the last journal.

"There has to be more," Yitzhak said as he closed the journal. "This one ends abruptly mid-sentence soon after recording the birth of their daughter."

"It must be hidden somewhere," Li said. "The question is where? It's obvious that he spent time down in that room writing. Did he continue to go down there to write in a new journal or is it hidden somewhere else?"

"I checked the bottom of the trunk and there's no hidden compartment," Yitzhak said. "There would have to be more than one journal that he wrote in after that. I've looked through the books of law and found the one in which King Ulric wrote the laws against women. Ambrose made some notations and even rescinded some of them."

"Writing in a journal is something one does in private isn't it?" Li asked and Yitzhak nodded. "The royal quarters has servants coming and going all the time."

"I don't think he wanted anyone finding a journal containing what he was feeling after Queen Lodena died," Yitzhak agreed.

"The office is more private," Li said.

"I've practically torn this place apart," Yitzhak said. "I've taken the books off of every shelf and found nothing hidden behind them."

"Is there anywhere else that he might go to be in solitude?" Li asked. "It might be a small space or room."

Yitzhak tapped his fingers on the desk as he thought about it. When he was a young boy he spent time exploring the castle, but he couldn't remember anywhere specific that would fit that description.

"I'll have to think about it," he said at last. "It's been so long ago since I've really explored the dusty corners of the palace. Once I turned ten Father spent more time teaching me how to be king. That put a stop to my exploring."

"I can help by taking on more of the duties you've had to do on your own until now," Li said. "That will give you a little more time to explore the palace."

"I noticed many of the audiences this afternoon involved women," Yitzhak commented.

"Why don't you go explore while I take the audiences?" Li said. "If I can't handle it, I'll make an appointment for tomorrow morning."

"That would be great," Yitzhak said. "There have been times I've wanted to get out of doing audiences."

"Let's go have lunch so you can start exploring."

Li had been increasingly more involved in the audiences so Yitzhak was confident she could handle it. He was eager to start exploring.

After lunch Yitzhak started his search by going to his old chambers. There were so many memories he had of growing up that came flooding back as he stepped into the bedchamber. There was a balcony that looked out toward the ocean. He went out on the balcony and the wind ruffled his hair. As he turned to go back inside, he realized that there was a small tower that started on the floor below, exactly where the sealed royal quarters were.

He went inside to go downstairs but when he reached the door, he stopped short. He went back over to the window seat and took the cushion off of it. He lifted the front and found the storage compartment. At the bottom was a compartment with a small journal in it. Inside the journal was King Ulric's handwriting. Yitzhak hurried down to the office to read it.

****

There was a bit of murmuring when Li opened the audiences.

"King Yitzhak had some pressing matters to attend to and asked me to take audiences without him today," she said and waited for the crowd to settle down.

Most of the matters were trivial and easily reconciled. Two women came up together with a basket between them.

"What have you come for today?" she asked them.

"We came to ask your permission to open a shop," one of the women said.

"We realized we could make things people would want," the other said as she drew a shirt out of the basket.

"We also make these under blankets that are very warm in the cold season," the other woman said as she lifted a blanket from the basket. "You put your regular blanket over it."

Li motioned the woman forward and the woman brought the blanket to her. It was made similar to the mats, but from finer material.

"You used a smaller hook?" Li asked quietly and the woman nodded.

"You may open your shop," Li said.

The women bowed and left.

"Are there any other audiences?" Li asked and two men came forward. "What is your matter?"

"He keeps stealing my horse," one of the men said angrily.

"The horse keeps jumping the fence between our yards," the other man said shaking his head. "I'm really not surprised considering how he treats it."

"Explain," she prompted.

"He doesn't feed or water it every day," the second man said. "When he handles it, he is rough and impatient. I've seen him hit the horse many times. I guess it got tired of that treatment. My horse gets food and water daily. I get cooperation from my horse because I'm patient and treat it well."

"Who are you to tell me how to treat my horse?" the first man shouted at the second man.

"Go get the horse and bring it to the palace courtyard," Li said, and the man stared at her. "Now!"

The man flinched at the tone in her voice before stomping out of the throne room. Li resisted the urge to smile.

"Are there any other matters today?" she asked, and silence fell. "Then we shall wait for the horse in the courtyard."

She stood and everyone bowed as she passed on the way to the doors. The man fell in step behind her, and the rest followed as she went to the courtyard. They didn't have long to wait before the man came dragging the obviously unwilling horse into the courtyard.

"Give me the rope," she said, and the man glared at her as he handed it to her. "Now you two stand at opposite ends of the courtyard. I will release the horse and we will see who it chooses."

Li softly stroked the horse's face and could feel it trembling. Its ears kept rotating around, listening to the crowd. Its bones were beginning to show beneath the dull coat. She gently put the rope across the horse's shoulders.

"It's alright," she said softly to the horse. "Go to your chosen master."

She stepped aside and the horse's owner started calling it. The other man said the horse's name once and the horse quickly went to him, pressing its forehead against his chest. The horse's owner started swearing and stomped towards the other man. Li pointed to him and two guards quickly grabbed him by the arms.

"You obviously have not been treating the horse well," Li said.

"What do you know about horses?" the man responded.

"I know starvation when I see it. I know dulled hair when I see it. You have a problem with your temper and with responsibility," Li replied. "The horse no longer belongs to you. If you harass your neighbor or the horse further, you will spend time in the dungeon. When we keep a living creature for our own, we must care for it. It needs a clean place to live, food, water and shelter. It doesn't matter that the creature cannot speak, it still deserves to have a good life and in turn it will willingly serve us."

The guards led the man to the gate and pushed him out. Li walked over to where the horse was being comforted by its new master.

"If he tries to get the horse back let us know," Li said.

"He's always had an evil temper," the man said. "He'll probably try to get King Yitzhak to reverse your decision."

"I'll discuss the matter with King Yitzhak," she replied as she softly stroked the horse's neck. "I'm certain he will agree with my decision. I may not know much about horses, but this horse has clearly been abused and neglected."

"You knew how to spot that in a creature and that is enough," the man said. "Your words display wisdom regardless of your knowledge of horses. Soon this horse will have a smooth shiny coat and a full stomach."

Li returned to the palace as the people left the courtyard. She found Yitzhak in the office reading a journal. He looked up and smiled at her.

"How did it go?" he asked.

"It went well. All but two were very easy. Two women asked permission to open a shop," she said.

"Which you gave of course," he said, and she nodded. "And the other?"

She told him about the horse and how she decided who should have the horse.

"I like it," he said. "I agree completely. If the horse was being abused, it needed to be taken away from him."

"So, you found something?" she asked, pointing to the journal.

"I found King Ulric's final journal," Yitzhak said. "It has given me the location of the missing journals, but I need to find the entrance to the hiding place. It must be somewhere in my old bedchamber."

"Did you find out anything more about Queen Lodena's death?"

Yitzhak shook his head.

"You've never shown me your old bedchamber," Li commented. "I never thought to ask about it."

"I'll show you," Yitzhak said and put the journal down.

She followed him down the hall and up some stairs. It was near the nursery. There was a small sitting room and a larger bedchamber.

"I found the journal in the window seat in the bedchamber," Yitzhak said as he put his hand on the wall near the corner. "There's a small tower on this corner outside."

"The floor seems dustier right here," Li commented. "I've noticed the servants seem to suddenly vanish or appear and watched more closely. I discovered there seems to be secret doorways in the halls."

"Yes, there are hidden passages for the servants to use to get around quickly," Yitzhak said.

"They seem to push the wall in a particular spot, and it opens for them. This wood paneling could hide a door," Li said as she began examining the corner area more closely. "Ah, there's a worn spot here near the corner on this piece."

She lifted gently and the panel swung out revealing a dark staircase. Yitzhak lit a lamp and led the way up the stairs. At the top they found a tiny room with a chair and a small table next to a bookshelf. There was a pen on the table and an ink bottle. Li picked up the first book on the shelf and opened it. She recognized the handwriting immediately.

"It's King Ulric's," she said. "It's a part of him he felt the need to hide from everyone else."

"Let's take all of these down to the bedchamber," Yitzhak said. "Maybe we'll find some answers at last."

Li took several more books and went down the stairs. The door had shut but she easily found the latch and opened it. She put the books on a table and turned to find Yitzhak behind her with his arms loaded with books. She helped him to put them on the table. One more trip and they had all of the books brought out of the tower. By then it was time for supper.

They spent some time with the children in the nursery. They were both growing so fast. Li enjoyed spending evenings with the children when they could. They continued to read King Ulric's journals, but the ones written after Queen Lodena's death made no mention of her death. It was as though he had erased her from his memory.

Chapter 22 – An Invitation to Union

The year since Tokar and An were born had been very busy for Yitzhak and Li. The changes they made to Mannton's laws changed the way women and girls were treated. There were more infants born and fewer deaths.

Yitzhak and Li had begun negotiations with Okiah which was to the north west of Mannton. They had been enemies in the past, but since both had peace treaties with Brinley they began to discuss their own treaty. So far they had not met in person, but only sent messages. Yitzhak had suggested meeting, but King Akar was hesitant. Yitzhak was becoming frustrated with the process. Li suggested that perhaps they should meet in Union instead of Mannton or Okiah. They sent a message to Marriah and Archelaus who responded with an invitation for the fifteenth day of the month of planting.

Kenner and Fi arrived at the palace in their wagon just as the last of the trunks were being placed in the wagon. Yitzhak was a bit anxious about taking An and Tokar since they had just started walking. They were bringing a coach for Li and the children to ride in. Joris and Yuri were leaving their wives home, but Lenar and Ka were coming to help. Fi decided to ride in the coach with Li and the children since she was soon to deliver her infant.

When they stopped for the night Yitzhak was surprised at how well Tokar and An minded Li. The next morning they were on their way shortly after breakfast. It took six more days to reach Union. Yitzhak was surprised to see how busy Union was and how new everything looked. They went to the largest building in the city. A man was coming out the front door with a pair of saddle bags.

"Do you know where we can find Queen Marriah and King Archelaus?" Yitzhak asked.

"I was just going to deliver something to them," the man said as he placed the saddle bags on a horse. "I'll take you there."

"Thank you," Yitzhak said as the man mounted his horse.

"My name is Fyodor," the man said as he began to lead them back down the plaza. "You're King Yitzhak."

"Yes," he replied in surprise. "How did you know?"

"You look a lot better than the last time I saw you," Fyodor said. "I was with King Burkhart the last time you and he fought."

"My wife stitched the cut in my side up and took excellent care of me while I healed," Yitzhak said.

"Queen Marriah speaks highly of both you and Queen Li," Fyodor said as he turned west toward the forest.

"I've been curious as to what happened to King Burkhart," Yitzhak said. "I received news of his death and Queen Aurita's search for Prince Langward, but never heard how King Burkhart died."

"He fell ill and died," Fyodor said. "I was his assistant those last few years and saw a side of him most people including Queen Aurita did not know. He felt very guilty about what happened when Prince Langward left Brinley. He never really got over that. I think the guilt finally consumed him. By the time he had fallen ill, he had completely lost his will to live."

"What did happen to make Prince Langward leave Brinley?" Yitzhak asked.

"Queen Marriah told me that both King Burkhart and Prince Langward wrote in their journals that King Burkhart frequently beat Prince Langward when they were young boys. When King Brook was killed, King Burkhart wanted Prince Langward to kneel before him, but he refused. King Burkhart ordered him out of the palace. Prince Langward swore he would never return. He kept his vow."

Yitzhak shook his head. In some ways King Burkhart treated Prince Langward as the men of Mannton had treated the women before Yitzhak had met Queen Marriah. The trees thinned revealing a beautiful palace built against a hillside beside a waterfall and small lake.

"Was this here before Union was built?" Yitzhak asked.

"No," Fyodor replied. "Edwyn built it for King Archelaus and Queen Marriah."

"But that's not long enough ago to finish such a large palace," Yitzhak said.

"Many people and even kingdoms contributed to building it," Fyodor said. "Edwyn studied the records and plans on Dracona's palace and learned new building techniques that were more efficient."

"Who is Edwyn and why would he do such a thing?" he asked.

"Edwyn is the cook from Burton," Fyodor said.

"The one who would beat King Archelaus?" he asked in amazement.

"The very same," Fyodor replied. "King Archelaus understood what Edwyn had suffered at King Gustave's hand. He forgave Edwyn."

Yitzhak shook his head. They approached a gate guarded by four guards. One of them spoke in the language of the northern kingdoms and Fyodor replied in the same language. The man nodded and the gate was opened.

"He will lead you to the guest's quarters," Fyodor said. "Supper will be in about two hours. You can get cleaned up and rested from your journey. I will inform Queen Marriah and King Archelaus you are here."

"Thank you, Fyodor," Yitzhak said with a smile.

Fyodor turned his horse to the right as the guard led them up the road on the left. It climbed partway up the hill before entering a covered courtyard. There were more guards at the doors to the palace. The guard spoke to them before leaving. Yitzhak dismounted and went to the coach.

"We have arrived," Yitzhak said as he opened the door.

Li smiled as both children walked over and hugged him. He kissed them both before picking one up in each arm. Kenner smiled as he helped Li and then Fi from the carriage. Fi looked very tired. They were led into a hall, then to a large suite. There was a large sitting room, a bedchamber and a bathing chamber. Kenner and Fi were led to another suite next door. Joris and Yuri were both given rooms as well. Yitzhak set the children down and they began to explore the room.

"Fi looks very tired," Li said.

"Yes, she does," he said as he drew her into his arms and kissed her. "You look a bit tired too."

"I am," she replied.

"Remember when I was injured and you said that King Burkhart deserved to die alone, ill in his bed, not in battle?"

"Yes."

"That's exactly what happened," he said, and she looked surprised. "He felt very guilty about how he had treated Prince Langward and causing him to leave Brinley forever."

"How did you find that out?" she asked as Lenar and Ka entered followed by men carrying their trunks.

"The man who guided us here told me," he said.

Another man and woman entered and bowed low to them.

"I am Ethan and this is my wife Kora," the man said. "We are here to serve you during your stay."

"My wife's father and his wife need assistance," Yitzhak said.

"They have been assigned servants also," Ethan said. "We noticed that she is with child and have called for a healer to stay at the palace to attend to her."

"Thank you," Li said.

"I will go draw a bath for you, Queen Li," Kora said.

"The children will need baths as well," Li said.

"We can do that first, and then send them up to the nursery for supper with Prince Bryant," Kora said with a smile.

"Tokar, An," Li said. "Come here."

The two children came out from behind the settee. Kora went into the bathing chamber followed by Ka. Yitzhak and Li each took a child and followed them. Yitzhak was amazed as he watched Kora turn a knob and water began to run into a large tub. She turned a second knob and then put her hand in the water. She smiled as she dried her hand on a drying sheet. When the water was just ankle deep, she turned off the water.

"How is it possible to make water start and stop like that?" he asked.

"Edwyn could tell you," Kora said. "I can tell you that it is so much easier than drawing water and heating it over the fire."

Soon they had the children bathed and Li was bathing. Tokar and An were looking tired. They both laid down on the floor and were soon asleep. When Li came out of the bath, she looked refreshed. She smiled as she saw the sleeping children.

"Oh, they'll miss supper," Kora said.

"We'll wake them," Li said. "They deserve a quick nap. They've been so good during the trip."

Soon Yitzhak was in the warm, soothing water. He looked around the bathing chamber as Ethan and Lenar bathed him. There was a small basin that was waist high with knobs similar to the tub and something that looked like a chair but had a large hole instead of a solid seat.

"What is that?" he asked as he pointed to it.

"It's kind of like an outhouse, but without the smell," Ethan said with a laugh. "When you're finished, you push the brass lever and water washes it clean again."

"I like that idea," Yitzhak said as they began to dry him.

Soon he was dressed, and they led him back into the sitting room. There was a knock on the door and Ethan opened it at Yitzhak's nod. He smiled as he saw Fyodor enter.

"Li, this is Fyodor," Yitzhak said. "Fyodor, this is my wife, Queen Li."

Fyodor bowed low to her.

"What beautiful children," Fyodor said. "We can take them to meet Prince Bryant before going to the dining hall. King Akar arrived just after you did."

"It is time they woke up for supper," Li said as she knelt next to them. "Wake up, Tokar. Wake up An."

Slowly the children began to wake up. An was the first to sit up, then Tokar climbed into Li's lap.

"Are you hungry?" Li asked as she hugged him.

Tokar nodded as An stood up. Yitzhak took Tokar from Li and offered her a hand. She smiled as she took his hand and stood up. After she picked up An they followed Fyodor through the hall to some stairs. They went up two flights of stairs. When they turned away from the stairs they found an open, crescent shaped room with doors around the outside. There was a railing with a gate in it forming a divider from the stairs. There was a boy not much older than Tokar and An playing with a miniature wagon. He looked up and smiled.

"Fyodor," the boy said.

"Hello, Prince Bryant," Fyodor said as he opened the gate and bowed. "I brought you someone to play with."

Prince Bryant stood up. His brown eyes contrasted his light hair.

"This is Prince Tokar and Princess An," Fyodor said as Li and Yitzhak put the children down.

Prince Bryant walked over to Tokar and smiled at him before saying something Yitzhak didn't understand. Fyodor replied.

"He speaks our language and that of the northern kingdoms?" Yitzhak asked in surprise.

"Children learn languages very quickly when they are very young," Fyodor replied as he nodded.

Prince Bryant looked at An. He smiled as he reached towards her and touched her cheek. Yitzhak glanced at Li, who looked pleased.

"Come play," Prince Bryant said as he took An and Tokar by the hand and led them back to the toys.

A woman came out of one of the rooms. Fyodor said something to her that included the children's names. The woman smiled and curtsied.

"They'll be well taken care of," Fyodor said as he led them back to the stairs. "Prince Bryant has been lonely since Katina took our son to Langward last week."

He led them$ down one flight of stairs and through a hall to a dining hall. Marriah and Archelaus were already there along with a man and woman that Yitzhak didn't recognize. A woman entered and curtsied before speaking. Marriah nodded.

"Welcome, Yitzhak and Li," Marriah said. "I've just been told that Li's father and mother will not be joining us tonight. This is Akar and his wife, Sofina. Archelaus and I felt that since we're all equal there is no sense in using our titles. We are all servants of our people and need to remember that as we work on the treaty."

Yitzhak smiled as he said, "It is so good to finally meet you in person, Akar. I'm certain that we can set aside the past and make some progress now."

"I was surprised when I received word from Archelaus and Marriah that you had asked to meet here in Union," Akar said.

"It was Li's idea," Yitzhak said.

"I thought that since both our kingdoms have a treaty with Brinley that it would be best to let Marriah and Archelaus help us work out our differences," Li said.

"Things have changed dramatically for all of our kingdoms," Marriah said. "Now Archelaus and I have joined Brinley with Burton, Union, Langward, Dracona and Merton, creating an entirely new kingdom which we have named Alessandrine."

"I've never heard that name before," Sofina said. "Where does it come from?"

"It was inspired by a letter from Yitzhak and Li," Marriah replied. "Alessandrine means 'bright dawn' in the language of the people who left Dracona and Merton."

Joris and Yuri entered with two other men and they sat down. They ate as they all got to know each other better. Yitzhak learned many new things about Okiah. He knew that it was Li that had made all of this possible. He was glad that he had not listened to Joris and Yuri when they told him to take a new wife. When they returned to their suite it was getting late. They found Ka waiting for them in the sitting room.

"Prince Tokar and Princess An are asleep in cradles in your bedroom," Ka said.

"Thank you," Li said. "Go get some sleep."

Ka smiled and left.

Chapter 23 – A Difficult Birth and a New Reason to Live

It had been a long week of negotiation. It had been decided that one new treaty would replace the two old ones. The new treaty would be between Okiah, Mannton and Alessandrine. Li was surprised and pleased that even Joris and Yuri listened when she spoke. All of her ideas were put into the treaty in some way. She was worried about Fi though. She knew that Fi would give birth before leaving Union. They were just finishing for the day when Fyodor and Ka came into the room.

"Come quickly, Queen Li!" Ka said. "Fi is calling for you."

"Is something wrong?" Li asked with alarm as she followed Ka out of the room.

"They've sent for a healer that may know what to do," Ka said. "The infant is turned wrong."

Li was frightened. She had known women to die when that happened. As they reached the hall, they saw a man with a small trunk hurry into the room. They followed him into the bedroom where Fi lay on the bed.

"I am here, Fi," Li said as she sat down near Fi's head.

She stroked Fi's hair as the man felt Fi's stomach.

"Lay on your right side while I try to get the infant turned right," the man said in an almost familiar voice.

Li helped Fi to turn onto her side. The man began to stroke her left side from the bottom of her stomach up. Soon Li could see the shape of Fi's stomach begin to change and shift from being too wide. She couldn't see much of the man's face other than his worried looking eyes above his beard and mustache.

"Lay on your back now," the man said with some relief in his voice.

As Fi rolled onto her back Li saw her stomach tighten again.

"That's better," the woman who had been caring for Fi said. "There's the head."

Li breathed a sigh of relief.

"It's a girl," the woman said.

The man took the infant and laid her along his arm with her head down. He patted her back firmly until the infant began to cry. Fi burst into tears. Li looked up to see Father in a chair in the corner. He was leaned forward with his head in his hands. The woman began to clean Fi up while the man gently washed the infant before wrapping her in a small blanket. As the woman pulled the blanket up to cover Fi, the man handed Li the infant without meeting her eyes. He washed his hands and picked up his trunk. Yitzhak came in as the man stood up. They both stood very stiff and still as they looked each other in the eyes. Yitzhak gestured for the man to follow him and went back into the sitting room.

Li handed the infant to Fi and said, "It's all over, Father. Everything is alright now."

Father looked up with tears on his face. He nodded and stood up. He went over to sit on the bed facing Fi.

"I was hoping for a girl," Father said softly as he stroked Fi's face.

Li quietly left the room and shut the door behind her. The trunk was on the floor. Ka pointed to the door opposite the hall door. Li opened the door to find Yitzhak and the bearded healer on a balcony. The man was on a chair with his face in his hands. She looked back at Yitzhak as she shut the door behind her.

"What is going on?" Li asked.

"Do you want to tell her, Kon?" Yitzhak asked.

Li's heart froze at the name. The man finally looked up and met her eyes. The last time she had seen those eyes they had been filled with anger, not the sorrow she saw now.

"Kervyn let me serve him for a week," Kon said quietly. "His friends found out who I was and beat me up. It took a very long time for me to heal. I worked at whatever I could find until I was able to buy a wagon. I have been working as a healer again, but now I treat mostly women. I have learned a lot since leaving Mannton. I learned how to turn an infant so it could be born. The first time was by accident and desperation really. When they sent for me, I had no idea it would be Fi."

"You saved her life and her daughter's life," Li said.

"Give her this," he said as he drew a folded paper from his jacket. "I've been training a horse that I was going to send to her with this letter. I'll leave it with the guards before I go."

"You're not going anywhere right now," Yitzhak said sternly. "You will stay right here."

Kon just nodded. Yitzhak led Li back into the sitting room.

"I think Fi and Kenner should know," Yitzhak said quietly.

"She may never forgive him, but I do agree," Li said.

They knocked quietly on the door. Father soon opened the door. He was holding the infant as it slept.

"Where is the healer who came?" Father asked. "I wanted to thank him for saving Fi and the infant."

"I want to thank him, too," Fi said.

"Sit down, Kenner," Yitzhak said. "There's something you both need to know."

Father sat down on the edge of the bed.

"The healer who turned the infant and saved both your lives was Kon," Yitzhak said.

"That was Kon?" Fi asked as Father looked shocked.

"He recognized you, Fi," Li said. "That's why he was trying to leave so quickly. He knew you would be angry."

"He's a changed man now," Yitzhak said.

"He asked that we give you this," Li said as she held up the letter.

"Read it for me," Fi said.

"Dear Fi," Li began to read. "I have learned the truth about myself at last. There are days that I wish you had succeeded in poisoning me for it is what I truly deserve. I will spend the rest of my life traveling from one place to another as I treat any woman who is ill or injured. I will do my best to save every life I can. I will never ask for payment, but I will accept what is offered. I pray that Kenner will love you as I should have. I now have seen life as you saw it, hungry, beaten and hopeless. I can never hope for your forgiveness. I can never hope to make up for the way I treated you. I now admit to you that I was wrong and am sorry for what I did. The horse I send with this is yours. I have trained it for you to ride. I shall never seek to contact you again, but I shall remember you for as long as I live. With all my heart, Kon."

The room was silent as Li folded the letter back up.

"Where is he?" Fi asked, breaking the silence.

"Out on the balcony," Yitzhak said. "He will obey my command."

"I am too tired to talk to him now and I am not quite certain what I would say, but I do want to talk to him before he leaves," Fi said.

"I will tell him," Yitzhak said. "You need your sleep. We will see you in the morning."

Li followed Yitzhak back out to the balcony. Kon was where they had left him, sitting with his head in his hands. He did not look up.

"Kon," Yitzhak said. "You will not leave this palace just yet. Fi wishes to speak to you when she has rested. I will find you quarters for tonight at least."

"I will go sleep in the kitchen near the ovens. Perhaps if I scrub the floor, they might have some scraps of food for me to eat," Kon replied. "That is where I will be when you send for me."

Kon slowly rose to his feet and went to pick up his trunk. Li could see his stooped shoulders as he left the room.

"He is a broken man," Yitzhak said as he shook his head. "He will not live much longer."

"I saw that look in the eyes of she who bore me not long before she quit eating and died," Li said as they went upstairs to the dining hall. "I think that he will live or die by Fi's will."

"Is everything alright?" Marriah asked as she met them in the hall.

"I have a new sister," Li said. "It was a difficult birth. It was Kon who saved Fi and the infant."

"Fi was Kon's wife before we sent him here," Yitzhak said. "It is unfortunate that Kon could not learn the truth before he was a broken man."

They were joined by the others as they entered the dining hall. Li was quiet as she wondered what Kon's fate would be. The next morning she still wondered what Fi would say to Kon.

"What's wrong?" Yitzhak asked as he joined her in the sitting room.

"I'm worried about Kon," Li said. "Although I never liked or trusted him, I do not want to see him die."

"I knew him for many years," Yitzhak said. "He never was a very nice person, but he did know a lot about healing. I don't want to see him die either."

"I think we should be there when Fi talks to him," Li said.

"Let's stop by to check on her before going up for breakfast."

Yitzhak nodded and they went to Father and Fi's suite. Li was relieved to see Fi sitting on the settee holding the infant.

"Have you named her yet?" Li asked as Father entered the room.

"We have named her Lo," Fi replied.

"That's," Yitzhak said, then stopped.

"Yes," Father said. "We named her after she who bore Kon. It was Fi's idea and I agreed."

"I have decided that I am ready to forgive Kon and that he is deserving of my forgiveness," Fi said. "I am ready to talk to him."

"I will have him brought to you," Yitzhak said and stepped out into the hall.

It seemed like a long time before Yitzhak returned followed by Kon. As he knelt down at Fi's feet Kon did not look up. He was dirty from sleeping near the ovens and his hands were trembling.

"Look up at me, Kon," Fi said.

Kon slowly rose up and lifted his head.

"I did not know if it would ever be possible for you to see the truth," Fi said. "I did not think it possible for you to truly care about other people, especially women."

"I am a stubborn and foolish man," Kon said quietly. "I am the one who is ugly, stupid and worthless. You are much smarter than I am, and you are beautiful. I know that you will now have the life you deserve, and I will have the life I deserve."

"Kon," Fi said. "Li read me your letter. I now know that you have changed. You saved me and my daughter knowing who I was. I now tell you that I have forgiven you and that you are deserving of that forgiveness."

Li could see the tears streaming down Kon's face.

"I never thought I would hear you say that Fi," Kon said with a tremor in his voice.

"Kenner and I have decided to name our daughter Lo, after she who bore you," Fi said.

Kon's head dropped to his hands and Li could see him shake as he cried. The room fell silent except for the sound of Kon's sobs. It was not something she ever expected to see. She went over to where he knelt on the floor. She placed her hand on his head, but he did not respond.

"Kon," she said gently. "It is now time for you to forgive yourself. You are not worthless. You have the skill and knowledge to save many lives. You are needed. If you decide to return to Mannton, then you are welcome there. If you want to continue to travel, then that is alright too, but first you must forgive yourself."

"I . . . I don't know if I can," Kon said hoarsely.

"Li is right, Kon," Father said as he knelt on the other side of Kon. "When I finally admitted to myself that I had caused she who bore Li to die, I felt as you do. I cried until I thought I could cry no more. I could not bring myself to eat knowing that she starved to death because I did not give her enough food. Li told me that it would not honor An to starve myself to death. She told me that I must honor her by helping teach other men how to treat their wives and daughters. I then realized that I could forgive myself. I sometimes wonder how Li became so wise, but I will follow her every word knowing that she is so much wiser than I am."

"I see in your eyes the same look I saw in the eyes of she who bore me not long before she died," Li said. "I know that if you cannot forgive yourself that you will soon die."

"I do not want you to die, Kon," Fi said and Kon finally looked up. "I do not want you to be dirty and miserable. When I first heard that you had fallen and broken your arm, I said it was too bad you didn't fall on your head. I even hated you for a while, but now I ask your forgiveness. Although I am no longer your wife, I do care that you live. I do care that you find your own happiness as I have found mine."

"I have long ago forgiven you for everything," Kon said quietly. "I did not think it possible for you to ever forgive me for how I treated you. I did not think you would want me to live."

"Kon, you have finally proven yourself," Yitzhak said. "I did not know if you could ever understand and admit the truth about yourself, but I am satisfied that you have. I will request quarters for you to stay in while we are here. You will get yourself cleaned up. Do you have any other clothes?"

Kon shook his head.

"I will pay for some new clothes for you," Yitzhak said.

Yitzhak and Kenner took Kon with them while Li and Fi went up to breakfast. Ka came along to hold Lo while they ate.

"Where are Yitzhak and your father, Li?" Marriah asked as the servers left.

"They are getting Kon cleaned up," Li replied.

"Kon is here?" Yuri asked.

"Why does he need to be cleaned up?" Joris asked. "I've never seen him with dirty clothes, ever."

Li explained while they ate. Yuri and Joris were very shocked. They postponed the meeting until afternoon. Akar said he was glad to take a break as they left the dining hall. Sofina asked where An and Tokar were. Li led them up to the playroom. There they found An and Tokar playing happily with Prince Bryant. They looked up from their play and saw her. As she opened the gate, they came over to her.

"How do you like playing with Prince Tokar and Princess An, Bryant?" Marriah said as Li picked up her two children.

"I like them, Mother," Bryant replied.

"Mother," Tokar said. "Father."

"Father is busy right now," Li said with a smile.

"They are beautiful children," Sofina said and Akar nodded. "Twins are so rare and usually one dies, but I can see that your twins are very healthy."

"It was quite a surprise," Li admitted. "We were only expecting one child. We did not even know that twins were possible."

"There you are," Li heard Yitzhak's voice from the stairs.

"Father!" Tokar and An both said.

Yitzhak looked very surprised.

"I think that they learned that from Prince Bryant," Li said.

"Come here," Yitzhak said as he held his arms out and took them from Li. "Are you being good?"

Tokar and An just hugged him.

Li smiled to see how happy Yitzhak was with their children.

"For as long as anyone remembers our people did not like the men of Mannton," Akar said. "But then for the last two years we began hearing that there were changes in Mannton. I was worried when you began to talk of peace that it was a trick of some sort. I thought you were trying to get more women since yours were dying off. I can now see that I was wrong."

"For a while the men thought I was going insane," Yitzhak said with a laugh as he set the children down. "Even Joris and Yuri."

"I've wondered where the changes started," Sofina said. "I was always very sad when I would hear of the way Mannton's men treated their women."

"It all began with Li," Yitzhak said as he put his arm around her waist. "When I took her for my wife she began to tell me that something was wrong. She had the courage to point out what no one else did. Because of that I was ready to listen to Marriah once she got my attention. Without Li Mannton would have died. Now, because of her, Mannton will survive and become a good place for both men and women to live."

"Where is Kon?" Joris asked.

"Sound asleep," Yitzhak said. "I don't think he slept at all last night. It took four of us to get him all cleaned up. I sent Ethan with some money to get him some clothes."

"Will he be alright?" Li asked.

"We found a deep cut on his leg that I want you to look at. It looks fairly fresh, but it was dirty. We got it all cleaned out and it started bleeding."

"It should be stitched shut, but watched for infection," Li said. "I would need a needle."

"Let me get my father's pouch," Marriah said. "It's got a curved needle and some sinew that Father used to use when we needed wounds stitched shut."

"You're a healer?" Akar asked.

"Not exactly," Li replied as they went down the stairs. "I learned to treat my own wounds. My brother once cut his forehead and asked me to stitch it shut."

"I had always realized what a clever woman Li was compared to other women," Yitzhak said. "But now I see that all women are clever in their own way just as men are."

Father met them at the door and led them in. They followed him into the bedroom where Kon lay on the bed. Lenar was standing nearby. One leg was not covered up and was propped up on a folded pillow. Li was taking off the bandage as Marriah entered with a leather pouch.

"I think there's some of the numbing herb in there too," Marriah said. "I have started taking it with us when we travel."

Li checked the wound and found that it was not yet infected, but she worried that it would become infected. She looked and found the leaves among the things in the pouch.

"Where is his trunk?" Li asked.

Father brought it over to her. She opened it and looked around. She opened several bottles and smelled the contents before finding what she was looking for. She looked at his face as he slept. It looked much older than she remembered. She moved closer to the head of the bed and gently shook his shoulder.

"Wake up, Kon," she said. "I need you to wake up." He groaned before his eyes opened.

"Queen Li," he said and tried to sit up.

"Lay down, Kon," she said as she gently, but firmly pushed him back down. "I want you to chew these and swallow them."

She held up two of the numbing leaves.

"I've never tried them myself," he admitted. "But my head feels like someone is pounding on it."

He took the leaves and began to chew them.

"I need to clean your wound before stitching it shut," Li said as she held up the bottle. "It will feel like you are being burned, but it will keep the wound from getting infected. Afterwards I can numb the skin where I will stitch it. Then you can sleep."

"Yes, My Queen," Kon said.

Li saw Yitzhak smile as she moved back to where she could get to the wound. She took some clean rags from the box and held them under the wound before pouring the liquid from the bottle into the wound and around it. Kon gripped the blanket tightly in his fists as his face contorted with pain. Li gently dried the wound before mixing the numbing paste. Soon she began to stitch the wound closed. She could tell that he felt it even with the numbing paste. At last she was finished and cleaned the leg with some fresh water. She dried it before bandaging the wound.

"You know you should have stitched it shut when you first got it," she said as he at last relaxed. "You must take better care of yourself."

"I know," Kon said. "I'm a coward. I don't know how you could stitch your own wounds shut. I couldn't bring myself to do it."

"It's a matter of will to survive," Li said. "What gave me the courage to try it the first time was the thought that perhaps it would quit hurting sooner than if it got infected. Sleep now."

"Yes, My Queen," Kon said.

Li led the others out of the room.

"I can't believe that is really Kon," Joris said. "He has changed since he left Mannton."

"He will need to be watched closely," Li said. "If he is to recover, he needs to regain his will to live. He needs to know that we care and want him to live."

"He's had a very difficult day already," Yitzhak said as he nodded. "Lenar, stay with him."

"I think we've all had a difficult week," Marriah said as Lenar went back into the bedroom. "I thought that we could go for a ride this morning and then take lunch in the garden."

"I like that idea," Akar said. "Perhaps we should take the whole day off."

"I agree," Yitzhak said. "It's one thing to be locked up in a room with each other negotiating a treaty, but I think we've made more progress while talking over dinner."

Akar began to laugh and said, "You are right. We need to get to know each other better. I almost didn't agree to come because I did not know Archelaus or Marriah."

"I've wondered if we could see the rest of this marvelous palace," Yitzhak said.

"Of course," Archelaus said. "Let's start down in the kitchens and servant's quarters."

They followed Archelaus and Marriah down the stairs to a busy hallway. There were many servants and guards in the hall. They all bowed as they passed.

"This floor is the kitchens and servant's quarters," Archelaus said. "The guards also stay here."

He led them into a large, busy kitchen. A man who was giving orders saw them and came over quickly before bowing lower than Li had seen anyone else bow. He said something and Archelaus replied.

The man blushed a bit.

"This is Edwyn," Archelaus said. "He was the one responsible for building this palace."

"King Archelaus is much too kind," Edwyn said. "Many people contributed to building this palace. I only put into action Queen Marriah's idea."

"I had a dream about building a palace near this waterfall," Marriah said. "Edwyn overheard me telling Archelaus about it and memorized the drawing I had made of it."

"Where did you learn to control the water in the bathing chambers?" Yitzhak asked.

"I was allowed to study the plans for Dracona's palace," Edwin replied. "I was able to adapt the design of the water system, but here we use the excess heat from the fireplaces and oven to heat the water instead of a dormant volcano like in Dracona."

"I sent workers from Okiah to help in the building so they could learn the new building techniques," Akar said. "It has proved most beneficial."

"We have a garden and small herd of cattle that provide all the food for the palace," Edwyn said. "The guards, servants and their children have all been learning to speak both Burton's language and Brinley's. We've been learning to read and write as well. King Archelaus and Queen Marriah have improved everyone's lives far more than we had imagined possible. This palace is simply a small repayment of their kindness and wisdom."

"We'll be taking lunch in the upper garden today," Archelaus said with a smile as he patted Edwyn's shoulder.

"I will have everything ready," Edwyn said.

Archelaus and Marriah led them back upstairs. They toured the rest of the palace. They even got to see the enormous water tanks that were fed by the river above the waterfall. When they reached the top floor, they were amazed at the beauty of the rooms that were the royal quarters.

"It's so completely amazing," Akar commented. "The workers tried to describe to me what they had built, but words alone can scarcely describe it properly."

"When Edwyn first showed it to us, we found it hard to believe as well," Archelaus said.

Li was over looking at things on the mantelpiece.

"What is this?" Li asked, pointing to something.

Queen Marriah smiled as she took it down and held it.

"This is my doll that I played with before Larkin killed my mother," she said.

Yitzhak could see that it seemed to be a girl made from cloth.

"Is that what girls play with in Alessandrine?" Li asked.

"Yes," Marriah replied.

Li looked up at Yitzhak and said, "The girls in Mannton should have dolls to play with."

"Where does one get these dolls?" Yitzhak asked.

"There is a toy shop in Union that sells them," Marriah said. "Many women make dolls for their daughters."

Li picked up the doll and looked it over closely.

"I can see it would be easy to make," she said. "What is inside?"

"They are stuffed with sawdust, cloth scraps or even sheep's wool that is too short to spin into yarn," Marriah said as Li handed the doll back to her. "Why don't we go get the horses and we will stop by the toy store before lunch."

Yitzhak smiled. He was very glad that they had come. Even though they had come to work out a peace treaty, they were learning so many things that would make life better for the people of Mannton, especially the women and girls.

It was getting close to lunch time before they stopped at the toy store. Li bought most of the small dolls similar to Marriah's doll and a nicer one for An. Yitzhak bought one of the larger dolls for Li. Its head, hands and feet were made of a very fine clay and its body was made of leather. It was wearing a dress similar to those Marriah had given to Li.

"I bought this for you, Li," he said as he held it out to her.

"For me?" she asked as he saw a tear begin to form in the corner of her eye.

She took the doll and stroked its beautiful face. She suddenly hugged him tightly with one arm as the other hugged the doll. He held her in his arms and patted her back. He knew she had never played as a girl. He could not change that, but he wanted her to know he cared.

"We should get back to the palace," Marriah said as Li finally released Yitzhak. "The storekeeper will deliver these to the palace later today."

"I want to take this one and An's with us," Li said.

Yitzhak smiled and nodded.

Soon they were on their way back to the palace. Li had both dolls held tightly with her right arm as she held the horse's reins in her left hand. Yitzhak was glad that she liked the doll he had given her.

They left their horses in the upper courtyard and went through a gate into the garden. As they walked there were a couple statues along the path. One was of a man and a woman with a small girl. They looked very happy.

"Who is this?" Li asked as she stopped to look at it.

"This is my father, mother and me," Marriah said as Kenner, Fi and Kon approached them. "Edwyn had Tarl carve it."

"Prince Langward certainly looks happy," Yitzhak commented.

"Father was a very happy man until Mother was killed," Marriah said. "A part of him died with her."

Kon stood and stared at the statue. He had an odd look of sadness on his face.

"Yes," Marriah said. "When I read his journal, I learned that he knew when he left Brinley that someday he would die protecting me. When Larkin came claiming a debt to return the cattle he had stolen, Father knew he would someday be beaten to death by

Larkin. Even days before his death he wrote that he understood that his death would insure my life and Brinley's future. He viewed Larkin as a farmer views the animals who hunt his livestock. Predators mostly kill the weak animals leaving the stronger ones to insure the future generations would be healthy. He knew that although he could have changed his fate, it was far more important to allow it to happen so that I would return to rule Brinley."

"How could he know that?" Kon asked.

Marriah drew a worn scroll and folded paper from the pouch on her belt.

"This was written by my grandfather, King Brook," Marriah said. "It contains a prediction given to him by Riva of Dracona. She was able to tell the future. It and this letter tell of Grandfather's future and that his true heir would be hidden but would bear the same heart-shaped birthmark that he bore. King Burkhart did not have a heart-shaped birthmark, but my father did."

"You also have the heart-shaped birthmark?" Yitzhak asked.

"Yes," she said as she put the scroll and letter back in the pouch. "Through reading the journals of my grandfather, uncle and great grandfather, I have learned much about what happened and how it prepared me to become queen."

Edwyn approached and bowed low.

"Lunch is served," he announced.

They followed him to a large table that was set up under a large tree. Two women were there with a cart of food. They sat down and began to dish up the food. One of the women seemed concerned about the other who seemed sad. As they ate, Edwyn and the two women waited a short distance away. The two women were quietly talking. Yitzhak could see Kon watching the women as he listened to the others talk. Yitzhak watched as the one put her arm around the shoulders of the other who turned to bury her face into the woman's shoulder.

"What is wrong with the woman?" he heard Kon ask.

"That is Tyrzah's sister, Marnah," Marriah replied. "Their parents recently died. Marnah had been caring for them and had never married. Now she is all alone. Tyrzah asked if she could stay in the palace and work, but I know she is not happy. She feels lost and alone."

"I think I know how she feels," Kon said quietly.

Suddenly Marnah collapsed, slipping from Tyrzah's arms to the ground. Kon knocked over his chair as he leapt to his feet. He ran over to kneel at Marnah's side. Yitzhak followed Li and Marriah over to where Marnah lay. Kon had his fingers on her neck before feeling her forehead.

"She just suddenly passed out," Tyrzah said.

Marnah's eyes began to flutter open, and she groaned softly.

"How do you feel?" Kon asked.

"Not good," she said before she rolled over and threw up a little.

"I will take care of you," Kon said softly as he helped her to sit up.

He took a handkerchief out of his pocket and gently wiped her mouth with it. She looked up at him.

"Have I seen you before?" she asked.

"I think I saw you last night as I scrubbed the kitchen floor," he replied. "I had a beard and mustache then. My name is Kon."

Kon and Tyrzah helped her to stand up.

"Have you eaten anything?" Kon asked.

"I haven't felt like eating," Marnah said.

"You must eat something," Kon said. "Come sit down."

"But I couldn't," she protested. "I am a servant."

"You are a person just like everyone else here," Kon said. "It doesn't matter what your job is. You need to eat now, even if it is just a little."

"Come sit down and eat, Marnah," Marriah said as she led her over to the table.

Kon sat down next to her and put his plate in front of her.

"But this is yours," she protested.

"You need it more than I do," he replied as Edwyn showed up with another chair.

They continued eating as they watched Kon feed Marnah. Yitzhak was pleased to see Kon seem more like himself as he took care of Marnah. They were almost finished eating when a woman holding Lo came leading An, Tokar and Prince Bryant. The two boys were carrying toys, but An was not. Li stood up and picked up the doll she had purchased for An. She went over to where the children were.

"Look what I brought for you, An," Li said as she knelt down.

"Mother!" An said and climbed up into Li's lap.

Yitzhak smiled as Li showed An the doll. An felt the doll's face and hands before hugging it. She climbed down and took it over to show to the boys. Yitzhak went over and helped Li to stand. He put his arm around her as they watched the children play.

"I never get tired of watching Bryant play," Archelaus said as he stopped beside them. "I can hardly wait until we have another child."

"Only about six more months, My Dear," Marriah said as she joined them.

"We should have our first about that time," Akar said. "I've been a little anxious about becoming a father."

"I was too," Yitzhak admitted. "So many things that Li and I are doing have never been done before in Mannton. It used to be that after an infant was about a year old, the men raised the boys and the women raised the girls. I was so completely in shock when Li gave birth to a boy and a girl, yet at the same time I was happier than I had ever thought possible. I understand love now as I never did before."

Yitzhak watched as Kenner took Lo from the woman and held her in his arms. He looked very happy as he and Fi sat together on a bench holding Lo. They watched the children play for a while before the woman took the children in for a nap. By then Kon had taken Marnah into the palace. Tyrzah looked a little worried.

"Will she be alright?" she was asking Archelaus.

"Yitzhak," Archelaus said. "Tyrzah is worried about Marnah and if she will be alright with Kon."

"In the last year, Kon has been through a lot. He is no longer arrogant and uncaring. He now understands how he treated women in the past was wrong. He will take care of her until she is feeling better. He needs to take care of her more than she needs to be taken care of," Yitzhak said. "Right now he is feeling guilty about his past. Unless he can see that his life has value, he will simply lay down and die."

"I have been so worried about her," Tyrzah said. "When we brought her here she wouldn't even get out of bed some days. I told her I needed her help just to get her out of bed. She could see how happy women with husbands were and it made her feel even worse."

"We'll have Lenar and Ka watch them," Yitzhak said.

"Thank you," Tyrzah said.

"I was wondering if we could go down to the lake this afternoon," Akar said. "If we are taking the day off, I want to go swimming. I haven't been swimming since I became king."

"I think that's a great idea," Archelaus said.

"I do too," Yitzhak said. "I'll talk to Lenar and Ka before we leave."

He took Li's doll to their suite and explained things to Ka and Lenar. They were glad to help out. Soon they were on their way down to the lake. Yuri and Joris were deep in conversation with Akar's two advisors as they rode. When they reached the lake, the women spread a blanket on the ground near the water's edge and sat down. Yitzhak and the other men stripped down to their pants.

"What is on your back?!" Akar asked as Archelaus turned towards the water.

"Marks like those are made by a whip," one of the advisors said.

"Yes, they were," Archelaus said before beginning to explain.

They talked as they swam. The water felt very good on such a hot afternoon. They all got to know each other much better. Yitzhak enjoyed being able to forget about being king for a while and just be like every other man. When they got out of the water at last, they found the women talking and laughing. It was good to see Li enjoying herself. By the time they returned to the palace, it was almost time for supper.

"What have you been doing, My King?" Lenar asked. "You're a mess."

"I've been swimming, Lenar," Yitzhak replied as they went into the bathing chamber.

"Swimming?" Lenar asked.

"I've had the most wonderful day," Yitzhak replied as he got undressed. "I've gotten to know Archelaus and Akar much better. I bought Li a toy called a doll. Girls play with them. We bought almost all the ones that the store had to take back and give to the girls in Mannton."

Lenar shook his head.

"How is Kon doing?" he asked as Lenar dried him.

"Better," Lenar replied. "He has spent the entire afternoon with Marnah. They've sat and talked almost the whole time. I think it's something they both needed to do."

"Good," he said.

When he was dressed, he went to the sitting room to find Li had changed into a new dress. They went out into the hall and found Kon and Marnah approaching.

****

"How are you feeling, Marnah?" Li asked.

"A little better," she replied. "Kon and I talked all afternoon."

"We've been worried about you," Li said as they followed Yitzhak and Kon to the dining room. "We've been worried about Kon as well."

"He mentioned that," Marnah said. "He told me a lot about his past and I told him a lot about my past. He said that he had a wife, but now she is married to your father."

"Yes," she replied. "Mannton has always been very different than other kingdoms. Yitzhak and I are working very hard to make it like other kingdoms. In some ways most men in Mannton did not deserve a wife, but things have changed."

"Kon said he was very ashamed of how he treated his wife but wouldn't say much more. He said that he did not deserve a wife and that your father did."

"Men in Mannton have changed," Li said as they arrived in the dining room. "Kon was just a little more stubborn than most, but now he has seen life as Mannton's women had. Kon now understands that he was wrong and feels true sorrow for what he has done. Fi has forgiven him. Perhaps now he does deserve to have a wife, but first he must forgive himself."

The conversation over dinner was light and everyone, including Kon, seemed to be in a good mood. Li was glad to see the children sleeping soundly when they returned to their suite.

"I think tomorrow we should be able to make real progress on the treaty," Yitzhak said. "We now know each other well enough to trust each other."

"I noticed that you were really enjoying yourself today," Li said. "You've been so tense lately. I've been worried about you."

"I've been neglecting you, My Dear Wife," Yitzhak said as he leaned down to kiss her lips.

Li could feel his hands unbuttoning her dress as she returned his kiss.

Chapter 24 – Forgiving the Past to Build a New Future

Li was glad as they finally signed the new peace treaty. It was similar to the one that they had with Brinley, but now included Okiah. She had enjoyed the time they had spent in Union, but now she wanted to go home. Fi was feeling ready to travel again. They were returning to their room to pack when they found Kon and Marnah waiting at their door.

"We wondered if we could ask you something," Kon said as he knelt and Marnah curtsied.

"Come in and talk to us while we pack," Yitzhak said as he opened the door. "What is it you wanted to ask?"

"Could we wait until Edwyn and Tyrzah get here before we tell you?" Marnah asked.

Yitzhak looked puzzled as he glanced at Li.

"Of course," he replied as Li began to gather up their things and put them in the trunks on top of the clothes.

It wasn't very long before there was a knock at the door.

Yitzhak opened the door, revealing Edwyn and Tyrzah.

"What's going on, Marnah?" Tyrzah asked as she sat down next to her sister.

"Kon and I have spent the last four days with each other," Marnah said. "We have come to a decision but wanted to ask your permission first."

"Since Marnah's father is dead, you are now the head of the family," Kon said as he turned to Edwyn.

Edwyn looked puzzled as he nodded.

"I know I have made many mistakes in my past," Kon said. "I know I may not be worthy in your eyes, but I must ask."

"Ask what?" Edwyn said.

"For your permission to marry Marnah," Kon said. "I swear upon my very life that she will be happy and well cared for. I will work very hard to make certain that she has everything she needs. I would rather die than do anything to harm her."

Edwyn looked at Marnah.

"It's what I want," she replied to his silent question.

"I understand your position perhaps better than anyone," Edwyn said. "I did not dare ask permission to marry Tyrzah. I did not know if I had earned such a privilege. When King Archelaus married us, it made me happier than I thought possible. If it is alright with Tyrzah, then it is alright with me."

"All I want is for you to be happy, Marnah," Tyrzah said as she hugged her sister.

"Would it be possible for you to marry us before returning to Mannton?" Marnah said as she turned to Yitzhak. "I want my sister to see my wedding."

"We have decided that we should go to Mannton to live for a while," Kon said. "I know it won't be easy to face everyone again after how I've behaved, but I must do it."

"I'd be happy to perform the wedding," Yitzhak said with a smile. "I think there's time today. We could leave tomorrow."

"Thank you," Kon said. "When you first sent me to Union, I was very angry. Now I see that I needed to come to Union to learn the truth about myself and women."

"There is something that I want you to do for me, Kon," Yitzhak said. "I'm glad you are returning to Mannton because you can teach me to speak the language of the northern kingdoms. I have realized that I really need to learn it. Mannton is no longer separate from the neighboring kingdoms. As king, I need to be able to communicate with other kingdoms in their language."

"I want to learn it as well," Li said. "I want to be able to teach it to my children while they are still young."

"I would be honored to do so," Kon said as he met Li's gaze.

There was a knock at the door and Edwyn was quickly on his feet to answer the door.

"We wanted to say goodbye," Archelaus said as he and Marriah entered the room.

"Actually, something has come up and we wanted to ask if we could leave tomorrow instead of today," Yitzhak said. "Kon and Marnah have asked me to perform their wedding ceremony."

"We want to help get them ready then," Marriah said with a mischievous grin as she glanced at Archelaus.

Within a couple of hours, both Marnah and Kon had been bathed and dressed for the wedding. Father and Fi were happy to help as well. While they were waiting for time to go out to the garden for the wedding, Fi took Li aside for a moment.

"I wanted to thank you for everything," Fi said as they stood out on the balcony. "You helped me to see that I deserved to be loved and you helped Kon to change so that he too deserves to be loved as well. I was Kon's wife for three years, but he never came to me as Kenner did."

"I met Kon when Yitzhak was injured in battle. He was certain that I would not care for Yitzhak. He did not think it possible for a woman to be trusted. I knew that Kon was not treating you well," Li said. "I am glad that he finally brought you to us so that we could help you. I am so grateful to you for making Father so happy. When I first met Marriah, she told me that change was not easy, but it must start somewhere."

"Kon certainly didn't think he needed to change until you sent him here to meet Queen Marriah," Fi said.

"I do not like to see anyone suffer as the women of Mannton have," Li said. "But I can see that was the only way for Kon to understand what he had done was wrong. Now he is seeing the truth and hopefully change will be a bit easier for him."

They took Marnah out to the garden for the wedding. As Li stood at Yitzhak's side, she could see that Kon was actually handsome.

They had lunch before Kon and Marnah went back to Kon's suite. Yitzhak and Li walked around the beautiful garden for a while.

"While we were getting Kon ready, we talked about being a husband," Yitzhak said as they walked.

"Fi mentioned that Kon did not come to her as Father did," Li commented.

"He had no idea what to do," Yitzhak said. "We told him what he should do and how he should do it. For a healer, he certainly doesn't know much."

"If he does what you and Archelaus told him to, Marnah is certain to be very happy," Li said as she began to laugh. "I'm glad that he is finally ready to learn new things. Fi said that she now cares that Kon will be happy and loved."

****

The next morning they finished packing before breakfast. Kon and Marnah arrived in the dining hall shortly after they did. Yitzhak had never seen Kon look quite the way he did this morning.

"He looks like you did after that first night you spent in Brinley," Archelaus commented with a laugh. "He must have followed our instructions."

Yitzhak just laughed. They left right after eating breakfast. When they stopped for the night, Kon came up to Yitzhak.

"I wanted to thank you," Kon said. "I admit that I was very angry and insulted when you first sent me to Queen Marriah, but I now understand why you did. I have been through a lot since leaving Mannton, but I can now see it was necessary. I will work very hard to help the women of Mannton. Now I understand what you see in Queen Li. Mannton is fortunate that you and Queen Li are our rulers."

"Mannton owes its future to Li," Yitzhak said. "If not for her, Mannton would still be dying and I would still be blind to it."

"Supper is ready," Li said as she joined them.

Kon knelt at her feet before going over to where Marnah stood. Li gave him a puzzled look.

"He is showing his loyalty to you as queen of Mannton," Yitzhak said before leading her over to where the others were.

The remainder of the journey was uneventful. As they passed through Brinley's city, Yitzhak could see Kon tense up. He grew even tenser as they entered Mannton.

"Why don't you and Marnah stay in the palace for a while?" Yitzhak said before they passed Kon's house. "Your house will need some repair before you can live in it again."

"Thank you," Kon replied with great relief in his voice.

Yitzhak noticed some of the men stopped to watch as they passed by. Some of them looked angry. He knew it would be difficult for Kon to settle his past, but it needed to be done. As he helped Li and the children from the coach, she looked worried.

"What's the matter?" he asked her.

"The men don't seem very happy," Li said as one man entered the courtyard.

"I have a question for you, My King," the man said as he quickly knelt.

"Ask your question," Yitzhak replied, wondering what was going on.

"Why have you allowed Kon to come back?" the man asked. "None of us liked him very well and the women all seem to hate him."

"Perhaps we need to make an announcement," Li said.

"Yes," Yitzhak said. "I think that would be for the best. Tell the men and women that tomorrow morning we will have a public meeting to announce the results of our trip to Union to meet with Okiah's rulers. We will at the same time explain why Kon has been allowed back."

Kon came up and knelt at Li's feet.

"Rise," she said.

"If it pleases you, Queen Li, Marnah and I will stay in the room you once used," Kon said.

"That will be fine, Kon," Li said. "It might need some cleaning."

"I can clean it," Kon replied and bowed before leaving.

"It ought to be an interesting explanation," the man said as he shook his head.

"I would not have allowed Kon to return if I was not satisfied that he was ready to," Yitzhak said. "Spread the word about the meeting."

"I will," the man said and left.

It was good to be back home. The children seemed happy to be home as well. They both went to sleep early after running around their playroom and bedrooms as if to make certain nothing had changed. Yitzhak and Li worked on an announcement and decided that they would begin to hand out the dolls at the meeting. They slept soundly until morning. After getting dressed the next morning, they discovered a very tired looking Kon and a worried looking Marnah waiting for them in the sitting room.

"You don't look well, Kon," Li said. "That wound isn't infected is it?"

"No, My Queen," Kon said. "I just couldn't sleep last night."

"Today will be a difficult day for you," Yitzhak said. "With your permission, I will read them your letter to Fi."

Kon nodded.

"We should have some breakfast," Li said.

Yitzhak noticed that Kon barely ate. He hoped Kon would make it through today. As they stepped up on the platform, he could see that all of Mannton must have come. Kon was shaking badly. Marnah looked concerned as she stood at his side.

"People of Mannton," Yitzhak said, and silence fell. "We have just returned from Union where we signed a new treaty of peace. This treaty is between Mannton, Okiah and the new kingdom of Alessandrine led by King Archelaus and Queen Marriah."

He paused to let the crowd settle down again.

"During the last two years, Mannton has undergone many changes that prepared us to sign that treaty. Other kingdoms have noticed the changes and are now more willing to trust Mannton. These changes have not been easy since every person in Mannton had to change to make it possible. Some of us have had a more difficult time than others during this time of change. Some have paid with their lives because they could not change."

Again he was forced to pause until the crowd settled down.

"Since healers are known to most people in Mannton, many of you know Kon," Yitzhak said and again the crowd was restless. "Queen Li and I sent him to learn from Queen Marriah that women are beautiful, intelligent and important."

He was forced to pause until the crowd quieted down.

"Since he left Mannton, Kon learned many things and has been through a lot," Yitzhak said before he told them some of what Kon had experienced and done since leaving Mannton.

Yitzhak then read them Kon's letter to Fi. As he read the letter, he glanced up to see shocked expressions on everyone's faces. When he finished, he glanced at Kon who looked like he would pass out at any moment if not for Marnah holding him up.

"Kon willingly returned to Mannton knowing he would have to face his past," Yitzhak said. "It would have been much easier for him to never return to Mannton. I am satisfied that he is not the same man he was when he left Mannton. While we were in Union, he met a woman named Marnah. They asked me to perform their wedding ceremony before leaving Union."

There was a lot of murmuring before silence fell again.

"We have made many changes and there are still more changes to be made when we are ready," Yitzhak said. "Part of what we must do is to forgive the past and each other. We must learn to forgive ourselves for our past mistakes. Kon knows that in the past he was arrogant and uncaring. He knows that he was wrong. All I ask of you is that you give him a chance to prove he has changed."

Yitzhak turned as a movement drew his attention toward the stairs. Kenner was holding Lo and following Fi up to join them on the platform.

"I am Fi," she said after Yitzhak nodded to her. "I was once Kon's wife. I admit that once I hated him, but I have chosen to forgive him. I know that he is worthy of that forgiveness. Kenner and I named our new daughter Lo after she who bore Kon."

Yitzhak walked over to Kon and put his hand on Kon's shoulder. He could see the tears running down Kon's face as he felt the man shaking.

"If we cannot accept and forgive Kon, can we expect other kingdoms to accept and forgive us?" Yitzhak asked. "We learned many new things while we were in Union. I have asked Kon to teach Queen Li and me to speak the language of the northern kingdoms. As your rulers, we need to know how to communicate to the rulers of other kingdoms in their own language. We also learned that in other kingdoms young girls play with something called a doll. Queen Li bought many of these dolls to be given to the young girls of Mannton."

Two guards brought a box containing the dolls out to the front of the crowd. Soon there were many young girls gathered around the box and taking dolls. Some of the older girls came forward as well. Soon there was only one doll left. As the crowd began to disperse one of the guards handed the doll to Fi.

"I think we had best get you back to your room, Kon," Yitzhak said.

Kon just nodded. Marnah wiped his tears before gently leading him towards the stairs. She slowly led him down the stairs. At the bottom of the stairs were several men.

"You really got beat up?" one of them asked in a disbelieving tone.

Kon removed his shirt to reveal the scars from the beating.

"I learned how stupid I really am," Kon said quietly. "I went many days with no food and no shelter. I'm not certain why I survived. Now I will spend the rest of my life taking care of Marnah and treating any woman who needs a healer."

The men looked at each other. One by one they laid a hand on his shoulder before leaving.

"Let's go inside, Kon," Yitzhak said gently. "I think you've faced everything you can today."

Kon nodded and allowed himself to be led back inside. Yitzhak was worried about him as he lay down on the bed and Marnah covered him up with the blanket. She softly kissed his forehead before gesturing for Yitzhak to follow her out into the hall.

"Thank you," Marnah said. "Kon did not think he had any friends in this world."

"I've known Kon for a very long time," Yitzhak said. "I haven't always liked him very well, but I know that now he needs friends more than anything else. Your love will give him the will to live. Let us know if either of you need anything."

****

It was a week later before Kon felt well enough to begin teaching Yitzhak and Li the language of the northern kingdoms. Li was very surprised at how patient Kon was as he taught them. She was also surprised to discover that she was learning more quickly than Yitzhak. They studied for a couple of hours almost every day. Kon had not left the palace, but several women had come needing a healer. A month had passed since they had returned to Mannton when several men showed up wanting to speak to Kon.

"Bring them in," Yitzhak said as Li noticed that Kon looked nervous.

He put down the pen he had been writing with as the men walked in. The men quickly knelt.

"We are not interrupting, My King?" one of the men asked as they stood up.

"We were just finishing for the day," Yitzhak said.

"We had something to show Kon," another said. "We came to see if he would go with us that we might show him."

Li could tell that Kon was still very afraid of the men.

"I'm in the mood to go for a ride," Li said. "Perhaps we could accompany Kon before going for a ride."

"Yes," Yitzhak said as he stood up. "A ride would be good. There's plenty of time before supper."

"We were wondering if Kon could bring his wife as well," one of the men said.

Kon looked puzzled by this request.

"She is down in our room," Kon said. "I will go get her."

They led Kon down the stairs and went to the courtyard as Kon went to get Marnah. Soon there were horses ready. Kon and Marnah came out of the palace. They both looked nervous. Kon helped Marnah to mount before getting on his own horse. They followed the men through the streets until they came to a house that was a little larger than most. Some of the boards looked newer than the others along with some of the roof.

"We've spoken to Kenner and Fi," one of the men said. "We decided that if Fi can forgive you then so can we."

"We knew that your house needed repair after being empty for so long," another said.

"I have no way to pay you," Kon said.

"I'll pay, Kon," Yitzhak said. "I haven't worried about it since you've been living in the palace, but I feel you should get paid for your time spent teaching us the language of the northern kingdoms."

"This is your house?" Marnah asked as Kon dismounted.

"No," he replied as he helped her from the horse. "This is our house."

Li and Yitzhak dismounted and followed Kon and Marnah into the house. There was an open room with a fireplace, chairs and tables just inside the door. Kon opened the door to the right. They followed him inside and found it to be another room with a fireplace, settee and a table with chairs around it. Through another door was a hallway. There was a kitchen and three bedrooms off the hall. There were curtains on the windows and a cloth on the table. There was firewood stacked by the fireplaces and oven. The beds were neatly made, and everything looked clean. Kon led them back through the first room to a hallway. The first room had a tall bed or short table with a thin mattress on it and cabinets along the walls.

"We didn't know what things you would need," one man said.

"The beds all have new mattresses, sheets and blankets," another said.

"I don't know what to say," Kon said as Li could see a tear forming in the corner of his eye.

"We all realized that King Yitzhak is right," one man said. "You've paid for your past."

"Life will never be what it used to be in Mannton," Yitzhak said. "Nor should it be."

"It's time to start a new life," Li said. "You have valuable skills, Kon. Everyone needs a healer at some time during their life."

"Perhaps you could even teach me," Marnah said. "I learned a lot caring for my parents, but I know there is so much I could still learn. Perhaps our children will become healers when they grow up."

"You want to bear my children?" Kon asked as he turned to face Marnah.

"Yes," she said as she put her arms around his neck.

He drew her into his arms and kissed her before holding her tightly for a while. Yitzhak motioned for the men to follow as he led Li out onto the porch. He shut the door quietly behind them.

"I want to thank you," Yitzhak said. "If not for Marnah, Kon would have laid down and died. Perhaps now he can forgive himself and see that he does have a future."

"There are those who are still uncertain about Kon, but they are willing to give him a chance to prove he's changed," one of the men said.

"We have all realized that what you said about Mannton is true," another man said. "There are not as many people as there used to be. We need every person we have."

"We need more children, too," the third man said.

"Few changes happen quickly," Yitzhak said. "I see that more women are with child and the girls are healthier. That is the way it should be."

Kon and Marnah came out onto the wide porch of the home.

"We want to move in as soon as possible," Kon said. "There is a lot of work to be done."

"As long as you still come to the palace at least three days a week so that we can continue our lessons," Yitzhak said with a smile.

"We will," Kon said.

Yitzhak helped Li to mount before mounting his own horse. They rode around the town watching the people. Li was glad to see that the women looked more like Brinley's women now. She smiled to see the girls playing with their dolls. When they returned to the palace, they went straight to the dining room. An and Tokar arrived just after they did. They were beginning to talk even more in both languages.

"Mother, Father," they said as they ran to them.

They each got hugged by both children as the servers brought supper out. After supper they took the children to their bedrooms to get ready for bed.

"They are so beautiful," Li said as they went to their own bedroom.

"Just like their mother," Yitzhak said before he kissed her. "I think it's time we have another child."

"Yes," Li agreed with a smile.

Chapter 25 – Missing Pages

It was an early morning when Li was rereading King Ulric's journal that ended just before Queen Lodena's death. She came to the end and as she closed the journal she noticed the back cover seemed a little loose. She opened the journal to find a sliver of torn paper and some thick thread.

"Yitzhak!" she called out. "I found something!"

Yitzhak came in from the sitting room.

"What did you find?" he asked.

"There are pages missing from this journal. It's the last one before her death," she said.

"I don't even know where we would look for them," Yitzhak said shaking his head. "It looks like a whole section was torn out."

"I think it is time to open the sealed royal quarters," Li said. "We've been going in circles without finding the answer to what happened to Queen Lodena."

"You are close to delivering and I worry about what we will find in there," Yitzhak said as he stroked her face softly. "At least let me go in first and have a look around. I don't want anything to frighten you."

"Alright," Li agreed with a sigh.

Yitzhak kissed her softly before leaving.

****

He went to the office where the key was sitting on a shelf. He dreaded what he might find in the sealed room. King Ulric had gone to great lengths to hide anything pertaining to his wife's death. Yitzhak went into the throne room and found Lenar directing some servants that were cleaning the room. Lenar hurried over to him.

"You are finally going to find out what is behind the door?" Lenar asked and he nodded. "I'll get a lamp."

Lenar was soon back with a lit lamp and they went behind the tapestry. He hesitated before inserting the key and turning it. He stood with his hand on the knob for a while.

"Thank you for being here when I open this. I didn't want to do it alone, but I don't want Li seeing anything that would get her upset."

"I'm glad I could be here," Lenar said. "I've been very curious about what lies behind these doors."

Yitzhak turned the knob and the door opened inward to darkness as the hinges protested. He stepped forward and Lenar followed with the lantern. Even with the lantern held high not much was visible.

"There are lamps on either side of the door," Lenar said as he pulled a stick from his pocket.

Yitzhak took the lantern from him and held it as he lit the stick then the two lamps. The light spread a little further illuminating a table and several chairs. There was a settee as well. Lenar found more lamps to light until the room was completely lit. Everything was covered in dust. Lenar found the curtains on the outer wall and opened them. One tore and fell in a pile on the floor. Yitzhak moved to the doors at the opposite end of the room.

He tried one of the knobs and the door opened. He pulled it open revealing another dark room. He opened the second door as Lenar joined him. Lenar began lighting lamps around the room and opened the curtains. Unlike the orderly sitting room, the bed chamber was in disarray.

"My brother had quite the temper and would tear apart our bedroom like this when he got angry," Lenar commented shaking his head.

"I believe King Ulric had quite the temper as well from the looks of the room and what I've read," Yitzhak replied as he spotted a paper under the edge of a tipped over table.

He lifted the table back on its legs and retrieved the paper.

"Look for paper," Yitzhak said holding up the paper.

"Here's one," Lenar said. "How many are we looking for?"

"I don't know," he admitted as he spotted another one under the edge of the bed.

"There seems to be furniture missing," Lenar commented.

"It's probably in that attic room," Yitzhak said as he went into the closet.

The closet was just as destroyed as the rest of the bedroom. He shook his head and went back out into the room. He noticed a broken vase on the mantle with dead flowers hanging out of it. Behind the frame next to the vase was something white. Yitzhak went over and carefully moved the frame. There was a neatly folded paper behind the frame. As he picked it up he realized there was more than one piece of paper.

"I found three more pieces of paper, but you need to see this." Lenar said behind him.

"I found something as well," he said as he joined Lenar on the other side of the bed.

There was a pile of wooden spindles and flat pieces of wood between the bed and the wall. Some of the spindles were broken and several had dark stains on them. There was a large area of the floor that was stained dark.

"It's a blood stain," Yitzhak said as he recognized it. "If that is all from one person this is where they died."

He heard rustling paper and looked up to see Lenar's face was pale and his hands trembling. He was pointing at the wall near the floor. Yitzhak turned to see something stuck to the wall. There was fine black fur or hair sticking out behind it.

"I think reading these might confirm that Queen Lodena and her infant died here," Yitzhak said as he took Lenar's shoulder and steered him toward the door.

"Do you think he did it?" Lenar asked.

"Hard to say," Yitzhak replied. "Hopefully these pages hold the answers. Let's go and lock the door again. I don't want anyone in here yet."

Lenar nodded and began dousing the lamps. Yitzhak felt better when the door was locked again. He went to his office and sat down to read the papers. He started with the scattered pages. They were in King Ulric's handwriting. It spoke of the birth of Princess Cora and how happy King Ulric was. At the end of the third page he found something curious.

'Today Lodena was having trouble speaking. Her face was drooping on her right side. Holding Cora to her breast to nurse was difficult for her.'

This puzzled Yitzhak. The next day's entry was written hastily and the size of the letters increased as it went.

'Lodena was still having trouble. She got up to put Cora in her cradle and fell. Cora was flung against the wall and Lodena was impaled on the cradle spindles. Lodena and Cora died in my arms. How can I go on? How can I explain this to Ambrose?'

That was the last entry. Yitzhak was curiously relieved that King Ulric had not killed his wife and daughter. He carefully unfolded the pages he found on the mantle.

'To whomever finds this, I feel the need to explain what has happened. When our beloved Queen Lodena and Princess Cora died King Ulric was inconsolable. It was a day before we were allowed to clean the bodies for burial. King Ulric demanded that everything belonging to them be removed from the royal quarters. He flew into a rage that we were not moving fast enough. He got the guards to take the bodies and put them in boxes to be stored in the cellars. I don't know what the future holds for this kingdom, but I fear King Ulric has lost his mind. Your humble servant, Marcus.'

Yitzhak let the paper drop to the desk and leaned back.

"What is it Yitzhak?" Li said as she entered.

"Queen Lodena died when she tried to put Princess Cora in her cradle but fell on top of the cradle instead. The infant fell against the wall and died as well," he replied. "The bedroom was torn apart when King Ulric was in the depths of his grief. At first I feared he had killed them himself."

She sat down.

"There was something wrong with Queen Lodena. She was having trouble talking and using her arms. I think her legs went weak as well causing her to fall. The boxes in that cellar room do contain their remains."

"Well, that explains it," Li said quietly.

"One of the servants left a letter hidden. He said he feared King Ulric had lost his mind. I think he was right."

Chapter 26 – A New Princess and Visitors

It was a couple of months later that Li gave birth to another girl.

Yitzhak smiled as he held the infant for Tokar and An to see.

"What is her name, Father?" An asked.

Yitzhak looked at Li who said, "Why don't we name her Ta after your mother?"

"I would like that," Yitzhak replied. "Your new sister is named Ta."

The children went back to their playroom and Yitzhak held Ta while Li slept. So much had happened in the last year. Both Carita and Garsha had given birth and Marnah was soon to deliver Kon's child.

Akar and Sofina had sent word of the birth of their son, Prince Onan.

Archelaus and Marriah had sent word of the birth of their daughter, Princess Bethany. Mannton's women were being treated as equals to the men at last and there were more babies being born that survived. Kon had attended most of the births in the last year. A few men tried to beat him up once, but others had stepped in to protect him.

Although Mannton was doing much better, there was still so much to be done. There were a few women that decided that they wanted new husbands. Each case was carefully considered after talking to both the man and the woman. They were able to work out the differences between two of the couples, but the rest could not work out their differences. There were some weddings. Some of the weddings were for couples who had been together for a long time, including Joris and Fa.

Li had recently suggested that they should set up schools like there were in Alessandrine. She said that most men taught their sons to read and write, but if there were schools, the girls could learn as well.

She suggested that other things might be taught in the schools. Although he knew it would be a difficult task, it was the right thing to do.

Kenner was right, Li was very wise. Yitzhak appreciated her help in ruling the kingdom. Often when he did not know what to do, Li would know exactly what to do. He looked down into the tiny sleeping face of his new daughter and wondered what Mannton would be like when she was a woman.

****

Li woke up and smiled as she saw Yitzhak looking down at Ta's face. She thought about the day he told her she was his wife. She had known then that her life would be so much better than before, but she had not dared imagine the life she was now living. Although he had been willing to listen to her then, now he asked her for her opinion on almost everything. Most of the time, he did exactly what she had suggested. Because he was willing to do what she asked him to do, now the women of Mannton were more like the women in other kingdoms.

Yitzhak looked up and smiled as he said, "She is so beautiful, just like her mother."

"And her father," Li said with a smile. "I know that all our children will grow up to be beautiful."

The next afternoon, a messenger arrived announcing Akar and Sofina would arrive the following morning for a visit. There was a flurry of activity as a room was prepared for them. Li was very excited.

The group from Okiah arrived just after breakfast.

"It is so good to see you again," Sofina said as she hugged Li carefully. "When was your infant born?"

"It is good to see you as well," Li said. "Ta was born just the day before yesterday. An was excited to have a new sister."

"Where are Tokar and An?" Sofina asked as a servant woman handed her Onan. "I bet they have grown."

"They are growing so fast," Li said as she led the way to the playroom.

"Mother!" An said as she looked up.

Tokar took An by the hand and they walked over to Li.

"This is Queen Sofina," Li said. "She met you when we went to Union and you played with Prince Bryant."

Tokar bowed and An curtsied.

"How adorable!" Sofina exclaimed.

"We thought we should teach them good manners as soon as possible," Li said with a smile as she sat down on a nearby bench.

Sofina sat next to her and set Onan on the floor at her feet. Tokar picked up a toy horse and brought it over to Onan.

"This is Prince Onan," Li said.

"Can he play with us?" An asked as she sat down next to Onan.

"He is still very young," Li said.

"I think that he would like to play for a while," Sofina said.

"I will take good care of him," said the young woman who was watching the children.

"Thank you, Ni," Li said.

When they were walking back down the hall to the guest room, Sofina said, "I have noticed that women in Mannton have very short names."

"That is how it has been for a very long time, but some of the new infant girls are being given longer names," Li said. "It will take time for things to change, but we have made so much progress so far."

"Why did you name both your daughters with such short names?" Sofina asked.

"An was named after my mother and Ta after Yitzhak's mother," Li said.

A guard came up and knelt.

"A message from Alessandrine, My Queen," the man said as he stood and held out a scroll.

Li read the brief message.

"What is that?" Yitzhak asked as he and Akar came towards them.

"Marriah and Archelaus are on their way here," she said. "They should arrive this afternoon. Tyrzah and Edwyn are coming as well."

"That's great," Yitzhak said. "I was going to take Akar and show him around the city."

"I'd love to see it as well," Sofina said.

"I'd like to go as well if we can take the carriage," Li said. "I'll leave Ta with Ni."

Soon they were in the carriage. Li was happy to see the women and girls looking so much healthier and happier. They stopped at a small shop.

"Two women opened this shop," Yitzhak said as he helped Li from the carriage.

They went inside to look around. The woman who was sewing a doll near the back of the shop quickly knelt.

"Welcome to our shop," the woman said as she stood up and picked up a small blanket. "Thank you for coming to see it. I would like to present this to you for our new prince or princess."

"The thanks should go to you," Yitzhak said. "You are showing the other women that they are capable of more than they have been doing. Hopefully more women will be as courageous as you two have been."

"I heard that a man and his wife were building a grain mill next to the river," the woman said. "She figured out a way to turn the wheel with water instead of using a horse."

"I'd like to know how," Akar said. "I don't like to see a poor creature tied up and forced to go in circles all day."

When they reached the site of the new mill next to a short waterfall, there was a man and a woman building a large wheel with what looked like trays along the outside edges. When they noticed the carriage, they both quickly came over and knelt.

"We heard about your mill and wanted to see how it would work," Yitzhak said.

"La can explain it best," the man said.

"This large wheel will go on the end of that square beam," the woman said, pointing to a beam that hung out over the river. "The water will catch on the trays and push the wheel so it turns. Inside the mill, a gear and beam system will turn both the grinding wheel and the flat stone."

"Interesting," Akar said. "This looks very heavy. How will you get it on the beam?"

"It is built in sections," the man said. "The trays will be the last thing to go on the wheel."

"How will you stop the wheel?" Yitzhak asked.

The woman led them around to the top of the hillside. As they looked back towards the mill, they saw something built of wood. It was wide enough for the wheel to fit inside it and almost as deep as the trays, but it ran from the upper part of the river, straight out to where the wheel was. As the woman pulled a board out of it, water began to flow towards the mill before falling off the end into the river. The water stopped as she put the board back in place.

"That is most clever," Yitzhak said. "And it doesn't need to eat, drink or rest."

"Do you mind if I send someone from Okiah to learn how this works?" Akar asked.

"We would be pleased to show them," the woman said. "I thought about using wind instead of the river, but there is not enough steady wind to do it here."

"We have a valley that is very windy all of the time," Akar said.

"I can show someone how wind could turn the wheel," the woman said.

As they were returning to the palace for lunch, Yitzhak said, "After I met Marriah, I began to wonder what things women could do if only they were allowed to."

"I am so glad to see how Mannton has changed," Sofina said.

"It is amazing how quickly things have changed," Akar added.

"There is still so much to do," Li said. "We've been talking about schools for the children."

"We have too," Akar said. "I'm glad that we made that treaty."

"Li is the one who made it all possible," Yitzhak said as he kissed her hand. "Because of her, Mannton will not only survive, but thrive."

It was nearly time for supper before Marriah and Archelaus arrived. Edwyn and Tyrzah had brought their son along. Yitzhak had sent a guard to invite Kon and Marnah to supper. They arrived just as the wagon was being unloaded.

"Tyrzah!" Marnah exclaimed as she saw her sister.

"You look happy," Tyrzah replied as she hugged Marnah. "It looks like you will deliver soon."

211

"Very soon," Marnah said. "We had no idea you would be coming."

"We wanted to surprise you," Edwyn said as he smiled.

"Come stay at our home," Marnah said. "There's plenty of room."

"We insist," Kon said.

"It won't be any trouble?" Tyrzah asked.

"Not at all," Kon insisted.

"Stay for supper at least," Yitzhak said.

There was more talking than eating during supper, but everyone seemed to be enjoying themselves. The next morning, they met to discuss the changes that had happened since they had last met. Marriah and Archelaus offered assistance in setting up schools in Mannton and Okiah. They decided that they should meet together at least every six months. Akar asked about the councils that were in Alessandrine.

"The first council was set up by my great grandfather, King Langward of Brinley," Queen Marriah explained.

"I remember my grandfather, King Onan, mentioned that he had been given the throne by the first King Burkhart who was an evil king," Akar said. "Grandfather always said that King Langward and King Brook were extraordinary men."

"The first King Burkhart's wife died giving birth to his daughter the same day King Langward captured the palace," Marriah said. "King Burkhart had no will to live as he gave the throne to King Langward. King Langward realized that one person with too much power would be tempted to use it as King Burkhart had. That is what inspired him to create the first council. He felt the people should have a voice in how they were governed."

"King Gustave proved the same thing to me," Archelaus said. "It was important to me that his greed and cruelty could not be repeated. It was important to me that Burton had a council as well. Once Alessandrine was created, every city and village elected a council of their own if they did not already have one. It has proved to be a valuable resource for us as rulers."

"It also makes it easier to enforce the laws and make the same basic laws in all cities and villages," Marriah added. "I read in King Langward's journal that he felt it very important that he not forget what it was like to live in a village and the struggle the villagers faced just to survive."

"I have noticed that each village seems to have their own customs and rules," Akar said. "One of my guards moved from one village to another when he was young. He said that it took a long time to learn everything that was new. He said he was in trouble a lot because he didn't know all the rules."

"By having a meeting for all the councils every other month, we have been able to change the local rules so that they are more consistent throughout Alessandrine," Archelaus said. "It has taken some time, but it is much easier for our people to visit other villages or cities knowing that the rules and laws are the same. Having two languages is still somewhat of a problem, but it is getting better."

"I like the idea of a council," Li said. "Although we only have one city now, there have been villages forming outside of the city. It will take time for there to be enough people to make them real villages."

"Apparently when King Langward formed the original councils, he divided Brinley in to eight districts, each with its own council," Marriah said. "Later each village had its own council."

"There are enough people to divide the city into two districts," Yitzhak said.

"I think councils would be a big help in Okiah as well," Sofina said.

"Definitely," Akar said.

"We've wanted to distribute a copy of the book of laws to each city and village, but we don't have enough people who want to sit and copy the book all day," Marriah said. "So far there are only three copies."

"We had the same problem with kingdom wide announcements," Akar said. "My scribe has been having trouble keeping up. He was writing so fast that the ink wouldn't fully dry before he put a new page on top. He noticed that the lettering was reversed on the backs of the page. He has some ideas about a machine to print an entire page at a time."

"Let us know if he gets one working," Archelaus said.

"We would be interested in such a machine as well," Li said.

They discussed the idea of exchanging copies of their laws and agreed that it would be a good idea.

Chapter 27 – A Place to Build a School

The following day they announced the birth of Princess Ta and that there would be a celebration feast in two days. While the women planned the feast, Archelaus and Akar met with Yitzhak and his advisors about creating a council.

"So the people will decide who will represent them?" Yuri asked.

"Yes," Archelaus replied. "You and Joris have been chosen by Yitzhak to serve as advisors, but the people need to choose someone to represent them."

"In time Mannton will grow and I will need to know what is going on with the people so I know how to better rule them," Yitzhak said. "It will give the people a voice. Li once told me that the women had no face and no voice."

"What if we ask for two representatives from each district?" Joris said.

"Why two?" Yitzhak asked.

"One man and one woman," Joris replied. "I know that Queen Li has done much to help the women of Mannton, but I know some still feel they are not treated equally. Fa mentioned that when the women talk at the well some still feel invisible to you."

Yitzhak was surprised by the revelation.

"I want to make certain everyone feels they are represented, especially the women," Yitzhak said. "I agree with your idea. I will announce that at the feast."

"I'd never thought about that," Archelaus admitted. "We have only a few women on our councils."

"That is something to consider when we set up our councils. I don't think I could rule without Sofina to help and advise me," Akar said.

Yitzhak nodded. Li was vital to ruling the kingdom. He knew that the women chosen would need to learn to read and write. Perhaps other women would want to learn as well.

When they met the women for supper Yitzhak mentioned Joris' idea of women on the council.

215

"I like that idea," Li said. "I know that life is better for women in Mannton, but that would help them feel more equal to men."

"We should have classes for the women to learn to read and write," Yitzhak said. "Once we set up schools all the young children will be taught, but the older women will need our help to learn if they want to."

"We have been offering classes two nights a week," Marriah said. "They are always full."

"I think women would like that," Li said. "It wouldn't take a lot of their time, but they would be learning something that in the past was forbidden to them."

On the day of the feast Yitzhak felt ready to make the announcements about the council and schools. He was grateful for Archelaus and Marriah helping with the plans.

Once it seemed everyone had taken their seats Yitzhak and Li stood up.

"We are gathering today to celebrate both the birth of Princess Ta and our friendship with Okiah and Alessandrine," Yitzhak said and there were cheers among the people. "We also want to announce that we are going to set up schools so that both boys and girls can learn to read and write. We will also hold classes two evenings a week so that all women can learn to read and write."

The crowd erupted in talk. It took some time for them to quiet down.

"It will take some time to get these set up, but we feel it important that everyone has the chance to learn to read and write," Yitzhak said. "We also want to form a council with four people chosen by you the people. We are going to divide the city in half so two representatives will be chosen from each half. We have also decided that from each district one of the representatives should be a woman."

There was stunned silence replacing the murmuring that had begun among the people.

"It has come to my attention that some women still feel invisible. This will help to correct that. Know that I value Li as a partner in ruling Mannton. I feel that having women on this new council will be a great asset to us."

"We'll give you a month to make a decision on who will represent you on the council," Li said. "For now let's enjoy this feast."

As they began to eat the delicious food there was much talk among the people. Yitzhak was curious to see who would be chosen. Li seemed happy but tired.

Their guests left the following morning. While Li rested Yitzhak took a ride on his horse to think about where they would start the school. While many of the homes were occupied, some were obviously still empty. None of the empty homes seemed large enough until he found two empty homes sitting beside each other. Yitzhak dismounted and so did his guards. One held the horses while the other three followed him into one of the houses.

There was a single large room with a fireplace. Highlighted by sunlight through a hole in the roof a broken chair lay under a table with two legs. In the corner there was a bedframe that looked on the verge of collapse. Yitzhak walked around and found that the floor was sound other than directly under the hole in the roof.

"This might work," he commented as he turned towards the door.

"Work for what, My King?" one of the guards asked.

"A school to teach children and women to read and write," he replied as he walked out the door.

"Women read?" the guard asked skeptically.

"My wife asked me to teach her," another guard said as they approached the other house. "I've been surprised at how well she's been doing."

Yitzhak entered the second house and found it was in about the same condition as the first. This home had a separate kitchen and one bedroom. This gave Yitzhak some ideas.

"I've seen what I need to see," he said as he left the house.

Once back at the palace he went to his office and got out a piece of paper. As he picked up a stick of charcoal he realized that a school would need lots of paper. He drew the outline of the two houses before pausing. He joined the back walls across the space between them. He then drew a new wall joining the front walls with a door in the middle. After a moment's thought he drew a wall enclosing the front with one door in the center.

Li came into his office quietly. He smiled at her.

"What are you doing?" she asked.

"I found two abandoned houses next to each other that can be joined and fixed up to create a school. One even has a kitchen and a bedroom. The bedroom can be used by the teachers or as storage and the kitchen can be used to prepare food for the children during the day."

"Perhaps families could contribute food," Li suggested.

"That's a good idea."

The following morning Yitzhak sent word out that some builders were needed to build the school. By afternoon only two men had shown up. It was a discouraging start, but Yitzhak knew it would take time for people to get behind the idea of a school.

"Thank you for coming," Yitzhak said as he met them in the courtyard. "Let me show you where I have chosen to build the school and the plans I came up with."

The two men glanced at each other and shrugged. People stopped and stared as they walked to the nearby houses followed by four guards.

"I know these homes are empty and need repair," Yitzhak said as he unrolled the plans, "but by creating another room between them and a wide hall in front I think the school could be finished more quickly than starting with empty ground."

The men looked at the plans and then began walking around the houses. Yitzhak could hear them quietly talking as they pointed to the plans and the houses. Finally they returned to where he stood.

"Some of the wood is rotted and would need to be replaced," one of the men said. "It might actually be better to tear these down and salvage the usable wood for constructing the new building."

"There are several other houses that are empty and in really bad shape," the other man said. "How would you feel about us tearing those down as well to get enough wood to build the school?"

"I think that's a great idea," Yitzhak said. "I think it will present a better image for Mannton as well as provide wood for the school."

"What's going on, King Yitzhak?" Kon's voice said behind him.

"We are going to tear these houses down and build a school," Yitzhak said.

"I was wondering who you had in mind to teach the classes," Marnah said. "I could teach half a day. I've already been teaching some of the women. Kyle's wife has been coming once a week for a month now and Marcus' wife just started last week."

"I would really appreciate that," Yitzhak said.

"That's why we decided to see what you had in mind for the school," one of the men said. "Our wives insisted they wanted the school built so they could take classes and so our children would learn to read and write."

"I know it will take time for the men to get very excited about the idea of building a school, but I think they might get excited about seeing these empty houses torn down," Yitzhak said. "There are few empty houses in Brinley and none in Union. I want Mannton to look more like that."

"We'll get started on this right away," the other man said.

"I'll send word out that the other empty houses can be torn down and the wood brought here," Yitzhak said.

He was deep in thought as he walked back towards the palace. He saw several women at the well as he approached it. They seemed confused as he stopped near the well.

"Is there something you want, King Yitzhak?" one asked with a trembling voice.

"I just wanted to wish you a pleasant afternoon," he replied. "I'm looking forward to having women on the council. I have learned so very much from Queen Li. I know that Mannton will greatly benefit from having women on the council that we are forming."

The oldest woman began to cry.

"What's wrong? Yitzhak asked with concern as he touched her shoulder.

"I never thought it possible," she sobbed. "You are the king and you are speaking to us."

"Li taught me that the world outside the palace walls held many things I was blind to," Yitzhak said. "She taught me that women are important and intelligent. It is her that made this possible."

He patted her shoulder softly and left as another woman drew her into her arms.

Chapter 28– The Storm

Li woke to the window shutters blowing open. It had rained for three days but there hadn't been thunder. Ta began to cry in the cradle as rain blew in. As Li comforted her. Yitzhak secured the shutters.

"Go check on An and Tokar," Li said. "They are probably awake and frightened."

Yitzhak nodded and pulled on his pants and left the room. He soon returned with An and Toker.

"The water is rising in the harbor and the river to the east of town is flooding," Yitzhak said. "The palace is on high ground so we should be safe."

"But those near the harbor and river are not," Li said. "There is room in the throne room and dining hall to shelter people until the storm passes and the water subsides."

He nodded and left. She worried about Rowan, Anunik and their families being right by the ocean. She hoped their homes would survive the storm. Ka arrived and helped Li get dressed while An held Ta on the bed.

"Have Ni get the children dressed," Li said. "I don't think anyone is going to get any more sleep."

Ka bowed and left. Soon Ni came for the children. Li went downstairs and found people shivering in the entrance hall. The open doors revealed the rain pounding in the courtyard.

"Come upstairs and into the throne room," Li said as a servant joined her on the balcony. "Make certain the fires are lit in the throne room and dining hall."

"How long are they staying?" the man asked.

"As long as necessary," she replied. "For now they need to get warm and dry."

People began to file into the throne room. They left a trail of water dripping off their hair and clothing. One little girl was so cold all the color was gone from her face.

"Get her next to the fire," Li said as more servants arrived. "We need anything that will hold water. These people need to wring the water out of their clothes so they will dry."

"We don't have enough clothes or even blankets for everyone," one servant said.

"Start with the children and elderly. Hang their clothes in the kitchen and return them as soon as they are dry or nearly dry," Li ordered. "We need mops to get this water off the floor and stairs."

Her words were punctuated by the palace door slamming shut and the panicked reaction of the people in the throne room.

More people arrived and soon the dining hall was nearly full as well. She found Yitzhak drenched and cold sitting on the steps. He looked up at her.

"Get out of those wet clothes and into some dry ones."

He nodded and slowly stood.

"The school is on high ground. Some people have gathered there."

"For now we wait out the storm," Li said. "We get people dried and warm. You are of no help until you are dry and warm yourself."

Li went back to the throne room to check on the people. Guards stood with spears supporting blankets to create some privacy for people to take off and wring out their clothing. Servants were passing empty pots and tubs in and full ones out. Others were passing out bowls and cups of warm broth.

Li made her way to the fireplace and found children huddled near the fire with some elderly women. She saw the little girl who had the pale face was warmed up and color back in her cheeks. She went into the dining hall. Some people looked warmer and dryer, but some still were cold and drenched.

"There is a place to wring out your clothes in the throne room," Li said. "Make your way in there. Once you are dry move away from the fireplace so someone else can get dry."

She saw familiar faces among the crowd but didn't see her father, Dreggen or Ti. She continued to direct people. She had some men move the dining room table to make an area to one side of the fireplace for the children to rest or play without being under foot of the adults. Soon there were several women watching over the children.

Li went out to the balcony over the entrance hall and found a few more people coming in the doors.

"Come upstairs," she called to them. "How is it out there?"

"Th-th-the s-s-storm is still raging," one man said through chattering teeth. "S-s-some homes are f-f-flooded. Everyone not on high ground is evacuated."

"Go into the throne room. There is a place to the left to take off your clothing and wring them out, then get a place by the fire to warm up," Li said.

One of the guards followed them up the stairs. Water was dripping off his armor.

"I want guards to watch the flooding and make certain we don't need to evacuate more people," Li said. "Quickly look and get back in so you don't get too cold."

"The armor keeps us mostly dry, My Queen," the guard replied.

"Even so, don't stay out so long you get cold," Li said.

"The wind has gotten stronger," the guard said. "The rain is coming down in sheets. I don't know how long it will last, but there are a lot of tree branches and debris that are blowing around. It is dangerous out there."

"Get everyone inside. Go to a tower and look out the windows before securing the shutters," Li said. "Keep me updated."

She hurried up the stairs to the royal quarters to find Yitzhak wrapped in a blanket near the fire.

"I couldn't stop shivering," he said.

"Everything is under control downstairs," she replied. "I'll get someone to bring you some warm broth. The wind is stronger and there is a lot of debris blowing around. I'm having them check the storm out of a tower window."

Yitzhak nodded.

"I haven't seen Father, Dreggen or Ti," she said quietly.

"I went by to check on them. They are on high ground and safe. The palace would flood before their homes. Rowan, Garsha, Anunik and Carita are there with all of their children. Everyone is safe."

Relief flooded through her.

"I had best get back downstairs," she said and kissed him before she left.

About an hour after she sent up the warm broth Yitzhak came downstairs. By then most of the people were dry and the few with damp clothing were huddled near the fire. The entry hall echoed with the rain pounding on the doors, but howl of the wind was louder.

A guard with wet armor came down the hall.

"Report," Yitzhak said as the guard started up the steps.

"It's still bad out there," the man said. "The water is still rising, but the rain is starting to die down. Some homes have been damaged and a couple nearest the river were washed away."

Yitzhak nodded.

"We won't know what needs to be done until the water recedes," Li said. "Do you have a map of the city?"

"Not really," Yitzhak said. "We have a rough sketch of the streets, but we really need to have a detailed map."

"Perhaps while we wait for the storm to subside we could work on filling out the missing details on the map," Li said. "The guards might be of help since they would be familiar with most of the city. We can also talk to the people here and label the homes by who they belong to and what they do."

"I'll get started on that map," Yitzhak said. "I'll have a guard tell you when I am ready to interview people."

Li nodded and headed back into the throne room. She could see that people were gathering in family groups. She went to the doorway between the throne room and dining room. She asked a servant for a chair which was soon brought to her. She climbed up to stand on the chair. People took notice and quieted down.

"We will wait out the storm here," she announced. "It has been reported that some homes are damaged and a few have been swept away in the flooding. King Yitzhak is working on a detailed map of the city to help with the recovery efforts."

There was murmuring among the people.

"We will soon be ready to have each family identify their home on the map along with what they do," Li said. "If we work together we can recover from this storm."

Li stepped off the chair. She moved among the people before heading to the kitchen.

"Queen Li!" one of the cooks exclaimed. "What brings you down here?"

"I wanted to see what you were preparing for supper," Li replied.

"Have you eaten today?" the cook asked, and she shook her head.

"No, but I am more worried about the people and what they will eat," Li replied.

"We are preparing a hearty stew," the cook said as she gathered a plate of bread and cheese. "Here is something for you to eat. Ni has made certain the prince and princesses were fed."

"Thank you," Li said as she took the plate. "I should share this with Yitzhak."

"If you take those stairs up they come out on the upper hall near the royal quarters," the cook said as she pointed to a doorway in the corner.

Li went to the corner and found the stairs. When she reached the top there was a door. She pulled on the handle and it swung in silently. As promised it revealed the hallway near the royal quarters. She stepped through the door and let it shut behind her. When she turned around the door looked like the rest of the wall between two columns along the hall.

Li went to Yitzhak's office and it was opened by one of the guards.

"I brought food," Li said. "I've made an announcement about the map."

Yitzhak smiled as he put down the charcoal stick. Li studied the map as they ate. She soon found the harbor, the well and her father's home. She reached out and softly touched the square representing her father's house.

"I'm certain they are alright," Yitzhak said. "I'm almost ready to start putting names on this. I realized that the paper maker is one of the flooded homes."

"That's a problem," Li said. "The school was set to open next week."

"I might have a solution to that," Yitzhak said as he stood up.

He opened a cabinet on the wall and drew something out of it.

"I used to play with these as a child," Yitzhak said as he placed a black square and a white lump on the desk. "This tile is of black stone from the mountains to the west. The white chalk is from the sea cliffs to the east of Anunik's home."

He picked up the white lump and drew a line on the black stone with it.

"How big can these pieces of black stone be?" Li asked as an idea came to mind.

Yitzhak shrugged and said, "As big as this desktop I suppose."

"What if we put one on the wall in each classroom?" Li asked. "The teacher could use it to show the entire class how to write a word or letter. Smaller ones could be used by the women and children learning to read and write."

"That's a great idea!" Yitzhak said. "That will let the school open without paper."

There was a quiet tap on the door.

"Come," Yitzhak responded.

A guard entered and said, "The rain has stopped but there are clouds above. The river is not rising as fast."

"Good to know," Yitzhak said. "Hopefully the worst is over."

The guard bowed and left.

"I should go check the damage to the town. I'll let the people know you are ready for them to come put their names on their homes. I'll see if the paper maker is among the people sheltering in the palace and send him up first if I find him," Yitzhak said.

Li nodded and Yitzhak left. A servant came in and took the empty tray. As she waited she worried about how they would deal with rebuilding their lives. Some would return to homes that could be easily cleaned, but others would return to nothing. Soon a man was guided into the office by a guard. His shoulders drooped and he didn't look up.

"Are you the paper maker?" she asked.

"I was," he muttered. "It's all gone, washed away. I nearly lost my wife and child to the river."

"Things can be replaced, but the people we love cannot," Li responded. "Come sit down."

"The school," he groaned. "There's no paper for the school."

"We've already got a solution for that," Li said, and the man looked up at last. "The school will open on time and without paper. Your job is still important, so we need a plan to replace your home and workshop."

He collapsed into a chair in front of the desk.

"We'll use this instead of paper for now," Li said as she pointed to the black rock. "Hopefully we'll soon have you back to work."

"You've given me hope," the man said as he looked over the map. "You're missing a home here next to the mill."

He pointed to a spot near the river.

Li drew in the missing house.

"As soon as the water recedes, we'll be able to see what can be salvaged," Li said.

"How far has the water gone?" the man asked.

The guard traced with his finger. Li was surprised at how close it was to the palace.

"There are a lot of people affected by the flooding," she said. "That's part of why I'm going to talk with everyone here. I don't want anyone to panic. This is the worst storm I can remember, but we'll get through it and rebuild."

"I had best get back down to my wife and child," the man said. "I feel better, and I know they need me to be strong for them."

Li nodded. After the man left, she asked the guard to bring someone else up. She had spoken to about a dozen families when a howl drew her attention from the map. A crashing in the hall announced the approach of a guard.

"The storm is back!" the guard exclaimed.

"Is King Yitzhak back?"

The guard shook his head and Li's heart sunk.

"Keep checking on the storm from the tower and notify me at once if he returns."

"Yes, My Queen," the guard said before leaving.

The day wore on as she spoke with each family about where their home was and if it was flooded. Some were worried about having enough seeds to replant their gardens that had just started sprouting. By evening she had spoken to only about a third of the people and Yitzhak had not returned. She prayed he had found shelter.

Li was exhausted as she told the guard she was done for the day. She went down to the throne room and found people were settling in to sleep. One of the women was directing some men to move the tables against the walls and put the chairs on top of them to leave more room for people to lay down. She went up to the children's room and kissed them as they slept. When she got to the bedroom Ka was waiting to help her undress. The bed was so empty and cold without Yitzhak.

****

The morning brought blue skies and news that the waters were receding at last. Li sent the guards out to search for Yitzhak and any others that needed help. It took the morning and half the afternoon to talk to the rest of the families. As soon as she finished Li ventured out onto the palace wall to look around. Li could see where the water had crested by the layer of mud and debris it left behind.

Her attention was drawn by a commotion. A group of men were carrying something towards the palace. Li hurried down the steps to the courtyard.

"We found him!" one of the guards shouted as they entered the gate.

"Yitzhak!" Li shouted as she ran to the group.

The blood drained out of her face as she saw him lying still and muddy on the thing they were carrying. She reached out for his face and felt his breath on her hand. There were splints on his right arm and left leg.

"He's injured, but alive," one guard said. "We sent someone to fetch Kon."

"Bring him inside. We'll take him to one of the rooms on the main floor," she said.

They followed her inside and down the hall to her old room. What they were carrying him on wouldn't fit through the door, but a guard brought two poles with some cloth. They carefully rolled him on his side and put a pole next to him. Li could see the fabric was attached between the poles. They rolled him back and picked up the poles to carry him into the room.

Li grabbed the bucket and got water from the courtyard well. She returned to find they had placed him on the bed with the blankets pulled back. She found some of the cloths she had used to clean with and began gently washing the mud from Yitzhak's face. Her efforts revealed bruises and scratches on his face. She wiped the mud from his clothes enough to find the buttons. A guard helped her to remove his shirt and jacket. She gently washed his body and left arm.

"I see you are doing my job again, My Queen," Kon's voice said behind her.

She looked up to see Kon set his bag down. He was dirty and disheveled.

"Is your family alright?" she asked.

"Yes," Kon replied. "Most of our neighbors sheltered in our home. How did he get caught in the storm?"

"He went out when the rain stopped and must not have seen the rain coming until it was too late," Li said as her throat tightened. "I'll let you do your work. I'll leave a guard to keep you supplied with fresh water. Come up to the office when you are finished."

"I'll stay," one of the guards volunteered.

"Thank you," she said as she stroked Yitzhak's face softly.

She stood and left while she still had control over her emotions. She quickly returned to the office. She looked over the map. There were many homes marked as damaged or gone. There were people that were marked as dead or missing. Tears were rolling down her cheeks as her mind kept straying to Yitzhak's condition.

Li suddenly remembered Tasia's prediction. He would live! She knew she had to be strong while he healed. A quiet tap on the door drew her attention.

She wiped her face and responded, "Come."

Kon entered. His expression of concern worried her.

"Tell me everything," she said.

"He has two broken ribs, possibly more," Kon said grimly as he sat down. "His left leg is broken in two places and his right arm is broken. He has two cuts that I've cleaned out, but I don't dare stitch shut for a couple of days. He's got a couple of good sized lumps on his head under his hair. I can't say if he will live or die."

"He will live," Li said firmly. "A dragon queen who can foresee the future told me he will give me five children."

Kon looked up at her at last, "It might be a couple of days before he regains consciousness. The guards found him in a tree near the river. There were two guards with him. They said he saved their lives by insisting they climb the tree and then lashing them to the trunk. They held onto him through the storm and through the night."

"They will be rewarded for their deeds," Li said. "I've been working on this map to record the condition of homes and families. Do you want to take a look and see what you can fill in?"

Kon looked at the map and picked up the charcoal. He drew in several more houses and added some names.

"Tomorrow I'll go out and check on my own family while filling in more of the map. This will help us make a recovery plan," she said. "I know I must rule while Yitzhak heals."

"There was a time that I would not believe it possible, but I have faith in your ability to rule," Kon said. "The people trust you to be their ruler."

"Go home and get some rest," Li said. "I know there are more wounded to care for."

"You look exhausted," Kon said as he stood up. "Take care of yourself."

"Tonight I will sleep better knowing Yitzhak is safely in the palace," she replied.

Kon bowed and left. Li looked over the map one more time before leaving the office. Silence fell as she entered the throne room.

"King Yitzhak was outside the palace when the storm returned, but he has been found," she announced loudly. "He is now safely in the palace and has been seen by the healer. He is badly injured but will recover. For now we must focus on finding others that were lost in the storm and rebuilding. Tomorrow is a new day and a new beginning for Mannton. Know that I will be working hard to help Mannton recover from this storm."

Li turned and left. She heard the room erupt in talk as she headed downstairs. The guard opened the door and let her in. Yitzhak was covered up with his right arm out of the blanket and wrapped securely. She sat on the edge of the bed remembering the last time he lay injured in this bed. She kissed his lips softly and he moaned.

"I am here, Yitzhak," she said. "You are home and safe. Rest and heal. I will take care of everything."

He seemed to sigh and relax. She kissed his forehead and left the room. "I want someone at his side at all times. Notify me immediately when he wakes."

"Yes, My Queen," the guards said.

Li went upstairs to visit the children.

"Mother!" An said as she entered the nursery.

"Where is Father?" Tokar asked.

Li knelt and drew them both into her lap.

"Father got injured in the storm. He is home now and will recover, but he needs lots of sleep," Li said. "As soon as he is awake, I'll take you to see him."

She kissed them both before letting them off her lap. She stood and Ni handed Ta to her.

"She is ready for bed," Ni said. "You look so tired. I could let her sleep in here so you can sleep."

Li kissed Ta's tiny face.

"I would appreciate that," Li said and handed her back to Ni.

She returned to the royal quarters and was grateful to find Ka and Lenar waiting there.

"King Yitzhak has been found," Li told them. "He is injured but will recover. He is in my old room on the first floor. A guard will remain by his side at all times."

Lenar collapsed into a chair with tears running down his face.

"I know," she said. "I think I'll be able to actually sleep tonight knowing he is safe. Tomorrow I'll need to go out into the city to complete the map of the city. I need to find out how many people are missing and dead as well as what needs to be rebuilt."

"I will come with you to assist you," Lenar said.

"I will watch over King Yitzhak for you," Ka said. "Let's get you ready for bed."

"Thank you," Li said. "It's been a really long day for me."

Soon she was settled into bed. It was so quiet without Yitzhak softly snoring beside her.

****

Li felt better in the morning but still tired and anxious about Yitzhak. Ka helped her to get dressed in one of her plainer dresses and Lenar brought her breakfast. She felt calmer after she ate.

"Can you gather the map and what we'll need to fill out details on it while I go check on Yitzhak?" Li asked.

"Of course, My Queen," Lenar replied. "I will meet you downstairs."

Li checked on the children before heading downstairs. The guard opened the door for her. Ka and one of the guards sat on either side of the bed.

"He still sleeps deeply, My Queen," the guard said.

"He will wake in time," she replied before she leaned over and kissed his forehead. "I am going out to inspect the town and find out if everyone is accounted for. If he wakes send someone to notify me immediately."

"Of course, My Queen," the guard said.

She heard the door open behind her and turned to find Lenar entering the room.

"I have everything you'll need," Lenar said. "I had horses saddled since I don't think all the roads are passable by carriage."

"Thank you," she replied as she glanced back at Yitzhak. "We should go."

Lenar followed her out of the room. There was a horse loaded with a pack along with four horses saddled. Two guards joined them. Li decided to go to the school first even though she was anxious to check on her own family. She found Marnah watching over a large group of children as they played inside.

"I see the children are well cared for while their parents are out cleaning up," Li commented.

"Everyone is worried about their neighbors that were not here last night," Marnah said.

"There are many who sheltered in the palace. I know we might be missing some people," she replied. "I'm making a map of the city and filling out names to go with the houses. That should help account for everyone."

"Come in here and spread the map out on the table," Marnah said. "I can send out some of the oldest children to bring people in to fill in their names. I think it will help for them to see names of people already filled in."

"Yes, that would be great," Li said.

Soon people began filing in. They expressed relief as they saw how many names were already on the map. Some drew a line around their homes that included their gardens. There were still a few houses near the river with no names by the time the people stopped coming.

"We may need to search further downstream," Li said with a sigh as Kon walked into the room.

"Marnah told me you were in here," Kon said. "There were some people that were brought to me this morning. Some are injured and two are dead."

Kon filled out the map with the names of the injured and the dead. He put an x next to the names of the dead.

"That leaves two families in this area unaccounted for," Li said. "I still need to check on my own family before returning to the palace. Tomorrow I'll check the other half of the town."

"This is a large map," Kon commented. "In Brinley many of the streets have names and the houses are numbered. If you named the streets you could number the houses and write out a list so the information could be accurately transferred to the map."

"That's a good idea," Li said. "The map is a bit awkward without a large table to spread it out on. Send word if these other two families are found."

"I will," Kon said.

Lenar folded up the map and put the cap on the ink bottle. Soon she was on her way to Father's home. As she passed the well, she wondered if the water would be safe since the line left by the flooded harbor was halfway up the side. Several small boats had been tossed out of the harbor against houses and one ship was sunk in the harbor with its masts sticking out at an odd angle. A woman was drawing up a bucket but gasped and dumped it out on the ground. Several small fish flopped and struggled on the muddy ground.

"Don't use that water for drinking," Li said. "It should be fine for cleaning."

"Yes, My Queen, but what will we do for drinking water?" she asked.

"I'll notify the palace guards that people will be coming to get drinking water," Li said. "The town is getting large enough to soon need a second well. Perhaps we should do that as part of the rebuilding."

The woman nodded. Li continued to Father's home. Rowan answered the door when she knocked.

"Li! It's nearly dark," Rowan commented. "What are you doing out at this hour?"

"And it's been a long day," she replied. "Yitzhak was out when the storm returned. He is injured, but safe and will recover in time. I had to check on all of you before returning to the palace."

"We're all fine," Father said as he hugged her. "The roof leaked a bit, but that's easily repaired."

"The homes along the river were not so lucky. A couple of homes near the harbor will need to be rebuilt as well," Li responded. "The dock probably will need repair."

"Anunik and I are going to check on our homes tomorrow," Rowan said. "Hopefully the height of the cliffs protected them from the waves."

"I hope so too," Li said as she hugged him. It was dark by the time they reached the palace. A guard was just leading a saddled horse out of the stables.

"King Yitzhak is stirring, My Queen," the guard said. "He's not quite awake, but we thought you would want to know."

"Yes," she said before dismounting.

She hurried into the palace and down the hall. The guard opened the door. She could see the guard and Ka trying to hold down Yitzhak. She rushed to his side.

"Yitzhak! Calm down!" she said as she put her hand on his cheek and then slid it down to his chest. "You are safe but injured."

He stopped fighting the bedding and began to relax.

"Li," his voice was a whisper.

"I am here, my husband," she said as she took his left hand and put it on her cheek. "The storm is over, and people are cleaning up."

He smiled softly. She tucked his arm back under the bedding.

"Sleep now and heal," she said. "You are home in my old room."

She kissed his lips softly and it almost felt like he kissed back.

"He should sleep better now that he knows he is home," Li said, and the guard nodded.

"There will be a servant and a guard watching over him at all times," Ka said as the door opened. "You look exhausted. Let's get you ready for bed."

She led Ka out into the hall. The two guards were standing near the outer doors.

"Please let all the guards know that people will be coming to draw drinking water from our wells," Li said, and the guards nodded.

"I'll let the servants know," Ka said as they climbed the stairs. "What's wrong with the town well?"

"There are fish in it," Li said.

Ka stopped suddenly and stifled a laugh. Li began to giggle.

"I must be tired. It really shouldn't be funny, but it is," Li said between giggles.

"Yeah, it is kind of funny," Ka said as she laughed.

Chapter 29 – Women on the New Council

It took several days of cleanup in the city before the houses that had only minor damage were repaired and the families moved back in. Other homes would take longer to make habitable again. There were so many houses that were missing. It would take several weeks or even months to replace those houses. Most of the families that didn't have homes were taken in by other families. More dead were found and buried. Li completed the map including borders between the homes and began naming the streets. Large thin pieces of the black stone were found and fastened to the walls of the school. Small pieces were made for the children to hold. Anunik and Rowan collected a large amount of the white chalk to be used. The school opened which gave the children somewhere to be while their parents worked to clean and rebuild.

On the third day after the storm a guard came to the office.

"King Yitzhak is awake and asking for you and the children," the guard said.

Relief washed over her.

"I'll get the children and be right down," Li said as she stood up. "Send someone to bring Kon."

Li hurried to the nursery to find Tokar and An playing while Ni held Ta.

"Mother!" An said and Tokar looked up.

"Father is awake and wants to see you," Li said.

Tokar and An began running around with excitement chanting, "Father is awake! Father is awake!"

"Calm down," Li said. "He has broken ribs, a broken arm and a broken leg. You need to be calm and quiet. Don't jump on him because it will hurt him."

"What are ribs?" Tokar asked as he stopped running.

"Here are your ribs right here," Li said as she put his hand on his side. "Do you feel those ridges? Those are your ribs."

"I have ribs too!" An said.

"Father's ribs are hurt so we need to be very gentle," Li said.

"Can you bring Ta, Ni?" Li asked. "He asked to see all the children."

"Of course, My Queen," Ni replied as she stood up.

"Come with me children," Li said as she held out her hands.

She led the children down to where Yitzhak waited. The guard opened the door for them. Lenar was sitting next to the bed talking quietly.

"They're here" Lenar said and waved them forward.

"Where are my children?" Yitzhak's voice said softly from the bed.

"Father!" Tokar and An cried as they pulled away from Li and ran to the bed.

"Stay off the bed!" Li reminded them as she rushed to follow them.

The children obeyed but leaned onto the bed with their feet on the floor. Yitzhak was smiling at them as they held his left hand.

"Mother said you have broken ribs," Toker said.

"Do they hurt?" An asked as Ni handed Ta to Li.

"Yes," Yitzhak said. "It hurts when I breathe too deeply."

"Why are you down here?" An asked.

"Because he could have gotten hurt worse from being carried up the stairs," Li said as Yitzhak looked at her. "It is so good to see you awake."

"I heard your voice in my dreams and the storm around me died," he said. "How long have I been asleep?"

"Three days," Li replied as she leaned closer so he could touch Ta's face. "You need your rest. Ni please take the children back up to the nursery."

"Of course, My Queen," Ni said.

Li handed Ta back to her and the children obediently followed her out.

"Lenar has been catching me up on what is going on," Yitzhak said. "You've been busy."

"Yes," she said as she sat on the bed and took his hand in hers. "I need to hear what happened to you. I know that you saved the lives of your two guards and they saved your life."

"The storm came back so suddenly," Yitzhak said after a few moments. "The river was rising again, and I knew the guards would drown in their heavy armor. We found a tree with low branches and climbed up it. I used some rope that had tangled in the branches to lash the guards to the tree. I had just finished when I heard a loud crack. I don't remember anything but pain after that."

"The guards held onto you until the storm passed and you were found," Li said as Lenar left. "You were covered in mud when they brought you in. You looked dead, but I felt your breath and knew you lived."

"I'm sorry to have worried you," Yitzhak said after he squeezed her hand. "You look so tired."

"I haven't been sleeping well," Li admitted. "Now that you are awake I will sleep better. I'll sleep even better when you are well enough we can sleep in the same bed."

He pulled his hand free and put it on her cheek. She leaned over and kissed him. His kiss was passionate. She was startled by someone clearing their throat.

"King Yitzhak will need time to heal," Kon's voice said as Li sat up.

The smile on his face betrayed the serious tone of his voice.

"How are you feeling, My King?" Kon asked as he took the seat Lenar had been sitting in.

"I've got quite a headache," Yitzhak said after a moment. "It hurts when I breathe."

"From what the guards told me you took quite a beating in the storm when a limb broke above you," Kon said. "They tried to protect you as best they could. If not for them, you would have died."

"We need to find a way to reward them for their efforts," Li said.

"Let's take a look at your arm and leg," Kon said as he drew something out of his case. "You might want to chew these."

Yitzhak took the leaves and put them in his mouth.

"There are a couple of wounds that I didn't want to stitch shut until I was certain they were not infected," Kon said as he unwrapped Yitzhak's arm. "It's still a bit swollen, but I was able to set the bones when you were brought in."

He rewrapped the arm. Li moved away from the bed so Kon could check Yitzhak's leg.

"It looks good," Kon said before rewrapping the splinted leg. "Let's check those wounds and see if they can be stitched."

Li held Yitzhak's hand as his wounds were stitched shut.

"All done," Kon said as he put his needle back in a small case. "The swelling should go down in about four to six days. It might be a couple of weeks before you are able to sit up for more than long enough to eat. Then you can be moved back up to the royal quarters. Thanks to a stubborn farmer, I know that a broken leg will heal faster if the patient starts putting some weight on it, but that is with a single break. Your leg is broken both above and below the knee. Once you are back in the royal quarters we'll see if you can tolerate putting any weight on it. To begin with it will be only for a few minutes at a time, but we'll lengthen the time gradually as you can tolerate it."

"I'll miss the first council meeting," Yitzhak said.

"Your job is to rest and heal," Kon said firmly.

"While you heal, I'll take care of the kingdom," Li said as she put her hand on his face. "I can come ask you if I have something come up that I can't handle. I've been letting the people know that you got injured in the storm but are safely in the palace and will heal in time."

"People have mentioned that they are very relieved to know that you are safe," Kon said. "Until those ribs begin to heal you will want to move slowly and carefully. If it increases the pain, don't do it."

"We should get a chair made to hold the chamber pot," Li said wishing they had bathing chambers like in Union's palace.

"Please," Yitzhak said.

"Definitely a great idea," Kon agreed.

Li spoke to Lenar about the chair, and he said he knew of just the person to build it quickly. By suppertime a chair was delivered with a compartment holding a chamber pot and a removable seat with a hole in it. There was also a solid cover that folded down over the seat. Li sent two guards to deliver it to Yitzhak.

The following morning Li went out to check on the town and the rebuilding. She noticed that often it was women directing the men. Near the river several women were discussing stones that the river had washed over the banks and into the road. She was curious.

"I saw you looking at these stones," Li said as she stopped her horse near them. "They need to be removed at least from the road."

"We thought that if they were built into a wall or even just covering the bottom portion of a wooden wall that would protect a home from the water," one woman said.

"We dug up a lot of stones as we tilled the garden and piled them against the walls of our house," the other woman said. "Our house is still standing but our neighbor's house was swept away."

"Yes, that does sound like a good idea," Li said. "It would get rid of the stones too. Let the other families along the river know so they can strengthen their homes too."

She saw the paper maker working on something nearby. He looked up as he heard her approach.

"I have found more of my equipment than I expected to," he said. "It needs cleaning and some repair, but it gives me hope."

"I'm glad," Li said. "I know so many families lost everything but their lives. I pray they can find something of theirs to give them hope."

From there she went to check on the harbor. The docks were being repaired. Efforts were underway to raise the ship from the harbor and there were smaller boats, tied to the dock. A couple of small boats were on land being repaired. Li continued toward her father's home until she came to a small group of men around a hole. A frame had been erected over the hole and there was a rope the men were pulling up using the frame. A large bucket soon appeared. One of the men dumped dirt out of the bucket into a small wagon.

"I didn't expect a well to be dug so soon," Li commented, and the men turned to her.

They all bowed.

"Our wives will be very happy to not have to walk clear to the palace for water," one of the men said. "It's not deep enough to get water from yet, but we're working on it."

"We will need to line it with stones and create the top," another added.

"Perfect," she said. "Most of the homes still standing in this area look like they are being repaired. Getting people back in their own homes is important. We need to get the gardens and fields replanted too. We will need that harvest to get us through the cold season."

"Having the school open has given our wives free time to help with the gardens and fields," one of the men said. "The men have been rebuilding houses and taking turns digging the well."

"That is good to hear," Li said. "I will be checking our progress every few days."

"How is King Yitzhak?" one of the men asked. "We heard he was injured."

"He is finally awake," Li said. "It will be a couple of weeks before he can do much. He has broken ribs, a broken arm and a broken leg."

"We are blessed that you are able to lead us while he heals," the oldest man said. "At first, I didn't think it possible, but my family was one of the ones that sought shelter in the palace. You saw my granddaughter on the brink of death from the cold and ordered her be put near the fire. Soon she had dry clothing and a blanket."

"I am glad to hear she is well now," Li said before turning her horse towards the palace.

The first council meeting was scheduled for just after lunch, but Li wasn't certain anyone would show up since everyone was so busy cleaning up from the storm. Li went to eat lunch with Yitzhak.

"How is the cleanup coming?" Yitzhak asked.

"I'm encouraged by how everyone is helping each other," Li said as servants brought in the food. "The harbor is still blocked by a sunken ship. I'm not certain how they are going to get it raised. The paper maker found some of his things were still usable."

Lenar began to sit Yitzhak up.

"Slowly," Yitzhak said. "I don't want to get sick again."

"Yes, My King," Lenar said. "That bedding is still drying."

He helped Yitzhak sit propped up by pillows and folded blankets against the head of the bed. His face looked pale until he had settled.

"Moving to try sitting up makes me nauseous," Yitzhak said after a few minutes. "I can't imagine losing everything and having to start over from nothing."

"I hope everyone will have enough food until the gardens and fields are ready to harvest," Li said. "We might need to request help from Alessandrine and Okiah."

Once they had eaten Li went up to the meeting room next to the throne room. She was soon joined by Joris and Yuri. The guard left the door open.

"I heard rumor that people have chosen their representatives," Yuri said.

"I wondered if the storm would delay their decision on choosing people to represent them," Li said as they heard footsteps in the hall.

A guard appeared in the doorway followed by two men and two women.

"Come in and take seats," Li said with a smile. "We're so glad you are here."

The two women sat together on one side of the table and the men on the other side.

"Let's start with introductions," Li said. "This is Joris and Yuri who have been advisors to King Yitzhak since before King Tokar died."

The women glanced at each other as one of the men said, "My name is Marden. I am a farmer."

"My name is Lazlo," the other man said. "I am a weaver I'm hoping these meetings don't take up too much time. My wife is still learning to weave, and I have orders to fill."

"The meetings will be once a month unless something important comes up," Li said. "If anyone brings something to your attention that needs to be addressed, let us know."

The man nodded.

"I am Ru," one of the women said. "I was very surprised to be chosen for this."

"I am called Mi, but I prefer MiMi," the other woman said. "I am not certain what is expected of us, but I'll do my best."

"These meetings are to help King Yitzhak and me know what is going on with our people. Here in the palace, we are isolated and we need to understand the lives of the people. We have made so much progress since I became King Yitzhak's wife, but there is still more that needs to be done," Li explained. "Joris' wife, Fa, commented to him that the women still feel invisible. We don't want that to continue. That is why we took Joris' advice to have women on the council."

The men looked surprised.

"Today's meeting will focus on the rebuilding efforts. Since Yitzhak was injured I have been inspecting the town and I have seen progress, but we need to know from you what needs to be done."

"We have been most grateful for the fresh water while the new well is being dug," Ru said. "We ran a fish trap down the old well and hopefully got the last of the fish out. We've been using that water and river water to wash clothes and wash mud from the homes still standing."

"In time the water should be safe to drink again," Marden said. "I tasted it yesterday and it was still salty."

"Actually it has relieved the lines for water since not everyone is drawing water for drinking," MiMi said. "Having the second well will help. It is good to know the water will be drinkable again."

Marden and Lazlo glanced at each other.

"Sometimes leaves and other things wind up in the well," Ru added. "I have wondered if a roof over the well would protect it from that."

"A roof over it and maybe a removable cover would protect the water," Li agreed. "I'll tell the men building the well to put a roof and a cover on the new well and the old one."

Yuri made a note of the decision. Li laid out the map she had been working on.

"When I was trying to account for all of the families and houses Kon, the healer, mentioned that in Brinley many of the roads have names and there are numbers on the houses," Li said. "I've been working on that to make it easier to find people and their houses."

"I've always called this road Hobble Road because my father found a pair of hobbles in the road once," Marden said pointing to one road Li had labeled Straight Road.

Li crossed out Straight Road and wrote in Hobble Road.

"I call this Spinners Lane because four spinners live on this road," Lazlo added pointing to a short road. "And this one Wool Circle."

Li added the names to the roads he pointed to.

"She who bore me, my mother, called this Mourning Way," MiMi said pointing to the road that passed the women's cemetery.

"Why?" Lazlo asked.

"This is where the women are buried," Li said, pointing to the cemetery.

"Oh," Lazlo said quietly.

"I've always called this road Water Way," Ru said indicating the road along the river.

"I've called it River Road." Marden said.

"Okay, let's call this portion Water Way and the other side of this bend River Road," Li said, and both nodded.

Everyone made suggestions and soon the roads all had names. After that they discussed the progress made in rebuilding homes for the people who lost theirs. The mill was still being repaired and dried out so flour could be made. Food supplies were also discussed. It was nearing supper time when they finished their meeting.

"This has been a most productive meeting," Li said. "I thank you all for your time and participation. We will meet again in thirty days unless anything comes up that we need to meet as a council to address. By then Yitzhak will be healed enough to attend."

Marden stayed as the others left the room.

"I had wondered what value my opinion would be to you and King Yitzhak," he said. "I'll admit that I wondered the same about the women, but I can see now you need all of us on this council."

"Even kings and queens have trouble making decisions sometimes," Li said. "Especially when we haven't experienced the problem ourselves."

"I noticed you were able to make everyone happy with the road names even when I saw a conflict," Marden said.

"Once the names are posted I'm certain there will be some conflict, but we'll work it out," Li said. "Soon everyone will be using the same road names and people will be easier to find."

"I'd best get back to Wool Circle before my supper gets cold," Marden laughed. "I found out that my wife really hates it when I'm late for supper. I'm really glad King Yitzhak changed the laws so women are valued as equals now. Now all the men know what I realized long ago, women are important. With sheep you only need one male, but without females you don't get any new lambs. The herd doesn't grow and eventually it dies out."

"Yitzhak once told me that without me he would still be blind and Mannton would not survive," Li said.

"Without you leading while he is injured Mannton would not survive," Marden said before he bowed and left.

Chapter 30 – Expanding the Map

The next morning Li went downstairs to have breakfast with Yitzhak. She took the map with her to show him what progress was being made. As he took a bite of the porridge he made a sour face.

"This tastes wrong and smells like flowers," he said.

"Let me see it," Li said.

She smelled the porridge and it smelled right to her. She took a small bite and could taste the honey mixed into the cooked oats.

"It smells and tastes fine to me," she said as she set it back on his lap tray.

The guard approached the bed and said, "Last year my father complained about the smell and taste of things after falling and banging his head on the floor. It was several weeks before he said things started smelling and tasting normal. He didn't like noise or bright sunshine either."

"I had been thinking about letting the children play in here while I'm healing," Yitzhak said. "It is boring just lying here with nothing to do."

"You are too used to being busy," Li said. "I'll speak to Ni about bringing the children down for a while. I will let them know they need to be quiet. I brought the map to show you what I've been up to."

The servant again began helping Yitzhak eat. Once they finished eating Li brought over the map. The guard and the servant helped hold it up for him to see.

Yitzhak reached out and touched a name with an x next to it. Then he touched the house with an x over it that was next to the name.

"There have been a few deaths and some homes were completely washed away by the storm and flooding," Li said and saw a tear roll down his cheek. "The harbor is still blocked by a ship, but they are trying to raise it. The docks are mostly repaired, and other ships are being repaired."

"You put names on the streets," Yitzhak said.

"With the help of the council," Li replied. "I'll number the houses and shops so we can find people more easily."

"What's this?" Yitzhak said as he pointed to a spot on the map.

"A new well," Li said. "The old well had salt water and fish washed into it during the storm. People have been coming to the palace for drinking water. This new well will serve many people and the old well will soon be fit to drink again."

"You have been busy," Yitzhak said. "I want to be up and helping, but just moving makes me so sick. The broken ribs hurt more than the broken arm and leg."

"You are helping me by healing," Li said as she began to fold up the map. "Your quick actions saved the lives of those two guards who in turn saved your life. You are safely home where I can consult with you when I need advice. You are already giving me the strength and hope I need to lead this kingdom while you heal."

Yitzhak reached up and stroked her cheek. Suddenly Li had an idea.

"I remember seeing some books among Queen Lodena's things," Li said. "Would you like them brought down so you could do some reading?"

"I'd like that," he replied. "We haven't read any of her journals. It might give us some more information."

"I'll have them brought down to you. I need to go get more filled out on the map before holding audiences this afternoon," Li said before kissing his lips.

He smiled and stroked her cheek before she stood up. Soon she had the servants finding Queen Lodena's books and went to talk to Ni and the children. Ni promised to keep the children busy with quiet toys while playing in Yitzhak's room.

Lenar was waiting for her in the courtyard. They headed towards the part of the city they hadn't visited yet. Repairs were underway and the mud was starting to dry. Someone found a table and fixed the legs so the map could be laid out. Soon people were filling in missing names and drawing in homes.

"What is this written on the road?" one woman asked pointing to the street they were on.

"We've named the streets," Li explained. "We named this one Center Street because it runs through the center of town. Soon we will put up street signs and even number the houses and shops. Mannton is growing and it will help everyone find the people or shops they are looking for."

"How will you number the houses?" someone asked.

"We haven't decided how yet," Li admitted.

"My grandfather was blind. He would count how many steps it took to get to places," someone else said.

"That could work well for numbering the homes and shops," Li said.

"Why is this road called Mourning Way?" a man asked.

"Because this is the women's cemetery," Li said as she pointed to the empty space.

"I always wondered why there was a border of stones around that, and no one had built there," he said. "It should have a stone wall or wooden fence. It should have a sign, so everyone knows."

"Yes," Li agreed. "With so much rebuilding going on we don't want someone trying to build there. Perhaps we can start with a simple wooden fence and a sign. After everyone is back in their own home, we can work on a stone wall and nicer sign."

"My son wants so much to help build something," one man said. "Maybe he and his friends could work on that after school."

"That would be a great help," Li said. "Over by the river some of the homes have stones stacked around the outside walls. It protected them from the worst of the water. I believe it would be a good idea to do that with any new homes built and to add that to the existing homes."

"My family has been tossing stones into the woods behind our home for generations, but that would be a great use for them," another man said.

By lunch time the rest of the map had been filled in, but Li realized that Rowan and Anunik's homes were not on the map. She returned to the palace to have lunch and take audiences. She had been a bit surprised that there were so many audiences with the cleanup and rebuilding going on.

When she opened the audiences the first audience was called forward. It was a man who was dirty and tired looking.

"My name is Rand. I come representing my family and neighbors," the man said after bowing. "We live a half day's travel to the west. We have five families living in the only house still standing. We need help rebuilding."

"Being isolated from the city would make it difficult to rebuild," Li said. "No family has remained untouched by the storm."

"You cannot understand how we have suffered with some of us injured and a couple dead," Rand countered in an almost angry tone.

"King Yitzhak went out to check on the people when the storm subsided not knowing the storm was not completely over," Li said. "When the storm returned, he and his guards sought shelter in a tree, but a branch broke and he was injured. He has broken bones and was unconscious for three days. That is why his throne is empty today."

"I am sorry," Rand said in a softer tone. "I did not know."

"I have been making a map showing all the homes and the names of who lives in them," Li said. "Now I will be working on recording those homes that are outside the city. My own brother's home is not yet on the map. It sounds like your immediate need is shelter while rebuilding."

One of the guards stepped forward and bowed.

"There are the tents that the army uses, My Queen," the guard said. "They will sleep six grown men."

"Even two of those tents would really help," Rand said. "It is difficult to sleep without enough room to lie down."

"You may stay the night here and return home with two tents," Li said. "After the audiences I want you to update our map."

"Of course. Thank you, My Queen," Rand said as he bowed.

Most of the other audiences had something to do with the rebuilding efforts. The last audience was two men wanting to build a shop.

"I am Ervin and this is Drake. We noticed a large plot of unused land near the forest," one man said. "It has a border of stones around it. That would be a good place to build our shop."

"If it is the plot of land I think it is, then you must not disturb that land," Li said. "I will have you point it out on our map to confirm my suspicions."

"Why?" Drake asked.

"Because it is the women's cemetery," Li said, and the men looked stunned.

"We definitely would not want to disturb the dead," Drake said.

"I have someone that will be building a fence around it to prevent it from being disturbed," Li said. "We will find a place for you to build a shop. What type of shop will it be?"

"I am a wheelwright and Drake is a blacksmith. We are looking for someone who is a carpenter so we can build wagons and other things," Ervin explained.

"I'm certain that there are many wagons and plows that need repair after the storm," Li said as she stood. "The map is in the office. Come with me. Rand, you come as well."

The three men followed her as the rest of the people dispersed. Lenar hurried on ahead and had the map spread out on her desk when they arrived.

"Rand, please use this to draw in the group of homes as they were before the storm," Li said and handed him a stick of charcoal.

Soon he had them drawn on the map. Li marked the damaged homes, and she got the names from him of the living and the dead.

"Lenar, please find Rand quarters for tonight and some clean clothes to wear while his are washed. Fill a tub for him to bathe in," Li said.

"Of course, My Queen," Lenar said.

"Thank you," Rand said with a tremor in his voice.

Li understood he had been through a lot. His wife was one of the dead. After they left Li turned back to the map.

"Show me the plot of land you were wanting to build on," Li said.

"You have it marked here as the women's cemetery," Ervin said. "I'm glad we decided to ask permission rather than just start building."

"I am glad as well," Li said as she looked over the map.

Soon she found an area that was about the same size plus it had an additional narrow area jutting out from it.

"This looks like a similar size," Li said as she pointed it out. "This long narrow part could be a row of stables to keep horses in or for storage."

"I like that idea," Drake said. "Sometimes horses need to be left if I can't get to them right away."

"It's tucked behind several gardens," Ervin said. "I hope that won't be a problem."

"This short end on the street can be the main entrance," Li said. "I don't know much about what you do, but it seems that there would be noise and smoke. By being behind gardens you will be farther from homes where people might be bothered by that."

"I never thought about that," Ervin said.

"There's definitely a lot of noise and smoke," Drake said. "I see the well is close by too."

"A second well is nearly finished here," Li said as she pointed it out. "That will shorten the lines at the old well."

She drew a line around the plot of land for the new shop.

"What are you calling your shop?" Li asked and the men shrugged their shoulders. "I'll just put 'Repair Shop' and your names for now."

"Thank you for finding us a place to build our shop," Drake said. "We should go talk to people living in that area, so they know what we are doing."

"It's important for people to help each other while we are rebuilding after the storm," Li said. "We can rebuild faster by working together."

The men left and Lenar returned.

"We need to check on the other isolated groups of homes," Li said.

"Perhaps you should send some guards to collect the information," Lenar suggested.

"That's a good idea," Li said. "I'm going down to talk to Yitzhak."

She found him propped up in bed asleep. The servant watching over him quickly met her by the door.

"He sleeps better propped up than lying flat," the servant whispered. "He says it hurts less to breath."

"That's what matters," Li said softly.

"Li," Yitzhak said as his eyes opened.

"We didn't mean to disturb you," Li said as she crossed to his side.

"I heard your voice," Yitzhak said as she sat down. "How were the audiences?"

Li told him about Rand and the two men building the repair shop.

"Lenar suggested sending guards out to collect the information on the groups of homes outside of the town," Li said.

"Definitely," Yitzhak agreed. "With me stuck in bed, you need to remain here to rule. It will take time for roads and trails to be easily passable again."

"It will be good to complete the map," Li said. "Already it has helped me make decisions. It is good to know where there are places to build within the town."

Yitzhak yawned.

"I should go so you can sleep. I need to speak with the guards and get some volunteers," Li said and leaned over to kiss his lips.

"Good night," Yitzhak said after kissing her.

Li stood and left the room. Two of the four guards followed her.

"I need to speak to the Captain of the guards," Li said. "Bring him to the office."

"At once, My Queen," one of the guards said and quickly headed towards the palace doors.

The other guard followed her to the office and waited outside the door. Soon after she sat down an older man came in. Although he was not in uniform or armor, he carried himself like a guard.

"Captain Ludwig at your service," the man said.

"I am in need of a few volunteers to collect information for this map," Li said, and he stepped closer to look at the map. "We have small groups of homes that are outside of the town."

She pointed out the homes Rand had drawn in and then Rowan and Anunik's homes.

"There are probably additional groups that are not on this map," Li said. "We need to know where they are, how many homes and the names of the people. We need to know how many homes were destroyed and who died."

"I know the perfect men for this job," Captain Ludwig said. "One comes from an outlying settlement and the other two were scouts in the army. They know all of Mannton and will be able to find other settlements."

"The man who came from this settlement said they only had one home for all five families to shelter in. I am sending two tents home with him, so they have shelter while they rebuild," Li said as she pointed to Rand's settlement. "I want them to take some extra tents in case they are needed."

"Since we are at peace with our immediate neighbors, we have little need of the tents right now," he said as he nodded. "I've noticed some of the people in town sheltering with others or in shelters crudely built against what is left of their homes."

"I'll trust your judgement on who needs the tents, but you have my permission to distribute them," Li said. "I also need some guards to pace out distances to assign numbers to homes and shops. I can explain it to them in detail."

"I'll get some guards assigned to distributing the tents and to pacing out for the numbering," Captain Ludwig said. "How is King Yitzhak doing? The men who were with him were not certain he could survive his injuries."

"He is anxious to get up," Li said. "When he tries the pain and nausea remind him to stay in bed. Once the nausea goes away, we'll move him back up to the royal quarters and see if his leg can bear any weight for short periods of time."

"It is a great relief to know he is healing," Captain Ludwig said. "I wondered how Mannton would survive, but you have restored my faith that we will."

"I know it took time for the guards to accept me as queen of Mannton," Li said, and he nodded. "I promise you I will continue to be a ruler you can have faith in. I consult with Yitzhak now that he has regained consciousness. We are a team and stronger together."

"All lingering doubts I had about you vanished when the storm struck and King Yitzhak was missing. You stood strong as a leader should," Captain Ludwig said. "I will arrange for the men to leave in the morning."

"Thank you," Li said.

He bowed and left. She leaned back in her chair and sighed. She was grateful she did not have to rule totally alone like Yitzhak and the kings before him had. She folded up the map before going up to the nursery.

Tokar and An ran over to her and hugged her tightly. She hugged them back. Feeling them breathe against her seemed to restore her. When they went back to playing Ni brought Ta over to her. She kissed the tiny face and smiled as Ta yawned before snuggling closer to her. She sat holding Ta watching the children play until a servant brought the children's supper in. As soon as Ni had Tokar and An eating Li handed Ta to her.

She went to the royal quarters and soon Ka brought her supper in to her. The food was good, but she was tired.

"I believe I will retire early tonight," Li said as she stood. "I'm tired."

"You have been working so hard and you are still recovering from giving birth to Princess Ta," Ka said as she followed Li into the bed chamber. Soon she was settled into bed and asleep.

Chapter 31 – Signs of Healing

After three weeks Li had completed the map and the guards had completed pacing out for numbering the homes and shops. Twice a week Li inspected the town. Rebuilding was going slowly, but the roads were passable by wagon and carriage. The fields and gardens had plants pushing up through the layer of dried mud but showed the effects of the storm with crooked rows. The old well had a new roof and cover. The new well had water and the men were working on adding the top and roof for it.

As the days progressed Yitzhak slowly got better. It was nearly four weeks after the storm that he no longer got nauseous when he sat up. He was having less pain while breathing and the swelling was down in his arm and leg. He was getting anxious to get back to the royal quarters. Kon checked on him once a week.

"So, when can I get back into my own bed?" Yitzhak grumbled and Li struggled to not laugh.

"I think you will survive being carried up the stairs now," Kon replied.

"Carried!?" Yitzhak rebelled at the idea.

"You are barely ready to start putting weight on that leg," Kon said. "It will be at least a week before I will adjust the splints to allow you to bend your knee."

"And when are you going to let me put on some real clothes?" Yitzhak asked in a bitter tone.

"I brought you a surprise," Li said and went to the table.

She brought back the pants and shirt she had made that could be fastened over the splints.

"The right pant leg is normal, but the left side wraps around and buttons down the inside of the left leg," Li said as she held up the pants. "The shirt opens on the right side and buttons up like the pants."

"That's much better than the robe I was going to suggest," Kon said.

"Yes, it is," Yitzhak agreed. "Thank you, Li."

Li helped Kon get Yitzhak dressed before calling in two guards to help him out of the room. Two more guards were waiting in the hall with a chair fastened to two poles. Yitzhak was able to support his left leg on the pole. They carefully lifted him and carried him upstairs to the royal quarters. Two of the guards helped him to sit on the bed.

"It is gratifying to see you are healing, My King," one of the guards commented. "I just wish we could have protected you better that night."

"You saved my life that night," Yitzhak replied.

"And you saved ours," the guard said. "My children still have a father because of your quick thinking."

"And so do mine," Yitzhak said.

The guard bowed and left. Yitzhak wiped a tear away just before Kon came into the room.

"I noticed downstairs you were putting weight on your broken leg," Kon said. "How was the pain?"

"Bearable," Yitzhak said. "I'm not ready to walk on it, but I can balance with it."

"I noticed you gripping the chair with your right hand. How painful was that?

"More than I thought it would be, but I can at least move my fingers now," Yitzhak said to Li's relief.

"Good," Kon said. "Now, just a reminder. Don't do anything that will aggravate your injuries. Take your time using your arm and leg. Bones take time to heal."

"I'm learning that," Yitzhak said with a sigh.

"And I am learning that kings don't make good patients," Kon said with a laugh. "But neither do healers."

"You are both stubborn and used to giving orders, not taking them," Li said, and Yitzhak finally laughed.

"I've got other patients to tend to," Kon said. "I'll see you next week unless you send for me."

Yitzhak nodded and Kon bowed before leaving.

"I'll sleep better now," Li said. "I've missed your snoring."

Yitzhak laughed.

"Go get the children," Yitzhak said.

Li passed several servants bringing up books and the chamber pot chair on her way to the nursery.

"Mother!" An said and ran to her with Tokar close behind.

"I have a surprise for you," Li said as she took Ta from Ni. "Follow me."

Ni followed behind the children. They seemed confused when she led them into the bedroom of the royal quarters.

"Father!" they cried in unison.

"You are wearing clothes," An said. "Can you get up and play with us?"

"Not yet, but I am feeling better," Yitzhak said. "Get up here so I can give you each a quick hug."

"Be gentle," Li cautioned them as they climbed up on the bed.

Yitzhak hugged Tokar and then An, kissing them both.

"I want to hold Ta for a while," he said as they got down off the bed.

Li carefully settled Ta in his left arm. She looked up at him.

"She has grown so much," Yitzhak said then kissed Ta's face.

"She has," Li commented as Tokar and An started exploring the room. "They all have."

"Yes, they have," he replied.

"I have a couple of meetings I need to go to," Li said and kissed him. "I'll see you later."

Li went to the office. Soon after she sat down at her desk the guards opened the door. Drake the blacksmith came in followed by another man.

"Thank you for coming," Li said as she opened a desk drawer and drew out two papers. "Please sit down. It's time for the women's cemetery to have both a name and a sign."

The men sat down.

"Drake, I noticed that the repair shop has been built and is doing a good business," Li said, and Drake nodded. "I want you to create a sign over the entrance to the cemetery."

"I noticed the stone wall being built around the cemetery," Drake said. "I saw there were two square pillars marking the entrance."

"I want you to work with the young men building the wall so the sign will be solidly connected to the stone pillars," Li said. "Here is what the sign should say."

"Queen Lodena Memorial Cemetery," Drake read aloud.

"I thought you were Mannton's first queen," the other man said.

"Actually, Mannton had queens before Queen Lodena, but her death began the enslavement of the women of Mannton," Li said as she passed the other paper to him. "Her story needs to be told and that is where I need your talents."

The man began to read, and Drake leaned over to read the page as well. Li gave them time to finish. Soon they looked up at her with wide eyes.

"I need you to carve that into a stone monument that will be placed at the entrance," Li said. "When the stone is placed, we will at last bury the remains of Queen Lodena and her daughter, Princess Cora. Their names should be carved on the other side. We will have a ceremony during which we will tell the full story to the people of Mannton."

"I'm grateful that the laws have changed," the man said, and Drake nodded.

"We are working to reverse the laws King Ulric made in his grief and despair when Queen Lodena and Princess Cora died," Li said. "It is time for everyone to know why and how it all began. I want the monument made from durable stone."

"I will start on it immediately, My Queen," the man said.

"I've never made anything quite like this, but I'm excited to get it started," Drake said. "How is King Yitzhak doing?"

"Much better," Li said. "He's anxious to get back on his feet, but it will take another three or four weeks at least. I want these ready so we can schedule the ceremony as soon as King Yitzhak is able to attend."

"We had best get to work," Drake said as he stood up. "I need to figure out how to make letters and assemble them into a sign. I think I'll start by making a sign for the Repair Shop. We decided to keep the name you gave it."

Li smiled and said, "I look forward to seeing what you come up with."

The men left and Li stood up. She picked up the map before heading to the meeting room. Several men were already waiting for her.

"Thank you for coming. It's time to put up road signs and house numbers," Li said as she laid out the map. "This is what I've come up with."

"So each house will have a number?" one of the men asked.

"Actually each property will have a number," Li said. "That way we can keep track of empty lots as well. We'll consider the palace as the center of town. We have Center Street that goes all the way through town and Main Street that does the same. They cross here in front of the palace. All the numbers start at the end of the road closest to these two streets and counts up."

"I see," another man said as he traced several roads with his finger.

"You've numbered the homes outside of the town," the first man observed.

"Yes," Li said. "As Mannton grows we need to keep better records than we have in the past. This is the start of that. What I need from you are signs with the road names carved into them and then painted. Then we need number signs for each home and business building."

"I have something that stains the wood red and lasts longer than paint," one man said. "It's a bit like dying fabric."

"Yes," Li said as she remembered the buttons she had made for Yitzhak's jacket. "That might be better than paint. I want the street signs on posts where roads cross or join each other. The numbers can be attached directly to the buildings near or above the doors."

"I don't know if people will like that," another man said.

"That's why we will start with the street signs," Li said. "If people ask about the street signs, tell them about the house numbers."

"I'll put numbers on my house," one of the men said and others nodded.

"Thank you," Li said. "Have all of you gotten your homes repaired or rebuilt?"

"I just started putting the roof on my new home," one man said.

"Mine still needs some repair, but it will be done soon," another said, and others nodded.

"While I want this done as soon as possible, do not neglect your duty to your family to provide them a sound home," Li said as she got out some paper. "Divide up who will carve which signs. The ones that are outside of the town can be installed by guards if necessary."

She got out a couple of bottles of ink and a pen for each man.

"I have another meeting I need to go to now," Li said. "There is a guard outside the door that can escort you out when you are done."

She left them to make their lists and went to the office. Soon the guards let in a young man who walked with a limp and a cane.

"Come in and take a seat," Li said.

"Thank you for making some time for me," the man said. "I know you must be very busy."

"Yes," Li replied. "I understand you are offering your services, but your note did not specify what services exactly you are offering, Nathan."

"I have been a fisherman like my father before me, but I was injured on one trip and lost my leg below my knee," Nathan said. "It happened about a month before the storm. I don't want to go back out on a boat even though I can get around on a wooden leg. I heard about the school and thought you might be looking for someone to teach the children."

"Yes," Li said. "We also hold classes for women who want to learn to read and write."

"I would be happy to teach them as well," Nathan said. "My home was destroyed in the storm so I am living with my family until I can earn money to pay someone to build me a home."

"I'll send word to Marnah that you will be starting soon as a teacher," Li said. "She has been teaching the classes, but we need more teachers so she can continue assisting Kon with his patients."

"I might know of a couple of people that might be interested," Nathan said. "Would you want more taught than just reading and writing?"

"I'm certain there are other things that would be beneficial to be taught in school classes," Li replied, intrigued by the idea.

"Write up proposals for any classes you think would be good. I will speak with King Yitzhak and we will discuss that idea."

"I'll get the proposals written up and delivered tomorrow," he said. "When do you want me to start teaching?"

"I'll speak with Marnah tomorrow," Li said. "Deliver the proposals the day after tomorrow and I will have an answer for you."

"Thank you," Nathan said as he stood up. "I will see you the day after tomorrow."

As he left a servant came in and bowed.

"King Yitzhak is asking for you, My Queen," the servant said. "He said it was important."

Li returned to the royal quarters. As she entered the bedroom something felt different. Yitzhak motioned her over to the bed.

"You met with the blacksmith and the stonecutter," Yitzhak said quietly, and Li nodded. "She is grateful. It is time to clean and repair the original royal quarters. She wants us to claim it as our own."

"I've never been in there," Li said.

"The key is in the top left drawer of my desk," Yitzhak said. "It's time for you to see it."

Li nodded. She put her hand on his shoulder for a moment before returning to the office to get the key. She found the strangely shaped key and went to the tapestry in the main hall. Two servants were coming down the hall.

"I need this tapestry moved," Li said, and they glanced at each other.

"Why would you want it moved?" one of the men asked.

"Because it covers the doors to the original royal quarters," Li said. "It is time to clean it up so it can be used again."

She pulled the corner back to reveal the doors.

"Where do you want it moved to?" the other asked.

"I don't know. Measure it and see if you can find some locations it would fit," Li said. "I'll decide after you show me where it will fit."

She unlocked the doors and entered the room. Light spilled in from the windows. The sitting room was dusty from being sealed for generations. There seemed to be a few pieces of furniture missing. The doors to the bedchamber stood open. She walked in and could see the room was wrecked. Much of the furniture that remained was broken. She walked over to the windows and noticed the remains of the cradle near the wall. She was saddened by the large blood stain on and around the cradle. She felt like she wasn't alone.

"It is time to set things right," Li said. "The nation is ready to know the full truth of the past. Your story will be known. Your bodies will be laid to rest where the women who died after your death have been buried. The cemetery will then be closed to new burials."

She felt at peace. The room would take a lot of work to clean and get it ready to be occupied. As she turned towards the doors a servant woman came into the room.

"What happened in here?" the woman gasped.

"The rage of a grieving man whose wife and daughter died," Li replied. "It is time for these rooms to be cleaned and readied to be the royal quarters again. I know it will be a lot of work, but we have several weeks to get it done."

"There's so little furniture," she said.

"Most of the missing furniture is in the attic storage room that had been sealed."

"I'll get some women organized to start cleaning them right away."

"Thank you," Li said.

"I came to tell you that your supper is ready."

"Deliver it to the royal quarters. King Yitzhak will be happy when he's allowed to eat at the table again," Li said. "At least he's back in the royal quarters."

Chapter 32 – Help Wanted

Yitzhak sat impatiently while Kon put the new splints on his leg. He had been putting a little weight on the leg when he was moved from the bed to the chamber pot chair and back, but it was still painful.

"Now you will probably be a bit stiff, but I want you to work on bending your knee," Kon said. "Keep your knee straight when putting weight on it, but as you are sitting on the edge of the bed or on a chair work on bending and straightening your leg."

"What about my arm?" Yitzhak asked.

"I don't even have to ask if you've been working with your fingers," Kon said. "If you feel the need to use it just be careful. If it hurts don't do it. There are two bones in your lower arm. You don't want either of them shifting. If you must put any weight on it as you are moving in bed, try to keep your elbow straight and your hand in a fist to keep the wrist straight. No twisting. Same goes for your leg, no twisting. Your lower leg has two bones that allow your leg and ankle to twist. Once the splints come off you can work on rotating your arm and leg."

"I still get bad headaches sometimes that last more than a day," Yitzhak said.

"You took a couple of hard knocks to your head," Kon said. "Your skull is hard, but the brain it protects can get bruised like any other part of your body. I can't say if those headaches will completely go away or if you will continue to have them periodically."

Yitzhak frowned.

"I know," Kon said softly. "My father had an evil temper. Once he hit me so hard I banged my head into the wall. I woke up three days later with a bandage on my head. After that he tried keeping his temper in check, but he would still beat us. I still get bad headaches sometimes."

"What do you do to relieve the pain?" Yitzhak asked.

"The numbing herb helps," Kon said. "I am most grateful to Queen Li for that. I stay inside with the curtains closed. Sometimes

263

I wrap my head with a wet towel. Mostly you just have to wait it out."

"Thank you for talking to me about it," Yitzhak said. "Li has had to handle everything. She talks to me about what is going on, but she is proving herself a capable leader. I don't know what I would do without her."

"You were most wise to choose her for a wife," Kon said. "I must be going, but don't forget my instructions."

"No twisting or rotating my arm or leg. No weight unless the knee or elbow is straight. Work on bending my knee and working my fingers," Yitzhak replied.

"Good," Kon said. "I'll see you next week."

Yitzhak ran the fingers of his left hand through his hair as he watched Kon leave. Li had been able to handle ruling Mannton as though she was born to it.

****

Li climbed the stairs to the attic storage room where Queen Lodena's belongings had been stored. Several men followed her. She directed them in moving boxes and furniture until everything was sorted into manageable groups of items. She began to recognize which pieces of furniture belonged in which room.

She got the men to arrange the furniture into three groups. One group belonged in the bedchamber, a second that belonged in the sitting room and a third that she wasn't certain of.

"That will be all for now," Li said. "As we get the rooms cleaned, we will begin to bring these down and clean them."

The men bowed and followed her out of the room. Lenar greeted her halfway down the stairs.

"The tapestry has been cleaned and rehung where you instructed us to," he said. "There might be a problem though."

"What is the problem?" she asked.

"Come see for yourself," Lenar replied and led her to where the tapestry was hung.

Li saw a tapestry with vibrant colors showing a battle scene. It looked nothing like the tapestry she remembered hanging over the doors.

"How did you clean this?" Li asked as she touched the tapestry.

"We used sponges to dab it with soapy water and then rinsed it with clean water the same way," Lenar replied. "When we were going to put it back up we noticed a corner had dragged on the floor through muddy boot prints. When we cleaned the mud off the corner, we realized the patterns on the tapestry weren't random. We saw a horse's hoof and tail."

Li looked around at other nearby tapestries. All of them were dull and dirty. She sighed knowing what had to be done.

"You and I both know all of them need to be cleaned," Li said, and he nodded. "Do them one by one starting in the throne room and front entrance. They can be rearranged as you clean them."

"We can start with the one covering the door in the throne room and put it in place of the next one to be cleaned."

"I'll let you determine the order they are cleaned and where they are placed."

"I noticed the back of the tapestry was cleaner than the front and easier to make out the scene. I'll get some idea of what the scene on each tapestry is about before starting and arrange the cleaning appropriately for where they will wind up."

"Perfect," Li said. "I want this to be a surprise for King Yitzhak. It will take him another several weeks to be able to come out of the royal quarters. There is a lot to be done in the original royal quarters too."

"I've heard there are some people that are still trying to get their lives back together," Lenar said. "Could I hire some of them to help?"

"Of course," Li said. "Getting paid to help clean the old royal quarters and the tapestries could help them get their lives back together. I don't see the need to make them commit to a certain number of days or to stay until the cleaning is complete. They can work as many or as few hours or days as they want. We'll determine an hourly pay rate."

Lenar nodded as Ka approached followed by several servants each carrying a tray of food.

"It is lunchtime," Ka said. "Will you be taking lunch in the royal quarters or in the office?"

"In the royal quarters," Li replied. "I need to find out what Kon told King Yitzhak."

She led Ka to the royal quarters. In the sitting room they found Yitzhak sitting in a chair bending his knee and then straightening it.

"Kon changed your splints!" Li said.

"I'm so looking forward to eating at a table," Yitzhak said. "Maybe the children could come eat with us."

"I'll go let Ni know and have their lunches brought in here," Ka said and left.

"I can't put weight on my leg while my knee is bent and I can't twist my leg to turn, but I can get around much easier," Yitzhak said with a smile.

"Father!" Tokar exclaimed as he ran in. "You are out of bed!"

"Father!" An shouted as she followed on Tokar's heels.

"Come sit down and eat," Yitzhak said as servants brought in the children's lunch.

Li enjoyed having lunch with Yitzhak and the children. She held Ta while the children chattered and asked Yitzhak questions. She could tell he was much happier to be out of bed. He even held Ta for a while before admitting his leg was hurting and he needed to put it up.

The children went back to the nursery and Li went to the office. She had started going over the finances of the kingdom. The taxes collected were enough to support the kingdom including paying the teachers. The servants had reported several leaks in the roof after the big storm. They needed to be fixed before anything was damaged. She knew that she really needed an assistant. Lenar had been so helpful but was busy with other duties.

"Does something trouble you, My Queen?" Lenar's voice broke into her thoughts.

"I really need an assistant," Li said. "You have your own duties. Even when King Yitzhak is back on his feet and ruling the kingdom, we need an assistant."

"Do you want me to find some people to interview?" Lenar asked.

"Let me speak to King Yitzhak first," Li said as she stood up. "Getting someone to fix the leaks in the roof is more pressing."

"Of course," Lenar said. "I expect someone tomorrow morning to start on the roof. I've been working on getting some additional help to clean the tapestries. I'm working on the list of what order to clean the tapestries and where they'll end up."

"Thank you," Li said. "I don't think I could keep things running as well without you. I know that first morning when you discovered I had slept in the royal quarters with King Yitzhak you were shocked and might have thought I had poisoned his mind somehow, but I'm grateful that you realized the truth."

"I am too," Lenar admitted as she walked toward the door. "I am so much happier than I thought possible because instead of simply being my wife, Ka is my friend and companion. That is all thanks to you."

Li smiled and patted his shoulder before heading to the royal quarters. Yitzhak was on the settee with his leg up on it. He looked up from his reading and smiled at her.

"I've been thinking that we need an assistant," Li said. "The kingdom is growing and even with the council we need someone that can run errands for us, help us keep records and run messages."

"I've never thought about that before," Yitzhak admitted. "That would be great, especially while I'm healing."

"Lenar offered to find some people to interview," Li said. "Perhaps a husband and wife might be a good idea. That way we know they already get along and will communicate with each other."

Yitzhak nodded.

"They could live in the palace, so they wouldn't have the stress of keeping up a household," Li continued.

"I like that idea," Yitzhak said. "Perhaps we should offer it first to a couple who lost their home to the storm."

"Perfect. I'll let Lenar set up some appointments," Li said. "We'll interview them in here."

"Now that I'm out of bed I'll agree to that," he replied.

She laughed and kissed his cheek, but he pulled her closer and kissed her lips. She smiled as she stood up.

"I need to go assess the cleanup progress," she said. "I'll be back for supper."

Li found Lenar and he agreed to set up some interviews. She went to the courtyard and soon was headed out the gate with four guards. She was pleased to see a post with the new street signs across from the palace gate. The homes and businesses were showing signs of repair and people bowed as she passed. When she arrived at the harbor the sunken ship was gone and most of the small boats had been repaired. The old men were on the dock mending nets again. A young man ran up to her and bowed before her.

"My grandfather asks if he could speak with you for just a moment," he said as he rose.

"You are Marvin," she said as she recognized him.

"Yes, My Queen," he replied as his cheeks turned red.

She dismounted and he led her to the dock.

"Thank you, Marvin," the old man said, and the boy touched his forehead before leaving. "My son has been to the island and found it to be even more devastated than Mannton."

"Was anyone left alive?" Li asked with concern.

"Yes. They had retreated to some caves in the mountain at the center of the island, but reported deaths and injuries," the man replied. "They sent someone with him. They arrived this morning."

"I want to meet them," Li said, and the man nodded.

He took an object out of his pocket and put it to his lips. He blew a series of whistles and a reply came from a ship tied to the end of the dock. Soon two men and a woman came down a ramp from the ship to the dock. The woman wore a very short skirt and a piece of clothing that covered her breasts but not her stomach. It had a strap over one shoulder. One of the men wore short pants and no shirt, but several necklaces. Between them they carried large shell cradled in a woven basket with braided handles.

"Go fetch a carriage," Li said and one of the guards who was still mounted galloped towards the palace.

The three stopped before her.

"Queen Li, this is Bok and Na of Poco Island," the fisherman said. "My father was right to be concerned about the effects the storm had on their people. I have been delivering part of my catch to them so they have time to rebuild their homes."

"I am happy to meet you," Li said. "I know what the storm did to the people of Mannton. I imagine being on the island would have been even worse. A carriage will soon be here to take us to the palace, but while we wait, I think you should see an idea one of our people had to strengthen homes against storms and flooding."

The man and woman glanced at each other. They followed her to a nearby home.

"There were a few homes that had rocks piled along the outside before the storm," Li said, pointing to the rocks stacked along the bottoms of the walls. "They stayed mostly intact while the homes next to them were washed away."

"That is an interesting idea," the man said.

"There are many rocks on the island, Bok," the woman said. "If it will protect the homes from storms it is worth trying."

"Thank you for showing us this," Bok said as the carriage arrived.

"I notified King Yitzhak of the visitors, My Queen," the guard said as he helped her into the carriage. "He asked that you bring them to meet him."

"Come meet my husband," Li said. "He is still healing from being injured during the storm."

Soon Bok and Na were settled in the carriage with the shell on the floor between them.

"What did you bring with you?" Li asked.

"A gift," Na said cryptically. "I will explain later."

Soon they were pulling into the courtyard. Bok and Na seemed intimidated by the tall walls and massive stone palace.

"I was a bit frightened the first time I came to the palace," Li said quietly as the carriage stopped. "You are my guests and under my protection."

The two nodded. A guard helped them out of the carriage and soon they were inside.

"It's bigger than the cave inside," Na said, and Bok nodded.

Li led them up the stairs. Lenar was waiting at the top of the stairs.

"We have guests for supper," Li said and Lenar bowed. "They will need a place to stay tonight. They might be more comfortable in my old room."

"Of course, My Queen," Lenar said and left.

"It has a fireplace and a well," Li said as she led them down the hall toward the royal quarters. "I think you'll find it spacious, yet comfortable."

Yitzhak was sitting at the table with his leg propped up on a chair.

"This is my husband, King Yitzhak," Li said. "This is Bok and Na."

Each nodded their head as they were introduced.

"I saw you in my dreams, your leg, your arm," Na said. "The next morning I felt we would meet."

They set the large shell carefully on the table. The shell had a toggle pushed through a loop to keep it shut. Na pulled the toggle out of the loop and opened the shell. Inside were dozens of small figures carved from gleaming polished shells.

"A gift of friendship," Na said.

"Please sit down," Yitzhak said.

Bok and Na sat in chairs on either side of where the shell sat on the table. Li took a seat on a chair near Yitzhak.

"We have recently uncovered a part of Mannton's history that had been hidden and forgotten," Yitzhak said. "Some of what we learned is that several generations ago all the unmarried women and young girls were taken to your island to protect them. Later some of the women were brought back to Mannton, but it was not willingly."

"Our stories tell of women and girls being left on the island and found by our village," Bok said. "The women told of an angry king who hated women. Some women were stolen back. Since then, our people have feared the land of the angry king. The fishermen have been kind, but we still feared them."

Yitzhak nodded.

"Since the storm the fishermen have come to our aid and asked nothing in return," Bok said. "They saved us by delivering food. The island is healing, but there is so much to do and some of the trees we relied on for food lost all of their fruit in the storm."

"The whole village met and decided that enough time had passed that things must have changed in the land of the angry king. We were sent to find out if the fishermen spoke the truth of the change and petition for aid," Na continued. "We see that things are as the fishermen told us."

"Yes, it is time the truth comes to light now that the damage done by that angry king has been healed," Yitzhak said. "We will help as we can, but we are rebuilding from the storm."

"Let's send messages to Alessandrine and Okiah," Li suggested. "They may be able to send some assistance."

"Yes," Yitzhak agreed.

Bok and Na exchanged worried glances.

"We have a peace treaty with two neighboring nations," Li explained. "We will explain the needs of your island and our nation. They will send what assistance they can. It might be food or men to help rebuild."

"We would be very grateful for any assistance they can offer," Na said as there was a soft tap on the door. "We have lived in fear of the angry king for so long that it is hard to trust others."

Li nodded as Yitzhak said, "Come."

Lenar entered followed by several people bearing trays of food. Bok and Na set the shell on another table and soon the meal was laid out. Bok seemed to enjoy the meal, but Na seemed distracted.

"Is anything wrong, Na?" Li asked after a while.

"There is a woman who is here but not here," Na said hesitantly.

Li glanced at Yitzhak who nodded.

"Queen Lodena," Yitzhak said and after a moment Na nodded.

"Sometimes those who are no more alive speak to me," Na said. "She is pleased with your plans, Queen Li."

"I am glad to hear that," Li said. "We know that her husband loved her very deeply and when she became no more he was a broken man who became the angry king you so feared."

Na nodded and began eating again. After the meal Li led their guests down to her old room.

"It is so large," Bok commented.

"There is a small courtyard out here with a well," Li said as she opened the door.

"Where do we," Na hesitated and blushed a little.

"Oh," Li said as she nodded. "There is a pot with a lid under the foot of the bed. The servants will empty it for you."

They looked at each other before looking back at her.

"I realize it's not what you are used to," Li said. "I found it a bit uncomfortable at first too. There will be a guard outside your door if you need anything."

"I didn't sleep well on the ship," Na said. "I'll sleep better here on land."

"Good night," Li said before leaving.

She requested a guard for the door before returning upstairs. She sent messages to Alessandrine and Okaih requesting aid for the island before returning to the royal quarters.

Chapter 33 – Executed for Treason

The next morning Li gave Bok and Na a tour of Mannton's city. They were interested to see how people were rebuilding their homes. That afternoon they boarded the ship that would take them back to their island. She was glad they had come.

As soon as she returned to the palace Lenar brought the first of three couples to the royal quarters for Yitzhak and her to interview. Yitzhak had prepared some questions to ask them. Li wrote down their answers.

Something about the first couple made Li uncomfortable, but she wasn't certain exactly what it was. She was glad when they left.

"What did you think?" Yitzhak asked.

"I hope the next two are better," Li replied.

"Me too," he admitted as the second couple was led in.

The second couple was younger than she expected, but the woman had been learning to read and write. They had recently gotten married and didn't have any children yet.

When they left Yitzhak said, "I like them."

"Me too," she replied as the third couple was led in.

Both had stitches in a couple of places but were cheerful and pleasant. They had lost their home, but their two children survived the storm. They were living with his father. The woman had been taking classes from Marnah before the school opened. She continued with classes at the school and was doing well.

When they left Li looked at Yitzhak and said, "I like the second two, but not the first couple."

"I liked the third couple the best, but their children will need care," Yitzhak said, and Li nodded. "Let's talk to Lenar about it."

"I'm going to see how the cleaning and repairs are progressing," Li said. "You should put your leg up and read for a while."

"I hate being stuck here," Yitzhak admitted as she stood up. "I don't know how you could stand to be locked up in your room for so long."

"It wasn't easy," Li acknowledged. "You'll survive it for a little longer while you heal."

She left the royal quarters and found Lenar waiting for her in the hall.

"We have settled on Makin and Su for our assistants," Li said and Lenar nodded.

"There is a group of people demanding an audience," Lenar told her in a worried tone. "They're in the entrance hall."

"I'll go through the old royal quarters to get to the throne room," Li replied. "Make certain there are some extra guards before letting them into the throne room."

Lenar nodded and hurried off. Li was worried as she followed down the hall. She could hear raised voices coming from the entrance hall. She entered the old royal quarters and found several people working on cleaning the sitting room. She slipped into the throne room as eight guards entered. After sitting down in her throne she drew a deep breath and let it out slowly before nodding to the guards.

They opened the doors and a large group of men jostled in and approached the dais. Li was grateful that four of the guards were stationed at the bottom of the steps.

"What matter do you bring before me?" Li asked in a stern tone.

Several men began talking in angry tones. She looked over the group. There was a scruffy man at the back with a determined look on his face who remained silent.

"Silence!" Li commanded and the room fell silent. "If you want your matter to be heard you must not all speak at once. You in the back with the dark blue shirt, come forward."

The men looked around before parting so the man could come forward.

"Now, are you willing to speak for this group?" she asked, and he nodded curtly. "Good. Speak."

"We are concerned that no one has seen King Yitzhak outside of the palace since the storm," the man said. "What have you done with him? Does he still live? Why have you taken his throne?"

"Broken bones take time to heal," Li replied thinking his voice was familiar. "It will be several more weeks before our beloved king is ready to leave the royal quarters. I consult with him daily. I have not taken his throne."

"We don't believe you," the man growled. "You are just a lying female who has no business even being in this throne room."

The other men began to advance and the guards stepped in to protect her. She glanced up to see Lenar in the doorway looking frightened. She knew the only way to satisfy their demands was to have Yitzhak brought in. She gestured Lenar forward. He skirted around the edge of the room to avoid getting too close to the group of men. He took the stairs two at time and was soon by her side.

"We need a chair with poles to get King Yitzhak into the throne room," Li said quietly. "It's the only way."

Lenar nodded and quickly left as the men jeered him for listening to a woman. They talked loudly among themselves. The bits of conversation she picked up were very rude. She let them talk for a few minutes as she observed them. She could tell which men were active followers of the scruffy man and which were afraid of him.

"Do any of you have a wife?" she asked sternly, and they all shook their heads.

"I had a wife that was killed in the storm," one man said angrily. "My infant son died with her."

"Then you understand what it is to lose someone you love," Li said. "The way women were treated for generations was started by a king whose wife and child died suddenly. In his grief he made the laws that subjected women to slavery. It is because of him that there are not enough women for all men to have wives."

"You lie! Women are weak and stupid. Hardly more than animals," the scruffy man blurted out. "That's why they die so easily."

"Without enough food any person will starve to death, men included," Li countered. "It is time that all of you realize that women are important and intelligent. Without them the nation will die!"

"You had best listen and obey what Queen Li says."

The sound of Yitzhak's voice made all of the men turn towards the throne room doors. They watched as Yitzhak was carried up to the thrones. With Lenar's assistance he was able to move to sit in his throne. He reached towards Li and she put her hand in his.

"As you can see, King Yitzhak is alive and healing," Li said. "We are partners in ruling Mannton and our kingdom is stronger because of our partnership."

"It's been several years since I last saw you Nokar," Yitzhak said sternly. "What is going on?"

"We all thought this female had killed you and stolen your throne," the scruffy man answered.

"I banned you from the palace when you tried to poison Queen Li," Yitzhak said sternly. "And what is in that bag you are trying to hide?"

"A gift for our queen," Nokar sneered as he tossed the bag onto her lap.

Something in the bag moved and a snake head soon emerged. Li quickly grabbed the snake firmly behind the head and pulled it from the bag. Most of the men gasped as she held it up. Nokar scowled.

"Another attempt to kill me, Nokar?" Li stated as much as asked. "This time such treason is punishable by death."

Nokar bolted towards the doors, but the guards soon had him and drug him back to kneel before her. Li lowered the squirming snake back into the bag and gathered the top around her fingers before releasing the head.

"Poisonous?" Yitzhak asked quietly.

"Deadly," she responded.

"Are you going to let her," Nokar stopped as he felt the point of a sword at his neck.

"She is correct about the law, you have committed treason by making an attempt on her life," Yitzhak said sternly. "You will die tomorrow morning. Your death will be by beheading."

"No," Li said. "He has chosen his fate and will die by snake bite."

Nokar's face lost all color and he slumped with his head in his hands.

"Yes, Nokar, I know exactly how deadly this snake is," Li said. "Take him to the dungeon."

Nokar offered no resistance as he was pulled to his feet and led out the doors.

"Lenar prepare an announcement to be read and posted around the city," Yitzhak ordered as he rubbed his temples with his eyes closed. "And take me back to the royal quarters."

"Headache again?" Li asked as she put her hand on his arm.

"Yes. It's too bright in here."

"Guards put out half the torches and lamps," Li said, and they quickly complied. "Take this snake and keep it safe until it is needed in the morning."

One of the guards took the bag with the snake in it gently from her. The men at the bottom of the stairs stood silently watching her as she helped Yitzhak from the throne to the chair. He stroked her face before the chair was lifted and he was carried out of the room.

"Is there any further matter you have?" she asked them.

Most shook their heads, but one stepped forward.

"We still have no wives," he said quietly.

"I cannot magically produce wives for you, you must go out and find them for yourselves," Li said. "We have a peace agreement with Alessandrine and Okiah. Perhaps you should do some traveling. You might meet a woman along your way. Just remember that women are equal in intelligence to men. They are capable of many things if only allowed to do more than cook, clean and bear children. Some might be perfectly content with that, but others will have dreams, interests and abilities beyond that."

The men began to leave, but the one who had lost his wife and son stayed behind.

"I know you are hurting," she said to him as she descended the stairs. "I'm sorry that you lost your wife and son."

"My daughter and older son still live, but they are staying with my neighbors," the man said. "I. . . I don't know if I can take care of them myself. My home is gone, my horses are dead. I feel like I have nothing left."

Li heard someone clear their throat and looked up to see Lenar.

"We are in need of someone to manage the palace stables and care for the horses, My Queen," Lenar said. "The guards have been doing it, but we really need someone dedicated to caring for the horses."

Li saw hope in the man's eyes as he met her gaze for the first time, then he bowed his head.

"I know that Nokar instigated this," Li said as she gently put her hand on his shoulder. "Your loss and pain made his ideas attractive. It is time to start a new job and a new life."

"You trust me?" the man asked as he looked back up.

She nodded.

"Even Nokar was given a second chance, but he wasted it," Li said. "Lenar will show you to the stables and what quarters are available while I work on the announcement."

The man knelt for a moment at her feet before rising to follow Lenar out of the throne room.

Li went to the office and found a fresh sheet of paper. She knew that she needed to word the announcement carefully so people would understand why Nokar was being executed. By the time Lenar returned Li was satisfied with the announcement. She handed him the paper and he nodded as he read over it.

"This is better than I would have come up with," Lenar said as he looked up. "All it needs is the official announcement proclamation at the top. I'll get it copied and send out guards to post it."

"Thank you," Li said as she stood.

Lenar pulled some paper out of a drawer and sat down at a table to copy the announcement. Li returned to the old royal quarters to see how the cleaning was coming along. The sitting room was nearly ready for furniture to be brought in and arranged. Sun streamed in the windows that were being cleaned. She found the bed chamber was cleaner as well. The wall had been scrubbed and debris removed. The bathing chamber smelled freshly cleaned, but the closet had not been touched.

"We don't know what to do with the clothes," a voice said behind her.

Li turned to find an older woman behind her. Li thought for a moment.

"Start by taking everything out and cleaning the empty closet," she said. "After that, start sorting the clothing. If any of it is worn out, ripped or has holes, put it in one pile. Make a second pile of clothing that can be repaired and a third pile of clothing that is in good enough condition to be worn. Anything else I will go through."

The woman picked up a dress that had a slash in the front of it. Li could see gems and beads sewn on the dress.

"Once the clothing is sorted out, we will go through the first pile to see if anything can be salvaged," Li said as she ran her finger along a row of gems near the neck. There is no sense in wasting anything that can be reused. There's enough fabric in that skirt to make a tablecloth for a small table or a dress for someone small."

The woman nodded and said, "I felt the same way, but wanted to confirm what you wanted done."

Li smiled and left to get a horse so she could inspect the repairs to the town. Four guards went with her. Li was pleased to see numbers on many of the freshly repaired homes. Some vacant lots still had piles of debris, but it appeared that people were salvaging what was usable from the piles. One lot had several men cutting large branches down into manageable lengths. There were people drawing water from the well near the harbor.

She paused near the well and asked, "Is the water drinkable again?"

"Yes," a man replied as he poured water into a bucket.

"Good to hear," Li said before urging her horse forward again.

When they got to the school, children were playing in the yard. It was good to see both boys and girls playing and laughing. Li stopped her horse and dismounted as Marnah came out of the school. She looked tired as she approached and curtseyed.

"I'll be glad to have Nathan start teaching," Marnah said.

"He sent me proposals for classes beyond reading and writing," Li said. "I'll go over them in the next day or so."

"I've been trying to teach the children to work with numbers as well," Marnah said. "Most of them are eager to learn. Some have a harder time."

"We all have our strengths and weaknesses," Li said as she nodded. "Each child should learn the basics. After that we can try to teach them the things that interest them. Certainly someone who weaves doesn't need to learn how to make horse shoes."

"Kon learned a little about a lot of different trades before we met, but healing is what he loves to do," Marnah said. "He said that it did help him to learn those other trades so he can talk to the patients and understand their needs in healing."

"Know that there are a lot of parents grateful to know their children are safe and learning something new while they are working," Li said as she patted Marnah's shoulder. "Nathan said he knows of a few other people interested in being teachers. It will take some time, but soon you will be able to go back to healing if that is what you want to do."

"I might still want to teach a little bit," Marnah said. "Maybe I can help some of the children that have a harder time learning things."

"That would be good," Li said. "I'd best be on my way."

Marnah curtseyed as Li turned back to her horse.

The rest of the city was showing good progress on repairs. They turned a corner and saw a sign that said Repair Shop in large metal letters. She heard pounding coming from inside.

"Go in and ask Drake to come out," Li said to one of the guards.

The guard dismounted and hurried inside as Li and the other guards dismounted. Soon the guard returned with Drake. The man was dirty and sweaty as he bowed to her.

"Your sign looks very good," she said as he rose.

"I've been working on the sign for the cemetery," he replied. "Would you like to come in and see it?"

"Yes," Li said and handed her reins to one of the guards.

Two guards stayed with the horses and the other two followed behind her. Drake led Li to a long table that was waist high. On the table were letters laid between two long bars. There were some pieces with curves and curls scattered around the table.

"I'm glad you came by," Drake said. "I wanted to do something decorative on the sign, but I just can't decide what."

Li looked at the extra pieces and had an idea. She picked up one that each end curled opposite directions and another with a curl on one end. She placed the double curled one so it was at the bottom of the sign on the very end and hung down. She took the other and placed it curl down on one side of the center.

"I see what you are thinking," Drake said. "It suggests an arch without the main portion being curved."

"Yes," she said as she picked up some short bits off the dirt floor.

She then assembled them above the center in a way to suggest a simple crown with three points.

"I get it," he said with obvious excitement. "I'll work on the decorative pieces and send you a message when I have them completed, but before I get it attached together."

"Thank you," Li said. "This is very important to me."

"Stanwick has been making good progress on the memorial stone," Drake said.

"Good," Li said. "I need to be going now, but I look forward to getting your message."

Drake bowed and she turned to leave. She noticed her hands were black from handling the metal. Drake held out a rag to her.

"It's dirty work," Drake said as she wiped her hands.

"I've never been too worried about a little dirt," she said with a laugh.

Soon Li was mounted and headed towards her father's home. One of the guards knocked on the door as she dismounted. Garsha opened the door and Rowan was behind her.

"Come in," Rowan said. "How is Yitzhak doing?"

"Healing, but still getting bad headaches," Li said as she entered. "I wanted to ask about how repairs are coming on your home. Are Anunik and Carita getting their home repaired as well? What about Anunik's ship?"

"The homes are taking time," Rowan said. "Both were so badly damaged that we tore them down and are building new ones. They will have stone at least halfway up the walls. The ship got thrown far up on the sand. There was some damage, but less than the homes got. We repaired the ship and dock first. While we are there working on the homes we stay in the ship."

"That is good to hear," Li said. "I've worried about you, but I've been so busy."

"You have more to worry about than us," Rowan said as Father came in. "You have the whole of Mannton to worry about."

"And everyone is grateful that you are a good leader," Father said. "I doubt we would be doing so well without you. Many people have said that you saved them by taking them into the palace during and after the storm."

"Not everyone has been happy," Li said with a sigh as she sat down. "There are still men without wives who have been unhappy. One tossed a bag in my lap hoping the snake inside would bite me. Tomorrow he will be executed by my command."

"What kind of snake?" Garsha asked.

"I'm not certain of the name of the snake," Li admitted. "It is bright gold and green with red stripes. I've seen a cow die very swiftly after being bitten by one. The meat was destroyed."

"A red death adder," Father said as he collapsed into a nearby chair. "I saw my own father die from a bite. It's a swift but horrible death."

Li nodded as the room fell silent.

"I must get going," Li said as she stood up. "Soon I'll invite all of you over for supper so we can relax and visit. It will be a while before Yitzhak can leave the palace."

****

Li woke early with a nervous knot in her stomach. She stood staring out the window knowing today Nokar would die by her command. She knew that most of the people were finally accepting her as their queen and hoped Nokar's execution would not shake their faith in her.

"It doesn't get easier," Yitzhak's voice said behind her. "I've ordered three executions during my time as king. I don't know how many my father ordered but I remember him saying the same thing each time."

"Life is precious and fragile," Li replied. "I hate to lose even one person, but. . ."

"He made the decision to waste his life," Yitzhak said. "Murder is against the law because life is precious. I feel better today and will be there if you want me to."

"I think it will reassure the people to see both of us in agreement," Li said as she finally turned around.

Li couldn't eat much breakfast. Yitzhak patted her hand before they got up from the table. The guards brought the chair on poles as Li settled her crown on her head. She put Yitzhak's on him after he was seated. When they reached the courtyard, she was surprised at how many people were there. She noticed Father there with Rowan, Garsha and their children.

"Bring the condemned," Li ordered and soon the guards were leading Nokar out.

He was fighting them as he was led before her and forced to kneel. There was murmuring among the crowd.

"Nokar, you have attempted to kill me for the second time since I became King Yitzhak's wife," Li said, and the crowd fell silent. "All life is precious, even yours, but murder is against the law. Your willful attempt on my life is treason which is punishable by death."

She motioned to the guard who was holding the bag with the snake in it. He came forward.

"Since you chose to throw a bag with a red death adder into my lap, your fate will be the one you wished upon me," Li said.

She cupped her hand under the bag and felt the snake in it. The guard loosened his grip on the top of the bag and soon the head of the snake emerged. She quickly grasped the neck of the snake and pulled it from the bag. The crowd gasped as she put her other hand under the body of the snake. She approached Nokar who fought harder against the guards. One of them grasped his hair to steady him. He screamed as he saw the snake near his face. She could see the vein in his neck and guided the snake's fangs to it. The snake latched onto Nokar's neck and chewed a bit before releasing. By then Nokar was struggling to breathe.

Li stepped back quickly and the guard held the bag under her hands. She dropped the snake into the bag which the guard quickly closed. Nokar was writhing on the cobblestones as blood began to come out of his nose, mouth and eyes. With a final convulsion he lay still as his blood drained through the cobblestones into the ground. Several guards brought a wooden coffin and roughly put his body into it before carrying it away.

Li's voice trembled as she spoke, "Set the snake loose in the forest away from the city."

As he nodded and left, she returned to Yitzhak's side. As she turned to the crowd, they all knelt.

"Remember that all life is precious," Li said trying hard to control her churning emotions. "We have all lost too much. It is by working together and helping each other that we will recover from the storm. That is how our nation will grow."

The people stood up. Li clenched her fists among the folds of her skirt in an attempt to control her trembling.

"We have begun to heal the dark past that isolated our nation long ago," Li continued. "We now have a peace treaty with Okiah and Alessandrine. Go home knowing that King Yitzhak and I are doing everything we can to build Mannton into a great and prosperous nation. We are doing everything we can to protect you from harm."

She felt Yitzhak stroke her hand with his. She loosened her fist and held his hand as people began to leave. She looked down at him and he smiled at her. She heard footsteps approaching and turned to see her family coming.

"I was terrified when you held up the snake," Garsha exclaimed as she threw her arms around Li. "I wouldn't have dared go anywhere near it."

"I knew if I had control of the head it couldn't bite me," Li said as she returned the hug.

"You have more courage than I have," Father admitted as Fi hugged her.

Li saw the tears running down his face.

"I know that must have brought back memories of your father's death," Li said as she hugged him. "I'm just glad to get it over with. I didn't want to execute him, but people needed to know I wasn't afraid to make the hard decisions and follow through with them."

Rowan just stood shaking his head before saying, "They know. What did it feel like?"

"It was awful to have to kill someone," Li said.

"No, the snake," Rowan said.

"Smoother than the fabric of this dress," she replied, and the children reached out to stroke her skirt.

"We should go inside," Yitzhak said as he shifted in the chair. "We'll all be a bit more comfortable."

"We were on our way to deliver some wood to rebuild our home," Rowan said. "The children wanted to go too."

"Why don't you come over for supper tomorrow then," Yitzhak said. "It would be nice to have some company. I'm not used to being stuck in the royal quarters for so long."

"Of course," Father said.

Fi nodded and said, "We were all so worried about you. I was so relieved to know you survived the storm. You saved my life and gave me hope."

Chapter 34 – Sorting Through the Past

Yitzhak sat impatiently as Kon removed the splints from his arm and leg.

"Now let me help you stand up," Kon said.

He took Yitzhak's left arm and Yitzhak tried to stand without leaning on Kon. His muscles protested and there were twinges of pain, but at last he was on his feet.

"Try taking a couple of steps," Kon said.

As Yitzhak lifted his right leg, his left leg felt weak, and he found himself leaning heavily on Kon.

"Okay. You'll want a cane until that leg gets stronger," Kon said. "Just remember that to strengthen that leg you need to use it. Walk slowly at first and make certain there is someone nearby to help you."

"What about my arm?" Yitzhak asked.

"It's going to hurt and be weak as well," Kon said. "The more you use it the faster it will heal, but don't overdo it."

Yitzhak sighed and Kon laughed.

"I know, but you need to learn to walk again before you can ride a horse," Kon said. "I don't think you could mount even with the horse laying on the ground right now."

"I'll have my assistant get me a cane," Yitzhak said as he sat down in the chair. "What about stairs?"

"Have someone with you until you are more sure on your feet," Kon said as Li entered with Makin and Su.

"Makin, I need a cane so I can walk without a splint on," Yitzhak said.

"I'll get someone to make one for you," Makin responded. "How long does it need to be?"

"I'm not sure."

"I'll have them make it long so it can be trimmed down to suit you," Makin said.

"We'll schedule the dedication and closure of the women's cemetery soon," Li said. "The stone wall and sign for it is nearly done. I do have a surprise for you if you feel up to going for a short walk."

"I can try, but I'll need to lean on someone," Yitzhak replied.

Makin took Kon's place and steadied him as Li led them out to the hall. The first thing he noticed was the tapestries had scenes stitched on them in brilliant colors.

"Where did you get the new tapestries?" he asked.

"They're not new," Li said. "They were long overdue for a cleaning. Lenar is getting all of the tapestries cleaned and rehung."

"That is quite a good surprise," Yitzhak said. "I never realized there were scenes on them."

"I don't think they've been cleaned for a very long time," Li said. "But that's not the surprise."

She led them down to the doors of the old royal quarters which were now uncovered. She opened the doors to reveal the sitting room had been cleaned and furnished, ready for use. Light streamed through the windows and the curtains had been replaced.

"The curtains are double layered so they can be pulled to block out the light," Li said. "Come see the bedchamber."

The bedchamber was as clean and welcoming as the sitting room.

"I did have some of the furniture reupholstered and the closet needed repair," Li said. "It is now ready for use."

"I need to sit down," Yitzhak said, and Makin helped him to a nearby chair. "This is beautiful. Now that I can start walking. I would be able to start doing audiences if we moved into here."

"That's why I wanted it ready for when your splints came off," Li said. "It's been hidden away far too long."

"Have the servants move our things in immediately," Yitzhak said.

Makin and Su bowed and left.

"I've got some meetings after lunch, but I need to go check on the wall and the sign before then," Li said before kissing his lips. "I'll be back in time for lunch. We'll have the children eat with us in the sitting room. You can direct the servants as they get things moved in."

"That I can do," Yitzhak said even though he was wishing he could go with her. "Maybe I can attend the meetings."

"That would be great," Li said with a smile before leaving.

Soon servants arrived carrying in their clothing and belongings. Lenar and Ka got the closet arranged while Yitzhak told the other servants where to put things. Some trunks were brought in that Yitzhak hadn't gone through in years. Soon he had a table brought over and was going through the trunks. Some items meant nothing to him, but others brought memories of his youth flooding back. He was still sorting through things when Li returned.

"I see you have been busy," Li said as a woman handed her bag. "Thank you."

She reached in the bag and drew out a wooden box small enough to hold in one hand. She stroked the box softly with a sad smile.

"What is it?" he asked.

"When I arrived at the palace the first time had my dress, my sleeping mat and this bag," Li said softly as she stopped next to the table. "So much has changed for me. I had no idea what would happen to me when I left my father's home."

A man brought a chair over to the table and she nodded in thanks before sitting down. She set down the box and drew a stick with a hook carved into the end out of the bag.

"This hook is what I used to make my mat with," she said as she laid it on top of the bag. "My mother used it to make her mat. This box and hook are all I have that belonged to her."

He reached over and took her hand in his.

"Choosing you as my wife was the best thing I ever did," he said. "You have changed everything you touch and made it so much better."

"Are these things from your childhood?" she asked as she picked up one of his toys.

"Yes."

"The shelves beside the fireplace are bare. We should put these things on the shelves along with the carvings Bok and Na brought," Li said. "Bring over that large shell box."

Two servants brought the shell box over and set it on the table. Li stood and started taking the carvings out of the shell. She reached in the shell and then gasped.

"Are you okay?" Yitzhak asked with concern.

Li lifted out a carving of a dragon. She set it gently on the table followed by two more.

"I thought all the dragons left with Regis Bryant's people," Li whispered. "Do you think?"

"That there are more dragons?" Yitzhak finished and she nodded. "There must be. There's no way for them to carve something they haven't seen. Even if someone described a dragon it would be difficult for them to have the carvings come out looking so much like real dragons."

"We'll have to ask the fishermen about it," Li said as Makin entered.

"Your lunch is being brought up," he announced.

"Help me get into the sitting room," Yitzhak said, and Makin hurried over to his side.

He heard the children coming down the hall as Li and Makin helped him sit down at the table in the sitting room where servants were setting out lunch.

"Where is this, Ni?" An's voice asked as the door opened. "Mother! Father!"

An and Tokar ran over to them.

"Where are your splints?" Tokar asked as he put his hand on Yitzhak's right arm.

"The healer took them off so I can start using my arm and leg again," he replied.

"Can you play with us now?" An asked.

"Not just yet," Yitzhak said and the excitement drained from her face. "I still need help getting around, but within a few weeks."

She sniffed and wiped at her eyes.

"Come here," he said gently, and she obeyed. "I know it's been hard for you to wait for my bones to heal. It's been hard for me too."

He put his arm around her, and she buried her face against him. He kissed her head and patted her back.

"I thought you were going to die when Ni told us you had been hurt," she sobbed.

"I'm not going to die, not for a long time at least," Yitzhak said as he held her tighter. "I was so scared when the storm came back, but knowing you were safe in the palace made me braver. Come on now, our food is getting cold."

She finally pulled away from him and Tokar gave him a hug before turning to go to his chair. Yizhak noticed him wipe his face on his sleeve before sitting down.

As they finished eating Tokar asked, "So why are we here and not in your rooms?"

"Because we are moving and this will be our quarters now," Yitzhak said.

"Long ago this is where the king and queen of Mannton lived," Li said. "It had been locked up for many years, but now we are ready to have it be the royal quarters instead of our old rooms."

"Why did they lock it up?" An asked.

"Something happened that made the king not want to see the rooms again and they were forgotten for many years, but that is a long story for when you are older," Li replied, and they looked disappointed. "I promise you will learn the story when you are old enough to understand it. It is a very important story that everyone will learn."

Chapter 35 – Dedication

Li was grateful that Yitzhak started attending meetings and even audiences with her. There were still days that he stayed in their quarters with the curtains drawn and only a few lamps lit, but he was getting better. After two weeks he was able to ride in a carriage around the city.

"There's the tree that we climbed up in to escape the flooding," Yitzhak said pointing to a large tree with low branches near the river.

"Perhaps we should put a small plaque or stone telling about the tree saving your life and the lives of your guards," Li suggested.

"I'd like that," he said. "I'm surprised at how many houses have numbers on them now."

"It's good to see most of the homes have been repaired or rebuilt," Li said as they approached the harbor. "There are still some that are working at rebuilding."

A young man came running up waving something in his hand.

"Hello, Marvin," Li said as the carriage stopped. "What have you got?"

"A message from Poco Island," Marvin panted as he bowed. "It arrived late last night. I was headed to the palace when I saw your carriage."

Li took the offered scroll and opened it.

> Dear King Yitzhak and Queen Li,
> We wanted to thank you for the assistance we have been given in rebuilding. The fishermen from Mannton and the other nations have been very kind in bringing us food and helping us rebuild. Some have agreed to future trades of baskets and carvings for food and cloth we cannot produce ourselves. We have hope for a bright future for all of us.
> With gratitude,
> Bok and Na

"My cousin wrote it out for them," Marvin said as Li looked up from the scroll.

"I am most pleased," Li said, and Yitzhak nodded. "Thank you. I will have a reply written out by tomorrow morning for them."

"I will be at the palace about this time of day tomorrow then," Marvin said with a bow before leaving.

"Take us to the Repair Shop," Li said, and the carriage started moving again.

Soon they arrived to see a large group of people crowded around the entrance.

"What's going on?" Yitzhak asked and one of the men turned around.

"King Yitzhak, Queen Li," the man said as he quickly bowed. "We came to see the sign."

Others turned around and bowed as well.

"What sign?" Yitzhak asked and the crowed parted until they could see a sign leaning against the building.

"Who is Queen Lodena?" a woman asked.

"The full story will be told, but it was her death that began the enslavement of our women," Li said. "We will be scheduling a public meeting at the women's cemetery very soon and at that time the full story will be told. There will be a memorial stone to explain the story."

Drake came out of the Repair Shop and quickly bowed.

"I am most pleased with your work," Li said. "This is perfect. How is Stanwick coming on the memorial stone?"

"He said it will be ready in four days," Drake replied. "By then the stone wall should be complete and the sign installed as well."

"Perfect," Li said. "One week from today will be the meeting at the women's cemetery."

They continued their tour of the city. Li was pleased with how the rebuilding was coming along. The gardens looked like they were growing well although there were obvious gaps in the crops that were growing in crooked rows. Many people greeted them and expressed relief to see King Yitzhak outside the palace again. Yitzhak looked happy, but tired when they returned to the palace.

Li wrote out a response to Bok and Na before writing out an announcement about the cemetery dedication to be posted around the city. She was just finishing when there was a tap at the door.

"Come," she responded.

Su opened the door and Captain Ludwig entered behind her.

"I need this copied and posted around the city, Su," Li said as she held up the announcement. "Please sit down, Captain."

Su nodded and took it from her with a curtsey.

"I came to give you a report, My Queen," Captain Ludwig said as he sat down. "Most of the tents have been returned. We have set up each one and made any repairs before placing them back in storage."

"That is good to hear," Li said. "It looks like repairs to the city are nearly completed, but I haven't been able to inspect the outer groups of houses."

"I've had regular reports from the patrols," Captain Ludwig replied. "I instructed my men that if the people needed an extra hand to report that need. I've dispatched a couple of volunteers, but they've mostly provided aid in the form of hunting and occasionally some heavy lifting to put a ridge beam up for a house. All of the tents have now been returned from the outer settlements."

"That is excellent news," Li said. "Thank you for taking that initiative to offer assistance. Even if they live far from the city by choice, they need to know they can turn to us for help and guidance."

Captain Ludwig nodded and said, "My men will continue to report on how the outlying communities are doing. I will let you know if there is anything that needs attention."

"Thank you," Li replied as she stood up.

Captain Ludwig was quickly on his feet. Li returned to the royal quarters to find Yitzhak waiting for her. The servants were beginning to set the table for supper.

"I think I'll retire right after supper," he said as she sat down. "I didn't expect the carriage ride to wear me out so quickly."

"You've been on your feet a lot today," Li replied. "It will take time to regain your strength."

"It is good to be able to eat with my right hand again," he said as he picked up his fork.

After supper she went up to spend some time with the children. It was good to let the worries of her duties slip away while she sat on the floor playing with the children. Ta was growing fast and interested in holding things and tasting them. So much had happened since she had been born. Li was glad that their children would grow up much differently than she had.

****

The day finally arrived for the dedication of the women's cemetery. Li chose a dark blue dress to wear. Yitzhak wore a matching dark blue suit. They had discussed what they would tell the people many times over the last week. Breakfast was eaten in silence. Yitzhak patted her hand after she put down her spoon.

"At last everyone will understand," Yitzhak said as he stood up. "The past can't be changed, but it needs to be known."

"Yes," Li agreed as she stood up.

They went out to the carriage that was waiting in the courtyard. The wagon containing the coffins of Queen Lodena and Princess Cora was waiting as well. When they reached the cemetery there was already a crowd waiting. The stone wall was finished and the sign was installed over the entrance. The memorial stone was covered by a large cloth. A hole large enough to put the coffins in was dug just inside the cemetery entrance. The crowd fell silent as Yitzhak and Li got out of the carriage.

"It is time for the truth of the past to be known," Yitzhak began. "The healing has begun, but with the dedication and closing of this cemetery we can take another step in that process."

He paused for a moment before continuing.

"Several generations ago King Ulric and Queen Lodena ruled Mannton. They had a son who became King Ambrose. Shortly after Queen Lodena gave birth to Princess Cora, her body weakened, and she fell while carrying Princess Cora to her cradle. Both died which drove King Ulric insane with grief. He made laws that enslaved our women. Some brave fishermen took all the unmarried women and girls to an island, but later some were brought back including a woman that became King Ambrose's wife."

He paused again.

"Recently Queen Li and I uncovered the truth and found the remains of Queen Lodena and Princess Cora," Yitzhak said. "King Ulric is one of my ancestors. It is up to me to bring this shameful past to light so it won't happen again."

Li tightened her hand around his briefly before speaking.

"Since the time of King Ulric women have been buried here and it is time that this cemetery is closed and women be buried next to the men," Li said and removed the cloth from the stone. "This stone will mark the final resting place of Queen Lodena and Princess Cora. On the back of the stone is their full story for all to read. We now dedicate this cemetery the Queen Lodena Memorial Cemetery and lay her and her daughter to rest here."

Women came forward and lifted the coffins from the wagon while the men stood watching. When Li met Yitzhak's eyes he smiled softly and nodded. The coffins were lowered into the grave and the women picked up flat stones from the border of the cemetery and began to push the dirt into the grave. Soon men joined in to help the women. When the grave was filled the stones were placed over the grave.

"Today I want to thank Queen Li for having the courage to tell me the truth about how women have been treated for these many years," Yitzhak said as he joined her at the memorial stone. "Without her this would not be possible. When I chose her as my wife, I didn't realize that I had chosen a woman who would prove herself the rightful Queen of Mannton. Because of her women are free and loved."

He bowed to her and kissed her hand before moving to her side and putting his arm around her while the people knelt. Li was briefly overcome by a feeling of joy and gratitude. As she felt a stroke on her cheek she knew Queen Lodena was at peace. The life she knew women deserved was now a reality in Mannton.

Through the courage of a single woman
loved by the one man who can enact change
the enslaved are given freedom
and a future filled with hope and love.

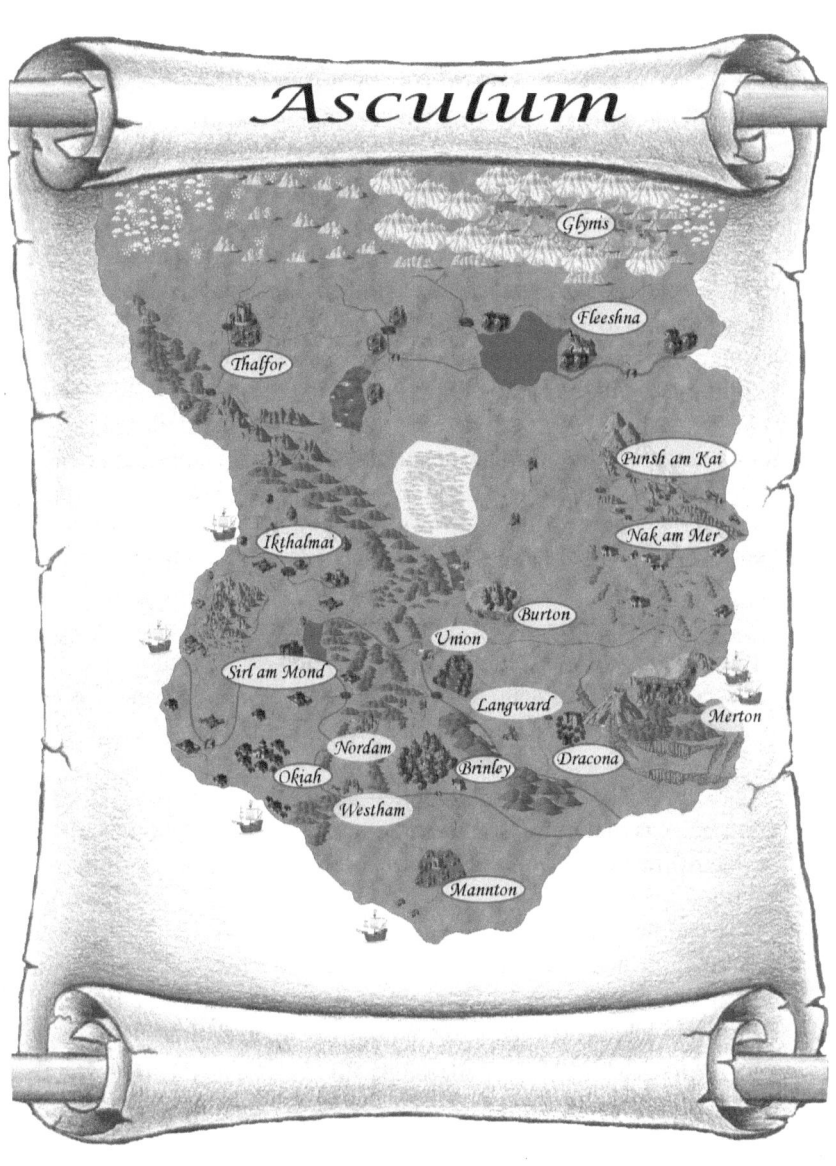

Tales of Asculum

A group of refugees stranded in the hostile snow covered north divide up hoping to find shelter on this world they call Asculum. All of the dragons and some of the people fly south in search of warmer climates while the rest of the people face a journey they are ill prepared for. They are lost and freezing as their leader urges them forward through the blizzard into the mountains for as a seer she knows that they will find temporary shelter there. They manage to stumble out of the snows into a paradise created by a ring of active volcanoes. Their magical talents become vital in building a city they name Glynis.

As they begin to settle into their new home their leader sends out small scouting parties to discover who inhabits this world. They find that while the people of Asculum look very much like them, they are a short lived primitive people. The people of Glynis learn what they can from these people without revealing that their past and magical abilities. They begin to make wagons and carriages for cargo and people. They even learn to make and use swords along with bows and arrows they've seen the people of Asculum using. As the people of Glynis search for a new home away from the volcanoes that could destroy their valley their past is forgotten.

It is in this environment that the **Tales of Asculum** are set. Each book is meant to be a standalone book involving a particular region of the planet and the characters that inhabit that region.

You would think the life of a prince would be great, but for the crown prince of Brinley that's far from the truth. The only others near his age in the palace are children of the servants who all tease him for having no name. When he goes into the military he must conceal his identity but finally gains some friends. When he is sent to deliver a message to the overthrown tyrant King Burkhart he falls in love with the one woman he knows he can't have.

Aurita knows everyone hates her and her father but everyone is forbidden to tell her why. What she does know is that for her and her father the village is their prison and to leave seals their deaths. King Langward controls their lives including who she will marry when she is of age but he is kind to her. When King Langward's son sends her a gift her father teaches her to read and write so she can send him a note to thank him. They begin to exchange letters. As the years pass she looks forward to the letters she gets from the prince but doesn't dare admit she has fallen in love with him. When she meets the handsome corporal sent to deliver a message to her father her heart is torn between him and the prince.

The last Lord of Dracona is a lonely man with a dark past who is thrust into unexpected responsibilities. He lives alone in an empty castle in the center of the deserted town of Dracona. He faces tasks that he has no hope of accomplishing on his own and no one to turn to for help. Lord Dracona's story includes a nation in search of the answer to an ancient riddle and another nation in the grip of a tyrant king. When he falls in love with a mysterious woman he goes from desperate for companionship and purpose to overwhelmed by new responsibilities as new citizens begin to arrive.

The new King of Burton is in search of a wife but is dissatisfied with the spoiled princesses sent by neighboring kingdoms to court him. At a dear friend's funeral, he falls in love with a beautiful servant girl that had a life of slavery and abuse. Through their love and perseverance, they are able to unite several kingdoms in peace.

In the dying kingdom of Mannton women are not treated as people. They work for scraps of food and sleep on woven mats that will become their burial wrappings. This all changes after Li is purchased by the king to provide him an heir. He soon finds that she is no ordinary woman.

For more information and social links see www.vjogardner.com

299

About the Author

Valerie J.O. Gardner is an award wining author of full length fractured fairy tale fantasy novels.
She has found success with both self published and traditionally published works.

Always fascinated by both medieval times and sci-fi she was an avid reader and enjoyed a wide variety of literature and authors. She began writing in in the late 1980's after graduating from Dixie State University in St. George, Utah, where she studied Fantasy Lit and Writing. Valerie is a member of the United Authors Association and LDS Publishing Professionals Association.

Valerie is a co-founder of V&E Enterprises a service to support and educate authors. She also does freelancer formatting and final edits for both publishers and for self published authors.

Valerie has been an invited panelist at Tree City Comic Con (Boise, ID.) and at Salt Lake Comic Con (Salt Lake City, UT.) She also has been a panelist at several writers conferences including LTUE (Provo, UT.) The topics she specializes in are World Building, Maps, Indie Publishing and Female Protagonists.

You can visit her at www.vjogardner.com.